I0573788

Rescued From Myself

Written by:
Kareen Lopez-Samuels

Cadmus Publishing
www.cadmuspublishing.com

PROLOGUE

I fall into the substantial and flawless snow. It fell earlier today and there are mountainous banks of it, stacked on a sea of ice, everywhere. Now that it is no longer snowing, it is strikingly cold—the kind of cold that stings like a wasp bite—but still breathtakingly beautiful. I feel like I've been drenched in hot water. The burning pain starts in my fingertips and resonates down to my toes. I'd almost forgotten about my toes, since I've not felt them in a while. My thick cotton hoody, grabbed in a hurry, is wholly inadequate to protect me against these temperatures. What am I doing outside in this weather? I am definitely underdressed for this occasion.

I'd actually had no plans to venture out tonight, but when he came at me what choice did I have? Just as in my worst nightmares, when I scream but my voice is stranded in the back of my throat, fear has taken control of my voice—as it often does—and holds it hostage. So here I am, running voiceless on a silent country road in Paris, Ontario, a stranger in a strange land being gracelessly chased by the man I love and whom I thought had loved me completely.

I hear his footsteps coming; he's not too far behind, and although I flee before him, his bloody mission causes him to gain ground. For sure he will catch up soon. Thankfully, my cellphone is in my pocket, but my fingers are frozen stiff. They look much like the chicken feet that Mommy used to put in the pumpkin soup. What I wouldn't give to be back home in the warmth of my mother's kitchen and her inimitable embrace. Certainly, if I try removing my phone from my pocket, it will stick to my fingers like metal to a magnet. So I keep running, not dragging my feet, and hoping against hope that someone will see me. However, I dare not hope too much, because the next house is miles away, in this area of L-shaped houses that stretches for miles, houses hidden behind groves that are inextricably connected to dense woodlands.

He's right behind me, now. I feel him rather than see him. When you have been intimate for so long with someone your body naturally senses when they are near. He's like a scent on me that grows stronger by the minute.

There's a river nearby, the Grande Valley River; it must be frozen now, but I have to take my chances. What other choice do I have? The river might be frozen, yet it is in no way antagonistic towards me. Underneath the ice I know it is calmly reflective, and therefore receptive to me. I am literally caught between the devil and the deep blue sea. I pick the river. I have always picked the river, even when I was a child growing up in Portland, Jamaica, surrounded by the beautiful Caribbean Sea. I will always pick the river.

He is just a few feet behind me now. I can hear him muttering and smell his sweat, mixed with his aftershave and cologne. I bought him that bottle of *Drakkar Noir* for his birthday just a few months ago. I am almost tempted to turn around and run into his arms. But how can I when he wants me dead—*eliminated?*

My only crime is that I fell hard for the wrong man, a man too damaged to be rescued. A harsh lesson, I know; still, like all erstwhile lessons, I am going to learn this the hard way.

We met years ago in my small community of Balcarres, Portland, Jamaica. He tried desperately to impress me. He pulled out all the stops, telling me about his family and friends. In fact, he'd told me about everyone else without revealing too much of himself, so much so that when I met them, I knew them because of all he had said. To think my family thought my ship had finally come in.

When we met, he was in Jamaica not only to take in the many and varied attractions, but also on business. He had come to investigate our thriving chrysanthemum industry in Portland. His family was in business with a big pharmaceutical company, with the potential to collaborate with more such companies, and they needed a reliable supplier of the beautiful plant. Apparently, although I was unaware at the time, the chrysanthemum has rich medicinal properties and has been used to treat a number of disorders, from respiratory problems to hypertension, and even nervous conditions. Portland was the best location to purchase the product since the industry was and is still not regulated.

I come upon the banks of the Grande River suddenly, and if it weren't for the rails to block me, I would have gone straight in, head first. He is right behind me now; he will be next to me within a few more strides.

At this point, he's yelling: "How could you do this to me? Why are you running away from me?"

I try to plead my case but my voice is still frozen, shut up in the back of my throat. Over time, I've noticed that it's not only my voice; sometimes fear takes my mind captive and locks away my memories, like a princess in a tower, hidden away until her prince comes to release her. Sadly, there is no prince coming to rescue me, not now, not ever. My prince is gone, he's become the villain in our love story. My silence emboldens him and so he continues.

"You are being selfish! Why are you doing this? Do you think I would just let you do this to me and my family?"

I don't even know what he's talking about. He's the one chasing me with a weapon. It is they who have become my enemy, not the other way around.

"I took you from your village, I saved you from a life of poverty. I made you into a lady and this is how you repay me? Us?"

I hear the pain in his voice but I can't stop now. As Lord Buxton said, "…*a purpose once fixed, and then—death or victory*.…"

He catches up to me. By now my hood, no match for the wind, has abandoned me and he grabs my hair from behind. Then he lets go and grabs my shoulders, spins me around roughly, holding me way too tight, and shakes me as if trying to shake some sense into me. If this were the movies, it would be the point where the lovers make up and pledge their undying love, but everything in me screams to *run*! So with strength I didn't even know I have I pull away, and just like that I jump over the rails, falling into the sleeping river. I don't know if he pushed me or if it's the adrenalin which sends me over the edge—but whatever the reason, I am falling. My hands instinctively reach out in front of me to grip something, anything. But alas, there is nothing, just a vast emptiness. The last thing I hear is him screaming my name.

Right before I hit the ice I think *this must be where I die, among strangers in a cold, distant land,* and I lose consciousness.

"*Nevaeh! Nevaeh!*"

CONTENTS

PART ONE

CHAPTER ONE

Ten Years Earlier

Neva, why you out here?"

"You not going to class?"

"Guys, could you please just leave me alone? Why should I go to be insulted by Ms. Shark?"

At this comment, we all burst out laughing. This statement, although obviously overused, always sends us into gales of uncontrollable laughter. My friends, Robin, Claire and Bridget, and I, have known each other since Providence Primary School and we've been through—as we always say—*mawga and thick.* We've dealt with the good, the bad and the ugly, which makes us as thick as Mr. Joe's molasses and as secretive as the Folly ruins located in our parish.

Our Literature teacher, Miss Shalk, seems to have it in for me. She is on my tail constantly, belittling me and calling me names. Last week, she called me a "pretty dunce," which made the class erupt into raucous laughter. I still don't even know why she hates me so much. I know that I am not the best student at Providence High School, but I am not the worst either. In fact, I have been in the top five in my grade for the past few years.

Claire declares, "Girl, don't listen to that witch, she is jealous."

Bridget interjects, "Yes, fe real! Come, go a class! The sooner you learn wha' happen to Romeo and Juliet is the sooner we can move on to *Beka Lamb*. My friends in the other grade eleven class say it is a really good novel."

Robin, the practical and sophisticated one, states, "Plus, you cannot just spend the rest of grade eleven hiding from class. You are this (she brings the thumb of her right hand and the index finger together) close to sitting CXCs, just one more year. It just does not make any good sense. It is—" she searches for the right word "—impractical."

At that, we all roll in the grass laughing (except Robin of course) not so much because of what she says but how she says it. She is so very stush that she pronounces her words like she's visited England at some point in her life, or like she's a broadcaster at RJR or JBC. We always laugh when she uses big words. We all know that she is the smart one who will definitely go places. Robin is the kind of person who has magic in her hands and will excel at anything she puts her mind to.

Eventually Robin stalks away, after declaring emphatically how "trifling" we all are, "a complete waste of her time, real Poppyshow". They all leave one by one, and I quickly weigh my options before chasing after them. Because, if Mommy has to leave my sick grandmother to come see about me, it is going to end in a beating. Mommy prides herself on having the "brightest and best" child in the family so I am not about to mess with that title. Mommy, despite her quick gap-toothed smile, is a strict disciplinarian in her own right. This I know for certain. I carefully consider who I am most afraid of: Mommy or Miss Shalk—and the former wins every time.

To be fair, it isn't that my mother isn't wonderful, but she is the sole caregiver for my grandmother, who has been ailing for long before I was born. She has some type of mysterious illness; at least, mysterious to me. All my aunts and uncles know what she has (even Daddy knows) but as soon as I enter a room where they are talking their big-people business, I have to leave. For Christ's sake, I am sixteen years old. I already know about the birds and the bees, so what else could there possibly be that I don't know yet?

My mother spends so much time with her mother, it's almost like nothing else matters. She spends hours applying various home remedies, from a concoction of rum, ginger, and pimento, to leaf-of-life leaves with Vicks and civil orange. We can be in the middle of a serious conversation, but as soon as my Granny calls she has to leave. Sometimes she is so worn out from attending to her all day that I just don't want to disturb her. There are lots of things going on in my life that I wish I could share with her, but why bother? As soon as we sit to have a conversation my Granny is in pain or she needs something. She always does.

Mommy spends the whole day feeding, cleaning, and applying and reapplying rubbing alcohol and lime juice to my grandmother's familiar grey hair, tied with her various tie-head, a leaf-of-life leaf, and sometimes a few soursop leaves. That's the other thing; her grey hair is my earliest memory of my very aged grandmother. I cannot recall a time when it was any other colour. Sometimes I go to visit and she is so completely snuggled in her blanket that all I can discern is just the white fluff on her head, sticking out unceremoniously from under everything that Mommy ties it with.

I swear, as soon as you get to the gate, all you smell is Genie floor polish (the dark brown stain we apply liberally to the wooden floor and shine with a coconut brush), Benjamin's bay rum, alcohol, Vicks VapoRub and castor oil. It is so embarrassing that I hardly invite my friends to my house. I visit them all the time, especially Claire, as she lives just down the hill from me. I have tried a few times but I don't even possess the words to tell them what is going on at my house. I think they understand in their own way as everyone goes through something at one point or the next.

Despite the fact that we share everything, I think we all have things going on at home that we are too ashamed to talk about. Or they are so painful that we can't allow ourselves to utter them, to give life to them, out of fear that they will wreck our fun, easygoing and laid-back time together. Once you give voice to these things, they tend to take on a life of their own and begin to consume the space which playfulness once occupied. For instance, in primary school Oretha Wilson told everyone that her mom had cancer, and things were never the same in the playground. We all avoided her like she had cancer by association; as if she were contagious. Balcarres is a really small community and the grapevine stretches wide and long, so we all know things about each other but choose not to say.

For instance, we all know that Robin's father is a married man who lives in America with his wife and children. He visits occasionally but doesn't dare stay with Robin and her mother. He usually stays in a villa in Buff Bay, and rumour has it that he is usually with his other family. We've been with Robin to visit a few times, but we've never actually met him. This duplicity has led to Robin's mother suffering from bouts of depression, as she is still in denial and believes firmly that they are a family. My father has always called her Cleopatra. Eventually, I had to ask, "Why do you call her that, when her name is Sabrina?"

He said, with a straight face, "Because she live on de-Nile."

Bridget's dad is a drunk, who pees himself whenever he is tanked-up and picks a fight with anyone who will give him the time of day. Of course no one in the community does, as they know that this is just his way. He is both harmless and powerless.

On the other hand, Claire seems to be a little more fortunate because *her* family secret is out there. Everyone is well aware that she lives with her mother, but it is her three aunts who take care of her. Her mom went crazy when Claire was just two years old. Community lore has it that the man Miss Cherry, Claire's mom, was in love with—mind you, not Claire's father, some other guy—went to *Foreign*, got married for "papers," promised he would get a divorce and then marry her and file for her. But he has never returned to Portland parish, or even Jamaica for that matter. He stopped communicating with her a long time ago. This drove Miss Cherry into depression; she stopped eating, stopped bathing and refused to comb her hair. To this day my mother believes that all Rastafarians are insane, because refusing to comb your hair is the last stage of insanity. Well, at any rate, Claire's secret is out there and everyone in the community knows it and shows her a lot of sympathy by not mentioning it in her presence.

This is despite the fact that the people of Balcarres, though very kind, can be loose with their words. They are neither afraid of nor slow at expressing their opinions—loudly. At any rate, it must be liberating to not have to live in mortal fear that your secret can be exposed at any time, which would leave you at the mercy of wagging tongues.

I enter Miss Shalk's classroom with a sinking feeling in the pit of my stomach, which I generally get any time I am in close proximity to her. Any time she's around lately, I try so hard to sound *bright* that I end up saying the opposite of what I mean. She literally makes me sick. I just sit quietly in the back corner of the room, where all the chairs with missing parts are stacked. I try not to breathe too loudly, lest my breathing disturbs her.

I look out the window to distract myself and avoid attracting her attention. Three trees stand like strong sentinels in the school yard: the bougainvillea tree, the mimosa, and the poinciana. The reddish-orange leaves of the bougainvillea are mesmerizing. They are all clothed in different shades of red, and I can almost smell the rich fragrances intermingling. They sway gently in the wind;

some leaves blowing around, littering the school yard with red like children running in the playground. I am so mesmerized by the opulence of the scene that I temporarily forget where I am.

Everything is going well; we're almost at the end of the class and she has not picked on me, not once. As far as I can surmise, she hasn't even looked in my general direction. I start to relax but still maintain a careful vigilance in my expression, to ensure that I look "engaged" as she calls it.

Eventually, I hear her say, "What do the light and dark images used in Romeo and Juliet allude to?"

No one seems to know. We all look out the windows at the same time, moving our heads simultaneously as if we're watching the same cricket match. I have lived in Balcarres all my life but I am always captivated by the green, rich vegetation that surrounds my school. For miles and miles there are rolling hills, home to a variety of trees: the classic *lignum vitae* tree with its beautiful purple blossom, the guango tree, and the dogwood tree. Combined they all look like miles of a well-kept garden, meticulously maintained by a dutiful gardener. The view is always breathtaking, calming and quite the distraction. So serene, so great a contrast to how I feel most of the time. To be honest, in my attempt to remain incognito, I not only have become distracted by the spectacular scenery outside but I have been daydreaming again so I've completely missed the first part of the lesson—I am really hoping that she does not call my name. I can only hope that she is in a really good mood so I will be spared her wrath.

Suddenly I hear, "Yes, Miss Nevaeh, what's the answer?"

With a sigh, I say in a quiet voice, "I don't know, Miss."

She has a really high-pitched voice, like a really strong soprano, but she says, just as quietly, "'Don't know, Miss.' Of course you don't. No surprise there."

At this comment, I don't know if it's her smug look, or the red blouse that she is wearing (the one she loves to wear the most, the one with a sickening red shade) or because it is my time of the month, or because I am sick of being taken for a poppyshow, but something snaps inside me. I do something stupid; I respond to her mockery.

"So, if you know that I don't know, then why did you ask, Miss? You could spare yourself the embarrassment."

"Spare myself the embarrassment?"

She counts each word, like she was measuring each against an invisible wrath-stick and testing their temperature before spitting them out.

I boldly say, "Yes, Miss."

I can hear my heart pounding in my chest and the sound echoing in my ears. I also hear the blood gushing through my veins like the water over Reach Falls. I am certain everyone around me can hear the sound of my interior plumbing, and that in and of itself is embarrassing. It is distressing to be so inexorably driven by fear that you feel all your inner thoughts and parts lie exposed for all to see. Not only that, but you are reduced to a miniature version of yourself, a mere replica, which negates all your potential and aspirations into nothingness. You are relieved of your humanity and dignity. I must be far more fed up with her, and her foolishness, than I've allowed myself to accept. I briefly wonder: who is Cleopatra now?

When I look up at her, fully intending to match her gaze and finish what I have started, I see her eyes are as red as her blouse and as big as apple seeds. Normally she is quite petite, very slim, just a little taller than me. I am five feet four inches, but today she is wearing heels so she seems taller, and in her wrath far more menacing. She has a very tiny waist that she loves to accentuate with big broad belts, giving the impression that her lower half might be permanently separated from her upper body. At the same time it highlights her ample breasts, which tend to sway with every move she makes. Right now, they are moving up and down rapidly with each angry breath. I get the feeling that at any moment she might evolve into a fire breathing dragon, with wings.

Miss Shalk has a beautiful, smooth, brown complexion, like the shell of a ripe tamarind. But right at this moment, somehow, she has managed to turn as red as an Otaheite apple.

"Get out!" she screams. "Get out of my class, this minute! You dunce bitch! You can fool all the other teachers and let them think that you are smart but *not me*!"

I move very slowly towards the door, almost mechanically, as all the heads swing towards me as if they are saying, *it's your time to bat*. With such a captive audience, I can't resist.

As I touch the door lightly, with half my body in the room and the other half just outside the hallway: "Well maybe if you were a better teacher, I would not be such a dunce."

I taste each word before spitting it out, much like she did, and they tasted bittersweet like jimbilin stewed in cane sugar. This last comment is the final straw. She completely loses it and her eyes take on a wild look, like a bulldog in heat. She does something that I have never seen a teacher do before: she bursts into tears, not the loud kind, but silently, so angry that she cries uncontrollably, the kind that says if I don't cry, I might end up hurting you. We are all stunned.

From my vantage point, standing at the door, I see that no one moves, not even to bat an eyelid, no one speaks, no one blinks, no one breathes. Everyone looks equally dazed and confused, like chickens just let out of their coop. Without moving my head, I see everyone has their mouths open. They look like they have an onion stuck in their mouths and they don't know how to get rid of it.

Dramatically, she rushes over to me like a gladiator, and slaps my face hard with her right palm: first my right cheek and then the left. Then she calmly walks back, taking her place at the front of the room, resuming her position as adult in charge and her lesson as if we both have passed the test. She seems quite satisfied with herself as she says, "Nevaeh, return to your seat. Please pay attention so that we don't have another outburst like this one. Do I make myself clear?"

All I can do is nod, with my head spinning and my ears ringing. Everything and everyone looks like they've been out in the rain and has water all over them. I have absolutely no words. Let's face it, I have been beaten by teachers before—a leather belt in the palm or across the back—we all have. It is a rare occurrence for me, but no teacher—no one, not even my mother—has ever boxed me in the face before. I am so embarrassed. I wish the sea would come in and cover the whole school. Naturally, I am silent for the rest of the class. In fact, everyone else is quite subdued, even Miss Shalk.

After class I just grab my backpack and leave without my friends, walking the many miles home. It seems like nothing. I get home purely on muscle and eye memory, because I don't remember anything from my journey. I just remember thinking of things I could have done or said in the moment, or to prevent the situation from escalating, and wondering how she could possibly have done that.

In Jamaica, one of the worst ways you can shame someone is to box them in the face. Shaming has been used as a weapon in the Jamaican culture from the days of slavery, to ensure submission and prevent rebellion. It has been passed down from one generation to the next, and as with everything else each generation has perfected their craft and sharpened the skill of shaming. But a slap or box to the face is still the epitome of humiliation, to put someone back in their place. To remind them of their station in life.

I go straight to my room, quickly, before my mother sees the ugly welts on my face. I am very quiet when I get home, but of course Mommy does not have time to notice, because Grandma is having a "spell." My grandmother has these spells, as my mother calls them, where she experiences sharp pains all over her body so she moans and groans the whole time, saying, "Me a go dead!

Duppy a go kill me!"

My grandmother believes firmly that every ill that happens in her world is as a result of otherworldly interferences; primarily duppies or ghosts. When I was a child I was always afraid to go into her room, fearing that one of her duppies might materialize when I entered and attack me as well. Both she and my mother are left exhausted after each episode because my diligent mother applies homemade salve to every area that hurts, massaging, soothing and "binding up" the duppies who are attacking her mother.

Plus, what would be the point of narrating what happened in class to my mother? She would immediately assume that I was in the wrong and give me a good beating for disrespecting an adult, especially a teacher, and causing people to think that I didn't come off of *good table* (not raised properly).

My mother comes from a generation with the prevailing idea that no matter what, the teacher is always right; therefore, they shouldn't *save the rod and spoil the chile only save the eye.* So, I am compelled to keep my secret. Yet another in the growing list of things that I wish that I could have discussed with my mother. I do understand that it is a lot for her; my father doesn't help at all. He is rarely ever home, and my aunties live in Kingston, a.k.a. Town. They moved away when they were young for better opportunities, but I am not sure what type of opportunities, because by their own admission they are still *struggling because tings tough.* From the snippet of conversation that I have been able to overhear, they both live in the same *big yard* or tenement yard, and they work in a factory packing diapers and baby food which is not hard work, but the environment is really stressful, *pure Ka sa Ka sa* (cursing and fighting). Invariably, they are unable to give Mommy much aid by way of financial assistance because by the time they pay bus fare and taxi fare to come to Balcarres their *likkle money done clean, clean.*

Most times, they send what little they have and I go to pick it up from the one taxi-driver that they entrust it to—disgusting Denver. He is always trying to grab my breasts, and not just mine but every girl wearing a uniform in his vicinity. He keeps promising to rape me one of these days but I know he's joking, and he knows that I know, because we are both aware that my father would kill him and my uncles would bury his body at sea. I wish I could tell Mommy all of this but then who would collect the money when my aunts send it? Or who would they send it with?

Thankfully, tomorrow is Saturday. I'll get time to rest and put balm on my wounded soul. We go to the local Market every other Saturday, so we won't be going tomorrow. I'll go to Swift River; the steady consistent flow and quietude of the river is always pacifying for my raw emotions. Just being near to any river, without exception, renews my soul and quells the unease in my mind. Although of late, no matter how hard I try, there always seems to be two warring factions within me. And just like I snapped today, I am always petrified that I am going to snap and split in two halves: one half going with my head and the other going with my heart.

Hopefully Claire won't visit tomorrow to check up on me, as I desperately need to spend this weekend by myself to convalesce. On the other hand, my mother will not allow me to go by myself. So of necessity I might need to lie—I'll just tell her that I am meeting my friends there. All the same, though, I hate lying to her. I might just invite Claire because I don't really want to go alone anyway; you never know what you might encounter by the riverside. Some people swear they have seen a river mumma or mermaid there. Although in all my years of going I have never encountered one, and I don't really know what I would do if I did. So far no one has said what the consequences are for observing one in her natural habitat, and I most certainly do not want to be the one who has to declare said consequences.

I'll see how I feel tomorrow. Tomorrow is a new day.

CHAPTER TWO

"Hi, Aunt Sher. May I talk with Claire?"

In the morning I feel slightly better, especially since the welts have gone away, and after I've vigorously cleaned our three-bedroom house—first wiping the floor with a bucket of soapy water infused with Fabuloso, then applying the red dye, and lastly scrubbing with the coconut brush until I can see my image in the hardwood floor. It must be the adrenaline, because I feel like a whole new person. I decide to lime with my friends today. After cleaning, I ask Mommy and she says, "Yes, you can go, but after you fry the dumpling and plantain wid di tin a' Grace mackerel."

I check in on my Grandma and she is fast asleep. Mommy says, "She never fall asleep until about five dis morning. I am so tired; I'm going to get some shut eye until she wake up. Be safe!"

First stop, Claire's house. I decide that if they bring up yesterday's incident, I'll just tell them that I don't want to talk about it. We meet at the gate; we always meet at the gate. It is a cool morning and the air is fresh and clean. While we talk the ground doves are heard nearby, making their consoling cooing sound, and the fresh breeze brings with it the smell of the Caribbean Sea saturated with fresh, new possibilities. She lives in a bright blue and yellow house. I've always wondered whose idea it was to paint their house in those colours. Her house is famous because of it, and it is sometimes used as a landmark. All alongside the front of the house both inside and outside the gate is a wide cross-section of flowering plants: the red ixora, Joseph coat, bougainvillea, chrysanthemums, hibiscus and the yellow fine-leaf stinking Mary, which is always the most overpowering. Also, there's the rich scent of mint and fever grass combined together, which always gives me such a relaxed feeling. I wish I were close enough to pick a mint leaf, hold it close to my nose and just breathe in the revitalizing aroma.

"Hey, Neva! You jus lef we so yesterday!"

"I just wanted to walk home, to clear my head."

"You walked all the way home? We looked for you after school but you just gone so like Sammie mout."

We are both bent over laughing at her last comment. Sammie is a figure in Jamaican folklore, and he's done everything: from planting peas and corn *dung a gully* to being quite talkative, but he is still wildly revered even though he died shortly after planting the peas and corn. After that, a comfortable silence sits over us; being friends for so long, we are always able to rest in each other's presence without forced conversation. Claire is my first friend, because her mother and mine grew up together so we were always in each other's company from when we were babies. However we didn't really become friends until primary school.

"Anyways, I was wondering if you wanted to go to Balcarres River with me today?"

"Gyal, look how many beaches we have in Portland, why you love go a river so much? You a mus mermaid!"

"I don't know, the river is always so clean, refreshing and

soothing! Me cyan explain it, me just love it."

"Well, me and my aunt plan to go to the beach today. You want to come?"

"Wait, which auntie? Not Collette?"

"No, you mad! Monepha, my youngest aunt!"

"Oh, okay, because Collette too strict and love tell people what to do! I swear she miss her calling in life because she should be a police officer."

"That is exactly why she is not married yet! Too many rules."

"Claire, leave you auntie business alone, you too fass, Ms. Nosy."

We both laugh some more.

"Alright, I have to go by the house to tell Mommy because I already told her that we were going to the river."

"Yes, good idea! You know how Balcarres people chat-chat, the last thing you want is for Mouta Massy Liza to tell her that you were at the beach."

"True dat! But Poppyshow, tell me something—"

"Yes."

"Who the hell is Mouta Massie Liza?"

Mouta Massie Liza is another figure from Jamaican folklore; no one knows for sure where she originated but I suspect that she was the creation of Ms. Lou, one of our most prolific poets and a spoken word artist.

We laugh so hard that I am in stitches by the time I leave her gate and walk up the hill to my house. I enter the house, check on both my mother and grandmother, and satisfied that they are sound asleep I leave a note on the dining table. I inform Mommy that we'll be going to Boston Beach instead and that we'll be going with Auntie Monepha. She'll be happy to know that we'll be accompanied by an adult.

By the time we gather everyone it is mid-morning and the sun is out and about in all her radiant glory, her beams reaching into every cell in my body. Everywhere she touches a feeling of warmth remains. This particular beach is a good distance away so we take a taxi. All five of us, along with the driver and two other passengers. At one point, since I am the *mawga* one, I end up sitting with the gear stick between my legs since I am the only one who can fit into that space. No one complains, though, because it is what it is: if it weren't me then it would be someone else who is as skinny as me. Taxi drivers pack passengers into their vehicles like sprats in a can because oftentimes they are working for someone else, so they have to make a profit that both parties can survive on. Hence they have coined the phrase *small up youself*. It is just the way things are.

The lush greenery is always invigorating and fortifying. I cannot picture myself living anywhere else. I often wonder how my aunts live in Kingston. I've visited them a few times and I couldn't wait to leave. It's all dust, noise and concrete. People are always angry at each other and why wouldn't they be angry, when there's no greenery around to rejuvenate and invigorate them?

I crane my neck to look out the passenger window as I watch the trees rush by, and I imagine myself floating above the trees—not in the clouds but just above the trees, a passive observer witnessing the birds taking flight. The bald pates and hummingbirds are my absolute favourite, but the latter are a rare find in these parts. The guys and even some girls in our community sometimes hunt the bald pates with a home-made slingshot, killing, roasting and eating them with white bread. I don't know how they could eat those poor, skinny, helpless creatures.

Before you know it, we are at the beach. It is still early but there are lots of people here already: sitting in small groups on large, colourful beach towels, talking and eating, or just standing around on the shore in various forms of beach-worthy attire, from shorts and T-shirts to short tights and tank tops, from one-piece bathing suits to the very daring two-piece swimsuits. Some people are wasting no time—they are already in the water, splashing around and playing beach volleyball, or just floating lazily, not a care in the world. We find a good location, spread out towels and leave our bags, and join the others in the water. We greet a few people from school and our community but we avoid long, drawn-out conversations because we are here to swim, not talk. We dive in. At first the water is surprisingly cold but gradually we get used to the temperature and the combination of cold water and hot sun is energizing. I always shiver involuntarily with unbridled pleasure after being in the water for a few minutes. The further I go from shore, the more I feel my shoulders dropping, a visceral reaction to stress leaving my body. Sometimes I think that if I could make it to the middle of the ocean, I would return completely and utterly stress free. I always test myself to see how far I can swim, but eventually when I am only a few feet from the line of demarcation indicating the danger zone everyone starts to wave to me like they're doing a new dance that they are inviting me to join. I feel so at peace here I wish everyone would leave. We join one of the groups playing volleyball on the shore and then we break for lunch; being in the saltwater sure makes me hungry. Claire has made corn beef sandwiches, there's strawberry syrup and there is also melon, of course. I really love melon, it's my comfort fruit.

I look to my left, where there are red mangroves. Palm trees and the seaside mahoe are growing wild and thick, and I see a group of guys whom I have never seen before. Someone says, "They come from Foreign." Anyways, we ignore them and continue our activities.

We plan to swim for another few hours and then head home. After we have had our fill, we pack up to leave, and the whole time Claire is complaining, "I hate the sand! It gets into everything and it is such a pain to get rid of."

I bite my lower lip before I blurt out, *that's why I prefer the river: no sand.*

The guys from earlier keep staring at us, one in particular.

However, I am not Michael Jackson and I don't want to be starting something, so I just keep my head down, avoiding eye contact as much as possible. In the blink of an eye, the morning turns to afternoon, the afternoon turns into evening and soon dusk is upon us. I really enjoy that time of the day, because dusk brings with it cooler temperatures and the calming chirping of the crickets. But the one setback is that the hungry mosquitos come out in droves with their vibrant buzzing sound.

Soon we're back in a taxi, saying bye to Bridget and Robin and then we're back home again. A day well spent.

CHAPTER THREE

In Portland we experience two dry seasons and two rainy seasons: July to August and December to April are dry months, and May to June and September to November are the rainy seasons. I hate the dry seasons; it is the rainy seasons that I live for, even though we don't get to do much of anything, because the rain comes down in drums. Sometimes there is flooding, which leads to landslides, and every now and again people go missing and then their bodies are recovered from the river. Sometimes it rains so much that the roof leaks, and they have to close the schools until someone from the Education Ministry in Kingston comes to look at the damage and puts in a work order to get the work done. This sometimes takes a while; everything is so laid back here, or the funds might just mysteriously go missing, so they have to find ways of replenishing them—usually by underpaying teachers. Our principal, Mr. Chambers, has decided to establish the *Mr. Rainy Day Fund*. That way there is usually some money set aside to at least start the work until the bureaucrats get to it.

Ironically, though I love the rain, I hate the mud. I hate the feeling of mud between my toes. The mud reminds me of worms, and the mud takes on a life of its own between my toes, hugging my feet and straddling my shoes like a second, repugnant skin. I immediately have to take a shower when I step in mud. The other drawback is that, of necessity, in the rainy season sometimes I have to stay home. This is especially difficult because, on top of the bay rum, Mommy has added Limacol and Tiger Balm to the Vicks VapoRub in her pharmacy. One thing's for sure, if this new formula doesn't heal my grandmother, nothing else will.

On rainy days, when I get tired of looking out my window at the slanting rain and the wind flogging the trees, causing the leaves and limbs to scatter in various directions, I mostly read. The sound of rain on the roof is always so soothing, like on old friend who doesn't visit often enough, but you know for sure that he will definitely visit at significant moments in your journey. We don't have a lot of money, but my parents have always invested in my education. They have always invested in me. I mostly read escapist fiction—anything to escape my reality right now. None of that Mills and Boons crap that most of the girls at my school seem to enjoy. There's nothing else to do. We only have two TV stations and my dad is always watching news, sports or *cricket, lovely cricket.* I assure you that there is nothing lovely about cricket, especially now that the West Indies team has been on a steady losing streak.

Moreover, the rainy season is typically my parents' fighting season, because Daddy is home most of the time. There is no work on account of the rain. My father works in construction, both residential and on business sites. They mostly fight about the inordinate amount of time that my mother spends with my unwell grandmother. I would never say this to either of them, but in a way, he is not wrong for wanting to spend time with his wife—which is what I want, to spend time with my mother. They hardly see each other as it is, and when he is home, she is caught between her devotion to her mother and her loyalty to her husband. I see her running from my grandmother's room to the living room, checking on both of them. This must be quite exhausting for her. But Mommy cannot comprehend his frustrations; she thinks he should understand her "sitiation."

"The sitiation that you are in or that you have placed yourself in is completely all your doing." My father explains as patiently as he can. But I can tell from his tone that his patience is waning.

"Fabien, don't talk so loud; you a go wake up Mama."

"But Bev, you really expect, say me a go keep quiet in a me own house? Jah know sey you tek me fe real poppyshow! Get your sisters to help you every now again. A no fe dem Maddah to? A jus you alone she have?"

"Fabe, see reason nuh! How much time me a fi tell you say, they are not in a position to help right now. You nuh see say dem a struggle right now?"

"So wait, we naw struggle to? Look from when me nuh get fe go work because of the rain. You want tell me say, every ting perfec wid we?"

"Not perfec, but we fine! We have food fe eat and de bills dem pay, so we good."

"We good? When las you sleep in a we room? Huh? You spen night after night in a you Maddah bed! So wait, me nuh have feelings like everybody else?"

That last comment and comments of that general nature are always my cue to close my door (not slam) just close because my parents always say, *ongly people who pay bills slam door.*

However, the closed door doesn't block out their words, it merely delays their entry.

Ultimately, when there's a lull in the rain, I ask, "May I go to Robin's house?"

They are so caught up in their argument that they both scream "*Yes!*" at the same time. I don't want to go all that way by myself so I invite Claire. She is more than happy to leave her house as well. Being an only child, at least I have my own room, my own space, but she shares a room with her youngest aunt, Monepha.

We get to Robin's house just before the deluge, which comes with gale force winds. Bridget is already there and we are just in time for a late lunch. Robin's mother is away so we have the whole house to ourselves to do whatever we like. Their house is located in another community in a new housing scheme, and it boasts a split-level concept promoted as a *Foreign Style Home*. There are three bedrooms—including the Master bedroom—on the lower level, along with two full bathrooms, and the kitchen, dining and living rooms are up top along with another very cozy bedroom. All the houses in this area look uniform, although they all sport different colours, but the tall black metal gates are the very same. They all have identical gardens and fruit trees, as if they share the same gardener. There is just one mango tree in each (East Indian), a star apple tree (this must be the only fruit I hate because it is sticky and sweet and gets all over your mouth and hands), an Otaheite apple tree, and a guinep tree off to the side—at the exact same location—which is currently in season, so we can hear the delicate fruits being tossed against the window by the angry winds. Also, they all sport a rose tree at the front, just inside the gate – the only difference being that there are a variety of colours. They all have a croton plant, a.k.a. a Joseph coat, creepers, hibiscus of varying colours, chrysanthemums, zinnias, lilacs, and some other purple flowers growing on the ground, but I don't know their names. Plus, the community has a wide cross section of trees: guango trees, a *lignum vitae* tree, a poinciana tree and bougainvillea plants that you can smell from a mile away. Oh and someone has recently planted a Julie mango tree close to the entrance of the housing scheme.

"Such a difference, girl, so much peace and quiet at your house."

Robin looks sad for a moment at Claire's assessment. Then she says,

"Really, do you know how much times I wish I had someone else to talk with or just hear other voices?"

We all look at our hands in our laps, avoiding eye contact with each other as we are all fully aware of the situation. Of course, Bridget comes to the rescue, quickly changing the subject. "Man, what a whole heap a rain."

"I love it though," I announce. "I have always found the rain so tremendously comforting—from the pitter patter on the roof to the whistling of the winds."

Claire rolls her eyes, "Of course you love it, you always love rain. You must be a plant or something botanical."

Robin jumps up and says over her shoulder, "Do you know that there is actually a name for people who love the rain? I discovered it last week and I've been meaning to tell you."

The rest of us say, "Really?" simultaneously. This happens a lot with us. She moves towards her huge computer. She is one of the few students at Providence High School who has one. We all read in a whisper:

Pluviophile—(N) a lover of rain; someone who finds joy and peace of mind during rainy days. The word pluviophile is a combination of two Latin words: "Pluvia" which means rain and "Phile", a slang word used to describe a lover of something.

"Wow! Who knew that that was actually a thing?" I say, still staring at the screen. In a way I feel relieved, because to be honest I was starting to feel weird as the only person I know who loves the rain. Everyone is always complaining about the mud and the lack of activity on account of the constant downpours.

We return to the living room to finish lunch: escovitched parrot fish with festival and soda. Of course there is a huge watermelon. I love watermelon. It is always so refreshing on a warm day. I love how the outside is green and the inside red. It is a messy affair eating a slice of watermelon, but I relish all the juicy goodness running down my chin and falling onto my clothes. I always imagine the watermelon just cleansing all my internal organs, making them brand new, invigorating my mind and renewing my muscles. Eating a slice of watermelon always takes me back to my childhood, when Mommy would cut the melon into chunks and feed me bit by bit like a bird feeding her baby. I have always associated watermelon with laughter and my mother's face, her gap-toothed smile. At that time I was her only responsibility and her focus was set primarily on me.

I love festival as well; I even got Robin to teach me how to make them, but mine are never as good as hers. I don't know if I am putting in too much cornmeal or flour or not enough baking powder, but they never come out right; the texture is always wrong. Being Jamaican we never use measurements—that's for people on TV to sort out.

Invariably, the conversation turns to boys. Astoundingly, Robin confesses that she is crushing on a boy who lives in Moore Town. We all gasp at the same time and our mouths gape open, like when the ackee pod is ripe. In a chorus we ask the same question, "You mad?"

Moore Town is a Maroon settlement. We all grew up with the Maroons basically right next door, never fraternizing with them because historically they are like the Rastafarians in a sense—a people who stick to themselves and maintain their own cultural, social, political and religious identity. The difference between them and the Rastas is that they live in their own town, on land they received from their ancestors. They are self-governed and do not choose to get involved with outside influences. If you were to look up *mind your own business* on Robin's computer, a picture of the Maroons would pop up.

From Mr. Wallace's History class we learned that they are the direct descendants of the Taino people, also known as the Arawak Indians, and African enslaved peoples who were, in the words of Bob Marley, *stolen from Africa, fighting on arrival.* The Africans were brought to the Caribbean when the Spanish sent the Conquistadors to the New World. They were released after the British fought the Spanish, conquered them and gave them a short time to pack up and leave the island. Those enslaved persons were either emancipated or escaped, depending on whose history you're reading. After which they fled to the hilly interior of the island and started their own community in the 1600s. Currently, Moore Town is one of four Maroon settlements on the island. There are: Accompong Town in St. Elizabeth, Moore Town, and Charles Town and Scott's Hall, which are both located in Portland as well.

Now that I think about it, Robin was asking a whole lot of questions in that class. The one that I remember the most because I have often wondered about it myself was: "Sir, why didn't the Maroons help the slaves more?"

She asked it in a way that suggested that she was weighing her mind, as my mother would say.

Mr. Wallace smiled his small, scatter-toothed smile and said, "That's a very complicated question, Robin, and the answer is just as complex."

He walked to the window, looked out at the big poui tree outside our east-facing window, with bright yellow leaves scattered all around. I've always imagined that they sit on the ground, looking up at the tree, like obedient children waiting to hear a story from their parents. He took a deep breath, as if fulling his lungs with much-needed oxygen—always an indication that he was going to give a very long-winded answer. I could hear sighs and groans all around, chairs moving and scraping the floor, as if everyone was getting comfortable to hear this tale. But unlike Miss Shalk's class, I feel at ease here. Maybe because I grew up listening to *Bredda Anansi Stories,* and stories about *Bredda Tacoomah* told by my dad, with all the inflections and actions. These mythical characters are larger than life and play a huge role in our oral history; they are like fables meant to instruct children and adults alike on lessons about ethics and human nature. To me, History class is all about storytelling, the only difference being that all these stories are based on factual events that affected real people and not just fictitious creatures.

He walked back to his desk, at the center of the room. The desk is made of solid brown wood and has seen better days. By now the room was so quiet that we could hear the squishing sounds his black leather shoes made, as if he were walking in water, or maybe there was too much space in his shoes because they are two sizes too big. He always walks with a sense of purpose, as if he has somewhere important to go and has to be on time. He cleared his throat and began. Generally, it's a sound I detest, but somehow not when he does it.

"Remember when we talked about the Transatlantic Slave trade."

More groaning.

Someone said, "That is so very depressing, sir, please don't tell us about that again."

He nodded, looking very serious, and said, "That's actually not what I want to talk about. I just wanted to give you context."

He appraised the room with a very somber look in his eyes, like a doctor about to deliver grave news; I guess he wanted to see if he still had our attention.

"To your question, Robin, and this is mainly my take on the matter: the Africans who were brought to the New World, a.k.a. the Americas and the Caribbean, their history did not just begin with slavery. I know when we discuss our history that it is where we tend to begin, at the inception of African enslavement, but like you guys learned in grade nine history, continental Africa has a rich heritage that goes back for centuries. Africa had the first civilized society, led by great kings and queens, and had a most thriving economy. They literally were here before anything else. The Africans had instituted a tribal system that worked for them in ways that we might never be able to comprehend. So guess what happened during the time of slavery?"

I blurted out, "They still had that tribal mentality when they came to Jamaica."

Mr. Wallace said, "Yes," looking quite pleased with my answer. I couldn't stop smiling.

He continued, "So, having brought the ideology of self-governance with them, they mainly focused on their own well-being, much like tribes would not interfere or intervene in the affairs of another tribe unless specifically invited to do so. Plus, to be fair, they did help many runaway slaves and they did fight many battles with the plantocracy, which invariably assisted to a large extent in first the amelioration and ultimately the abolition of slavery."

There was a pregnant pause as he was collecting his thoughts. By now we were all sitting on the edge of our chairs, because with him it is never what he is saying, so much as the way he is saying it. He is always so passionate and there is a resonance to his voice that is quite endearing. His voice tends to pull you in like the wind transporting the tide in the evening. Plus, he always leaves us with something to "muse on," as he calls it.

"Imagine, if you will, the enslaved who were taken from Africa: their confusion as they were thrown on huge ships, final destination unknown. They'd watched their loved ones die at the point of entry—choosing death over the unknown—families separated, daily waking up to the stench of death and excrement. Finally, they arrive in the Caribbean. The land mass seems similar but it doesn't feel quite the same; it is still not home, because it is not where their ancestors are buried, definitely not their ancestral lands. They are beaten and berated daily, their way of life severely disrupted, they own nothing, and they have no hope of owning anything. Then, one fateful day, someone says: *there are people on the island who look like us but they are free.*"

At this last comment he laughs, not a belly laugh but one that indicates pleasure.

"Everyone who hears this must have berated him and laughed him to scorn. They must have asked, *how could this thing be?* But after the laughing finally stopped, they must have sent out brave scouts to confirm this myth with strict instructions on how to communicate their findings since they couldn't send telegrams or make phone calls—"

Robin stirred in her seat, then asked, "So then, sir, how did they communicate?"

"Great question, Robin. They used a system of signaling, singing and signing to get word back of their findings. To this day, that is why so many of our people sing when they are working. It was passed on to us by our ancestors."

The lazy-eyed boy in the back yelled, "I thought that was my mother's way of annoying everyone."

There was polite laughter and Mr. Wallace continued.

"Ladies and gentlemen, can you imagine how empowering that must have been to discover, that at a time of bondage and despair, there are people who look just like you, who are living right under your nose, living their lives in freedom? Soon after this discovery, the enslaved people started to sabotage the plantations, breaking equipment, maiming animals. At first just little things, but eventually this sabotage became a hallmark of their act of rebellion, and they later graduated to bigger things, like setting fires. Initially, the Maroons did not get involved in the affairs on the plantations—"

"Because of their understanding of how tribes work."

"Yes, Bridget, that's correct. But later, people used to go missing from the plantations, and after an investigation it would be discovered that the Maroons had been helping them. Of course the plantocracy got involved and the British waged war against them just to maintain their dominance. Also, when war did not break the Maroons and curtail their actions, treaties were signed which helped in cutting down the number of enslaved people who were running away to join the Maroons in the mountains. Nanny of the Maroons being one of the heroes of those battles. However, the very presence of the Maroons had a very profound impact on the mindset of the enslaved, so they were energized to act, and as they say the rest is history. So to your point, Robin, the Maroons did help the enslaved, in more palpable ways than can ever be measured. They reinforced their rightful position as humans, entitled to being treated with dignity, which enabled them to rebel—to take back their power and their sovereignty."

"That's amazing!" Robin looked like someone coming out of a dream.

Mr. Wallace laughed the laugh of the contented, someone who had accomplished his mission in life, and he ended the class by saying: "Yes, it sure is, Robin. So you can understand that, after spending a huge part of their history fighting wars, now the Maroons just prefer to live their lives in obscurity and enjoy the labour of their ancestors. They prefer not to let anyone else into their world, so there is no doubt as to whom their legacy belongs. Sometimes when you allow people into your space, that only leads to complications. So, as much as possible, they avoid whatever issues they can."

Robin interrupts my cogitation.

"I know it sounds insane to be in love with a Maroon, knowing what we know about them—knowing there is no future in it. Plus, Mummy would be so incredibly disappointed if she found out, but I can't help it. The heart wants what the heart wants. Love is like the rain; you don't know when it's going to come pouring down."

"We know you can't help how you feel, but you must stay away from him," declares Bridget. Bridget has always been closest to Robin. They were friends first, just as Claire and I were friends first, and then the two friend groups just merged. Not so much because we are alike, but more so because we are so different. All our differences just seem to work well together.

"On top of that," Claire reasons, "based on what you are saying, you don't even know exactly where he lives, whether or not he already has a girlfriend, who his parents are—nothing."

"Has he ever invited you to his house? Have you guys ever been on a date?"

My time to chime in. She didn't need to answer, because her mother will literally kill her if she ever discovers that she'd been to a boy's house; especially a Maroon boy, who spells trouble for her daughter. Robin getting involved with this boy would be perpetuating what her mother had done, getting involved with a man who is both physically and emotionally inaccessible to her. This is so very much out of character for Robin, the sensible one who weighs all the pros and cons twice then weighs them again in reverse. I conclude that it must be hormones: either that or she is just sick of her mother, so this is her way of rebelling.

To ease the tension that has surreptitiously invaded and desecrated our space, I ask: "How exactly did you guys meet?"

She thought for a moment, as if searching for the right word, not so much to convince us but to convince herself that this relationship is actually worth fighting for.

"I went to Port Antonio to do some business for Mummy, as she was having one of her episodes."

I know all too well about episodes.

"After I was done, I felt so drained that I just sat on the side of the road."

We all exclaimed, "You? Really? Wow!"

Claire proclaims, "Wonders never cease!"

"I was on my period! You guys know how weak I get during that time of the month."

We nod vigorously as we all have experienced the horrible feeling of lethargy at some point or the next.

"My mother wants to force-feed me liver, because she says that helps with the exhaustion but no star, no way. Anyways, he was passing by and saw me, stopped to find out if I was doing okay. I have seen black people before but this guy is blue black, hair of wool lustrous and vibrant, the whitest teeth, cherry lips and the kindest, darkest eyes I have ever seen. Just for his eyes alone he could be a supermodel."

Claire mocks, "Not the eyes," making kissing sounds.

We all giggle, and the tension that had occupied the room earlier knew it was time to leave. I could feel it leaving the room while looking back to see if there might another opening.

"Since then, anytime I get a chance I meet up with him. He hangs out in Port Antonio most times because he helps his uncle to transport people when they need to access services that are not readily available in their community. When he's not there, I give his uncle a note for him, letting him know the next time I will be away. A few times I have told Mummy that I am going to meet up with you guys."

"The fact that you have to lie to your mother is an indication that this is not a good idea. Also, I have so many questions: does he go to school? Does he work? How old is he?"

All this had to be said. I would not be a good friend if I didn't say it aloud. I know that we all are thinking this.

She looks very sad, which makes her appear so vulnerable. Again, completely out of character. "I know that all of what you are saying is correct and eventually I will tell her, but for now it's just nice to have someone to talk to."

"So wait, who are we… scandal bag?" Bridget goes on the offensive, as she should.

"You know that's not what I mean. You guys will understand when you meet him."

"So when do we meet him?" Bridget says, grudgingly.

"Today. Since Mummy is going to be away for a while, I invited him over."

"You did what?" Bridget asks, sounding almost offended.

After that, we all looked at each other, dumbfounded. Who knew Robin was so brave, to bring a boy into her mother's house? This I had to see.

It is so funny how people change over time. The Robin I knew would never even consider doing anything so risky. Things are really changing, and I don't think I like it. None of us do, but she's her own person, so what can we do?

CHAPTER FOUR

It's the second week in December and the community is fully engrossed in preparations for the Christmas season. Christmas is a big deal in Balcarres and the celebrations start early in December. There are always many activities in the homes, and in the community at large. The community events are held in the town square, and people from neighbouring communities, mostly smaller ones, join in. Mommy said that back in the day they used to have to travel to either Port Antonio or Buff Bay to take part in the festivities. We start prepping for the next Christmas from early in the year by setting the fruits for the Christmas cake or the Black cake, by blending raisins, cherries, and prunes in Red Label wine and letting them soak until it's time to bake the cake. Also, there's always a goat or a cow set aside for the celebrations.

In addition to all the sweet aromas of food and pastry, there is also the ubiquitous smell of burning wood that is evident all year round, but certainly more conspicuous at this time. Many people in our community cannot afford to buy cooking gas so they cut down trees and burn them, which produces charcoal. Burning wood and the smell of fresh rain on dry soil are my all-time favourite scents. I can literally smell the rain coming in from miles away as soon as the first drop hits the ground. Moreover, ever since I was a little girl I have always loved the smell of charcoal, for reasons that I am not fully aware of; it reminds me of Sunday and Christmas dinners.

Charcoal is black and hard like rocks, but sometimes, I get lucky and I find a soft piece. Generally, I start off by holding it up to my nose for a few minutes, and then take a quick look around to see if anyone is nearby. Ultimately, the smell and the texture are so tempting that I sometimes pop a piece in my mouth and just let it sit there for a while. At first I chew, ever so slightly, until I can't resist any longer and I swallow. I used to induce vomiting after having a small piece, but after some time had passed I abandoned that practice altogether. I am so embarrassed about eating charcoal at my age, but I always have a nice juicy piece with me and any time I feel stressed I throw a piece in my mouth. I have to be careful, though; I always have to wash out my mouth because it stains my tongue and teeth jet black, like the black shoe polish I use to shine my school shoes. Anyways, so far this is my one vice, my only guilty pleasure, and at least I am not out there engaging in unprotected sex like some of my peers. Thus I deserve to have this one little secret that no one needs to know about. After all, I am not hurting anyone; charcoal is burnt wood, and I am pretty sure everyone who eats jerk pork or jerk chicken unwittingly ingests some of the charcoal as well.

I especially love the Christmas season, as it is the only time that my mother and I actually spend time together, and of course my aunts come home to spend the holidays with us. We start by washing all the baking tins, then we combine all the ingredients: flour, the fruits, nutmeg, cinnamon, molasses for colour, salt and cane sugar. We use most of the fruits, but whatever is left we use to bake a pudding. The pudding is generally more textured, not as rich, but just as flavourful. We usually have both because some of our family members don't like Black cake. They prefer the pudding.

Once we have sorted out the baking it's time to thoroughly clean the house inside and out, from top to bottom. Every other year my dad whitewashes the verandah and the gate and paints the living and dining rooms. We use a dye to colour the floor and wash all the bedding and the curtains. Most times Mommy asks Miss Agatha to sew new curtains, and my aunties bring home fancy satin sheets: red, green and pink, mostly, which are only used during the Christmas season. There is always so much laughter during the holidays. I never want them to end.

We also make a special drink from the rich red sorrel plant. People have a variety of recipes, but we mostly just add ginger, cane sugar and Red Label wine; usually the sorrel drink is made in two different containers, one with alcohol and the other without. Being the taste tester for the family, I normally get to try both. However, I am looking forward to the next few years when I turn eighteen and become eligible to have the adult version.

A few days before Christmas Eve, my father and his brothers kill the ram goat that they have been grooming specifically for this occasion. This is the part that I hate the most. Every year I tell myself that I am not going to watch but every year I do, and end up with nightmares for weeks. I don't know what it is that I find most hypnotic: if it is the act of using a sharp machete to separate the goat's neck from his body with swift precision or if it's the innocence of the goat itself that keeps drawing me to witness its gruesome death. Sometimes I wonder if the goat knows all year that he is being prepared for his death. Do the other goats know that he is the chosen one, to be sacrificed to celebrate the birth of our Lord and Saviour Jesus Christ? Do they treat him any different? How does he feel about his impending demise?

The irony is that Jesus died so that people wouldn't have to sacrifice anymore. But when I asked my mother, she said it is the purpose for the death that is significant—to sustain people who might not have a meal if the goat isn't killed. It's for the good of the cause, and the cause of the many. She thinks Jesus is fine with it because it is not really a sacrifice, seeing that the Bible says, we should "eat of the fat of the land." However, that doesn't make it easier to watch.

I can't even have any of the meat, which always smells so delicious with curry, scotch bonnet peppers and the other seasonings; you can smell it from miles away. I keep seeing the goat taking its last breath with tears in his eyes, although I think the tears might just be in mine. The meat is quartered and shared among my dad and his two brothers, each getting a fourth, and the extra is given to the poor in the community. From the goat we get a variety of dishes: mannish water (a special soup made from the brains and the intestines), and tripe and beans, served with white rice and broad beans along with the other parts of the animal, none of which is ever wasted. This is the season that brings out the genuine kindness in our community. There is an unspoken rule that no one should go hungry on Christmas day. Some people kill pigs or cows and share the meat as well. The meats are parceled and seasoned to perfection with thyme, garlic, scallions, scotch bonnet pepper, red onions (that always cause my eyes to water) and salt, because the only powdered seasoning we use is the curry. We only use what we grow as seasoning. The bags of meat are refrigerated until Christmas day when we have the *big cooking*.

On the eve of Christmas there is usually a huge community fair. There are pageants and parades, and the centrepiece is the Junkanoo dancers, men on stilts who are as tall as giants. They wear masks that completely change them into monsters, and they appear in every child's nightmares for weeks and even months after. The name Junkanoo has evolved over the years from John Canoe, a historic folk festival: a combination of British and

African influences. As a child they always scared me—even now I am not too keen on seeing them, but I always attend the event with my friends. When I was younger my mother or my Aunt Yvonne (my dad's youngest brother's wife) used to take me to the event, but now I just go with my friends. However, I am a little embarrassed to admit that I am still afraid of the Junkanoos, especially Pitchy Patchy. Sometimes as a part of the entertainment they will randomly select an audience member to antagonize.

Claire usually comes up the hill very early in the morning so we can get a front row view so to speak, but after a while she's stopped coming to get me that early. I think she figured out that I was afraid, so she just gave up on trying to convert me. Claire thoroughly enjoys going; she never misses a year. I once asked her why and she said, "They wear masks, and everyone knows that they wear masks and are acting out a role. It is quite similar to real life, to me."

"How so, Claire?"

"Everyone in life is playing a role, acting. At some point, we all wear masks to protect us from the glare of the world and the gaze of strangers. People can be so judgmental and it hurts, especially when it's your own."

"So let me get this straight, out of fear of being judged we are compelled to wear masks—to roleplay—to protect ourselves?"

"Yes, basically."

"So why not just be yourself, and whoever loves you will understand your shortcomings and whoever doesn't love you, to hell with them?"

"Neva, sometimes that's easier said than done. Let's face it; we all have this need to be loved. Remember when Shalk talk to us about Maslow's Hierarchy of Needs?"

"Yes, but what does that have to do with wearing masks?"

She sighs, obviously frustrated with my lack of understanding.

"Well, it means that, because we all have this intrinsic desire to be loved, and out of fear that we will be rejected if we don't somehow measure up, we all wear a mask at some point to protect us from the cruelty of rejection."

"I still don't get why people feel the need to pretend, to fake a persona, to fake their whole life. Wouldn't it be much simpler to just be yourself, accept who you are and then others will catch up later?"

At this she shakes her head as if in utter disbelief of how dense I am. But I am really just trying to understand what is going on here.

"Nevaeh, you're an idealist and I love you for it."

"That's unfair! Who is judging who, now?" I say as I feel the anger rising in me. I hate when people call me an idealist, because all I hear is that I am naïve and stupid.

"Don't be offended, girl, I don't mean anything. I just mean that you are a pure soul and you see things and people from that perspective. You don't understand roleplaying because you have always been loved and appreciated by your friends and family, so you've come to a level of self-acceptance. However, there are people in our world who have not attained that level, and still struggle with who they are. Therefore, out of fear of not being loved, they wear masks. Sometimes they don't even know that they are. It becomes automatic for them, especially when they feel threatened by rejection and abandonment. It becomes a compulsion after a while."

I do understand that idea of a compulsion. That I cannot argue with.

"So you mean the mask, the roleplaying, is all a part of our coping mechanism?"

"Yes, exactly."

She says this with a brilliant smile as if I'd just seen the light.

The Junkanoos wear very loud and colourful costumes. The movement was founded during slavery, as Christmas was one of the few times when the slaves were allowed to have free time and celebrate their culture. The dance includes a king, a queen, and courtiers, and they don a cow's head, a horse head, an image of the stereotypical devil, and warriors and Indians. The central character is known as Pitchy Patchy. He is the most feared, by young children and adults alike, because of his flamboyant attire and outlandish antics. Jamaicans describe his antics as *prancing*. You will often hear parents accusing children of prancing around like Pitchy Patchy if the children can't keep still.

The Junkanoo dancers perform in the day, into late evening, and we attend *Gran Market* in the night. The Gran Market involves loud music and a sea of people bumping into each other—some people save all their pennies for this one night. There are a variety of vendors selling everything from food to clothing and cosmetic jewelry and this includes my favourite snacks: gizarda, grater cake, coconut and peanut drops, sweet potato pudding, cornmeal pudding and duckuno (also known as blue drawers). Duckuno is made by binding cornmeal, sugar, and spices in a banana leaf and cooking it in hot water; it is more like steaming, though. They also sell fruits like locust (or stinking toe), June plum, jackfruit, custard apple, sugar cane, coconut water and jimbilin (a tiny fruit that is yellow and quite tart). We use jimbilin to make jams and other sweet snacks.

This particular year, we are all excited about the Gran Market. We all plan to meet up at our usual spot and start the night. Also, Kwame and his friends will be there, so that's a bonus. Claire is so excited she couldn't wait for me to come down the hill. She comes to meet me, wearing a bright red lipstick that somehow compliments her beautiful dark hue, her hair is done in long single braids; definitely Monepha's handiwork. Collette must be having a fit. She is also wearing the white T-shirt that we all bought so we could look like a team—Robin's idea.

"Girl, what is taking so long?" She storms into my room while I am towel drying.

"Poppyshow, it is not even 6 p.m. yet. Relax, we'll get there in time."

"Not at the rate that you're going, Poppyshow!"

"Don't worry; Daddy is going to take us, so we don't have to wait on those full-up taxis."

With that she seems to visibly relax.

"I am so excited to hang out with the guys."

I can't help it, I giggle. Every time there is any mention of *the guys*, I giggle. For the first time ever, our girl group now includes guys.

"Robin must be beside herself this evening." Claire declares, giggling as well.

All of a sudden she looks serious and then she says, "Do you think that they're doing it?"

Now it was my turn to be serious, and might I add, confused. "Doing what?"

"You know! The wild thing!"

I was so shocked. I'd honestly never thought of Robin being the type to do that.

"No, of course not! This is Robin we are talking about. Can you even imagine her in that very compromising position?"

We both burst out laughing.

"You're right, not stush Robin. Plus, they really only just met recently."

We get to the town square and everyone meets up and we walk around for a while, but sadly before the night ends we all go our separate ways. This has never happened before. Robin goes with Bridget and Kwame and his friends, which just leaves me and Claire to hang out for the night. I guess that's fine but it is not the night I had planned. Claire seems disappointed as well, and who can blame her? This is not usually how we spend our night—but for the first time ever, I see her slip on a mask of nonchalance, and I quickly follow suit. After all, life goes on.

The other event popular among both young and old is the Watch Night Service. This is a church service held at all the churches in the community, starting at 10 p.m. on December

31 and ending on January 1. These services are always well supported, because people like to ring in the New Year in church. They seem to be of the view that the Rapture is going to come on either the last few hours of the old year or the first day of the new, so they rush to church. The pastors are always well prepared for the influx of potential new converts, and they always preach the most terrifying and soul-searching message that they can find. This year is no exception. For the first time in ages my whole family will be at church, including my father. My aunts, uncles, and even Grandma will be there. We get to church at around nine in the evening. Daddy is already grumpy because he has to make two trips to get everyone to church in good time.

We all sit together in the middle. I sit closest to Mommy so that she can translate for me. I see Claire and her aunts and Bridgett and her mother; no trace of her father, which is generally a good sign. I look around but there's no sign of Robin; her mother doesn't usually attend. I guess it's too many people, too many prying eyes, and too many wagging tongues for her level of comfort. This service is generally fun and terrifying all at once. There is singing, dancing, praying, and preaching, but best of all the testimony service never fails to deliver comic relief.

It is during one of these testimony services that we discovered that church people are visiting the resident Obeahman, to which there is an audible gasp, usually a sign of unanimous disapproval. I pull on Mommy's skirt and try to get her to explain about this Obeahman business but she is too engrossed in the service. She whispers, "When we get home I'll explain."

We also discover who is having an affair with whom. This causes more gasping, some whispering accompanied by raucous laughter.

As always, at 11 p.m. exactly, Pastor takes the mic, and his sermon is taken from St. Luke 15:11-32. His text is always the very same, and while the focus of the message might vary, it always comes back to the wrath of God being poured out on an ungodly, unjust and sinful world. Generally he needs a full hour, sometimes more, to expound the Word and change minds. I look over and Daddy looks so uncomfortable; every year he doesn't attend because he says, "Pastor a preach pon me." Although I don't know how he could arrive at that, because there are hundreds of people in attendance, many of whom are standing outside and participating through the open windows. So I don't know how or why Pastor would be picking on him specifically. I will need to ask Mommy to explain that as well. Pastor takes a while to "warm up," but once he's all revved up and gets going full throttle he sounds like his lungs are about to explode. There is a loud sound, maybe it's a sigh, I can never be sure, but it punctuates almost every other word, like a tambourine. Currently, he is in high gear.

"Bredren, God is a jealous God!"

The congregation cheers him on with a loud shout of "*Amen!*"

This assurance that his audience is with him prods him on. Seemingly, he is getting louder and louder.

"Some of you are still living like the prodigal son!"

More amens.

"You are going to lose out on your birthright like Esau, because uno love to fernicate! Fernication is a sin, children of God. Don't be fooled, don't stay out in the worl' and eat pig food, when the table is set with a lot of special treats. Fernication keep us from coming to the table, sistas and broddas."

He keeps saying, "fernicating" and "fernication." I don't even know what that is. I have never heard that word before. But then again, Pastor says a lot of words that I have never heard before. This I need an immediate explanation for, "What's that Mommy?" I yelled, competing with the cheerleaders.

She looks at me for a while then says, "He means fornicating."

I said, "Oh, oh, okay," although I still have no idea what it means. I'll have to ask Robin; she will know. Immediately, I scan the faces of the congregants, but there is still no Robin. I even glimpse Auntie Sabrina—tucked away in an inconspicuous corner of the church—but no Robin. I'll have to ask auntie for her at the end. This is strange, because even if it's just her or she's a little late Robin is usually in attendance.

"We have to be like the great speckled bird, children. We can't act like John Crow all year, eating dead, rot meat, and expect to be treated like dove."

At the John Crow comment there is lots of laughter, especially from the people standing outside looking through the window. I bet that's going to be the only take-away from this message. After what seems like an eternity, and a lot of yelling and screaming from Pastor, it is finally 12 a.m. Time for us to wish everyone a happy New Year; there are hugs and kisses all around.

But I feel so disturbed, and this is not the first time that Pastor's message has left me upset. Instinctively I know I should feel blessed not bruised after the message. I look around and everyone else seems fine—but I bet if they looked at me, really looked at me, they would see blood dripping from the bruises I have sustained, so they could tell. My parents have never beaten me, and very few teachers—only on occasions when they are administering a congregational flogging and I'll get the least— but I have seen what a beating looks like and the end results for the recipient and that's exactly how I feel: bruised and battered.

Every time I sit in the hearing of one of Pastor's sermons, I am left wondering if God is always angry with His people, because Pastor always sounds so angry even when he's expounding the love of God. Consequently, I've grown up fearing God.

To be honest, at this point in time, I don't even know if it is God or Pastor who is angry. I always see him as a sad little man with virtually no joy or power in his ordinary life, in his ordinary little house, with his ordinary wife and children. Therefore, the little joy and power he has is only in church where he is—apart from Jesus—the most dominant force.

CHAPTER FIVE

We met Robin's boyfriend Kwame in November, and since then we've spent a lot of time with him and his friends, Aja (which means goat), Thandwe (which means beloved) and Sankofa (which means "to get back"). I think they have such unique names; for once I am not the only one in the group with a *strange* name that people generally ask me to *repeat again*. From the moment we met Kwame, or as we call him, Kwa, I can see why Robin loves him; he and his friends are just so cool. Our girl group has never had boys who are our friends before, so this is quite refreshing. Sometimes it's hard but we always find a way to hang out with them. We all share this secret, because our parents cannot know that we are spending time with them and their parents can never know, either. Our two worlds, although close in proximity, are just not a good fit. I think we all strive to keep them separate; we live with a certain amount of fear that they will one day collide and this is both frightening and exhilarating all at once. In our world everyone has their place, has their role, and there is no uncertainty about that.

*   *   *

It is Thursday evening, and as usual I am helping to clean the science lab at school. It's a beautiful afternoon, not a cloud in the sky for miles—you know those days that everything is so perfect that you feel like you can do every- and anything all at once. I just love science and all things related to it, just being in the room with all the equipment and books and paraphernalia makes me feel smart. Everyone has left for the day and it's just me, Jasmine and Equiano who are left. Of course, almost every Jamaican has a pet name, so they are affectionately known as Jas and Equi for short. They are mostly together, not in a relationship way but in a friendship way. I admire Jas so much; I could never have a male friend that I chill with all the time. Maybe my mother would be understanding but my father's heart would attack him. Anyway, they are the science brains at our school and I am grateful for every moment that they allow me to spend in their presence.

It is almost 6:30 and we are just about ready to leave. But as soon as I step out into the hallway, I feel an eerie presence, just like a strong gust of wind. I ask, "Did you guys feel that?"

They both look at me like I have patty crumbs on my face and bulla stuck in my teeth.

Jas says, "What? I don't feel anything! Do you Equi?" He just shakes his head and walks away. Generally, he doesn't have the patience for any foolishness; his head is always in the clouds. He has big dreams of being a top scientist and he is already on track to receive a scholarship. So no, he has no time for nonsense.

Jas is a little more sympathetic. She walks beside me and says: "Maybe, it's just a draft. After all, this is not exactly a new building."

But as I am about to respond, I see a quick movement at the corner of my eye and when I turn around, I realize that it is Miss Shalk. My heart drops. I have been avoiding her since our last encounter. She steps out of the shadows and says, "Hi ladies," with such a huge smile, my stomach flips twice, my heart starts racing and my legs feel like coconut custard.

We both say, "Hi Miss." I can feel tension emitting from Jas, like standing in front of a bonfire. I guess I am not the only one intimidated by her insanity and her current level of duplicity. It is funny, but Miss Shalk is one of those people who would never achieve any success in the acting world. Her emotions always show in her eyes. Every time she looks at me, her eyes aim darts at me which is so disquieting it leaves my mouth as dry as parched corn.

"What are you ladies doing here at this time of night?" Still the repulsive smile, and as usual the perfect enunciation.

Jas offers, "We were cleaning the science lab, Miss."

Miss says, "That's great that you're helping out, Jas."

Jas is in the middle of saying, "Thanks Miss—" when my teacher turns directly to face me and declares, all the while with that repugnant smile,

"As for you Ms. Nevaeh, it's good practise because it's the only job you'll ever be qualified for: janitor."

With that being said, and clearly her mission accomplished, she walks away, head held high, humming. I am rendered speechless. Apparently, so is Jas, as we both turn to watch her leave and Jas' mouth is open as in a farewell greeting, but no sound is heard.

Even when we finally catch up to Equi we are still silent. Not a single word passes between us, to the point where Equi asks, "Are you guys okay? You both look like you've seen the same ghost." Which for him to notice is quite telling.

We both manage to mutter, "Mhm. Mhm."

We get to the town square where all the taxis and minibuses are parked and we go our separate ways, a foreshadowing of Miss Shalk's prophecy. They are both moving on to great things; meanwhile, I am not going anywhere—at least that's how I feel. We manage to say goodbye while Jas and I avoid eye contact.

I get in a taxi going my way but I don't want to go home, not with how I'm feeling. I decide to go by Claire's house before heading up the hill to mine. Mommy won't be too worried because she knows that I am staying after school. All the joy I had while cleaning the lab has now vanished like the sun taking a bow and hiding behind dark clouds.

I knock on the gate for a while, as no one expects a visitor at this time of the day.

Eventually, someone says, "Who is there?"

I respond, "Me, Neva!"

Then it's Claire's voice saying, "Come inside, girl." I have very rarely been invited in, but today is not a good day for a visit.

I don't feel like going inside. "No, please come out! I need to talk to you."

I hear the front door open and then close. She must have gone back inside to put on her yard slippers—her flip flops.

"What happen, Neva? I wasn't expecting to see you this evening."

"Me neither. I wasn't planning to stop by, but girl, I need to talk to you."

As she comes closer, it is obvious that she has just had a bath, as the strong scent of carbolic soap competes with the mild smell of Johnson's Baby Powder, the white powder smeared all over her neck and chest.

I just cut straight to the point. "Girl, you would never imagine what Shark just said to me."

I am still so shaken, I am whispering.

"What?" She sounds like she wants to hear, yet doesn't want to hear.

"Well, she basically just prophesied that I am going to be a janitor for the rest of my life. Which means I should just quit school, right now. Can you imagine?"

"What? This woman mad to rhatid! What kind of statement is that to come out of an adult's mouth, let alone a teacher's mouth?"

"Tell me exactly how she said it."

I tell her, withholding nothing.

"Me nuh know why she hate me so much to granny. But I feel strongly that she just put a curse on me!"

"I hope say dis time you tell Auntie Bev. She needs to know."

The thought had flashed across my mind but I'd decided against telling her because she just has too much on her plate. Plus, I am really afraid that she is going to be disappointed in me. That somehow, she's going to think that I am a fraud, that I have only been pretending to be smart this whole time.

"No man, it's nothing, I feel better now that I have said it to you," I lied. "Mommy have too much on her head right now." This is not a lie.

Claire does not seem convinced. She looks at me with so much sympathy in her eyes, I almost erupt into tears. It is as if she has seen clear through me, and how could she not? I would have to convince myself first before I would be able to persuade someone else, especially my forever friend.

"But what if she fails you out of spite? Remember that if she fails you, the school won't send your name to CXC. Because they are not going to risk lowering their passing average."

"I had forgotten about dat! Claire, what am I going to do? To rhatid, this woman is so vindictive that she is likely to do any and everything to disqualify me."

"So tell you Maddah, Neva."

"No Claire! That will not work. Shalk will just put on her fake smile and disingenuous demeanour of care and concern for her student. Remember the incident with Tricia Gordon? Do you remember what she told Tricia's mother?"

"Yes! She told Tricia's mother that she spends too much time hanging out with the boys and that's why her grades are dropping."

"Poor Tricia, she so fraidy-fraidy, she would never hang out with pure boys."

"But you see what happen though! She was so convincing that even Tricia own Maddah believe her and beat de girl in front of everyone."

"So, who else was there with you this evening?"

"Just Jas, Equi was walking too far ahead. But you know how she timid and stay. She would never rat out Shark if she feels like her scholarship would be or might be affected, and who could blame her?"

"A bet say if it was one of us standing there, she would never dare to say dat!"

Being so focused on the situation at hand, I'd almost forgotten about the gathering darkness, until the mosquitoes started buzzing around us. At first, just one or two were nipping on Claire, attracted by her white powder, but pretty soon there is a whole circle of mosquitoes and more flying in from every direction. Their loud singing was also attracting other insects.

"Anyways, it's getting dark so me ago up! See you tomorrow."

"Alright girl. Be safe. See you tomorrow."

I walk home in the dusk all the while my head spinning with the idea of failing English. I absolutely need to pass English for the school to allow me to take it at the CXC level. Not even Mommy's precious gap-toothed smile would be able to pull me out of this dark mood. I am even more scared that I might permanently obliterate that smile. My parents are depending on me to graduate from high school with high marks in the CXC exams so that I can attend college; something they were unable to do, and I would be the first member of the family to do so. As I make my way up the hill, I can't help but think, how could such a perfect day go so horribly wrong? When the day started there was no indication that anything like this could have happened. No indication that I would be so down in the dumps before I went to bed. If I had known I would have probably just stayed in bed today.

* * *

I arrive home to the smell of my favourite: stew peas with pigtails, white rice and I am sure coleslaw will be served on the side. But I am way too upset to eat. The full weight of what might happen is crashing down on me like when the tide comes in the evening and brings with it the rage of the sea. Another reason I prefer the river; the sea is notoriously temperamental. Mommy meets me at the door, not smiling but quite concerned.

"You come home so late!"

"Mommy, remember that today is Thursday and I help out at school on Thursday evenings."

"Yes, but you've never been this late before! You alright?"

"Yes, ma'am, I am fine."

"Mama had a good day today, so I had time to mek you favourite dinner."

"Thanks but I'm not hungry."

She looks so disappointed, I quickly add, "Because we were at school so late, the teacher bought us box food. There was so much to do today, he knew we would be there for a while." I lie, careful not to mention any teacher by name. Praying she won't ask for a name.

"Well, okay! It will taste better tomorrow when you heat it up."

"Yes, Mommy, that's true."

"You can have some watermelon for dinner then. Me know say you always love melon."

"Yes, Mommy," I said with my lips, but my heart says *not even watermelon will soothe me; not tonight.*

After I put my backpack in my room, I go to check on Grandma. She is sound asleep, looking so peaceful, and the rhythmic motion of her breathing so soothing. She really does look better. I stroke her soft grey hair. I return to the living room. I see my father heading toward the kitchen.

"Hi, Daddy."

"Hey star girl. How you do?"

"I'm good, Daddy."

"I hope say, you a study hard." He always says this.

"Yes, Daddy, always."

He questions, "You see you grandma?"

"Yes Daddy!"

"You see how she just come around and look good?"

"Yes, Daddy!" Although this is more of a statement than a question.

"A dead she soon, dead you nuh!"

"What! But she looks fine, I just checked on her!"

"Then nuh dat, me a try tell you! Anytime, people sick bad and den all of a sudden, dem jus start look betta; a dead dem a go dead!"

My father says all that with a straight face. I burst into tears; I can't help it. On top of everything else that has happened today, to discover that my grandma, who has been a fixture in my world, my entire life, is going to die. Immediately, I start to wonder if this is somehow my fault, if I have caused this by wishing she would die so I could get my mother back. My mother has always told me that my thoughts are very powerful and that just by thinking about something long enough, I can call them into existence. But I've only thought about it like once, well maybe more than once, but still, I didn't really mean it at the time. I just wanted my mother back.

My mother rushes out of her bedroom because by now I am howling like the wind in a thunderstorm and big heavy boulders are rolling down my face like stones rolling down a hill.

"Is what? What happen?"

Even Grandma is now wide awake and calling, "Bev! Bev! Bev! Wha happen? Why is dat likkle gyal crying and a disturb me sleep?"

Between sobs, I gush, "Daddy… said grandma… is going to

die… because she look good." More bawling.

However, thankfully my mother is not as upset as I thought she would be.

"What wrong wid you, Fabien? Why would you sey sum ting like dat to the chile about Mama? You a eidiat Fabien? For a big man, you a real poppyshow sometimes!"

"Bev, don't get upset because you done know sey a true!"

My mother hisses her teeth and gives me a warm hug.

"Nuh listen to him baby! That is ole wife fables!" She then looks at him and says, "Poppyshow, you should a shame a youself."

My grandma continues, "Bev what's wrong wid de likkle gyal?"

"Nutting Mama, she's fine!"

"Sen her in here, mek me see her!"

"Wipe you face and go mek she see sey you alright!"

But I'm not. Anyways, I do as I am told and go to say hi to grandma. Mommy goes with me to make sure I say the right thing.

"Why you crying likkle girl?"

My grandmother still thinks I'm a baby.

"Nothing, grandma."

"She's fine Mama! Just a likkle misunderstanding."

She says this while simultaneously glaring at my father, who has quietly entered the room, looking sheepish. But Grandma is not convinced.

"Mek sure sey you nuh have no boyfren, enuh cause man a problem."

Dear God, what is happening today!

"No Grandma, no such thing."

"You betta mek sure!" A declaration I have heard many times before, from many people, many of whom aren't even family members

"Yes, Grandma."

"Den Bev, why she sound like dat, like she's been to England to visit de queen."

At that comment, she bursts into raucous laughter, so much so that she coughs uncontrollably for a few seconds, which seem more like minutes. No one is surprised! She always does this.

"Well, Mama, she's a high school student now, the top of her class so I will not have her up here chatting like she work in the cane fields. Because we pay too much money to have her sound uneducated."

Apparently, Grandma has amused herself enough. She starts sounding proper. She says, "You know you right. I like to hear a young lady sounding proper, not vulga."Bev, a when we a go eat? Chrismus?"

Thankfully, my father is just as sick of the nonsense.

"Come eat, me star girl."

"She's not hungry."

"So me wait whole evening fe nutting!"

While we are heading through the door, I hear Grandma saying, "Bev, mek sure dat gurl is not prignant!"

"No, Mama, she's fine."

*　　*　　*

I take a bucket outside and draw water from the cement tank and have a refreshing bath outside. We do have internal plumbing but sometimes the water pressure is too low to come up to the house, as our house sits on top of a hill. From my vantage point, I can see all the houses with their lights, some lights flashing while others are ablaze with intensity. The light gives each house a specific personality. Combined, they look like a huge lighthouse. There's a gentle breeze playing in the leaves. The Pentecostal church where my mother is a member is *on fire* as they say. They are singing one of their favourites: "Pentecostal Fire is falling. Praise the Lord it fell on me." Mommy won't be going tonight or else she would have left already. I guess because I was late getting home. I sigh, as a tinge of guilt grips me.

That night my sleep is restless and I dream that I fall into a river, fully clothed. Although I am not quite sure which river, and no one comes to my rescue. I keep yelling: *Help! Help!* But the words are stuck in my throat and they are not coming out. I wake up with a start, just before I drown. I shake myself as if to dislodge all the water that has soaked into my clothes, my skin, sinking into my lungs. I have had this dream a few times and I often wonder what would happen if I were unable to rouse myself in time. As much as I try, I cannot shake the thought from my mind that I would literally drown, just slip into oblivion, in my sleep and no one would know. That thought like a throbbing headache keeps me awake for the rest of the night; afraid to venture back into the world of dreams, afraid to find out what the outcome might be. Eventually, I get out my copy of Shakespeare's *Romeo and Juliet.* Maybe a greater tragedy than my own will settle the quiet storm brewing in me.

CHAPTER SIX

For the rest of the school year, I avoid Miss Shalk as much as possible. She is still my Literature teacher so it is really hard to escape her. We have not had a run-in since that Thursday evening when I stayed late to help out in the lab. However, staying to help out has somehow lost its appeal, its value suddenly diminished by the events of that day. I don't go as often as I used to and I avoid Jas as much as I can. Equi has never been one to be friendly but a few times I have seen him looking at me in a strange way. I guess Jas must have told him. I am so worried about failing high school. I cannot help but worry, seeing that I have failed the last assignment—a book report—of all the things in the world to fail.

"How do you fail a book report? Are you sure you submitted it? Because once you submit it, there's no way you should fail," Claire questions me, looking confused while absently stroking a *shame old lady* plant (which we learned in Biology class is called the *mimosa pudica*, but I still prefer our name for it). This plant closes when touched, just like it is closing its eyes on the world, blocking everything out. At this precise moment, I wish I could close my eyes to the world and forget school, forget Shalk, forget everything.

It is lunch time and as is our custom we sit under the shade of a huge, ancient guango tree, protected from the merciless rays of the glaring sun. All around us, girls and a few boys are playing all sorts of games: from skipping and dandy-shandy, to A Brown girl in the Ring, while the boys play football and cricket.

"That's true!" says Robin. "Technically, a book report is a summary, an in-depth discussion of the themes in a book, and you can only fail if you fail to submit your book."

Bridget is sucking a guinep seed—a cousin to the lychee fruit—so she has to push the seed to her right cheek before she is able to speak. It is rumoured that if swallowed the guinep seed can lead to instant death. She looks like when Miss Mavis down the street from her house had the mumps and her face was swollen for weeks.

"That woman really have it out fe you girl! What are you going to do? You certainly need to take drastic actions before she fails you and blights you future."

Robin and Claire both nod in agreement, as they are too busy chewing to speak with any certainty of clarity. We are respectfully quiet for a few minutes; however, the air is charged with the tension we are all feeling. A slight breeze picks up and I hear a bald pate's soothing cooing nearby. Both the cooing and the gentle breeze are so alien to the topic at hand that I feel like I am in a dream that has taken a turn for the worse.

Robin looks so concerned that there is a crease in her forehead; even her cheeks look red. "Why don't you just tell your Mother? Let her handle it. I think things are really getting serious and she needs to know."

"Or else," Bridget almost shouts, which alerts us to the fact that she is getting an idea—usually a bad idea, a really bad idea.

Her sudden outburst reminds me of when the chickens lay their eggs. They always make a loud sound as if to alert everyone to the presence of a new egg. "You should go see an Obeahman; I hear there is one in our community, so you don't even have to go to Port Maria. Because it sounds like Shark a work Obeah to destroy your future."

Robin screams, "*What?*" her whole face turning red, like she has been slapped in the face. "Why would you even suggest that? Where is that even coming from? That's crazy talk!"

After a deep breath she continues, "That is exactly what is wrong with Jamaican people. Everything that ails them, they blame either gas or Obeah."

Bridget is starting to get upset. "You can stay there, Ms. Robin, and act ignorant. These things are real, you hear! Why else would a bright girl like Neva suddenly be failing? Do the math, it is just not penciling out as my Granny used to say. She used to be in the top five of all her classes and now you can hardly find her in the top twenty, which clearly makes absolutely no sense."

Claire jumps in. "I have known Neva the longest, from primary school, and she has always done well. Right now, I am doing better than her, so like Shalk would say: this is situational irony."

We all sigh at the same time. I break the silence which now looms over us like angry clouds threatening to burst and spill water everywhere.

"To be honest, the thought has crossed my mind but my mother says, 'Belief kills and belief cures,' so I never really wanted to dwell on that idea too much," I hear myself confess for the first time. I take ownership of this idea which has been pursuing me for the last little while. "Plus, my mother is a staunch Pentecostal so it would be the death of me if I ever mention anything like that to her."

"Nevaeh, this is completely up to you. It is your choice but I would steer clear of Obeah, Obeahmen and their balm yards.

You hear me?" Robin says as she bites into her patty and coco bread. Claire bites into her bun and cheese and looks perplexed as she does so.

After chewing, swallowing and drinking her favourite Juciful flavour, fruit punch, Claire solemnly declares, "I agree with Robin, but you know we are your friends and we will support you no matter what."

She pauses, looks out at the sea of students in front of us and she seems to have made a decision. "As you guys know, Mama has not been well."

We all look at our black shoes in disbelief, and some discomfort, that Claire is actually broaching the topic of her mother's illness which has been taboo up to this point. We all wear the same uniform at Providence High School: green tunic, grey blouse with gold epaulettes and black shoes.

"My aunties all agree that someone worked Obeah on her and if they had checked things out in time maybe Mama would not be at the stage she is right now."

At this admission, we are all too stunned to speak—including Claire, who has gone rigid with her mouth shut, looking everywhere except at us—I don't think she has ever allowed herself to verbalize this to anyone before, not even her family members. There is a stillness in our group which seems oddly out of place in the busyness of the school yard. Luckily, Robin recovers quickly, and clears her throat as if to clear away the strain which now hangs over the group, threatening to rob us of our camaraderie.

"Claire, so very sorry to hear that about your mother, girl. If there is ever anything we can do, please let us know."

Bridget and I nod in solemn agreement. Claire looks up at the guango tree as if to confirm our allegiance there.

Soon the bell rings, signalling the end of lunch, and our harmony. It is time to go to face the music again—but at least it is History class—the only class I am not failing. I miss most of the lesson as I am still regurgitating our discussion at lunch. Still mesmerized by what Bridget suggested and stunned by what Claire confessed. I keep wondering, though: could any or all of it be true? What if it's all a coincidence, and Claire's mother quite possibly just needs the right medication? I bet they keep feeding her on bush tea, every bush in the book: hibiscus, fever grass, lemon grass, orange leaf, sour sop leaf…. Jamaicans believe that there is a bush out there to cure all that ails humanity.

All jokes aside, though, Obeah is not something that is talked about in my family. In fact, I have never heard my mother or aunties mention Obeah. Come to think of it, my Grandmother has been ill for a long time, yet they have never taken her anywhere but to see her doctor. Grandma is always yelling about duppy this and duppy that but she has never attributed any of her visiting apparitions to Obeah or anything remotely related to the occult. Of necessity, I am going to have to find a creative way to bring this up to my mother. After all, don't Obeahmen require monetary payment? I don't have any money, so I am going to have to get my mother involved in one way or the next.

It is the weekend and I am so grateful. I used to love school, but these days I don't even know if I am coming or going, or going or coming. The only thing that keeps me going is the hope that things will turn around next year once I get to grade twelve. My mother and I are having a rare moment together since we have to go to the market and supermarket today. We both enjoy the hustle and bustle of the busy marketplace. Most fruits and vegetables are grown either by ourselves or our neighbours, so we barter with them, but we get other produce that we do not grow, like codfish or saltfish, beef, rice, flour and cornmeal, at the store. We get our milk, eggs and chicken from a farmer down the road from Bridget's house. We know many of the vendors in the market, so we just go directly to them to purchase what we need, but I always find it hilarious how so many people selling the same produce have found creative ways of garnering customers. For instance, a young woman selling shrimp declares that hers are the best because "they come from the bottom of the sea where it is nice and clean." I always wonder who has done the research. Other people selling the same Otaheite apples that most people grow in their backyards declare that "dese sweeter than cane sugar"—again, I wonder who has made enquiries into it. After the noise and various smells of the market, it is good to be heading home. My father is at work, so we take a taxi that leaves us at the foot of the hill. As we are walking up the hill, trying to balance the bags (we have to make two trips), for some reason maybe emboldened by the intimacy of the day, or maybe buoyed by the casual conversations we've been having, or maybe the heat has gotten to my brain, who knows? But I muster the courage to broach the topic.

"Mommy what do you think of Obeah?" There, I just come right out and say it. At the question, my mother stops in her tracks, the stillness of the moment momentarily disrupted by a passing vehicle.

Her ready smile disappears even before it has a chance to shine. "What? Wha you sey? Obeah? Nevaeh, please stay away from things and people like dat, ok! Please promise me!"

"Okay, Mommy, but I was just asking."

"Why? Why would you ask me about something like dat? That is not normal, everyday conversation."

"It is for a project at school." I lie again.

"What? That is what dem a teach a school? Out of everyting else on God's green Earth, a dat dem a teach uno? Which teacha is dat? I want to talk to him."

"No, no Mommy! It's not a big deal, I can pick a different topic. I just wanted to say it to you first."

"Well please do, Neva, because Obeah is not some ting fe play wid. You hear me?"

"Yes Mommy."

"The Bible says, '*Their sorrows shall be multiplied that hasten after another god'*. It says so right dere in Psalms sixteen and the fort verse. So please do your research on a odder topic me darlin. Do me a beg you, stay away from dat."

"Yes Mommy, I will."

I feel bad to be the one to take away her gap-toothed smile, even temporarily. But even as I say yes, I know for sure that I will continue to think about it. It was like I had suddenly stumbled upon a secret island, and despite the dangerous wild animals lurking around, threatening to devour me, I just cannot stay away. My mother quoting scripture to me means nothing; it does not serve as a deterrent because it does not answer all my questions.

It is early Sunday morning and I awake from another fitful sleep. It had taken me forever to fall asleep the previous night and once I did, I had vivid dreams of men dressed like Junkanoo, wearing brightly coloured clothing and hideous masks that glow red and change from one unsightly creature to the next intermittently. They were all trying to capture me while I did everything I could to escape.

But as much as I try, I cannot free myself, because after a while I am captivated by their mesmerizing presence and, just like I have been magnetized, I am drawn to them. They cluster together like wild grapes, and pull me in like the sea coming ashore and taking sand back with it. Luckily I wake up before I commit to or accept anything being offered to me in my sleep, because my Grandmother once confided in me that evil spirits called demons sometimes visit us in our dreams. They negotiate with us for our souls and before you know it, we are captivated by their proposition in our sleep. She always warns, "Neva accept food in your dream, no matter how delicious and tempting! Don't do it. Evil spirits use food to a trap and catch people."

She claimed that not only food but money and jewelry are often used to seal the deal. I don't know where she gets this nonsense from, but still as a precaution I try not to eat food or fruits in my dreams.

I yawn and stretch, feel for my slippers and go to look out my window at the old Otaheite apple tree. The heart-shaped fruits are all clustered together (like the Junkanoo in my dreams) covered in varying shades of red—from light pink to blood crimson—as they sparkle in the morning sunshine. I have always enjoyed this time of the day: so peaceful, so relaxing, so quiet. But this morning my sense of peace and tranquility is under attack. I feel anxiety rising in me at the thought of returning to school tomorrow. My palms are sweaty, my heart is racing, and I think I am running a temperature.

Generally, church attendance is mandatory, although these days if I tell Mommy that I am working on an assignment she will allow me to stay home. But today I feel a great need to attend church, to take part in the worship and the fellowship. I am not baptized or anything; my mother says, "I am not going to force you, it is a personal choice, and it has to be your own choice and yours alone. But gettin' baptized is the best decision a young boy or a young girl can make."

Plus the praise and worship is always soothing, the familiar choruses, the rich voices blending, the singing, the clapping and the dancing. It's like a complete workout, going to church, which never fails to dispatch the dopamine to my brain, leaving me feeling happy, my thoughts clearer and my mind more focused. I always leave church feeling relaxed and composed. Some of my schoolmates say that church is boring and they view attendance as a chore, but I genuinely enjoy going. I have skipped weeks because I am trying to study and work hard, yet with all that extra effort I am still failing. I might as well just go to church.

So today, when my world is topsy-turvy and everything in my world is coming unglued, I decide to go to church. Plus I have so many questions. Maybe someone will discern my distress and rescue me. They are always discerning when people have demons or when people are *fernicating* so maybe, just maybe, someone will be able to help me. I get a quick shower in the bathroom before the water pressure drops. It is freezing, but so relaxing. It is amazing how we live in Portland, surrounded by water, and the rain falls all the time, but still we have problems with plumbing. I put on my straight red dress, the one my auntie brought from *Town*, and pull my braids in a high ponytail to show off my high cheekbones. Pretty soon I am going to have to take out my braids and I am not looking forward to that.

I keep begging Mommy to straighten my hair but she keeps insisting that "hot iron will fry you brain and turn you into a dunce." Too late for that, though. I try to explain that that is a scientific impossibility but she never listens. With a sigh, I apply a small amount of the homemade castor oil, not too much because the scent is pungent. I brush my hair. These days my life has been so chaotic that I take great pleasure in the mundane. I savour every ounce of boredom I can squeeze out—moments spent not thinking about my current dilemma are quite rare.

Of course, Mommy is quite pleased to see me dressed and ready for church. She is grinning from ear to ear. She is always so proud when I am able to go, so that she can show off to her church sisters how well her baby girl is doing in school—well, I used to do well in school. I hope and pray that she will do nothing of the sort today.

Normally we would walk the two kilometres to church, but since I am going, as a special treat she wakes my father and makes him drive us to church in his silver Honda. At first he pretends to be upset (it's a game he plays quite well, feigning anger) but we all know that he is always happy when I attend church because, "Star Gurl, me nuh want you get in a trouble and church is a safe place." By trouble he means get pregnant.

Daddy almost never attends church. He goes on three occasions: funerals, weddings and Easter Sunday. I asked him why Easter Sunday, why not Christmas, and he said, "Well, if someone died for our sins, the least I can do is go to celebrate His recovery."

When I asked, "Don't you mean resurrection?"

He laughed and said, "You know weh me mean Star Gurl! You a bright gurl so you know more about dese tings dan I do."

This thought makes me feel so guilty that I feel nauseous. Guilty for not doing well in school, guilty for being a disappointment, guilty for failing, guilty for not being the star girl that my father has always thought I was—just guilty in general for being such a "pretty dunce." One time, Shalk told me that, "Your light skin is wasted because you don't have the brains to deserve it."

So far I have managed to keep the fact that I am failing from my parents. I have been able to intercept my report cards in the mail and tell my mother that they got soaked in the rain, and the fragile paper destroyed. Thankfully, the rainy weather in Portland has been my co-conspirator as this has actually happened twice. But what I don't tell them is that each time I just watch it happen by carrying the envelope in my hand instead of concealing it in my backpack. They believe me every time because they trust me. I feel even more horrible for doing that.

The second time my Grandma was having a "good day" and she said, "A how you so unfortunate that the same thing happen to you so much time?" She sounded utterly unconvinced. She was about to pick my story apart some more but thankfully Mommy shows her the envelope with the damaged contents: the ink spilling through the paper and running zigzag in all directions, successfully demolishing each negative word written about me.

Today, we get to church and Mommy gives Daddy strict instructions on how to care for Grandma.

Dad asks, sounding really annoyed, "So yesterday when you and Neva went to the market, who tek care a her?"

Mommy angrily snaps, "You well know it is Miss. Mavis who stays with her when I go to the market so stop this! Cho man!"

We get there before Sunday School starts and as we are going in I glimpse my basic school teacher Miss. Parker, who was also my first Sunday School teacher, approaching. I groan inwardly because just like my parents she is always singing my praises. She is always saying, "You are so smart Nevaeh! I just know that one day you are going be someone in this world, someone we all can be proud of."

However today, even from a distance, she doesn't seem proud and when she catches up to us, she doesn't greet me by saying, "Is this my bright girl Nevaeh?"

On the contrary, she appears to be quite perturbed.

She addresses my mother first (in my experiences dealing with adults, that is never a good sign). "Bless the Lord, Sister Bev. How are you doing?" Deliberately avoiding eye contact with me (another telltale sign).

"How is your mother doing, Sister Bev?"

"She is doing okay. She had a few rough days last week but God has been faithful."

Mommy always uses her "best" English when talking to any of my teachers, both past and present. I asked her why once and she said, "Because I want them fe know that you come from good stock. I want them fe know that you are not just a odder pretty brown skin girl. You come from quality."

I hate when she mentions my skin colour. It is almost like she is suggesting that if I were not a "browning" then I would not be considered pretty, which Shalk has also said to me. Robin and I are basically the same complexion and I have never heard anyone mention anything like that to her.

I try to go in the building while Miss. Parker is talking with Mommy but she suddenly takes my right hand gently in hers, looking me squarely in the eyes for the first time. She speaks quite firmly in her teacher voice, a subtle change but one I would never miss, seeing how she is my first memory of what a teacher looks and sounds like. "Nevaeh, can you kindly hold on?" To any onlookers, including my Mother, it sounds like a question, but the intense look in her eyes indicates that it was more of an order than a request. "I want to talk to you for a bit."

"Yes, Miss. Parker, of course."

I look at Mommy, although I know it is futile because she is always ecstatic when "important people" want to talk with me, because somehow that indicates to the world how important I am. As if my value is in some way linked to what other people think of me and not who I am as an individual, as a person with a soul, a sentient being.

"Okay, I will leave you ladies. Nevaeh, please come to my Sunday School class before you go to yours. I want to give you your offering."

"Yes Mommy, I will."

I desperately want to hang onto her dress and cry, "Don't leave me," much like when I was a little girl being left at infant school and later at basic school. But I know I can't; it wouldn't be dignified and Mommy would be angry. Plus, I have so many secrets that I don't even want her to start asking any questions.

Miss. Parker and I walk towards the mango trees that grow wild in the church yard, and she leads the way. We stop at the spot where a mango tree and an orange tree converge, making an arch. The orange tree is just starting to blossom and the citrus smell intertwined with the sweet aroma of the mangoes washes over me and gives me a heady feeling. I close my eyes for a second to savour the rich smells. Miss. Parker clears her throat (I hate it when people do that) and with that sound I am brought back to the severity of the moment, because somehow one of my chief cheerleaders has stopped cheering and this could only mean one thing: she has discovered my deception and she sees right through me for the fake that I am. In a sick way, I am happy that she knows, which means that I don't have to pretend anymore; pretending is so exhausting. I tell myself that she must hate me now, so I don't even care anymore.

She says, "Nevaeh, is there anything going on that you want to discuss with me?"

I say, "No, Miss, everything is fine," more out of habit than anything else.

"Don't lie to me, Nevaeh. I cannot help you if you are lying to me. What is going on with you?"

"What do you mean, Miss?" I can't believe how good I am at playing this game. Plus, I am not about to make things easy for her. Suddenly, she does something that I have never seen her do before. She hisses her teeth, much like Claire would as a sign of annoyance. I am starting to regret my decision to attend church.

She continues, "I saw your Biology teacher last week and as usual I asked her how you are doing in school. Generally, she would not discuss her students because that is unethical; however, she reached out to me out of concern for you, Nevaeh. She says you don't even help out on the lab after school anymore. You used to enjoy doing that."

Her harsh tone gradually becomes less stern, less disappointed and more solicitous.

"She tells me that your grades have been dropping, Nevaeh. That you are now struggling in Mathematics, Chemistry, Physics, even Biology, which has always been your favourite subject. She also said that you are completely failing English Literature. Nevaeh, what is going on? You have been reading way above your grade level since you were four years old. I know this because I taught you how to read."

On the last sentence, she reaches out and takes my hand gently into hers. I was hoping she wouldn't notice the tremor. I avoid her eyes. She has big puppy dog eyes that share all her emotions, all she feels on full displa,y and right now, I know she feels hurt. I can discern that even from the quick glances. She is deeply wounded, a hurt that I have managed to inflict even without trying.

"Is it a boy?" she says, almost a whisper, startling me back to the moment.

"No, Miss, not at all."

What is wrong with Jamaican people? Why do they always

assume that in every situation a boy is always somehow involved? They are misguided if they believe that I can't be egregious all by myself.

She snaps, "Well, what is it then, little girl?" She sounds so disappointed that it is not a boy. I guess she'd practised a pep talk about boys and now she is out of her depth. "I want to help you! We want to help you! But how can we if you won't let us?"

I can't help it; all the tears I have been storing up over the last little while just come gushing out, like the water toppling over Reach Falls. I feel like the tremendous burden that I have been carrying on my shoulders has just taken wings and flown away—moving swiftly like the hummingbird. With my eyes brimming, I watch it leave and whisper farewell because I have unexpectedly and instantly arrived at a decision.

Just as quickly as I start crying, I stop and confess to Miss. Parker, "I have not been doing well lately and I don't know why."

This next part I say while holding her gaze for the first time today. "But I promise you that as of this moment, all that is about to change. Thank you so much for reaching out. Please do not tell Mommy because I have been distracted, but from now on, I am going to do better. I solemnly swear that I will do better, just give me time to work things out on my own, Miss. Please!"

She hugs me and whispers, "I know you will. I have faith in you." I hold onto her for a few more minutes just to savour the moment and solidify my decision. As we are walking back to the front of the church she abruptly stops and declares, "I trust you, but I'll be checking in from time to time and if things don't improve, I will definitely need to speak to your Mother. You are her whole world, Nevaeh, and if things are not going right then you should tell her. She has a right to know. Okay?"

I nod in agreement, knowing as I do that things would never come to that. I won't let them.

I go to get my Sunday School offering from Mommy. I sit attentively in Sunday school. A lesson about the woman with an issue of blood and the miracle she experienced just from touching the hem of Jesus' garment. I zone in and out. Close to the end, they mention Lazarus, his death, burial and resurrection. All stories I have heard all my life, so at crucial points I am able to interject, contributing substantially to the discussion. I even mention Job and his patience and endurance in suffering. Job's story is really resonating with me right now. The only difference is that I would never be so duplicitous as to call myself righteous. A distinction that's about to further separate us after what I intend to set in motion. The teacher (Sis. Marsha) beams with delight. However, mentally, I have already left to execute my plan. After Sunday School, some girls my age hang around for a bit and ask if we can hang out some time. I say yes, a little too quickly, and we all know that it is never going to happen. I should feel bad for lying at church, on a Sunday, the designated Lord's Day, but I don't.

The service later in the day is lovely, the singing is on point, the dancing and clapping so contagious that I join in, the preaching as usual a work of art, with the appropriate tongues and pauses for emphasis. It's like I've left myself on autopilot. As always, I am sure that there is a lot of yelling about hellfire and the dangers of "*fernicating.*" But today I don't feel battered and bruised. There is more socializing after church. Someone has baked a sweet potato pudding, someone else has brought a cornmeal pudding, a toto was there as well but I am not a fan, and there is pineapple juice and guava juice. Of course there is a big sweet watermelon, and I have a huge slice. I smile and laugh in all the right places, being careful not to get my dress messy, give and receive hugs, hear a million times how "pretty" I am and that my dress is gorgeous. Also that I could even be Miss Jamaica or Miss World or even Miss Universe with my brains and beauty. I flatly refuse to even locate Miss. Parker after our encounter. I am certain she's observing me from a distance, or not so distantly, but since I am at peace with my decision, I don't even care anymore. As a matter of harsh cold fact, I couldn't really tell anyone what was said or specifically who said what, because the whole time, as the song goes, *my mind was on the other side of town.*

It is beyond astounding how one incongruous encounter can change the trajectory of your life forever, and take you into unfamiliar territory where you have to sink or swim. Obviously, I am Jamaican and I have been swimming my whole life; therefore, I know with all assurance that as much as I will always choose the river, I will always choose to swim.

CHAPTER SEVEN

I tell Mommy that I have left a textbook at Claire's house that I need urgently and I absolutely have to pick it up right away.

"But it is getting dark, Nevaeh. Why didn't you go earlier?"

"I just remembered, Mommy."

"Okay den, well, wait until you fader come home and him, we drop you over dere!" she says this with her voice dripping with uncertainty.

"No Mommy, I can just run over! Plus, we don't know what time Daddy getting home and I need the book right now to complete my assignment."

She looks really concerned and disturbed. For a minute I think she is going to flatly refuse and insist that I wait until Daddy gets home. But her features soften and she says, "Hold on! I'm going wit you! Let me go change out of my yard close."

I panic because this was never a part of the plan and I didn't budget for this happening. If she comes, my plan will be ruined. *Think! Think! What I'm I going to do?* I pace for a few minutes (which I hate so much because other people pacing leaves me feeling anxious). I've got it!

My Grandmother is sleeping peacefully in her room. I slip in quietly and start pushing books off her nightstand. They hit the wood floor with a bang and clatter. She is startled and awake instantly.

"Bev! Bev! Is dat you?"

She listens silently for a minute and in the silence I push more books off the table. It is pitch black with the curtains drawn and the windows closed, so she does not know that I am in the room. I feel like that weird guy in Allan Edgar Poe's poem "A Tell-Tale Heart" who visits the old man's room every night and stands in the same position, waiting for an opportune moment to kill the old man.

"Bev! *Bev!*" She screams, her voice hoarse from sleep, cracking.

My mother comes rushing in, oblivious to my presence and as she enters the room and leaves the door open, I slip out the room, just in time, as she flips the light switch.

"Mama! Mama! A wha? Wha happen?"

"Duppy, Bev! Duppy in de room!"

"Mama—"

"No! Don't tell me not to talk foolishness! I heard dem Bev, wid my own two ears, as plain as day. First dem bang the floor and den dem push off me book dem. Look, de books dem still on de floor!" I listen from just outside the door.

I imagine Mommy looking around the room at my handiwork.

"Okay mama! Everything is fine! I will stay wid you tonight."

I hurriedly make my way to the verandah before she sees me lurking outside Grandma's bedroom door.

"Nevaeh!"

"Yes Mommy! Are you ready? I'm on the verandah!" I yell back in the house.

"No chile, I have to stay wid Mama! She is not feeling well."

"But I thought she was asleep, Mommy." I feign innocence so

well, I surprise myself.

"She was but she's wide awake now."

"Alright Mommy! I understand! You do what you have to do! I'll be quick."

"Here, bring de flashlight just in case, and remember to scream if you see any ting dat you not comfortable wid."

"Okay, Mommy."

I leave my mother on the verandah. The shadows at dusk are casting just enough light for me to see how conflicted she is: between her only child and her only living parent. I sail down the hill before she is able to think of a different plan. All the time questioning: *why am I like this*? When did I become such a monster as to torment an old lady? I appease my raging conscience by saying that by this time tomorrow all will be well and I will repent and read as many scriptures as she likes to her by way of atonement.

*   *   *

I meet up with Claire. All four of us are going to this appointment. We went earlier but the assistant said, "Come back at dusk." I'm not sure why and we were already physically present. I couldn't see if there were other people there, seeking assistance like I was.

"What took you so long?" she whispers.

"Mommy wanted to accompany me!"

We meet Robin and Bridget at the crossroads where four streets merge. We are all extremely quiet. There is no need to talk. We have already laid out the plans, both plan A and B. We are definitely doing this. Thankfully, it is not a church night so there's hardly anyone out and about. That's the beauty of a small-town community; everyone knows everyone's routine and most people are in their homes before it gets too dark as there is not much by way of nocturnal amusement.

We get to the gate for the second time today and there is an eerie silence. There is no wind tickling the leaves to make them giggle, no crickets chirping, not even an annoying mosquito making a nuisance of itself; nothing. I am ever so tempted to not enter through those gates because breaching them is similar to a bride crossing a threshold—the point of no return. However, if I don't things will go from bad to worse and I will always wonder what might have been, how things might have been different. I picture myself a bundle of disappointment ten years from now, looking old and frail like Grandma, and with that I steel my resolve.

The same assistant from earlier comes to the gate and says, "Yes?" which is more of a declaration than a question. As if we didn't just see him a few hours ago and had been forced to explain at length what my problem is, or more specifically who my problem is. Therefore I am forced to explain again. Earlier he had said, "There is no payment, Healer (that's what they call him) will tell you when and how to pay for the treatment."

"Treatment?"

We all screech at the same time.

"You never said anything about any treatment earlier," Robin asserts.

"Relax ladies, Healer will tell uno wha fe do! No need to fear, the Healer is here."

Bridget pushes me to the front and establishes, "She, only she need de treatment."

We all look at her in the darkness; so much for thick and thin. What happened to "We will support you no matter what your decision"? I honestly can't even be mad at her, because I am scared stiff. My legs have turned to jelly and I am afraid that any minute now they are going to give out on me.

The Assistant (we never did get his name) is a short man about my height, and I am five feet five inches. He has really broad shoulders and now that I have a closer look at him, his face is broad like a bulla cake and his lips are thick like liver. However, if there were ever a disconnect, it would be his voice; his voice doesn't match his body. It's calm and reassuring, like someone on the radio would sound. When he speaks, I am tempted to look around to see if there's a ventriloquist at work. However, this lulling quality does nothing to alleviate my fears and calm my racing heart.

We all step over the threshold and enter through the small wooden gate attached to the huge metal one. So many gates. I don't know why they need so much security; no one in their right mind would enter this place without a very good reason. The moon starts to play a game of hide and seek—one minute it's peeping through, the next it is completely concealed behind viscous dark clouds.

We enter gingerly, looking around, and from the small ember of light that occasionally flickers in the sky we can see many tall trees and short bushes. It is hard to determine in this light, but if I were to hazard a guess I would say that there are palm trees, coconut trees, that I can smell hibiscus, chrysanthemums and the potent *pyrethrum* aka stinking Mary (which I learned recently in Science class is not the correct name). Why couldn't we have done this in the daytime? Well, on second thought maybe not, because for one thing people would have seen us entering this locale which has been taboo all my life. I didn't even know of its existence until earlier today. I have always passed by and considered it just another house in our community. It is one thing to be seen passing the gate and probably stopping to pick up something off the ground or tie my shoelaces—but it is a completely other story to be seen entering through the gate. That's another level of *bare face* as my grandmother would say.

Between the gate and the house, we almost trip several times, because the yard is not paved and there is loose gravel everywhere. The Assistant takes us around the back, past the fever grass, spearmint, and the rosemary bushes, where it is even darker.

It feels like since we set foot through the gate the night itself is darker. Suddenly we see a very tall object, like Pitchy Patchy, moving towards us. We stop in our tracks, poised to flee. We bump into each other, Bridget screams and when Robin enquires why, she moans, "Me buck me toe!"

Claire whispers, "Which one?"

"My left big toe."

I almost expect them to race towards the gate, because bucking your toe is one thing, but bucking your left toe is never a good sign; in fact, it is a sign of bad luck, just like seeing a black cat or walking under a ladder. For that reason no one ever admits to owning a black cat. Despite the commotion, the Assistant keeps going full speed ahead, so after commiserating with Bridget we try to catch up. I am tempted to use the flashlight that Mommy gave me earlier but think twice because I still don't want to garner any unwanted attention. Although at this point I don't know from whom. But as Grandma always says, "Guilt will bring strong delusion, so that you believe a lie."

Eventually, we come to realize that the tall object moving towards us is the Healer himself, and without a greeting or anything, he pronounces, "Just the person in need of my help is allowed in my workshop, and I only take care of one problem at a time."

I must admit, at this point the fear hasn't given way. Still, I am left in wonderment. Because really, this man speaks so well. He sounds like one of the male teachers at Providence High, with his clear and resonant voice; a radio announcer, even.

Robin bravely proclaims, "We are not going to leave her with a complete stranger."

The Healer seems unmoved although I can't see his face. He says, quite firmly, "My house, my rules."

It's strange but for a tall man his voice is really soft. When he speaks, I imagine honey coating velvet. Previously, I'd decided that he would have a big booming voice like thunder before the first drop of rain. We all stand there for what seems like an eternity evaluating each other. I sense that he is assessing my level of desperation. I probably reek of it. He could possibly smell my despair from all the way up the hill to my house. I measure his credibility. I feel the raindrops. At first, they are light, intermittent drops, like standing next to a waterfall, not too close but close enough to feel the spatter, but then it feels like a dam is breaking.

"We can't just stand here in the rain." Bridget shouts to be heard. Her voice is hollowed by fear.

The Healer starts to leave. Apparently he has been waiting on me to make a decision and has decided that I am not worth his time. He probably senses that I am an impostor just trying to change my fate.

I disconnect from my friends, or the girls instinctively pull away from me; either that or they all simultaneously take a step back. What other choice do they have? What other choice do I have? From my short life here on Earth, I've gathered that life is a series of choices, and not choosing is not a justification because that in and of itself is a choice. I look at them in the dark and through the pouring rain, as if it is the first and last time that I am ever going to see them, knowing their individual features distinctively—features I have effortlessly memorized. I follow the Healer's footsteps, fear again taking a stranglehold on my whole body, and I wear it like a second skin. Automatically, I reach for the small flashlight that affords me very little light. It looks like a *blinkie*, also known as a *Peenie Wallie*. My Biology teacher said that they are fireflies, a type of beetle. We understood the term blinkie because the creatures appear to be blinking, but where on God's green Earth did Peenie Wallie come from? I've asked both Mommy and Grandma and they didn't have a clue.

I get to the back of the house and thankfully he has turned on the lights. There is a type of shed, a wooden structure that is not particularly high but which is fairly wide and painted grey. The door is open, so I enter. There are candles everywhere, as colourful as the rainbow, and while the lighting is quite poor in the shed, I do get a chance to look around. There are shelves covering the wall, with multi-coloured vials, and unique images are posted helter-kelter above the shelves. There is not much in the way of furnishings; a few chairs are haphazardly placed around the room on a wooden floor which is in pristine condition. The shed even smells clean. It smells like damp soil after the rain has cleansed the Earth.

In due course, I take a close look at the Healer. Obviously he is very tall, the tallest person I have ever seen in my whole life. He is jet black, or to be more accurate blue-black, like charcoal fresh out of the pit: beautiful, baby-bottom-smooth black; just like Claire and Bridget. I have seen black before but his black is immensely beautiful. His lips are cherry pink, his teeth are Christmas lily white and his eyes a light brown. Once more we evaluate each other, and as I stare at him, he is staring directly in my eyes, digging into my soul and excavating my deepest, darkest secrets. Yet again, under the glare of candlelight, he gauges my substance or worth. He seems, no, more like feels very familiar.

Eventually I have to look away, not only because of the intensity of his stare and the sense of being naked, but also because of his masculine beauty. I have to admit that I have never before seen a man wear this type of beauty before; it is like an aura on him. No wonder he hides it behind gates, trees and plants, for fear that people won't take him or his craft seriously. Mind you, I have seen handsome before—there are handsome boys at school, Robin's boyfriend and his friends are handsome, and my father with his light complexion is generally considered handsome. In fact, Mommy said that when she brought him home, her family and friends were amazed that such a light skinned guy was "… interested in her, considering that she is on the darker side."

I asked her, "On the darker side of what?" She doesn't know either, she was just happy to find a man who adores her, and he adores her even now. Sometimes he calls her his Coco Tea.

However, this Healer is in a whole different league. He could easily take your soul and you would never know that he had left you empty. To be honest, I am not prepared for him to look like this and for me to feel like this. When I look away, I hear a sound and when I look up at him, I realize that he is chuckling. Instantly, I regret my decision to look up at him because on top of everything else, this man has a dimpled smile and gap teeth just like Mommy. The chuckle and dimpled smile are short lived, because abruptly he puts on his serious face and is back to business, as if he has suddenly remembered why we're here.

He now speaks with his back turned to me, while he is busy throwing herbs in a huge, metal bathtub. "Usually I do not allow anyone back here, but under the circumstances I guess there is always a first."

I am not sure what he means by *circumstances*. He doesn't explain and I am too mesmerized to ask.

He proceeds, "Your friends will be safe. My assistant will take them to the back porch, where they can shelter."

So if *they* are safe, what am I?

"Your friends can stay on the porch but you and you alone are allowed into my studio."

He looks straight at me while he says this—to underscore the point that I am the most troubled among my friends.

He takes the opportunity to question: "So tell me, exactly what is the problem?"

"My English teacher!"

I look up at him for a reaction but he seems unmoved; seemingly this is not a grave enough problem for alarm. It is so funny how life is, you could be crushed under the weight of a problem but other people think it is a light thing. When he just stares, I look at the mud which has accumulated on my sandals. I take a deep breath and breathe it all through my nose before taking another breath to continue.

"She hates me! She has always hated me, but a few months

ago she promised me that I would fail high school and become a janitor."

He says, "I see!"

"Yes!"

"So you believed her?"

"I guess! But—"

He interrupts.

"So what do you want me to do for you?" He suddenly asks, although from my vantage point it would appear that he has already arrived at a decision. Apparently he is choosing to include me in the decision-making process—as if underscoring the point that whatever the consequences are, I have chosen. Also, that we are bonded to this moment for all eternity: confederates.

"I don't know. Do what you would usually do under these circumstances."

"Let's see, you need my help but you don't know what type of help you need, correct?"

"I want you to make it stop! Make her stop!" I suddenly scream, surprised at the echo in the shed.

"I want to go back to being an exceptional student! I want to be in the top five again in my class and throughout the whole school. That's what I want! It's all her fault that I am not!"

Had it not been for the echo, I would not have realized I was yelling. I had not known how angry I had been about the situation. I'd thought I was perplexed, but now I realize that I am more enraged than perplexed. How dear Shalk had come and changed all the rules without my permission.

"First, I have a few questions."

"Go ahead."

"What is your name?"

"Nevaeh."

He raises a very bushy eyebrow, his left eyebrow and then says, "Heaven spelt backwards," and I nod. I am not sure if this means he's impressed.

"How old are you? Have you told your parents about your troubles?"

"Sixteen, almost seventeen." I quickly add. "And no!"

"Why not?"

"I guess I don't want to worry them or disappoint them."

"You keep guessing!"

"I definitely do not want to disappoint them, okay!"

"Why do you think your teacher is picking on you? What has changed?"

"*I don't know!* Okay? You are the Healer, you should have all the answers!"

He looks at me, still expecting an answer despite my outburst. But he looks at me as if we have an eternity. Still testing and measuring me.

Then he says, "Alright, I am going to help you! But you *cannot* question my techniques or strategy and you *can not* tell anyone (not even your friends who are waiting outside) what we do here. Is that clear?"

I am so completely and hopelessly desperate that at this point I am shivering with anticipation, and I would agree to absolutely anything. I am so absorbed in the moment that I even forget my friends and the harsh rain on the roof until I hear a peal of thunder accompanied by a flash of lightning, as if capturing the moment forever.

"Yes," I say, endeavouring to be heard above the elements.

"The first thing we are going to have to do is give you a bath."

"A what?"

"A bath."

"But I just had a shower at my house!" I exclaim at the unorthodox request, which invariably would entail me undressing in front of a stranger.

With a sigh, which I observe rather than hear, he replies, "I thought you just agreed not to question my techniques!"

I am tempted to say I am on my period but I am too resigned

to my fate.

"Alright."

He points to a little room off to the right and he informs me that in the room I'll find a full-length white dress to change into and that I should remove everything including my panties. I cannot help but wonder: *what if he rapes me?* What if he is baptizing me into some type of cult? I don't hear him on account of the rain but in my mind I see him busying himself with the preparations for the bath. When I am done, I look in the mirror, sunken cheeks and darkened circles around my eyes, all telltale signs of the chronic stress my body has been subjected to over the last little while. I think just being here they have been magnified. I also question my sanity: what have you become and what will become of you? I tell myself that it is now or never; I can either do as he says or I can run out screaming like a bulldog is after me.

I slowly return to the main room, just outside the entrance, and the huge tub is now filled almost to the brim with water. From the looks of it he has sprinkled crushed, dried and fresh herbs in the water. I move closer to take a look at the herbs. I don't know all of them but from our garden I recognize primrose, fever grass, thyme, hibiscus, chrysanthemums of various colours, pimento seeds, ivy, nerve plant, and creeping figs, which all combined exude a rich scent, with a tinge of lavender. There are other seeds and leafy plants but I do not recognize them.

He extends his hand, an indication that the bath is ready. He helps me into the tub and I wish the dress were not this hobbling, it feels like I am in a straightjacket. With his help, his grip both firm and gentle at the same time, I am eventually able to sit in the tub.

The water is surprisingly warm and some spill over the edge as I make myself comfortable. Forthwith I feel so relaxed, like the elephant in the room has left my shoulder. I feel completely light-headed. I close my eyes. For the first time in my life I feel at one with myself, at one with the moment. I don't feel like the present is happening to me—like I usually feel—I feel like this moment is specifically for me. I feel like I am one with the moment. Sometimes, I feel like I am just floating in mid-air, watching my life happen, but at this moment I feel like I am in my life, not just a witness to the events in my life.

After about fifteen minutes, he starts to pour some of the water on my head, soaking my braids; the abruptness startles me, but it is not at all horrible. Thank God for the rain; how else would I be able to explain my hair being wet or damp to Mommy? Following that, to my absolute surprise, he whips out the Bible, and I have to say after all the strange things which have transpired tonight, I find this to be the most bizarre. A Bible in the hands of an Obeahman or Healer is paradoxical. He reads Psalm 91, very slowly at first.

"He that dwelleth in the secret place of the most High shall abide under the shadow of the Almighty.

I will say of the Lord, He is my refuge and my fortress: my God; in him will I trust.

Surely he shall deliver thee from the snare of the fowler, and from the noisome pestilence.

He shall cover thee with his feathers, and under his wings shalt thou trust: his truth shall be thy shield and buckler.

Thou shalt not be afraid for the terror by night; nor for the arrow that flieth by day;

Nor for the pestilence that walketh in darkness; nor for the destruction that wasteth at noonday."

Then as he gets more worked up, more frenzied, he speeds up and the well-known verses start to sound exultant in his rich cadence, like an incantation. He transforms into an angelic being, awashed in brilliant light. It is both him, yet not him, simultaneously.

"A thousand shall fall at thy side, and ten thousand at thy right hand; but it shall not come nigh thee. Only with thine eyes shalt thou behold and see the reward of the wicked. Because thou hast made the Lord, *which is*

my refuge, even the most High, thy habitation; There shall no evil befall thee, neither shall any plague come nigh thy dwelling. For he shall give his angels charge over thee, to keep thee in all thy ways. They shall bear thee up in their hands, lest thou dash thy foot against a stone. Thou shalt tread upon the lion and adder: the young lion and the dragon shalt thou trample under feet. Because he hath set his love upon me, therefore will I deliver him: I will set him on high, because he hath known my name. He shall call upon me, and I will answer him: I will be with him in trouble; I will deliver him and honour him. With long life will I satisfy him and shew him my salvation."

This is a text I have heard all my life and I know by heart. All the verses seem to merge into one; there's no pause. I don't even know where one begins and the other ends. At this point, I feel like I am pinned in the bath. I am enthralled by his voice, by the familiar words, now pulsating through me. I am feeling so languid that I don't even want to move and it isn't that my brain has turned to mush, it is an overall feeling of ataraxy. I am at one with myself, with the bath, with his voice, with his words, with my path. Unexpectedly, the incantation ends and he is back to himself; his regular honey-rich, velvety self.

"Alright! That's it! Your treatment has ended."

He says it so calmly, as though the moment before had not just happened. I am most disappointed and deflated. I am not ready for the moment to end. He commands,

"Just read Psalms 23, 35 and 91 every night before going to bed and you'll be fine."

I question, "That's it? That's all you're going to do?"

"Yeah, that's it!"

By this time, the water is freezing. It's lost all its warmth. I do not wish to leave despite the cold water, getting colder by the minute. Greatly desiring to prolong my stay in the water, I try to keep him talking.

"So how much do I owe you?"

"Nothing," he announces quietly.

"Are you sure?"

"Yes!"

"Well, how much do you usually charge?"

"It depends on the situation!"

"Well, how much does my situation generally cost?"

At this last question, he takes a break from cleaning up the herbs which have fallen on the floor.

"The treatment is finished, ok! That's it!" He comes closer. "Everything will be alright, just stay focused in school. This one is on the house with the expectation that you don't ever return!"

That last part is said with finality, and something tells me not to keep pressing. He returns to his chore.

I still press on because I have been alive long enough to know two immutable facts: there is nothing free in this world and nothing last forever.

"Is this for real? At some point are you going to summon demons to haunt me because I owe you money?"

He throws back his head and laughs so loudly that for a moment I don't hear the rain. After he is able to control himself, he says, "Okay, tell you what? Those herbs in the bath, bring me some, especially the rosemary. I am running out and it's not growing back fast enough."

"When?"

"When, what?"

By now I am shivering!

"When should I bring the herbs?"

He thinks for a moment. "In seven days."

"What time?"

He sighs, obviously frustrated; something previously foreign to him. Clearly, he is a man who is unaccustomed to explaining himself. He looks over at me again. Then he shakes his head like my dad when he's annoyed.

"At dusk like when you arrived here tonight."

I sigh with relief because I do not want to owe Obeahman. There are too many scenarios where people allude to the consequences of owing Obeahman, or Healer man or whatever the heck he calls himself. Juxtaposed with the relief, I feel a huge sense of loss rising up in me, from the pit of my stomach to the top of my braids. I guess there is nothing left to say. I cannot prolong the inevitable any longer.

"Thank you, sir."

I get dressed slower than I got undressed.

When I am ready to go he says, "Remember, just stay focused on your schoolwork from now on! Do not allow yourself to get distracted anymore, you have a goal, never give up until you attain it. There is a word in Swahili which means greatness, *ukuu*—so find the *ukuu* in you. It is already there, you just need to look beyond the clutter and locate it in yourself."

I think, great, more pressure from a complete stranger to excel in school.

"Thank you sir, I will."

There are so many questions that I want to ask. How does he know Swahili? Why is he so well-spoken? But I think *he is done*, he has turned his back and is busy returning bottles to their original place on the homemade shelves that line the walls. Just his demeanour stipulates that he's done, his role accomplished. Like Shakespeare pontificates,

All the world's a stage,
And all the men and women merely players;
They have their exits and their entrances;
And one man in his time plays many parts,
His acts being seven ages.

The Healer through his bearing has made it abundantly clear that his *part* or role or segment in my life has been masterfully executed and accomplished. Hence there is nothing left to be said.

The rain has stopped, the Assistant is waiting by the door with a torch, and silently we walk to my friends. The torchlight reflected on half of his face gives him the look of a bulldog. I can't help but wonder if he were listening to the proceedings the whole time. From the light on the porch which has now started to attract a barrage of insects, my friends all look like they have endured the same degree of torture and they have aged as a result. I pull them all into a group hug. The short man—a stark contrast to his boss—walks us to the gate and once he has deposited us safely on the other side, as if with an afterthought expresses: "Focus on your schooling at this point, dat is all dat mattas, and don't come back here again!"

His voice a low whisper but we all hear him loud and clear. I was about to ask how I'll be able to deliver the plants that the Healer requested—but the torchlight is already disappearing around the back. For a short person he sure walks briskly.

My friends are scared and still nervous but wanting to hear what has happened and if I am okay. I am unable to say much and I tell them so but I take the opportunity to inform them of the new Swahili word that I just learned. I already know it is going to be our new catchphrase. *Ukuu* has a fresh sound and it sits in my mouth for a while. I wish I could share more because it was such a profound experience, but a promise is a promise and while we didn't seal it with blood or anything, I feel compelled to keep my word.

*   *   *

I get home as Daddy is about to drive up the hill.

He asks, "Nevaeh what you doing outside dis time a night?" Luckily, dependable as ever, Robin had remembered to bring a textbook.

"I had to get this from Claire." I say holding up the evidence. "And then it started to rain so I stayed until it cleared up some."

"I hope so! I hope a nuh bwoy you go hang out wit or me might affi go a prison."

I giggle at this! Daddy always says this and he always makes me laugh. He laughs as well but quickly adds, "A nuh joke me a mek doe."

Mommy is happy to see that I am with Daddy. She hugs me and ask, "What's that smell in your hair Nevaeh?" I am stumped for a minute. Then I quickly recover, "Claire's auntie adds peppermint to her castor oil so I wanted to try it."

She sniffs my braids again and says, "Tomorrow, please wash your hair before school. I don't want you up dere smelling like dat, fi people tink you nuh come from a good home."

"Okay, Mommy."

Of all the problems I have that is the least, and the most easily attainable goal.

At least I sleep very well, with no disturbing dreams tonight. A feeling of peace and tranquility replaces the guilt and disappointment that I have been carrying. I think I left it in the Healer's bath.

CHAPTER EIGHT

The next morning, I wake up at the crack of dawn to the cock crowing. I used to be so resentful of the light of a new day, always looking so bright and gay, so many possibilities like anything could happen. But not today. Today, I feel so overwhelmingly rested. I arise early to shower and wash my hair. I almost do not want to wash away the smell of the herbs but I must. I'd read my Bible before bed and I read it as soon as I wake up. I pray that my day will be grand and Shalk will be irrelevant to my existence. I venture outside to take a bath at the tank. The cold water is invigorating, infusing vibrancy into my skin. There is a gentle breeze and the birds are chirping. One of those days that promises to be amazing, and for the first time in months I am excited to go to school to start a fresh page in my academic journey. I feel like on a day like today I could actually win.

It is a Monday morning so it is a time for general devotion, when the whole school comes together to sing worship songs, read a scripture and left with a Word of exhortation. Today, the Prefects are in charge of devotion: we sing, "I am running for my life," one of my favourite choruses. I feel like I have spent the past months running. As is our custom, we sing it over and over again and do the actions. The morning lesson comes to us from the book of Exodus.

"And Moses said unto the people, Fear ye not, stand still, and see the salvation of the LORD, *which he will shew to you today: for the Egyptians whom ye have seen today, ye shall see them again no more forever."*

(Exodus 14:13)

I have always loved this chapter and verse. It describes the children of Israel's directive from God and the day they triumphed over the Egyptians. The Egyptians, after enslaving Israel for so many years, all miraculously died that day. Sometimes I feel bad for the Egyptian soldiers. Had they known that such a horrible death was awaiting them they might have done things differently. Plus, they were just following orders. Also, the Bible also said that it was God who had hardened Pharaoh's heart so whose fault was it that they actually died? Was it fate or was it a case of being in the wrong place at the wrong time? The head boy prays the closing prayer, a powerful prayer of protection for all of us. Then it is all over and the principal takes the podium. A rather anticlimactic feeling tends to linger after such an amazing devotion. I always feel a bit disappointed at this point, although I know that this is not church and we cannot sing and pray all day as the business of school must go on.

After that, the principal, Mrs. Pascal, (our new principal, who has replaced Mr. Chambers after he retired) comes to the podium and shares the announcements for the week. As usual I am standing with my friends, commenting intermittently after each announcement. Then all of a sudden, the auditorium goes quiet, but of course we missed what was said. I had to ask the girl on my right who is closest to me what had happened. She looks at me disapprovingly as if to say, "You and your friends should not be talking during the announcements." Whatever, girl! The people on my left were already commenting and it took me a while to understand what the words meant. Because they were spewing ridiculous nonsense that Miss Shalk had died, that she had died over the weekend. The principal manages to take back control of the proceedings like only she can.

Principal Pascal proceeds: "At the moment, the details are sketchy at best and her family members are requesting prayer and privacy as they mourn this sudden, devastating loss!"

The silence in the room is pulsating, mockingly rhythmic. My friends and I look at each other in utter disbelief. How could Shalk be dead? Is it my fault that she is dead? All of a sudden, I can't breathe. I am fighting for air. I push through the sea of students. I feel eyes on me but I don't have the lung capacity to care. I am outside in the open and glorious fresh air and take a combative stance to access my lungs. Soon my friends are next to me, all around me. I see them between my legs because as the air enters my lungs my breakfast is induced to leave. Claire grabs my braids which were supposedly in a ponytail but some unruly ones have escaped. Luckily she captures them in time, keeping them out of the way. Afterwards, a feeling of immense weakness spreads throughout my body. I try to sit but they grab me and take me to one of the seven benches scattered around the schoolyard. Robin is fanning me and Bridget brings me cool and refreshing water that I cannot finish because my throat is closing. Claire hugs my shoulders. We sit in silence which is only interrupted by a light breeze and the muffled sounds coming from the school's public address system.

In due course, I am able to right myself, to quell the turmoil in my brain. I ask the one question that's been rocking my brain since Mrs. Pascal said those fateful words, turning my insides into mush.

"Is it my fault?" First, it's a whisper and then I am screaming. *"It is my fault that she is dead!"*

Robin slaps my face, so hard it feels like I've been stung by a hive of wasps. She grabs my shoulders, shaking me, shaking me back to my senses, back to myself. Because at the moment it feels like I am about to lose myself, lose myself to turmoil and guilt.

"This is not your fault, so stop this!" Her voice is just a decibel higher than a whisper but the intensity burning in her eyes speaks to me loud and clear. The slap restores my equilibrium. My other friends echo her words and add their own pieces of advice.

"Plus, we don't even know exactly what happened to her," Bridget says, sounding really sad.

"True! We also don't know when she died. We went to the place last night; meanwhile, she could have been dead on Friday. You mustn't blame yourself. You did nothing to her." Claire admonishes, touching my face, a welt rising from Robin's slap.

Robin takes my face into her warm palms and demands, "Promise me, you will not allow this to destroy you." She adds something that I never thought that I would ever hear her say and I know that long after, I will wonder if she actually had said it or it was just my mind playing games with me, games inspired by grief and loss. Luckily, the other girls are here. They will confirm or deny the veracity of my memory. Because at this point, I cannot trust my senses. "I know this situation is different in many ways but I have watched my mother allow herself to be destroyed by my father and the life he chose. Nevaeh, we all have a choice in what happens in our life, so you can either see this as an opportunity to grow or you can choose to fold. But you know what? I refuse to watch you fold. This is not your fault!"

The last part she almost hisses at me, spittle spraying across my face like a waterfall.

She commands, "Say it with me!"

Like a small child, I say, "It is not my fault."

She picks up where she left off, "From now on, I want you to say it every single day until you believe it!"

I dutifully repeat the phrase but at the same time I couldn't get this other nagging thought out of my head: *what if I have unleashed something bigger than myself, with Shalk being the first casualty.* As horrible as she was to me, and she was extremely horrible, I have never wished her dead—never.

Robin seems to have said all that she was about to say. She seems to take a deep breath to collect herself, then she takes a few steps towards the auditorium and barks: "Are you guys coming or not?"

Just like that, Robin was over it. She has moved on from Shalk and everything Shalk-related.

She quickly adds, "We will never speak of what happened that night ever again. Not even among ourselves. Do I make myself clear?"

We all follow her obediently, the answer resonating in our swift movement. The whole time I am wondering, who died and left her in charge of us? While still being grateful for her fierce steadfastness because it is indeed sobering in the face of adversity.

We return to the auditorium to rueful stares and I am forced to pretend that all is well. To pretend that I don't know what I know. That I hadn't taken part in a ritual that might have initiated someone's demise. That I might have required someone to surrender their life.

∗　　∗　　∗

Life advances in leaps and bounds. We are assigned a new English teacher, Mr. Remi, whom everyone adores, which is not difficult as he is the exact opposite of Shalk. He is approachable, patient and kind. We all behave as if we have just left an abusive relationship and have found solace in his big strong arms. However, I can't help but feel a deep sense of loss. At least Shalk saw me for the fake I am and did not pretend like everyone else that I am something I am clearly not. She was brave enough to be honest, even if that meant she would stick out like a sore thumb.

Pretty soon my grades are back to being worthy of sharing. I attend church more frequently now. I am even considering being baptized soon, since church is so altogether stabilizing with all her rituals. But I am still undecided. There's a lingering feeling of being unworthy, unworthy of salvation, unworthy of God's love. I often see Miss Parker and she is once again quite proud of me. We both pretend like the last seven months hadn't happened. Of course I know that she is proud of my marks, not of me as a person. After all, when my marks dropped, she is the one who was quite disappointed and threatened tell my Mother. I am even starting to think that my Mother doesn't love *me*, not the way I need desperately to be loved. There are all these variables that come with love. Therefore who can be their most authentic self in the face of all these accoutrements? You have to be pretty, you have to be smart, and if not, you are labelled a disappointment. I never want to feel that way again. I've vowed to never be a disappointment ever again, no matter what is at stake. I don't even feel close to my friends anymore. That one night and everything that happened has altered us in ways that not even the Healer could have prognosticated. They too don't love me the way I wish to be loved. They don't love the vulnerable Nevaeh, the out-of-control friend. So if they don't want that part of me, the part which might be the most authentic me, then clearly, they want none of me. Because to love me is to love the whole me: the broken parts, the damaged parts and the whole parts.

I continue to read my Bible, study hard and keep my head up. They had a memorial service for Shalk at school but I just couldn't bring myself to go. I sat in the shade of one of the guango trees until it was done—it would have been too overwhelming—rubbing salt in my gaping wound. A wound I must strive to keep hidden. Another disappointment to my friends. They kept saying, "We kept looking for you!" their words dripping with judgment.

I bring the herbs for the healer at dusk as he had requested. I was hoping to be able to speak with him, tell him all that has transpired. I even go twice, but each time the assistant, looking more and more like a bull dog, simply says, "Leave de tings outside de gate! The Heala is unavailable right now."

I keep wondering if the Healer is in some way angry with me. Angry because I have caused him to break some type of rule by not collecting any money which has somehow invoked a spell. But there is no way to know because his guard dog won't let me in. Imagine, such a powerful man needing protection from little old insignificant me. It is laughable. Yet I cannot laugh because of this gnawing ache I feel.

Mr. Remi wastes no time in getting into the thick of things. He launches us into Shakespeare's Hamlet. Pretty soon the discussion is centred around whether or not Hamlet is really crazy. Also, how come Hamlet is just putting on *an antic disposition* while Ophelia is so *distracted from herself?* Is Shakespeare saying men are stronger? I don't have answers to any of these questions but what I do know is that Hamlet is smart to act crazy so that he can get *direction through indirection*. There is a saying in Jamaica, *play fool fe ketch wise* which is exactly what Hamlet does. In this class we never arrive at any definitive answers. Mr. Remi likes to begin these discussions by setting his one and only ground rule: "There are no wrong or right answers. I just want you to be able to think critically about the characters and by extension think critically about the people that you will encounter in your own life. So that people don't take advantage of you because of your inability to discern their motives."

I like that; finally a teacher who is more interested in teaching us life skills rather than just textbook knowledge. Life skills that most of us can relate to. A teacher who wishes to hear what we think rather than a regurgitation of what he might think or what he might prefer to hear.

However, one fateful afternoon, just as I am wrapping my head around the whole incident, while going up the hill on my way home, I stub the big toe of my left foot on a reckless stone.

This is never a good sign. Just like when my left eye is twitching, that too is always a bad omen which means sad tears are in the forecast. For years I wondered why, but when I question Mommy her response is always the same, "A so ole people say, and it seems to be true."

I get home and my whole yard is covered in a sea of people. As a matter of fact, from just a few kilometers from the gate, I hear my mother screaming at the top of her lungs.

"Mama gone! Mama gone!"

My grandmother had died, right after I left for school that morning. She just up and left us, left me, without a care about what would happen to us, to me. I saw her in the morning and she was fine. She was smiling her lopsided, toothless smile. She had gotten a stroke a few weeks back. Everyone had been amazed that she had survived it and had seemingly recovered. But as usual my father had his theory about her sudden recovery. Initially, we all thought that this was it, she was going to die the day of the stroke; but she hadn't. She'd gotten our hopes up that she had some type of superpower that sheltered her from the cold and chilly hands of Death. This morning she had been looking bright eyed and bushy tailed, yet this evening she is gone. She is no longer in her room. The only thing that reminds us of her presence is the smell of the concoction that Mommy used to slather all over her every day. I wonder what she will do with those ointments now that Grandma has vacated her room.

The night before the funeral, we have a *Nine Night* or a *Dead Yard*. There is singing, drumming, and lots of food. Everyone in the community is in attendance to celebrate my grandmother's life. There are commentaries on her life throughout the night that I hear snippets of when I go to serve soup or food: that it was well lived, that she had strong children who loved her up to the end. Some of them don't even know her because she hasn't interacted with the community members in years.

I busy myself serving mannish water, which is a crowd

favourite so it goes really fast. Robin's mother sends fried fish and I hear it is delicious. I haven't been able to eat anything, not watermelon or charcoal. In fact, ever since Shalk died I haven't had any charcoal. My way of inflicting private punishment on myself. Bridget brings a crate of soda, and Claire and her aunts bring fried chicken, fried dumplings and festival. I am deeply touched by their kindness and for a brief moment things feel like old times, but we all know that it is not. It is no longer same old, same old. There is a newness to our fellowship. A newness that we are too cowardly to investigate. We even share a laugh at the drunken antics of Bridget's father. Momentarily, she seems unmoved by his recklessness as if it is not a problem. We have all perfected the way of the thespian, the fine art of mask-wearing. We have learned that there are some things that we don't share, no matter how close we are. I can't help but wonder if they blame me for our new normal.

This funeral I have to attend. I hate funerals. My mother and aunts cry for the entire service but my mother in particular is inconsolable. I think she will miss more than anything else not having a crutch so that she will now of necessity need to live her own life. I read the eulogy. I allow tears to flow at the appropriate places but I don't really feel the pain like I want to. I feel like I have grown scales that prevent me from being in touch with my emotions. My friends are in attendance. They cry with me and once again I am grateful. I am also reminded of what we have lost and I feel so much guilt that I actually cry because the guilt feels like a flame throbbing in my heart. I don't go to the grave, that would be too final and I am not ready to let go; not yet. I know eventually it will come home to me that Grandma is really gone, has left her room empty, but for now I will bask in the presence of my erstwhile friends.

*   *   *

At school, our girl group hardly hangs out anymore. We see each other in passing now, sometimes avoiding eye contact. They have found other friends to occupy their time. It is like those Mills and Boon romance novels that Claire's aunt Monepha loves to read: when friends become lovers and then lovers become strangers; now we're strangers. I don't even pay attention, really, because I have had a lot of catching up to do in almost all my classes; plus since Grandma passed things have been weird at home. My mother seems like she has just returned from a long, arduous pilgrimage and all she wants to do is sleep. Sometimes when I get home in the evening, she has been in bed all day so I end up doing the cooking, cleaning and sometimes the laundry. If my father has noticed, he does not feel the need to comment— although with him you can never tell, at least not for sure. These days he too seems to be exhausted all the time. So after school I no longer have the time, energy or the desire to just hang out anymore. There's so much to do and so little time.

Before you know it, it is late June when the mangoes are ripening on the trees and the fruit flies are everywhere. Guinep is in season as well, and everywhere you go parents are warning small children about the dangers of swallowing the seed. The sun is merciless to humans, plants and animals alike. Final exams are approaching and I am even more zombie-like than ever before, my head constantly in a textbook. Robin seems to be the only one trying to rekindle our friendship but that's just been over the last two weeks.

It's Saturday and I am home alone, my parents having decided to go to the market and supermarket together, so I am catching up on some much-needed rest. I decided from Monday that I was going to take the weekend off to rest my brain. My head keeps throbbing and I see stars when I close my eyes. I wake up at around eleven, read my Bible and then just look outside at the trees and the flowers. The huge apple tree standing guard, overlooking the property, a few coco plants growing sparsely in the yard, the coconut tree trying to compete with the apple tree to touch the clouds, the solitary coffee tree that took forever to grow, and the naseberry tree, all familiar and comforting. There's a light breeze but I can tell that it is going to be a scorcher.

As I stare out the window a memory takes shape, and I don't resist it, I let it take up space in the landscape of my mind. After Grandma died most people kept saying, at least you'll have the memories that you shared with her forever. Well, I don't want memories; I want her, in her room, laughing, talking or sleeping. I want her, not memories. Just like memories of Shalk; I block those out as well. Hence I have been resistant to memories these days, because they sometimes bring with them strong arms that take my breath away. And so I avoid them.

But not this day. It was my sixteenth birthday and my friends and I decided to spend the day at the river. It is always such a sensory pleasure to be at the river: the fresh water, the water flowers, the tall stately bamboo trees and most of all there is neither sand nor salt—hence there are fruit-bearing trees clustered around. There is a perpetual scent of freshness (except during the rainy season when the river sometimes turns brown because of all the mud). Grandma once told me that the river cleans itself by depositing what it doesn't need on land. It was a beautiful calm day with little to no wind. So we were swimming, talking and eating when all of a sudden there was a rumble and a bubbling sound that disturbed the tranquility of the moment and I heard people yelling, "Get out the river!" My friends and I said, "Why?" simultaneously because that was back when we were in sync. A guy near to us was almost running out the water and then he turned around to say, "Di river a come down". We all squealed at the same time and chased after the man. The river coming down meant that it was raining somewhere else and water was coming fast and furious from the source of the river. We got out just in time before the deluge.

But even now I shudder to think what might have happened if

we hadn't listened or if we were too far away from other people. People sometimes go missing in a storm and their bodies are located days later in a neighbouring parish.

I have to put a pause on my perilous pondering. But I cannot shake that idea of alienation. What might have happened if we were somehow alienated or isolated from others. Momentarily, it is as clear as if I were still standing in the river, all by myself after everyone got to safety, that I have been alienating myself from my friends. I suddenly miss them, miss our merriment every time we meet. Instantly, I know why Robin has been trying to reignite our friendship. It is almost her seventeenth birthday and we had planned to celebrate it in fine style. I fill the plastic bath that we keep in the bathroom for when the water pressure is low and have a quick bath; it is not as refreshing as a shower but at least I am clean. I leave a note for my parents. I stop by Claire's but no one answers when I knock on the gate and call, which is really weird. Someone is always home with her mother.

I take a taxi and hope and pray that Robin is home. I get to her house an hour later and the whole gang is there; even her mom is there. She answers the door.

"Hi, Nevaeh. How are you doing? How is your mother coping?" She gives me a brief, warm hug that almost brings me to tears. "Please say hi to Bev and let me know if there's anything I can do, okay?"

She then calls, "Robin, Nevaeh is here!"

There are running sounds and then all my friends are around me, hugging me and asking if I am okay. I did not expect this welcome at all after how distant I have been. I don't deserve it. I spent the entire taxi ride over here wondering if I were making the right choice, and now I am sure I did. After the hugs, they catch me up on the plans for Robin's birthday event but it is a different plan.

"Why? What? A hike? Why?" I stutter. She wants to do a hike up the Blue Mountain for her birthday.

Claire observes, "That's exactly what I said. Why? Of all the places in Jamaica, why do we have to go there?"

Something is off with Robin, now that the greeting is out the way; I can tell. I can always tell with Robin. I don't know what it is. Maybe because I have been away that things are still strained between us. Maybe she is still angry with me for being such a weakling. Even her face looks kinda chubby. She probably has been cooking again. She cooks when she is stressed and since it's just the two of them they have to eat all the food. I guess I don't even deserve the right to question her demeanour since technically I am the one who left. I am starting to realize that there are many and various ways that one can leave and that leaving is not just a physical act, it is emotional and spiritual as well. Hopefully, we can get a moment alone and she can tell me what is going on. With any luck, I have enough credit in my friend account to warrant her telling me.

Robin is explaining, "Guys come on! I have grown so much over the last little while." She looks at me, "We all have. So I decided that I don't want to have a big bash at a hotel, I want something small and intimate, more personal, memorable. We can do this hike and then there are cabins on our way to the peak and at the peak as well. We can bring our own food and just chill and have a picnic."

Her mouth is saying all the right things but her eyes are telling a different story.

"Okay, fine! But are Kwame and his friends coming? I feel like I have not seen them in a while," I complain.

"That's because you haven't! You haven't been around in a while." Claire and her smart mouth.

"Yes, I get it Claire! It's been a while but I am here now."

"I missed your red face."

We all laughed at Claire's description of my face, but deep down I couldn't help but wonder if she would have missed my face if it weren't as she said "red." Maybe I am taking things too personally. I see every comment as an attack.

"So when is this trek?" I ask.

"The weekend after final exams. Can you imagine? I am going to be seventeen and then we have only one more year left in high school."

Again Robin is saying all the right things but the eyes don't lie. I also notice that after I brought up his name she didn't take the opportunity to gush about Kwame like she usually would. I can't help but wonder if they are still together. But I don't feel like it is my place to ask. I feel like I lost that privilege on that fated night. Most notably, instead of escovitched fish and festival, we have stewed fish for lunch. Robin hates stewed fish, especially with white dumplings and ground provision, yet that's what we're having.

*   *   *

It is July and exams are behind us, and I feel good about my performance. I have been spending more time with my friends. After the eventful year we've had, everyone is back to normal or as normal as can be. But there is still something odd about Robin; still no talking about Kwame. All she keeps saying is, "We're fine, just trust me."

However, I have learned two things about trust: it is a two-way street, and never trust people who say, "Trust me." Even Bridget is starting to look concerned. Although they are still tight, so I don't know how much she really knows about what is going on with Robin. Anyways, my Grandmother always used to say, "What don't concern you, Ms. Nevaeh, leave it alone." So I opt to leave this alone. This is not my battle.

The day of the trip comes and I have to admit that I am quite excited. I wake up early; it is an ordinary Saturday, the same sunrise, the same trees, the same breakfast of smooth cornmeal porridge, because since Grandma died Mommy just makes the basics for breakfast and dinner. Occasionally my dad will complain and she'll make something sumptuous, but mostly she's too exhausted. I plan to pamper her over the summer holiday.

There are two routes to get to the Blue Mountain Peak. The short route, which starts at Whitfield Hall, goes through Jacob's Ladder which is quite steep and dangerous, with many twists and turns, but it is also quite scenic. There are a number of endemic plants that line the road leading up to the Peak and trees of various sizes and heights. Then you pass Portland Gap, Breezy Gully, then on to Lazy Man's Peak where there is an old broken-down shelter. Shortly after this point you'll be at the peak enjoying a panoramic view of the island. The longer route is via Mavis Bank which is more dangerous because of the rivers that you would have to cross (the Yallahs River and the Green River) also known as the Twin Sister Rivers. They say you can never cross the rivers twice in a day as their temperament changes constantly from complete calm to mild irritation to being downright enraged in no time.

We opt for the short route. The plan was to summit the Peak and spend the night at one of the log cabins. But then Robin decides that she wants to spend the night in her own bed. So the plan is to summit the mountain, take in the breathtaking views and eat a hearty lunch to refuel for the trip down. I did not want to go down Jacob's Ladder in the dark but Robin was taking her own sweet time and since it is her birthday treat, I did not want to complain and seem rude. She decided that the Peak was a perfect spot to have lunch. To be honest it was great, just like old times. We talk just like in the old days about everything, except Kwame and the Healer. No one mentions Shalk. We share monumental secrets that were previously kept hidden and before we head home I am able to comprehend why Robin has been looking and acting so out of the ordinary. I honestly wish that I didn't know but what is done is done and cannot be undone. That too must be kept a secret and never mentioned ever again.

"This view is so stunning; I could stay here forever." Robin says, with a look of faraway places in her eyes, holding a half-eaten chicken leg in one hand.

We all say, "Me, too," at the same time. Followed by heartfelt laughter. Robin has brought her expensive new camera—just like her computer and cellphone, another guilt-derived gift from her father—so we take turns taking photos and posing. It is really cold at the Peak so we huddle together most of the time.

I don't know if it is the air, or our close proximity to each other, but while we devour our elaborate lunch of fried chicken, festival, bun and cheese, Claire shares, "My Mother is not living with us anymore. My aunts decided to send her to an institution, seeing that she is not getting any better and she is starting to become a danger to herself."

Now it made sense why no one was at the house the Saturday when I went to get her so we could visit Robin.

"So sorry to hear that, girl."

Being the nearest I reach out for her free hand. And I mean it. I am really sorry to hear that. That must I have been really hard for her and I was the closest to her in terms of proximity but the furthest in terms of emotions. Just when she must have needed me the most. We all commiserate with her. I thought she would cry but she didn't.

"I guess she has been gone for a long time now. I just didn't want to see because I didn't want to let go."

Claire says this while looking at her chicken leg as if it is the most beloved chicken leg in the whole wide world.

Robin clears her throat and says, "I know how you feel; my Mother was gone for a long time too. But we had a long, excruciatingly painful talk about it and she went to get help because I won't always be around." I look at her meaningfully and she quickly adds, "I'll be done with high school soon and off to UWI. So she is now on meds. It took a few months to find the right dosage but she's doing alright. At first there were days when she existed in a fog, but now she is more or less lucid most of the time."

Another grim reminder of how much I have missed. Bridget doesn't ever talk about her family but she declares, "I know how you feel, Robin. I've been thinking more about what will happen to Mama once I go off to college." She looks at Robin apologetically, "I have to go to teacher's college because it is heavily subsidized and I wouldn't be able to afford university right away."

Robin had been so sure from our first day in high school that she was going to the University of the West Indies (UWI). There are three campuses: Cave Hill, Barbados; Mona, Jamaica; and St. Augustine, Trinidad and Tobago. Meanwhile, I am still so unsure of where I am going and what I am going to do after high school. I am just generally unsure about my place in the world. Claire has always wanted to be a nurse and that program is subsidized as well, and especially now that her mother is away, I know for sure that she is going into the medical field. I am almost sure at the back of her mind she still thinks that she can save her mother, somehow rescue her from herself.

Bridget continues, "My dad's drinking is getting worse and I am so worried that he might get physical with Mama."

"He has never done that, so you shouldn't worry too much about it," Claire says reassuringly.

"No, but there were a few nights when he was so out of it that he didn't recognize her and when she tried to help him, he shoved her hard. But of course in the light of day, he doesn't remember what he has done. He has even lost his job because his boss got tired of giving him a bligh."

I feel so bad for Bridget; it must be very hard to be a bridge between her parents. Essentially that's what she is, and she too wishes she could rescue them from themselves. I don't share about my mother, about her exhaustion, about the lost look in her eyes. I don't want to cry and I don't want to admit that our relatively stable little family is coming unhinged. All throughout our friendship, I have had the most stable home life, yet the most unbalanced emotionally.

In the blink of an eye, it starts to get dark. Eventually we're packed and ready. It has been a great day! We all give Robin a gift although she had said not to. I give her a brand-new copy of *Beka Lamb*, our class novel. The school rented them to us so we had to return them at the end of the school year. For some reason, Robin fell in love with Toycie, the character who dies at the beginning of the book from an abortion gone wrong. I actually feel bad for Beka Lamb, the friend who is left behind to mourn her death and pick up the pieces. Claire gives her a journal so she can record the journey of her seventeenth year and Bridget gives her a hairbrush set, her favourite perfume, *Imari* by Avon, and a ball point pen. We all use the facilities but Robin says she's fine.

During the gift-giving I start to feel a headache coming on, a bit of nausea is creeping up on me as well and by the time we're done and I try to get up, I feel dizzy. I really don't want to ruin the mood so I keep it to myself. I don't want them to think that I am so self-absorbed that I want to make everything about me so I grin and bear it, like Mommy used to say.

We are finally on our way down and it is more treacherous in the dark. My symptoms do not improve on the descent. At Jacob's Ladder, we almost turn back to find a cottage. But just as we're trying to decide, Robin moans, "I have to pee."

"Really girl, why didn't you use the facilities earlier," Claire yells. Just like old times. Robin says, "Just hang tight, I'll go over there in the bushes. I'll be back soon. It's because it's cold, I always have to go often when it's cold."

We wait for the required ten minutes, and since peeing is somehow contagious among females we all have to go again. I remember that I still have the little flashlight that Mommy gave me, I use it to find a spot. We go in different places along the trail. It is neither hygienic nor ladylike but nature calls and we all have to answer in the affirmative. But at this point my symptoms have gotten worse, and I feel like I am about to faint.

When we are all done, we gather in the spot where Robin left us. Everyone, that is, except Robin.

It's been about fifteen minutes, so we call her. We start to yell, *"Robin! Robin! Ro…b…in."*

I use my flashlight and try to locate her but there's no sign of her. She is gone, disappeared in the dark.

"Well, what now?" Bridget asks, sounding really calm. I guess she is now immune to drama.

"I don't know!" Claire explodes.

"Where could she be? What if she fell over the edge?" I asked, getting really concerned by the fact that she is missing and the calmness of our friends.

"Wouldn't she scream on her way down?" Claire's logic is impeccable.

"Let's return to the Peak!" I know I'm reaching.

"Why? What good will that do?" Bridget muses.

"I don't know! It's just a suggestion!"

"Sorry girl, I didn't mean to snap!"

"What if she came back before us? After all we didn't tell her that we were going to leave this spot!"

Bridget doesn't sound convinced but it sparks hope that our friend is well.

"That sounds plausible! She probably looked and didn't see us so continued on the path. Let's try to catch up."

Even Claire is grasping at straws.

The path that she is referring to is both narrow and treacherous; one misplaced foot could see us toppling to our demise, especially at night. I don't know why we ever allowed Robin to delay us. Pretty soon the insects will come out and it will be too dark to see, except for the lights in the sky. We trek on down the path we came up, hoping that Robin is ahead of us waiting at the cabin, so we can finish the journey and head home. However, as hard as

I am trying to be optimistic, I have this nagging feeling in the pit of my stomach that something is exceptionally wrong and we are not going to find my friend.

* * *

It turns out that my intuition was right. There was absolutely no sign of Robin in any of the cabins. We ask around, disturbing couples and various groups, even individuals who seem to be seeking solitude, but no one remembers seeing her. And she is quite difficult to miss, with her beautiful terracotta-coloured skin, full, molasses-dark eyes, her high cheekbones and her shoulder-length charcoal hair. Eventually it starts to rain and we have to tell one of the soldiers who is on his way to Newcastle for training. He alerts his superiors and they start a manhunt which is tremendously hampered by the rain and the fact that it has gotten really dark. That night, they put us in a cabin and decide to do a thorough search in the morning. I try to protest that in the morning it will be too late, but none of the adults is listening. The cabin is freezing, the water is like ice. I hate it when it is this cold; like Robin, I have to pee all the time. I hardly sleep a wink. My mind keeps racing, retracing our steps, trying to figure out where we went wrong. Where I went wrong.

At dawn, a lieutenant comes to find us. He says he has assigned a cadet to take us home. He is so tall, his voice so deeply masculine, and it is so early and so very cold I have trouble focusing on what he is saying. I still feel ill: I'm nauseous and the obnoxious headache is still plaguing me.

"But how can we leave without Robin?" I argue. "This was not supposed to happen," I lament.

"Don't worry, we will be looking for her. But it is important that you ladies go home and inform your parents of this new development."

New development; that's how the lieutenant puts it. I have

been willing myself not to think of Robin's mom. Fortunately, the cadet will be the one to deliver the bad news. On our way, Claire declares, "Maybe she is already home," with so little enthusiasm that she looks pathetic, like an abused puppy. We all look at her. She looks a mess. We all look a mess, like clothes left on the line overnight and battered by the rain.

The coward in me almost asks the soldier to take me home first, but I don't have the heart to abandon my friends; not this time, certainly not now. We get to the house and I hope against hope that Robin will answer the door and say it was all an elaborate prank, a test of our loyalty—but she doesn't and her mother does. After she hears that Robin is missing, she looks at first like she doesn't understand and then she shakes her head and says, "Missing! Missing!" in a whisper and then the sound that comes up out of her curdles my blood. I have to cover my ears. Soon the neighbours are rushing out of their pristine houses. I can't take it, it is too much, so my body and my mind bond together, to fight for me, for my sanity. Everything is a blur and then there is silence.

I drift in and out of sleep. I wake up a few times to cold hands and warm eyes, faces amplified by their nearness. I hear voices and words that are hard to discern in the fog. But words like "exhaustion," "dehydration" and "shock" waft over me. My sleep is fitful. I am either running or drowning, because I hear Robin's voice, so I keep chasing after her yet the more I chase after her the more elusive the voice is. Sometimes she's in the sea, right where the sea embraces the sky and I try to get to her but each time I am near, she either disappears or I wake up. Other times, I am tracking her across the school yard, down to the main road then on to the town square, but then I lose her among the many people in the town. Where did so many people come from all of a sudden?

In due course I start to gain strength and I wake up from the haze. Mommy says it's been a week but it seems longer. Dr. Moore, who comes to the house, says I need to rest and take things easy because I have suffered a great shock. I couldn't disobey him even if I tried. As it turns out, the soldiers searched the whole area and still found no sign of Robin. They did find her bag close to the edge of a precipice but still no trace of her. There was some speculation that she might have accidentally fallen over the ledge in the dark but there is no evidence to support that theory, so now she is listed among the missing. My friend, listed among the missing. I don't ask about my other friends; I don't want to know. I don't ask about her mother, either, because I really don't dare to know. How could Robin be missing? Where could she be? Maybe if I had insisted that we left the Peak before it got dark— just maybe she might still be here.

I stay in bed a few more weeks. I am too weak to go anywhere. Gradually, my strength starts to return and my mother decides that it is time to allow me a visitor. A few actually. Miss. Parker visits, a few kids from school, and even Mr. Remi and Mrs. Pascal. Every time Mommy says I have a visitor I think either Claire or Bridget will come straight to my room, but they never do. I know for sure that Robin would have visited. Maybe they blame me, blame me for being weak, for being the weak link in our friendship. Maybe if I hadn't gone on the trip with them none of this would have happened. Maybe if I hadn't gone to see the Healer none of this would have happened; Shalk would still be alive and so would Grandma, and Robin would still be here. When I think of the weeks I spent avoiding her and the others, now I desperately ache for her presence. I wonder how Kwame is coping. By now he must have heard. But I don't even know where he lives.

I guess Mommy was right about the dangers of seeking after another God.

CHAPTER NINE

It is my first week at Mico College. My grade twelve year passes in a blur, while I strive desperately to forget everything that has happened the year before. I am getting used to the ragging. I've actually started my program of study later than everyone else because the CXC results were delayed this year and the other students are older than me. I was lucky to get a space at the much-in-demand Women's Hostel just around the corner from the college. The well-kept grounds of the college are beautiful, with trees and flowering plants everywhere. I could get used to life in this very well-concealed gem in the heart of Kingston city. At first I was terrified to live in Kingston, and even more fearful that I would have to "kotch" with my aunts, Sabine and Sebouney, who are actually fraternal twins, at their tenement building. These days there are always stories about shootings coming out of the capital city.

The political climate is so tremendously tense that there are shootings every day, even in broad daylight, and they are centred around my aunts' community. Apparently there is an ongoing gang feud, which is heightened by political affiliations. I don't know how they can live there. The day when I came to register at the college, my father took me to their house to decide if it were a plausible idea to stay with them, just in case I did not get a space in the hostel. Mommy hadn't come with us; since my grandma died, she's been getting progressively worse. The doctor said it is her nerves that are damaged, the shock of the sudden death and years of being overworked, just constantly pushing herself, have conclusively taken their toll. I try not to think about leaving her, but Monepha, Claire's youngest aunt, has promised to take care of her. Especially since Claire's mom is now in an institution, she has the time to keep an eye on my mother. I feel so conflicted about leaving her, but everyone, Mom included, insists that I leave. They insist that I go out into the world and make a life for myself.

Claire would be two bus rides from me, at the Kingston School of Nursing, but after Robin went missing our group just seemed to disintegrate. Bridget has gotten a job at the Post Office in our community so that she could be close to her mother in case anything happens, and she is trying to save enough money for college. She had been accepted to the Mico, the same as me, but she couldn't attend—not this year, not with everything going on at her house. If her mother would only leave and go live with her family, then Bridget would be free to attend college. But as long as her mother is at that house with her father, then she won't leave. I know for a fact that she would never forgive herself if anything happened to her mother. So she is desperately trying to save her mother from herself, but she keeps frantically holding on when there is nothing left to hold on to. Bridget has always been the designated bridge between both parents; being an only child can be so oppressive. I guess we all carry burdens and we have to do what we have to do. It's just the way life is.

Aunt Sabine had stayed home in anticipation of our visit.

When we got there, she was so anxious that she seems ten years older. She says, "You came right on time, because someone just got shot a few steps from our gate."

She says all this while pulling us into their cramped two-bedroom apartment. It is not the first time that I have wondered if they would ever get married and leave each other. Their apartment is located in a row of units and theirs is at the front, attached to another unit, then there is a single unit, a much bigger one that houses two big families, and a single unit on the far side of the yard. The layout is in the shape of a C. There is not one tree in sight. I start worrying about how I could ever live there; no trees, not one plant in view, hence no wind. Just scorching heat all the time, and it rarely rains. Just going from the car to the gate I am sweating. Sure, my aunts, being from the country, have a croton and a few other potted plants placed around their unit, but that just would not do for me.

I start praying earnestly that the secretary at the college would call with good news. We do not have a phone at the house but we've made arrangements for them to call the Post Office and Bridget would deliver the message. I am really praying that by the time we get back to Portland, Bridget would have received the call.

She offers us a drink and there is some small talk, which both my father and I hate, so pretty soon we are on our way with a promise to visit again soon. Before I leave my aunt gives me a lingering hug and whispers in my ears, "I am so very proud of you. You have broken the curse by being the first to go to college." Great, more pressure, more expectations. I wonder what she means by *break the curse*. But before I am able to process a question Daddy is ushering me out the house, holding my hand, almost dragging me to the car. The whole time he has been uncomfortable, constantly looking out the window to see if someone is trying to steal his car or parts of it. As soon as I get in the car Daddy says, "Don't you ever set foot back in this place."

"There's no need to worry, because I have no desire to die right now."

Daddy drives so fast that at one point, I think we are being chased by the police.

By the time we get back to Portland it is already dusk. The Post Office would be closed by now. All the way home, I kept wondering about the curse that auntie had mentioned. But I know it was pointless discussing it with Daddy. He always says, "Your mother and her sisters ole before dem young. Dem *always* have some ole wife's fable to share," with a huge emphasis on the "always." Hopefully, Mommy will be able to shed some light on this. Since she is the oldest, she should know.

Just as we clear the hill, I see Bridget sitting on the verandah, and my heart starts to race. I hope it is good news. She stands when she sees the car approaching. I can't wait for the car to stop.

"Hey girl."

"Hi, Neva. Hi, Uncle Fabien."

I am so impatient. "Any news?"

"Yes, I just got here. The college called and they said they found a spot for you at the Annex."

"What's that?" I ask, not really caring.

"Apparently, it is a house that is next to the hostel and a girl decided that she didn't want to live there because there is no privacy."

Daddy chimes in, "Well, her loss, your gain. I don't care how much people live dere, it has to be better dan where your aunties live."

I am so relieved. I give Bridget a huge hug and she reciprocates. Our first act of closeness in months. We look each other in the eye for the first time in a while and I can see how much older she looks, and although there's a smile on her face, her eyes are not smiling.

"Thank you so much."

"No problem, my pleasure. Hopefully, I'll be able to share

room with you soon."

"Yes, I hope so too."

"Well, I have to go now. I came straight here. Mama must be wondering what happen to me."

"How is your mother doing?" Daddy asks before I can get the words out.

"She is doing alright, all things considered."

There was a moment of silence and neither Daddy nor myself knows what to say. Mommy would know.

"Well, alright, I guess I'll see you, Uncle. And Neva, I'll see you when you're home on weekends."

"Yes, of course."

Bridget has such a sad look in her eyes, such a longing that I am tempted to look away. I know she is happy for me but I know she can't help being even a little jealous. After all, this was her dream, to go to teacher's college, the Mico in particular, and now it seems like someone else is living her dream right in front of her. She must feel like Hamlet after his father died and his uncle took the throne, when he, Hamlet, should have been the rightful heir. No wonder Hamlet says that Denmark is a prison. Bridget by now must feel like Balcarres, Portland in general, is a jail or a microcosm of a prison.

"It's getting late, Fabe, you should carry her home," Mommy says, sounding quite weak. Those nerve meds are really strong. They make her so frail that sometimes she can hardly make it to the verandah, one of her simple pleasures. I am not sure how long she has been standing there. I hope she did not hear what Daddy said about living with my aunts. I quickly go up the steps to greet her with a hug. That's when I allow myself to see how much weight she has lost in such a short time. I hold her and she's just skin and bones. I have never seen her like this.

"Alright, come Bridget. A soon come back," Daddy says, closing his door. Bridget waves as he does a three-point turn and then heads down the hill.

While putting on her seat belt, Bridget says, "Neva, remember *ukuu*."

I can't believe she remembers that. "*Ukuu*," I say in response with a huge smile, while clutching my tiny mother. Our roles are now reversed.

"How are you, Mommy?"

She allows me to lead her into the living room.

On her way, she questions: "Me alright chile. How was the visit to the school? Do you like it? How is your auntie dem doing?"

She asks all these questions with such urgency that she is left breathless. We have to pause for her to catch her breath. It's almost as if she is running out of time and she has to know everything right now.

"Let's talk in the living room, Mommy."

She nods in agreement and I have to hold her close and lead her to the floral couch, still wrapped in the original plastic it came in. These days, I rarely see her gap-toothed smile anymore and her hair has started to grey at the roots; I am certain it will look like grandma's did really soon and I don't think I am ready for that. As I help her to sit, I realize that the plastic on the chair doesn't groan when she sits on it like it used to. I tell her about the college grounds and how picturesque it is. I tell her that my aunties are doing well. I am careful not to mention anything about the shooting or their living arrangement. I don't want her to worry about her sisters. I so desperately want to ask her about the curse that auntie mentioned earlier but she looks so fragile, like a premature kitten; I don't want to say or do anything that might break her. So I decide to leave it for another time, because one thing about us as humans we always think that we have time; until we don't have any.

*　*　*

It is the Wednesday of the first week and my left eye has

been jumping—never ever a good sign. I get up early to get a shower because there are always so many people in line to use it. The Annex is literally a house, with many bedrooms, and some bedrooms have an en suite while others don't, so we have to share the facilities. Our room houses six people: four older ladies, me, and another girl my age. It has the smallest en suite, but it is generally the cleanest and most well-kept; hence it is always in demand. Now I understand why that other person didn't want the room; there is little to no privacy, but surprisingly I don't mind it at all. I guess the constant chatter and laughter coming from the other ladies and girls in the adjoining rooms keep me from remembering things that I don't want to, and from thinking about things that I shouldn't. Our room is generally quite quiet as well.

I walk to school and it is such a lovely day. There is a slight breeze, and although there is traffic it is not bumper-to-bumper so there is considerably less use of horns this early in the morning. The flowering trees are blooming all along Marescaux Road, the street that links the hostel and the college, which is close to National Heroes Circle. This is where many of our national heroes and prime ministers are buried, and it is also the largest park on this side of the island, home to a lavish botanical garden. It is such a welcoming place, yet sometimes seems so out of touch with the hustle and bustle of life in Kingston. I plan to visit after school. I still haven't really made the effort to form any friendships and I doubt I ever will. I really don't mind my own company; as long as I am able to keep memories at bay, I am fine. Many of the ladies are quite congenial, but I am not in the mood to have friends right now. I just want to bask in my alone time because it is true what they say, that *because I am alone doesn't mean that I am lonely.*

I stop by the office to see if there's any mail or messages for me. There's a note from Bridget; it is dated the day before. It is written in very neat script, but it's very terse:

Nevaeh, your father will be visiting you tomorrow around noon. Please be available.

Bridget.

Why would Daddy be visiting me in the middle of the week? In the middle of my first week? I make my way to my first class but I cannot shake this feeling of foreboding, one that indicates that something is not right. I look outside the window where there is a very aged guango tree that conceals most of the other buildings: the tuck shop, the administrative offices and some of the other classes that face my classroom. To all intents and purposes, it is a very ordinary day: the same sun, the same cool breeze, the same birds, even the same lizard crawling up the tree. But it doesn't feel ordinary.

At about 11:30, I see my dad standing at the door. He is my father but he is not my father. I ask to be allowed outside and my professor says yes. Daddy hugs me, which he never does, and he tries to make small talk, which he fails at because it is not in his nature. Eventually, he lets go of the charade and says, "You maddah dead."

I am silent for what seems like an eternity. I just stare straight ahead at the trees growing only a few meters from my face. I could reach out and touch them. I hold the rails that frame the building to keep from falling.

A single word breaks the silence, "When?"

He says—looking out at the other buildings where we can see people engaged in discussions; one student is gesticulating with his hands and if it weren't for the distance, I can tell that he is shouting—"Yesterday around noon. Monepha went to get her lunch ready and when she came back, she was on the floor… a stroke… like your grandma…. The doctor said that… you know… it seems like… death was… instant… there was no pain."

At this he pauses and we look at the same student, now standing to emphasize his point. We are quiet for another eternity.

"What now?" I hear my voice ask. I sound like a child again. But I don't know when my brain processed the question because I seem to have separated from myself; one part of me is here standing, holding the rails for support but there's another part of me that has somehow left me. I seemed to have divided into two personas. Where has the other me gone? Did she fly home to see if this idiocy is real? What will happen to me now? Doesn't the Bible say, a house that is divided against itself cannot stand? How will I stand all these things which are to come in my life? How will I be able to stand without Mommy to hold me up? She has always held me together. I hope and pray that I don't faint as I fight back bile and a sudden desire to throw myself on the ground and weep uncontrollably. I remember Mommy weeping for Grandma. Maybe that is how I am supposed to weep. Maybe that is the only way to demonstrate great sorrow and brokenness. If Mommy were here, I would ask her how to mourn for her, how to be away from her. Yet I cannot weep. Because I get this sudden feeling, this knowing, that if I start crying now I might never stop. So I keep everything bottled up inside. I cannot cry, although my umbilical cord has been severed from my mother without the aid of anesthesia and the pain is excruciating, more so because I was woefully unprepared.

Everything from that moment is a blur. I know that, somehow, I collected some of my things from the Annex and stopped to pick up my aunts but I am not sure how or when I got home. I woke up screaming for Mommy in my bed. Both my aunts rushed to cuddle me, to give me comfort but their arms feel odd, like they had claws where hands should have been, because they hold no comfort for me. Nothing will ever bring me comfort again. Nothing will ever be the same. That's really how I mourn my mother; I never wept in my waking moments, only in my sleep when my subconscious gives way to the overwhelming rush of tears, like when the river came down.

I attend the funeral but it's only a part of me. The other

part has still not returned and I feel unbalanced without her, incomplete even. I don't know when to eat or what to eat. It seems like she was in charge of that part of me and she just up and left me, just when I needed her the most. What am I supposed to do right now? Everything is foggy, even faces are dubious. My friends are there but I am no longer sure if they are my friends or they belong to the part of me that left. But they are there, I can also feel Robin as well. For the first time since she disappeared, I can sense that she is near. I want to tell them that Robin isn't dead, Mommy is dead, I can sense her too but her aura is different from Robin's. But I can't because the words are stuck in my head. I see them prancing around in my mind but I cannot get them to flow in the right order. They are all jumbled like a crossword puzzle.

I sit perfectly still throughout the ceremony. Every now and again, someone touches my hand, or my forehead, or rubs my back; I guess to check if I am still breathing. The singing, the clapping and the dancing that once brought me so much comfort all fall flat. The praise and worship is off key, the singing is pitchy in parts, the music is too loud, and the dancing is too much. It seems like everyone is doing way too much; overcompensating for my mother's absence. Somehow trying to show that they loved her the most and will miss her the most. All the while not knowing that I am the one who is left without my soul.

After the funeral rites are completed, my aunts decide that it would be best if I return to school, so I do. But just before I leave, I get a message through Claire that the Healer wants to see me. It is a strange and utterly unexpected request and it jolts me back to reality for a minute. I go to see him at dusk, just like old times. This time, the Assistant isn't there to meet me; the Healer himself is standing tall just inside his gate. I am startled for a moment, as I've forgotten how stunning he is and framed against the backdrop of the setting sun with the hues of light pink and greys behind him, he is nothing short of hypnotic. It's getting dark and pretty soon it will be quite difficult to see; I wish I could see his face more clearly, and see what is written in his eyes. We stare at each other for a while, one of those moments that seem longer than they really are.

He breaks the silence: "We can talk here." With the gate separating us, I think.

"Sure."

"I heard about your mother. Accept my condolences."

"Thank you, sir."

"I hope you don't think this is your fault; none of this is."

How does he know this? I open my mouth to question but he raises his hand, in the dark, it looks like a sword, an indication for me to be still.

"Life happens, Nevaeh, and so does death. One never punishes herself when a child is born, when a new life enters this cruel world, but at death, people tend to experience survivor's guilt. Do you know what that is?"

"Yes, sort of. It is an intense feeling of guilt and remorse that you are alive but a loved one has transitioned."

"Exactly! Do not allow this to destroy you, your mother would not want that…"

He pauses, I guess waiting for a response. I forget that he might not be able to see me so I nod in agreement.

He continues, "It's getting dark and you have to go soon. But here is a chrysanthemum plant. Plant this to honour the memory of your mother. Every time you see it, it will remind you that she is watching and that she is doing fine."

I notice that he didn't say, watching over you, like everyone else.

"Thank you, sir, this is very kind of you. You didn't have to, so for that reason, I am eternally grateful."

I accept the container.

"It is about eight weeks old, an ideal time to transplant it, and it should be fine."

He turns to leave and as if struck by a thought he pronounces, "Remember *ukuu*." I say, "*Ukuu*," like a chant or a secret language between us.

I leave because I have to. I don't want to. I wish I could stay here, ask him questions, learn from him. Suddenly, the memory of the bathing process comes flooding back to me and I am homesick to be back in that shed among the vials of herbs, sitting in the metal tub and absorbing all the plant life in the water; just to be held captive by the tranquility of the moment. But I have to leave. I turn around and he is already slipping away as the darkness swallows him up.

The next day, I transplant the chrysanthemum plant in honour of my mother's memory at the front of the house, right below her bedroom window, where it will be sheltered from the rain and direct sunlight. Everyone watches me plant it, and no one questions its sudden appearance or my disappearance the night before. My father volunteers, "Nuh worry, Star Gurl, me we tek care of it fe you."

I thought about what the Healer had said about life and I figure that when children are born in our community, they plant a fruit tree with their *navel string* as they call it; as for me, my coconut tree still stands tall in the yard, right across from my bedroom window. So it is only fitting and appropriate, and appropriately fitting, that I do this for my mother. I rationalize that Mommy will always be right there to greet me anytime I am home from college. After all she will always be there watching out for me. I just wish that she had picked me and chosen not to die. How could she leave me, her only child, right when I needed her the most? This whole experience reminds me of that song—

… You left me just when I needed you most

Now   I   love   you   more   than   I   loved   you   before
And   now   where   I'll   find   comfort,   God   knows
Cause you … left me just when I needed you most….

I sit through all my classes in a haze. I basically leave when everyone else does and follow the masses to the canteen or out through the gate. I collect my lunch and smile at everyone but all the time no one knows that I have died inside. My aunts come to check on me weekly. They take me to the movies; the Carib Theatre (before the fire that destroyed the inside) is just about ten minutes from school. We watch *The Titanic*. I feel so bad for Rose after the love of her life dies; she had that faraway look in her eyes, the one I am pretty sure I have in mine. My aunts feed me all the time; they bring me money just in case I don't want the cafeteria food which is subsidized so everyone eats for free. Also, at the Annex the food is subsidized and we take turns making our meals.

I go home less and less. Each time I go home I am amazed at how big my chrysanthemums are getting, and the colours. My father has certainly kept his word. I stay with my aunts who were forced to give up their old apartment because of the violence, which works in my favour because they get an apartment closer to school. I spend most of my weekends and holidays with them. I feel really bad for Daddy that I can't be with him right now. I have to heal first or else I will be of no use to him or anyone else. I guess the discipline from high school has really paid off; I never miss a class and I complete and submit all assignments on time. The work is significantly more demanding. I no longer get As but at least I am not swimming in a sea of Cs. Despite the emotional turmoil I fail nothing. I am completely shocked at the end of the first semester.

My aunts and I celebrate by throwing a party. They invite all their friends to celebrate their "bright niece." They ask me to invite my friends, but the truth is I have none. I seem to have forgotten how to make friends. I am completely cordial with everyone, but no one strikes me as a true friend. I don't sense Bridget, Claire or Robin in any of them. I smile a lot more now because a smile will always fool people into thinking you're happy. Plus, I am so damaged that I just mostly stay out of people's way.

Yes, that is what I am—beautiful and broken. Sometimes I look in the mirror and see a complete stranger staring back at me. Sometimes, we even smile at each other and make believe that we know each other.

Time moves at warp speed and before you know it, I am in my third and final year. My aunts used to gently suggest that I make friends. By that they mean, get a boyfriend. Aunt Sebouney warns, "Do not become us. Look at us, two old hooman without a man. You try mek sure you end up married with children."

Aunt Sabine adds, "Mek sure, you nuh just leave school with a Diploma, mek sure you leave with a man."

Dear God, one minute they say stay away from boys, next thing I have to find a man. The pressure is unreal and I have never done well under pressure. I make stupid choices that everyone is hurt by. Plus, I don't know the first thing about being flirtatious so I am not even quite sure of how to acquire a man and I am quite certain that they wouldn't know either because they don't have any. If Robin were here, I am sure she would know how to go about doing that, but as it turns out she is not, so I don't know what's going to happen in that department.

In my second year, I did make a few friends, some Pentecostal ladies, but they seem way too intense so I try to minimize contact with them. However, they are adamant about taking me to church and taking me to *the water to be baptized*. More and more I have been thinking about baptism but I am still not sure. Now in my final year, my aunts order me to take part in the Socials at school. I attend a few and a boy in my class catches my eye. He is tall, dark and handsome, with a ready smile that he whips out at will. He has the darkest skin I have ever seen, since the Healer, and the brightest eyes. He seems to have a lisp, but he is so articulate it hardly shows. I only know this because I have been spending a lot of time looking at him and analyzing his every move. He walks with such a laid-back gait, almost swaying, always with a bounce—the very epitome of swag.

He could never be interested in me.

But somehow, he always seeks me out and comes to sit next to me. So very confusing. He is hilariously funny, charming and brilliant. All qualities that I tremendously admire in people and more specifically in the other gender.

His cologne is tantalizing.

Before you know it, when I am not thinking about Mommy and her absent gap-toothed smile, he is all I think about. People start to speculate that we are together. I have never had a boyfriend so I am not quite sure if we are an "item" like everyone is saying. I play along to see where it leads. I start to like him more and more. I don't know what to do. I don't want to tell my aunts; they are going to make a big deal about it. I can't tell my Pentecostal friends because they are going to bind and rebuke the spirit of sex and I really don't want to lose that warm tingling feeling that I get when he is in my line of vision. At least when I am tingling, I am not missing Mommy as much. Yet she is always there in my mind and in my heart. I still haven't seen that part of me that disappeared that fateful day. The coward has left me to face life on my own. The Bible is right, though, because a house divided against itself cannot stand.

I couldn't tell anyone so I tell Mr. Tall, Dark and Handsome. It was one evening after our class had ended and we decide as at other times to stay back to jest.

So I say, "I need to tell you something."

He replies, "Go ahead. I'm listening."

"I don't know how else to say this."

"Just say it. You have a mouth."

We laugh at his nonsense.

I play with the implements on the desk: my notebook, textbook and pens, which gives me an idea.

"So," I begin with a sigh. He starts to look very concerned.

"Yes, tell me," he demands.

"Well, let's just say, I was over here where the textbook is and you came over. Then you brought me to where the notebook is and we seem to be heading to where the pens are."

I thought he was going to laugh at me but he doesn't. He just says in a very quiet tone, "I can't talk about this right now." And with that he says, "We should leave, I should get you back to the Annex, it is getting late." Just like that.

As it turns out, he too has issues. As soon as I make my feelings abundantly clear to him, he backs away. No, he runs away, and leaves me all alone again and even more confused. He doesn't come to find me anymore; I am the one who is always looking for him. He avoids me, even in class. He has moved seats. I feel so stupid and broken, even more than I felt before. I feel like I have a gaping hole in my chest and everyone is staring at it and laughing behind my back. I wish Mommy were here, I could probably tell her and she would know what to do. Robin for sure would know what to do.

I think of hanging out with Claire sometimes, but I don't have the energy to make the effort. Plus, it wouldn't be fair to her, to dump all this drama in her lap after I have been avoiding her all this while. So on top of the fact that I am deeply saddened at the passing of my mother, I am now heartbroken; even more divided than before. Life just doesn't quit, does it? So I do what I always do when emotions are involved and threaten to overwhelm me: I throw myself into my schoolwork. I tell myself that he was a mere distraction sent by the devil to tempt me. Well, I certainly hope I passed that test, because I drove him away in one evening. That experience has taught me a few lessons, though: primarily that it doesn't matter how I feel about people, they still have the right to choose whether or not they want to be in my life, and sometimes they choose not to. I have also learned how to survive armed with a smile. Mr. Handsome just didn't want me. I knew he was out of my league. I've learned that in this life even if you love someone, it doesn't matter, and it doesn't mean that your love will magnetically pull them to you.

* * *

At the end of my three years, I left college and Kingston far more broken than when Daddy had deposited me at the Annex the very first day. It's like all the hurt that I was supposed to accumulate over the course of my lifetime had just found me all at once. I went back to my community and a lot of people trekked up the hill to see me. They came looking for me, all the while not knowing that that was the old me. How could I blame them? For all intents and purposes, the smile and the face all looked the same, so how could I blame them for missing the obvious fact that they came looking for the old me?

So many things have happened, so much hurt and pain, that now all I want to do is forget. I want to forget all the people who have either died or left me without a clue as to how to move on without them. I make a decision on my first week back home, that I will forget all the people and experiences that have left me spent and raw. I will have to live in my small community but I will put all the harsh realities of the past behind me and pretend that they never happened. I will not allow anyone to force me to remember the things that I need to forget, even if it means leaving my friends behind; not necessarily in a physical sense, but emotionally I will be far removed from them. I will become like Aunt Sabrina, now far more removed from the realm that is considered the present.

As a result of my sojourn, I discover two things: Jesus, and sad soul music. Lyrics that are song with so much passion, so much achingly raw emotion, that they search the depths of my soul and rub salve on my wounds. My Pentecostal friends would say that type of music is of the devil, because it doesn't bring glory to God and it celebrates the flesh. But how could that be when God Himself created everything, including the devil and music? Doesn't the Bible say that God created both good and evil, including the waster to destroy? Doesn't that allude to the fact that everything serves a divine purpose—it just depends on usage? Doesn't the Bible also say that all things work together for good? I have so many questions, and possibly that's why I still haven't chosen to get baptized. Also, because I feel like baptism would make our relationship too public, and what if Jesus rejects me like Whatshisname? Then where would I be? Plus, there are still too many unnatural rules at my church, too many don'ts without a reason.

Furthermore, while I was growing up, I could just accept what was preached from the pulpit, but now that I am older it is a lot more difficult to accept certain "truths" as they are presented. For instance, Pastor is of the view that God is going to kill everyone. Every time he takes the mic I imagine that any minute now there will be brimstone and fire falling around us. But based on my experiences, based on all that I have done and all the grace that I have received, I cannot imagine that Pastor is talking about the same God that I have come to know and love. Plus, he doesn't believe in dating, and I still don't see how two people can get to know each other well enough to determine if marriage is an option for them without it. Unsurprisingly, he is still going on about all the people who are "fernicating." It seems to me that he is of the view that that is all people do when they get together.

I return home to my own room, my own bed, and my own plants that I have planted and watered. My chrysanthemums fill the length and breadth of the front yard, spreading viciously to below my window at the east side of the house. They are beauty being colorfully displayed. I returned home to pomp and pageantry. My aunts have ensured that everyone has been made aware of my accomplishments, of our accomplishments. My success seems so personal to them that I can't help but love them for being my biggest support system when I needed one the most.

Daddy has aged so much; his gait is slower and he seems to

have lost his sense of humour. He is only a shadow of himself. My return home seems to help, especially because I bring my aunts with me. My dad says, "It is nice to 'ave people around again."

I feel horrible every time he says it. When I should have been visiting my dad on weekends, I was at school obsessing about some boy who didn't even care.

Miss. Parker gets me a job at the new high school in our community. She'd suggested working at Providence, but the memories are still too fresh, the ghosts all too real, so I graciously declined. I spent so much time planning what I would say at an interview, but I didn't even have to. The principal just wanted to meet me, and the job teaching Grade 11 English Literature was mine, which both terrified and exhilarated me at the same time. I'd spent three years preparing to teach: planning lessons, writing both the unit and the lesson plans, but otherwise I am ill-prepared for the actual execution of the lessons.

However, like most humans long before me, through trial and error, I settle into a routine. But soon I begin to worry that life was passing me by. My aunts start to complain that I need to get married. Daddy's sense of humour has slowly returned and even he (the same man who planned to go to prison not so long ago) wants grandchildren. Everyone at our local assembly is asking when they are going to eat a slice of my wedding cake (a Jamaican euphemism for marriage). Being a very small community where everyone knows everyone by name and nature, I can't go anywhere without enquiries about marriage. A few ladies even tried to interview me for their sons, but I respectfully declined, seeing that I was still traumatized by my own misguided choices.

I have never been one to thrive under pressure, so one Saturday morning it all got too much for me and it all came to a head. I decide to visit the river, with no intentions of returning home. But before I do, I go to check on Auntie Sabrina, Robin's mother. I feel like I at least owe her a visit, because since Robin's sudden disappearance and my breakdown, I have not had a chance to speak with her. I am sure she was at Mommy's funeral but I can't remember. I don't know how she will receive me, but at least I have to try to see her before I go. She too has aged rapidly, but is still such a beautiful woman. Warmth still exudes from her and her embrace is so welcoming. I wonder why I have been so afraid to see her all this time.

At first we sit in a respectful silence. Then she looks at me with that infectious smile. "How have you been, baby?"

"I have been well," I lie. She smiles one of those I-know-you-are-lying smiles, but we won't talk about it right now. I say, "How have you been, Auntie?"

"Not good! But I have been getting better and better every day."

"Sorry to hear that, Auntie, but I am very happy to hear that you are getting better. I can only imagine."

Let's just say that I am quite shocked at how candid she is, which must have lingered on my face.

"Thank you. I have decided that I am going to be honest about my feelings. I am no longer going to be living in denial. Because maybe, just maybe, if I had had the courage to be honest, I wouldn't have lost my only child."

She looks at her hands in her lap then back at me. I don't know what to say except, "So sorry about that, Auntie. I wish I could have done more…."

"You must not blame yourself, Nevaeh. There is absolutely nothing that you or anyone else could have done. Everyone has a choice in how their life story plays out. Please do not take on other people's stories. My child, my one child, is gone, and there's nothing that any of us could have done. Just like how your own dear mother is gone. For a long time I thought it was my fault, my own doing, and in part it was. Looking back, I should have made better choices, I should have seen all the signs—"

"What signs, Auntie? What do you mean? Did Robin leave a

note?"

She looks at me, as if she's on the verge of going off script, but this is something that she has rehearsed, a message she is compelled to deliver. The significance is weighing heavily on her.

"Just signs of my neglect. A child should be allowed to be a child. My child should not have felt that she was the adult in the house. I spent so many years being focused on the wrong thing, seeing but not wanting to see, hearing but not wanting to hear… but now I am choosing to live my life differently. I miss her every single day, but what is done is done and cannot be undone, so the best thing to do is learn the lesson and move on. Do you hear me, Nevaeh? Learn the lesson and move on. Do not waste your life carrying guilt; life is way too short."

After that, she is silent again. I have so many questions. Did I miss something? Did they find Robin? How can she be so unaffected, detached even? I guess the meds she is on have really helped her to focus. She seems to have said all that she had intended to and has that far-afield look in her eyes like she has forgotten I am here. So not wanting to wear out my welcome, I say, "It's been great catching up, Auntie." She looks surprised to see me.

"Yes, it has, chile, please come again."

She walks me to the door and enfolds me in another warm embrace. Then she whispers in my hair, "I am very proud of you, and remember that your ancestors were slaves." Then she pulls away to look me in the eyes and hold my hands in hers.

"They were determined to never give up, never surrender, never throw in the towel. They were determined to fight for their freedom. The Maroons living so close to us, but on their own terms, are a shining example of the strength that lies in us."

Needless to say, I change my mind about ending my life. I decide that I will make the choice to start living again. So far I've been locked in survival mode—a meagre way to live. I guess having contemplated giving up so many times, Auntie Sabrina can now discern when the spirit of surrender is present, when it sits in the room and makes breathing difficult. So I figure, if she has had to endure so much for so long and still has the perspicacity to want to live, then I should at least honour her and the memory of my mother by being bold enough to hang on for dear life.

I visit the Dry River, in Comfort Castle, a bit out of my way but so worth the trip. The river is surrounded by greenery, plant life that seems like a nest around the river, a mini waterfall gushing from the rocks. The whole area seems to have emerged from a fairy tale—wrapped in hues of viridescent plant life—from a distant land, surrounded by steep ridges and verdure of the rarest find. To think that this is where I had planned to end everything: all the pain, all the bad memories. I came for solace and I am instantly refreshed just by looking at its vastness and perceiving how many years it's been around, how much the flora and fauna depend on it. Yet it is never overwhelmed, it never gives up, it never gets weary and runs dry. Even in the dry season, there is a spring somewhere, waiting to feed and be fed.

I won't give up, not now, not ever. I will fight for the life I want; the one I deserve.

CHAPTER TEN

I get home from my trip and even from the foot of the hill I can tell that there is a stranger at my house. I can tell, even in the gathering dusk, that there is car parked in front of it. I make my way up the hill, but not as quickly as I used to. I get home panting. A stranger sits on my verandah looking down on me.

Daddy says, "Star gurl, where have you been?"

My daddy's use of the formal way of speaking is strange indeed but not uncommon when we have visitors.

"Hi, Daddy. I went to the river and lost track of time."

"There is someone here who wants to speak to you."

I reach the verandah and the stranger stands and extends his hand. His voice is deeply masculine and he sounds like an older person, not as old as Daddy but maybe older than me, although it's hard to tell from the disappearing sun.

"Hi, my name is Rayva. My friends call me Ryva. Nice to meet you."

"Hi, I am Nevaeh. It's a pleasure to meet you."

Daddy says, "He's been waiting all afternoon. He's here about your chrysanthemums. But I told him that they are very special so he would have to speak with you about them. I'll go inside so you both can speak."

"Okay, Daddy."

I take the patio chair on the far side of the verandah. I guess living in Kingston for three years has made me wary of strangers. Plus, it is a good position for observation.

"So how can I help, Mr.—"

"It's Barron, actually, but you can just call me Rayva."

His accent sounds American but not quite.

"Okay, Rayva, what can I do for you?"

Someone turns on the verandah light. I see that he is not old at all, around my age, although it's hard to tell. So handsome, with terracotta complexion like Robin, and lips that look decorated— lined and coloured. Full lips that he licks every now again.

"Well, first of all, deepest condolences on the passing of your mother. I am so sorry to hear of your loss."

"Thank you."

He pauses and then continues.

"I am here because of your magnificent chrysanthemums."

"Oh!"

"Yes, I am a buyer. I buy chrysanthemums and I have been asking around and I hear that yours are the best: the most healthy and the most vibrant."

"Well, you must also have heard that I planted them to honour my Mother's memory, so they are not for sale."

"Yes, but hear me out—"

My aunt Sebouney comes out with a tray, and from the smell of it it is homegrown and homemade guava and passionfruit juice. We both say "Thank you," at the same time.

She gives us each a glass and without saying a word she goes back into the house. I don't know what she thinks this is. After a few sips and sounds of approval, he continues, "This is delicious."

"Yes, it is."

"Now, as I was saying. My family has a contract with a pharmaceutical company that's based in Canada. By the way, that's where I'm from."

That explains the accent. He seems slightly familiar as well.

"They are harnessing the medicinal properties of the chrysanthemum plant, and are using it to make life-saving drugs for a wide variety of illnesses, ranging from hypertension, seasonal allergies, and nervous conditions to inflammation, just to name a few of the things. The research is ongoing and they are now trying to determine if it could be useful in treating some types of cancers."

"That's great and all, but my plants are not for sale."

"I hear you. But if you could just listen for one sec."

Not wanting to seem rude, I urge, "Go on!"

"So I was talking to your dad, and I was telling him that it would be a great way to honour your mom's memory, to hand over these chrysanthemums to the science that could help others, so that someone else's mom would not have to die prematurely, that someone else would not have to suffer the emotional torment that I am sure you have suffered. Plus, your soil seems to be so rich that from this one plant thousands of lives can be saved. Certainly, it will grow again."

He pauses here for effect. I look away from the intensity of his gaze, from his passion, out at the darkness that is slowly spreading across the neighbourhood. I have not seen so much passion in a person in a long time, not since Robin. Come to think of it, he reminds me so much of her. Everything from his personality to his terracotta skin tone and full eyes.

"They are not for sale!" I say, standing up. My indication that I have heard enough.

"I am so sorry, Nevaeh. I can tell that you're upset and I really didn't mean to upset you."

"Yes, you have… very much."

"I am really sorry. Here is my card. It has my cellphone number. Maybe you can text me if you want to discuss this further."

"Text you…? I don't even have a cellular phone."

"Really, you don't have a cellphone?"

He looks very amused, which is more irritating than him trying to buy Mommy's chrysanthemums.

"Mr. Barron, some things just cannot be bought. I am sorry that you've wasted your day waiting for me and coming here but Mommy's chrysanthemums are not for sale. Thanks for your time."

"I understand, but still keep my card, just in case."

He hands it to me but I turn away. He places it on the windowsill that faces down the hill.

"I'll be going now. Please say goodnight to your dad and thank your aunt for me. I really feel horrible for upsetting you. That was never my intention."

"Goodnight, Mr. Barron."

"Goodnight, Miss Francis."

With that he does this cute thing, like a kind of nod or a slight bow of his head. Why did he have to be so adorable? It's the Healer vibe all over again. I go inside. Everyone is waiting for me, for an update, but I head straight to my room. That man has triggered so much raw emotion in me. I need to lie down.

The next day over breakfast all my family can talk about is how handsome Rayva is and how respectful he was. But from our very brief encounter, there is something about him that deeply disturbs me in ways that I cannot articulate. He seems too composed, like he wears a facade on the outside while he fights to quell the quiet storms inside him. A veil that he takes off at night and replaces at the crack of dawn. And having worn one for most of my life, I know how to discern a mask when I see one. However, unlike the Junkanoo dancer whose mask is present and visible for the world to witness, Rayva's mask is invisible to the naked eye and can only be detected by a similar mask-wearer. I guess Claire was right after all.

Daddy finally asks, "So what do you plan to do, Star Gurl? Are you going to sell?"

I had just put a spoonful of creamy, smooth and rich cornmeal porridge in my mouth and I had to swallow quickly to respond.

"No, Daddy, how could you ask such a thing? Those plants are important to me. I don't want to sell them to a stranger and I don't want to discuss this anymore. It is quite upsetting for me."

"But why, Nevaeh?" My dad almost never calls me by my Christian name.

"Who knows, this might be your ticket out of this small town, Neva," Auntie Sebouney says, and Auntie Sabine nods in agreement.

"Who says I want to leave, though? I went to college and I came back. This is my home and I am not ashamed to be here."

Aunt Sabine pipes up, "No one is saying you are or that you should be ashamed of your home, but Neva, you can have more, you can be more. You don't have to settle for life as we know it."

She takes my hand gently into hers. "Our way doesn't have to be your way. This is where we were born; your aunt and I left for a long time but we came back. Because this is where we were born and this is where we will die, but it doesn't have to be so for you, Neva. You have so much more to offer the world. Like your father always says, you are a Star Girl."

Both Daddy and Aunt Sebouney say, "True."

It's times like these that I wish Mommy were here to help me decide. So much pressure. Why do they want to complicate things by allowing this stranger into our lives? I get the distinct impression that our lives are about to change in ways that we could never imagine. Sadly, they are all fooled by Rayva's charm and a huge part of his appeal is his foreign accent. Some Jamaicans love every accent except theirs. If he were some guy from another parish they wouldn't be so enticed, they wouldn't be so giddy to sell.

"Okay, I'll think about it."

"That's all we ask, Star Gurl. Don't close the door to an opportunity before first looking into it," Daddy says, looking very somber. They have already made up their minds, so they're just being gracious by allowing me to feel like I have a say in the outcome.

Prior to last night those plants have always been a source of comfort for me and usually I sit outside and read, but today I can't bear to see them, so I spend the day reading in my room. Late in the afternoon, I hear a knock on my door. It's Aunt Sabine and she says in her high pitched happy voice, "You have a visitor."

I wonder who would be visiting me at this time of the day. When I make my way to the verandah, it is Mr. Barron himself, talking to Daddy with a gift bag in his hand. He says,

"Hi, Nevaeh, how are you doing?"

Daddy says, "I'll leave the two of you to talk."

He is really starting to work on my nerves. Where is the man who used to threaten to shoot boys for me?

"Hi, Mr. Barron. I am well. How are you?"

"I am very well, thank you. Here, I brought you a gift. My way of apologizing for upsetting you last night. It was certainly not my intention."

He hands me the gift bag. I say, "You really shouldn't have, Mr. Barron—"

"I should have, and call me Rayva. Here, open it."

It's a small cellphone, green with Motorola written on the front.

I am in the process of returning it to the bag and preparing to return it to him.

"No, thanks! I cannot take this. This is too much."

"No, I insist. This is second generation Motorola and I think it's perfect for you. Please accept it. It is my way of apologizing. If you don't accept it, I am going to feel really horrible."

He seems so genuinely hurt that I acquiesce and take his gift.

"Thank you. That's very thoughtful of you."

"It's my pleasure."

We stand around for a few awkward moments and then he says it's time for him to go.

Before I can stop myself, I say, "Would you like to stay for dinner?"

I don't know why I just spoke before my brain was sufficiently engaged, but as it turns out I did and there was no going back from there. Sometimes in life just one action triggers multiple others, and once they are set in motion there is no undoing what's been done.

From that time on, Rayva becomes a fixture at our house. In addition to the cellular phone, he buys me a car. I try to refuse but he would not have it.

"Thanks so much, but I can't drive."

It is a 1999 Honda Accord. Apparently all the rage at the moment.

"That's fine. I'll be happy to teach you."

"But don't you have to return to Canada?"

"As a buyer, I am allowed to travel on an open ticket, so I don't have to return right away."

"I don't have a licence, even."

"Nevaeh, I will take care of everything. Don't worry about it. A lady of your calibre should not be walking or taking public transportation." If only he really knew me, he wouldn't have said that. I know with time he will run away, fly back to Ontario and abandon me. It's only a matter of time.

Days turn into weeks and weeks turn into months, but every time I turn around he's right there, driving up the hill, sitting on the verandah, or walking around taking pictures of my chrysanthemums and my aunts' now thriving bougainvillea plants. Our yard looks like a big, beautiful, fragrant garden, which can be discerned from the foot of the hill.

One thing is for sure, Rayva is quite persistent and determined to get what he has concluded is his. In his mind, us being together is a foregone conclusion; fate, as he puts it. At a point I realize that it is no longer just about the chrysanthemums, as he intends to not only take all the plants he can but he fully intends to pluck my heart as well. He doesn't seem to have any concept of no and what that potentially means. I surmise that this is how things work when you're born with a proverbial gold spoon in your mouth. I cannot get rid of him, and in this regard my family members are of no help. They are all so enthralled by him and it is annoying to me how contagious their enthusiasm is. I have not seen them this happy in a really long time. I feel delighted that I am in some way responsible for their new-found bliss. My father is beside himself with glee.

Over the summer, we see each other every single day, sometimes twice a day. Day by day, little by little, he wears down my defenses and weakens my resolve, and despite my misgivings, I allow myself to believe that this is real love. The fairy tale that Hollywood has sold us and that Mommy bought, repackaged and gave to me. She told me that, if I were a good girl, stayed pure, kept my head up, the *right one* would come along, sweep me off my feet and it would be a long and lasting love. I believed her because after all, isn't that her and Daddy's story? She was very proud to share with me that she was indeed "the little black bird that stole his heart" and he had remained faithful to her even after death.

I bring Rayva to all my favourite places. We visit the many rivers in my parish. He takes me on a cruise, island-hopping. He teaches me to drive and he displays all the patience of Job in accomplishing this feat. We have our first kiss under the streetlight at the foot of our hill the night before he is to fly back to Ontario. He wants more but I make it clear that I am not that kind of girl. He smiles and says, "Aren't you all not that kind of girl, until you are that kind of girl?" Framed like a question, but the impact is more of a conclusion.

"What does that mean?" I'm completely shocked at both his tone and his words. But he laughs and says, "I am joking with you, English teacher. It's a play on words."

"That's the worst pun I have ever heard in my whole life."

He insists, "I am just kidding. I know you are not that kind of girl. Now can we please drop this? Don't go ruining the moment by being moody."

He has not brought up the chrysanthemums but I feel obligated to offer them. At this point, I hope he understands me enough to say no; but he says. "Yes! That's amazing. I knew eventually you would see reason."

He hugs me, picking me up off the ground in the process and whips out his phone, already making arrangements to cut down Mommy's memorial.

Early the next day, two young men come to do the deed. I cannot watch. I feel like that time at Christmas when they slaughtered the ram for Christmas dinner and to share with the poor. A sacrifice for the good of the cause. One that is painful to watch but I understand that it needs to be done. But this feels like a sacrifice for all the wrong reasons. Thankfully, they are respectful and leave the original plant, but they remove all the overflow, which is a whole lot. I can't believe how much that one plant has yielded. It seems to have been cared for by supernatural hands.

Later, on his way to the airport, Rayva comes to pay. I can't even look at him so I tell him to talk to Daddy. I go to my room but I still manage to hear the exchange. It sounds like when the Higglers haggle in the Marketplace with potential customers. I hear Daddy refusing vehemently and Rayva objecting just as fervently. Eventually, Rayva gets Daddy to see reason and before you know it Daddy has accepted the money and Rayva comes to say goodbye.

He says, "I'll call as soon as I get to Toronto." Apparently, he has to catch a connecting flight in Toronto. Before, he leaves, he looks me straight in the eye and says, "You are not that kind of girl and I know that you will remain faithful to me, to us. You are my forever."

I wasn't quite sure there was an *us* but I say yes, to not prolong this discussion with my aunts and my father within earshot.

After he leaves, I pray silently that he will go home and forget about me. The summer holiday has come to an end, I return to work in two weeks, and so I will do what I always do, throw myself into work and try to forget him. But even as I pray I know it is a waste of breath, because I know that I am already in love with him and I will love him forever.

CHAPTER ELEVEN

The night before our wedding, my sleep is fitful and I think it's because I am not in my room, not in my bed. We are staying at a hotel in St. Ann. That's where we'll be having the wedding ceremony, not in a church but under a gazebo, my dream wedding. I know that if Mommy were alive she would have insisted that we have the ceremony in a church. Well, it's too bad that she abandoned me; she no longer has a say in my choices. If she wanted to have a say then she shouldn't have left me just when I needed her the most.

It takes us just a little over four months to plan the wedding. Rayva has done most of the planning, because all I had to do was just agree. He took care of everything: the location, the outfits, the rings, the food, everything. The wedding is at a beautiful villa overlooking the Caribbean Sea, with the most beautiful palm trees, hibiscus, chrysanthemums and other flowering plants. The location is so tranquil and peaceful that I could stay here for the rest of my life. The hotel is located in the town of Ocho Rios, St.

Ann, but seems so isolated all at the same time.

I have not had a dream about my mother since I sold the plants to Rayva. The plants did return, although not as vibrant. Somehow they have lost their shine. After the rehearsal dinner, I toss and turn in bed. I read my Bible and a novel that I have in my bag. I always have a novel in my handbag.

Yet sleep is still playing truant. Therefore all the rogue thoughts that I have tried to avoid find their way into my mind. I think of everything that could or might go wrong in my marriage. The worse part being that I would have to leave my island home. Rayva has already put in the paperwork and he is just waiting on the wedding certificate and the wedding pictures to complete the package.

Naturally I remember every mistake I have ever made. All the sad memories come flooding back, bringing company with them, to the point where I literally feel them walking around in my room. Eventually, when I think I am going to lose my mind and look horrid on my wedding day, sleep finally rescues me from myself. However I instantly realize that it is trap, because all the dreadful images have come alive in my dream and they all have faces. As it turns out sleep is the gateway to these villainous apparitions.

First, I see the Healer, then his assistant. I see Robin, and she is the only ray of sunlight in my dream world. I see my grandmother and she looks really angry. She is so angry that she doesn't speak, she just shakes her head and folds her arms. My mother appears next but she is not really my mother. She looks like Claire's mother. Her hair is a mess and her clothes are unkempt. I know my mother would not be found dead looking such a mess. She speaks and tells me the most colourful expletives I have ever heard in my whole life. I am so afraid of her. I close my eyes and cover my ears.

Just before I wake up, I hear her say, "You a go sorry!"

I wake up to sunlight streaming into my room and a knock

on the door. My aunts have come to help me get ready. Claire and Bridget are here as well. I feel so scared that I don't want to remember my dream. Could my mother's spirit be angry about the chrysanthemums? Does she feel betrayed because I sold them? I don't want to share the dream with anyone, not today, not ever. I am trying to rationalize my dream but in order to do that I have to think, so it cannot be now. It has to be when I am alone. But I remember that today is my wedding day, my big day.

"Why do you look like that?" Claire is speaking.

"I couldn't sleep last night."

If things had been different I probably would have invited both her and Bridget to sleep in my room so we could laugh and talk all night. But that was a different time, when we were all in a different place.

"It's from all the excitement," Aunt Sabine declares.

"You'll sleep later, but right now you have to shower so we can help you get dressed," Aunt Sebouney exclaims.

I watch everyone moving around the room, removing this, packing that. A whole lot of nervous energy at work. Everyone is distracted except Bridget. She looks like she wants to say something but there's too much going on at the moment.

By the time I am ready, it is already an hour after the original start time for the wedding. Rayva must be livid. Rayva hates to be kept waiting.

"Don't worry, every bride is allowed to be late on their wedding day!" Claire says after seeing how agitated I am becoming.

"Well, I'm not every bride, am I?"

I see the crushed look on her face. She is so hurt that she can't even apply her mask of nonchalance. I say these horrible words to my friend, my best friend, in a tone that I do not even recognize in myself. When did I become this mean girl? I think I have turned into Shalk. Instantly, I regret saying them but the deed has been done. I see Claire shrink into herself, like a turtle. I tell myself that later I'll get an opportunity to apologize but even as I think it, I know that later will never come. I'll just will myself to forget what I've said so that I won't feel bad anymore. I have been doing a lot of that lately, willing myself to forget things that hurt me or in some way bother my conscience, or that simply don't fit into the narrative of who I should be. I often feel great shame in my speech, and sometimes my conduct, but I feel powerless to change so the best I can do is forget. I am actually getting pretty good at forgetting all the pain and hurt. But all that effort to forget leaves me feeling exhausted and numb; numb to my pain and the pain of others.

I so wish that Robin were here. She would know precisely what to say and what to do. Robin would know how to fix me. She would tell me what to do to fix myself. And to think that I used to resent her for always telling people what to do. This is so not the wedding I dreamed of. My mother is not here, neither is Gran, nor Robin. I feel like crying, just a good old fashion cow bawling. But I will myself to be strong. This is my new life, now, and life must go on. I cannot help but wonder how much of a difference it would have made if I did cry. Looking back, so much has happened that I should have been crying over but I stubbornly refuse. What good would that do? Also, as always, I am afraid that if I start crying, I would never stop. I think that is fundamentally *the* reason, the only reason that I keep my tears at bay with every fibre of my being.

The show must go on. I step out of my room, which is covered in pink—pink curtains, pink paint and pink bed linen— with my aunts and Bridget and Claire behind me on what should have been the most amazing day of my life. The sun embraces me and the warm breeze soothes me. I take a deep breath and move towards my destiny with my friends behind me. I already know that a part of my life has come to an end. I feel like I am at a tipping point, at the precise moment when momentum is finally going to swing in my favour. So if that's the case, why don't I feel happy? Where is my joy? Why don't I feel fulfilled?

I think and almost feel bitter that here I am, stressed and stretched beyond measure, and no charcoal in sight. I've quit punishing myself by withholding it a while back so I usually have a small piece in my purse but I'd consumed that last bit before bed.

PART 2

CHAPTER TWELVE

PRESENT DAY

I hear voices and beeping sounds around me. I try to open my eyes but they feel like they've been glued shut. One voice says, as if in response to a question that I hadn't heard, "No, doctor—no change, not yet."

Another more authoritative voice interrogates, "Was there any ID found on her that might help to locate friends and family members?"

"No, nothing! The detective said there was only her cell phone but that was so badly damaged it might be irreparable. She's wearing those very expensive earrings so that might be a clue."

"Okay! Hopefully someone will come forward soon. After all, it's been two weeks already."

I try to fight it, the sleep I mean, so I can wake up and say something. But what? The sleep slowly drags me under and I feel like I am drowning again.

The next time I try, I struggle against sleep for a while but this time I win. I open my eyes slowly. I feel like I have been hit by a bus and dragged for miles. I have such a horrible headache. In fact my whole body aches. I try to move but my hands are stuck and my legs are as heavy as lead. What is happening to me? Where am I? I can't feel my legs. I can't breathe either.

"Well, hello there, sunshine!"

A middle-aged white lady says this to me with a brilliant smile, like I am the prodigal child whom she is happy to embrace again. She has freckles on the bridge of her nose and kindness sparkling in her eyes. She is wearing dark green scrubs that reflect her hazel eyes.

"I'll go get the doctor."

Doctor? I think of saying it but the words are stuck in my throat. I am in a hospital, but why? *What's that sound!* I look around and see I am hooked up to so many machines, flashing red, green and blue lights. They hurt my eyes. Not to mention the bright light in the ceiling. Panic rises in me like lightning coming out of the sea when I feel that there's a tube protruding from my mouth, and I feel it in my throat. That's why I cannot speak. A new fear rises in me: *I'm going to stifle.*

"Hello, so nice to see you awake—"

A brown man steps confidently into the room. He is wearing blue scrubs and a stethoscope. He has light brown, tired eyes.

He must have seen the look of sheer terror in my eyes as I move my head from side to side. The doctor, as I assume he is, rushes to my bedside and says in a calm but firm tone, "I'll get rid of this tube for you. Robin, a little help here, please."

The middle-aged lady moves into action like she's been activated. They both remove the tube from my throat. I choke as they remove it and fight for air. I feel like I'm drowning. The machines scream angrily while I struggle for air.

"It's okay! Just breathe." Robin demonstrates for me how I should take a breath.

"Two seconds in and four seconds out." She does this for a few minutes, using her hand as a guide, while I mimic her, which surprisingly stabilizes my breathing but does little to calm my fear. I try to speak but something like a croak comes out.

"It's okay, don't try to speak yet. Take your time. Hi, I am Dr. Wheeler." He has a very sympathetic tone.

"Do you know where you are?" I shake my head, afraid to speak as I cannot trust my voice to cooperate.

"What is your name?" *Name. I don't know what my name is.*

Dr. Wheeler must see the look of trepidation on my face. He exchanges a glance with Robin, who has lost her smile and looks really worried. He takes out an instrument and looks into my eyes, tells me to follow his hands. Tells me to squeeze his hand. He hits my knees and the bottom of my feet as well.

He questions, "Can you feel this at all?" while touching my legs.

Again, I shake my head in the negative. Again, he and Robin make eye contact.

The doctor pulls up a dark blue chair that makes a scraping sound on the floor, which hurts my head and my teeth even more. *What is going on?* He smells of aftershave and sweat.

"Someone brought you in two weeks ago. Apparently, you had washed up on the shores of Lake Eerie, Pennsylvania, but they didn't have the resources to treat you so they flew you here to New York, New York." He takes a breath and swallows loudly.

"Since then you've been in and out of consciousness, plus you didn't have any ID on you so we've been calling you Jane Doe. You had a phone in your pocket but it has sustained severe water damage. We've been working with the police to try to locate your last destination to potentially find your family."

The police! New York, New York. How the hell did I get here? But where did I come from?

"Sweetie, do you have any idea where you came from and how you got in the lake?" Robin interrupts.

"No," I wheeze. "I have no idea where I come from or how I ended up on the shore." I say this slowly, unsure of the cadence of each word.

They both smile as if I had revealed the secrets of the universe. "At least you got your voice back," they both say at the same time. Which feels oddly familiar but my head is so empty I cannot seem to make any connections. Why won't my brain work?

"Your accent sounds like you might be from the Caribbean. Can you remember being in the Caribbean?" Dr. Wheeler asks, looking quite hopeful. But the only thing that comes to me is what seems like a river, with water gushing through the rocks, draped in greenery. But I don't reveal that because I don't even know how I know it's a river. How would I explain that? Dr. Wheeler sighs loudly and looks at me for a minute. Then he says, "Robin, I am going to refer her to Neurology for a consult. Please page Dr. Sonni."

"Yes, will do, Dr. Wheeler."

Robin leaves and for some inexplicable reason, I miss her already. She reminds me of someone, but who?

Dr. Wheeler turns to me: "We are going to try to get to the bottom of this. You might have amnesia but there's no way to tell since we don't know your history. A neurologist will be able to shed some light on your situation. Also, I am quite concerned that you've not regained feeling in your legs. Being in the frigid water will do that to you, but we'll work on it. I was afraid that might happen. Hopefully there's no permanent damage."

He gets up from the blue chair, ready to leave, but as an afterthought he says, "Don't worry. We'll take care of you; just try to get some rest. Rest sometimes help the brain relax enough to release information." With that attempt at reassurance, he leaves the room. But I don't feel reassured. Not at all. I don't even know what amnesia is. How did I get it? Is it contagious? I feel really confused. I sigh and close my eyes. I will myself to remember who I am and where am from. I must come from somewhere.

No one just falls out the sky, or in my case tumbles out a lake.

But nothing. There is a hollowness inside my mind, like a vacuum, a void; there's nothing there, just space. Shouldn't someone be looking for me? But who might that be? And how could they allow me to fall into a lake? So many pointless questions, because I have no answers and no one else here has any either. My brain has gone on a faraway journey and has left my body to fend for itself.

Suddenly, I feel very exhausted. All this effort to remember has depleted my already frail resolve. I close my eyes and try to rest. I don't know for how long. The next time I open my eyes an old white man with a clean-shaven head and a grey beard is standing there with a tall lady. The tall lady has dark hair and green eyes. She is stunning and seems out of place amidst the machines and all the accoutrements.

"Where are Dr. Wheeler and Robin?" I ask, panicking.

"Shift change. They left. I am Dr. Sonni and this is nurse Hibbert. We have made arrangements for you to do a series of bloodwork and a CT scan. We might have to do an MRI as well but that's usually a last resort. Then hopefully the results will yield some answers, because I understand that you have no recollection of what might have landed you here in the first place." Again, sympathetic stares from both of them.

"Okay, sir," I mumble. What else is there to say?

As if on cue, two men dressed in a darker shade of blue come in and wheel me out into the hallway, where the light is blinding, there is too much talking, a lot of movement, and way too much going on, which only serves to confuse me more. I feel like I want to just rush back into my room. I will myself to go back to sleep since sleep is the only thing between me and insanity right now. The procedure and the rest of that evening are nebulous.

The next day, when I wake up, both Robin and Dr. Wheeler are standing over my bed.

"Hi, sleepyhead," Robin says in an exuberant tone, with her

now-familiar smile.

Dr. Wheeler holds a folder in his hands that I assume is my docket, outlining all my symptoms, meds and potential treatment. "What do you want first, the good news or the bad news?"

"Good news, I guess."

"Good call. The good news is that your tests don't reveal any permanent damage to the brain or legs. Also, there is no obvious evidence of trauma to the brain. Which would typically arise from the water and frigid temperatures." He shows me an image on his device but these images make no sense to me so I just nod and try to look attentive.

"So does this mean I won't remember anything at all, ever?"

"No, it doesn't. Because obviously you still remember words and how to put them in the correct order to make a coherent sentence. Some people who suffer from amnesia forget everything. Therefore, I am somewhat confident that there are memories there, but for some reason they just happen to be suppressed at the moment and with time and patience they will come floating back. Maybe all at once, or little by little. The body knows how to heal itself."

"What now?"

"Well," he says, and pulls the blue chair close to my bed, taking a seat and clearing his throat as he does so. This time he smells like aftershave but no sweat. "Dr. Sonni has recommended extensive physical therapy for your mobility, and counselling to help you remember. You've been lying in bed for a while, which might have contributed to your lack-of-mobility issues, so starting today we're going to get you moving, young lady. Not too much at once but little by little. Immediately after breakfast we'll introduce you to Shane, who will be your physiotherapist. He's from Jamaica. You'll love him. He's hilarious and extremely good at what he does. We've seen him work miracles here, so to speak."

Wheeler is so optimistic and confident that he is smiling with not only his lips but his eyes as well.

Robin pipes up, "That's the other thing: we discovered that your accent is Jamaican."

"Yes," continues Dr. Wheeler, "Shane will work with you, and Sandy as well."

"Who is Sandy?" I ask.

"Sandy is a nurse and also a Jamaican. We figured that just maybe through your interactions with them it might potentially jog your memory. It has happened in the past, quite rarely, but we're hoping it will happen again if luck is on our side. Plus, they are very good at what they do. Really good people as well who won't take advantage of you but will care for you with all they've got."

I am Jamaican. At least that's a start. But what does that mean to be a Jamaican? There seems to be a lot of pressure and expectations of being Jamaican.

Wheeler shifts gears and he becomes quite serious. "The bad news is there was something else in your bloodwork, but we'll leave that for our resident psychologist to discuss with you."

Robin says excitedly, "Her name is Imka and she is South African." With the little laugh that I have come to associate with her, she adds, "We'll let her tell you her last name since we can never get it right."

At that they both laugh and I laugh along with them. I don't even know why, but for some reason it seems like the natural thing to do. But that is short-lived.

"What do you mean, something else? Is it bad?"

"I am not sure, but she'll be better able to explain things to you. She'll be working with Dr. Sonni to take care of you. We've put together a great team to restore you to optimal health."

"Also, now that you are awake, Sergeant Dennis would like to have a word with you," Dr. Wheeler continues. "He wants to get to the bottom of your situation as soon as possible. He's going to be here in the noon hour, right after you have lunch. He might even have some good news for you."

"But who is he?"

Robin jumps in. "He is the detective working on your case, to help locate your family members and find out how you ended up in the lake. Since you can't remember, he is investigating to help figure out what might have happened."

"Oh, okay!"

With that said, there's nothing more to say and after a few awkward moments, they both pat my shoulders and leave, saying I'll be fine. I wish I could feel as optimistic as they seem. How can I be fine ever again? I don't even know what my name is, but for sure I know it is not Jane. At least now I have something to fill the void in my head; *something else* echoes over and over in my head. I wonder what that could be. What else could have been discovered? The morning goes by really quickly and I meet a whole slew of professionals that I will be working with—all those that Dr. Wheeler mentioned and then some.

It is hard to keep track of who is doing what. I just go with the flow. I meet everyone, that is, except Dr. Imka, whom I really want to meet. Apart from her unusual name there is that whole business of the *something else* to be addressed. I also start physiotherapy as I have to learn to walk all over again, just to teach my legs to move as I still can't feel anything in them. They say it might be paralysis but it's still too early to tell. Being in the water for such a prolonged period has strained and weakened the muscles in my legs, but Shane is hopeful that I will make a full recovery. Sandy was the one who brought me to physio and we chatted for a while.

I like working with Shane. He's short and muscular with wavy hair (waves he's happy to report that he'd created). He's quite jovial, with a big laugh. The first time he laughed, it startled me and that made him laugh even more. He said, "A so you easy fe frighten man. A wha kind a Jamaican you be?"

I said, "I don't even know right now." At that we all have a good laugh. They both surmise that based on how I speak, I am definitely not a Kingstonian because apparently there is a specific way to how they speak and conduct themselves. Sandy could be my age or maybe a little older. She too is quite jovial and matter-of-fact in her approach to things. The way she explains it, the fact that I am still alive is a miracle. Shane thinks that I must come from a coastal parish to be able to swim that well; although we don't even know where my journey began.

He says, "That's both frightening and cool at the same time. You sure you not an undercover mermaid?" We all laughed out loud. I'm not sure what cool means but I like being on the receiving end of it.

Sandy says, "All jokes aside, though, it is a miracle that you're still alive. One day, when you're stronger, I am going to show you on the computer where they found you." Sandy is definitely the type of person who would prefer to break your heart with the truth than mislead you with a lie. She is taller than Shane and they seem to have an ongoing feud about that. Sandy has short dreadlocks, a beautiful dark complexion and a space in her top front teeth. All in all, I am happy that they are on my team. I sense that I am in good hands all around.

After lunch, I am about to doze off when I hear a very harsh knock on the door, and without waiting a very tall, skinny man comes into my room. He extends his hand right hand and says, "Hi, my name is Sergeant Dennis." He puts on what I think he believes is a smile but his overgrown mustache gets in the way. The smile seems crooked. Apparently, unlike Sandy, Shane, Robin and even Dr. Wheeler smiling is not something he is accustomed to doing.

He gets down to business right away. He doesn't even pull up the blue chair.

"We've been investigating your case ever since you washed up lakeside. We intend to pursue this thing to the end to discover whether there was any foul play involved. Now what can you tell me about what happened? Were you pushed into the lake or did you fall in? Were you alone at the time?"

He says all of that using the same breath, and his voice is big and gruff. You can tell that he is a man who is accustomed to having his own way.

"I am sorry, but I don't remember anything." My voice comes out quiet in light of his thunderous sound.

He continues, "Okay, so now that you are awake and more or less alert, we're going to post your picture all over; from here straight to Canada to see if someone is missing their daughter, or wife or sister. A photographer will come later to take your picture."

I catch my breath as soon as he says Canada, although I don't know why.

"What? Did you remember something?"

"I don't know, sir."

The Sergeant's bedside manner is so abrasive that I wish he would just go away. I wish Robin would come back with her easy smile and infectious laugh. He stares at me for what seems like an eternity then simply says, "Okay, don't worry. We're looking into this for you." He attempts to leave but then turns suddenly as if he almost forgot. "We're still trying to resurrect your phone but the water and the cold temperatures sure did a number on it. I think it's in worse shape than you are."

With that he leaves as abruptly as he came.

Now with his severely intense energy out the room, I can process what happened when he mentioned Canada. But first I must nap. All the activities of today have worn me thin. Later today I am supposed to meet Dr. Imka. I am so anxious to meet her, to figure out what else is going on. That might be the key to unlocking my memories.

As it turns out Dr. Imka can't make it today. She was called away on an emergency. Apparently, one of her patients at another location was experiencing a crisis. I couldn't help but wonder why he or she couldn't have a crisis tomorrow or another day.

I immediately feel horrible for thinking that. But she should be here after breakfast tomorrow so that's not too bad.

I have such a huge expectation of Dr. Imka so that she has become a monster in my mind. Right after breakfast, she comes into my room with a radiant smile. Actually, she doesn't exactly come into the room; she leaves half her body outside in the hallway and just admits her top half.

"Good morning, Jane. How are you? I am Dr. Imka Mawelah." After she says this, she permits herself to enter the room fully.

"So sorry I couldn't come by yesterday, but I really had to attend to one of my patients. She's just thirteen years old and she wouldn't allow anyone else to approach her."

I feel horrible about what I thought yesterday, hearing the age of her patient.

As she explains being called away, I take the time to analyze her. She is beautiful, not in a way that strikes you immediately, but being in her presence you feel she emanates warmth. She is about my height, five foot five, of light brown complexion with just one dimple on her right cheek and shoulder-length wavy hair. She has what sounds like a British accent but that must be how South Africans speak. I don't think that I have ever met a South African before. Once again I wouldn't be able to explain the British reference. She has a big butt but quite shapely. However, her most striking feature decidedly is her eyes, not the colour or anything like that but the way they stay focused on you and make you feel like you are the most important person in the world. I love her already. I literally feel energy enter my body when she walks in the room.

"Nice to finally meet you, Dr. Ma…le…wah."

She laughs and clasps her hands, happy with my attempt to pronounce her name correctly.

"Yes, that's exactly right. Very few people get it right the first time around. Even now Robin calls me 'Maweah.' But please call me Imka."

"Imka is a very beautiful name. If you don't mind what does it mean?"

"Oh, not at all. In my language it means water."

"What is your language? I thought it was English."

"Yes, we have a few official languages and English is just one of them. But my mother tongue, the language I grew up hearing around me, is Afrikaans."

For lack of a better word, I repeat what Shane said earlier, "That's cool." She smiles again.

She asks if I am comfortable and I tell her yes.

"Well let's begin then, shall we?"

"Yes, let's begin."

Dr. Imka pulls the blue chair closer, without scrapping the floor—an action that I have gotten accustomed to by now, which foreshadows a serious discussion.

"How are you feeling? From your chart, I understand that you've been having headaches, so do you have one now?"

"No, my head feels weird but there's no pain."

"Okay, good to know." She says this while scribbling on her notepad.

Without looking away from her notepad she states, "I understand that my colleagues think that you have amnesia. But the good thing is there is no obvious damage to the brain so I am somewhat confident that your memory will return. The body has a way of healing itself."

"So why do you think I developed amnesia?"

"Well, there are many things that could trigger amnesia in a person. One being a traumatic brain injury. However, we have seen no sign of that."

"What's that? A traumatic brain injury?"

"It is generally caused by a blow to the brain, a blow that is so aggressive that it damages parts of the brain, and depending on the part that is damaged the symptoms will reflect that. Also, there is a whole technical explanation with a lot of medical jargon used to explain amnesia but I won't bore you with the details."

"Please give me the Coles Notes version."

She laughs at that comment.

"What's funny?"

"It's you saying Coles Notes. I have not heard that in a long time; not since I left Medical school."

"Okay." I smile at that. Imagine the irony. I am causing her to remember things; meanwhile, I can't remember a thing about my personal history. I don't even remember how I know about Coles Notes.

"So, the Coles Notes version is this: sometimes when we encounter something that is quite painful or emotionally draining, quite traumatic, the brain jumps into overdrive and tries to protect us from ourselves by blocking out painful memories."

She explains all this without sounding condescending.

"So apart from the cold water, you think something horrible happened to me so that my brain was forced to shut down the part that houses all my memories?"

"Precisely! And by the same token, I am of the view that when the brain feels that the body is safe it will then start to release the memories. So your memories might come back all together, or in chunks; in that, little things might trigger a memory and little by little you might start remembering everything. However, at this point I cannot make any guarantees and apart from counselling I cannot offer any other treatment options."

"Okay, Imka, that kinda makes sense. So what is the thing you wanted to discuss with me?"

"Oh yes, I got a chance to look at your bloodwork," at this she looks in my eyes and holds my gaze, "and there was something in it that I find quite interesting, an anamoly if you will."

"So what is it? I've been dying to hear what it is."

"There is no easy way to say this, but there was gasoline in your bloodstream, Jane." That stupid name again. I cannot wait to remember my own name.

"We are very concerned because at this point we don't know if someone was trying to kill you by forcing you to drink it, or if you were being fed it a little at a time in your food, or—" At this point she takes a breath and looks at me, deep into my eyes as if she might find the answers floating there.

"Or what?" I interrupt.

"Or, you might have been ingesting it yourself—"

"What? Why? How?'

"It could be as a result of a condition called pica."

"What? No! At least I don't think I would drink gasoline. I don't remember a lot of things but I know for sure that gasoline is definitely bad for you. So why would I drink that?"

"Well, pica is a psychological condition which sometimes begins in childhood, where some people might have a craving for dirt or paint chips, or some people have even eaten their own hair."

She says hair like *hay*.

"These cravings could indicate the presence of anemia."

She hastens to add, "But in your specific situation, that is not the case. From the bloodwork, you seem to have had an excellent diet. There is no indication of a vitamin deficiency. Also, the craving could just be a way to relieve stress. Everyone has a different way of dealing with stress and the body usually tells us what it needs, which indicates what is happening to us at the moment. Plus, craving these… peculiar things… doesn't make sense to other people because these substances in and of themselves have no nutritional value, but it makes perfect sense for the person suffering from this condition. Of such, it is a disorder and it can be treated."

"Okay, wow!"

"I know it's a lot to digest at the moment but does any of this ring a bell, Jane?"

"No, I don't have a clue what you're talking about. Is that why I can't remember?"

"Not necessarily, but like I said, sometimes when the body goes through great trauma, as a defensive measure the brain forgets, it shuts down to shut out the pain."

"So, am I going to be in… in this… this state forever? Also, I don't even know how or when or where I could have had access to gasoline!" On that last statement, I catch myself shouting.

"Not necessarily. There have been documented cases where when the brain feels safe it will start to remember. I feel confident because there doesn't seem to be any scarring on the brain—" she looks back at the image among the sheets of paper in her hands, "—that would indicate any kind of permanent damage, so I strongly feel that in time you will remember. But it is a little-by-little and one-day-at-a-time process. It is not a process that can be rushed."

But it seems like the more I deny the idea of the gasoline and fight against it, the more it unleashes a reaction in me. I feel so very offended, so violated, so exposed, and so angry as a result of the fact that she has unearthed this, that I could cry. There is something else as well, a feeling that I cannot quite put my finger on. I really want her to leave now. I am so agitated I cannot stop the tears.

"I am so sorry Jane. I didn't mean to upset you. I am just trying to help, to get to the bottom of this. This might be the trigger—"

"What's a trigger?"

"In this particular case, a trigger can be anything. It can be a word, a smile, a touch, a particular food, an image, an action, it could simply be how someone speaks, their tone or cadence that unlocks your memory. Because in this case, if consuming gasoline is something that you've been doing for a while, then there will not only be a physical response but a neurological response as well. This is what doctors call a compulsion, something that the individual knows is harmful but can't help themselves."

"Are you trying to say that I am crazy? If that is the case, please leave!"

She looks at me for a while and then says almost a whisper, "No, Jane. There is no judgment here."

My words are laced with venom, but hers with sympathy. I am slowly getting sick and tired of all this goddam sympathy.

"Plus, that is a word that I don't even use in jest. I am so very sorry that I have offended you as that was never my intent. I am simply trying to explain the situation that has manifested itself which is cause for grave concern at this point. This practice could potentially lead to permanent neurological damage and even death."

I turn my face to the wall as an indication that the meeting has ended. I weep. I am so angry, but why? At my own behaviour? I need time by myself to process my reaction. I don't remember myself very well but somehow I think this is quite out of character for me. I wasn't even this way with Sergeant Dennis, when he was the abrasive one. He sounds like the wind when it's angry and loud. Imka is definitely the quiet and gentle one; even her voice is soothing. It sounds like the cooing of a ground dove. How could I be so rude to a complete stranger who is only trying to help me? Could she be right? Could I have been ingesting gasoline? But why? I weep more, because now I have a headache and I have figured out the feeling that had eluded me earlier; I now know what it is. It is disappointment. I am so embarrassed at my very uncouth behaviour that it has led to an intense feeling of regret. I am so disappointed in myself. Something is going on here and I wish more than anything else that I could remember. Remember what it is that has triggered this reaction in me.

CHAPTER THIRTEEN

Life moves in quantum leaps. Pretty soon, they move me from the ICU and place me in a room upstairs, which is great because there is less beeping and it overlooks a river. I still have my team. My legs are starting to obey me so I can walk, now. Thankfully it was not a serious paralysis. I still see Shane three days a week for therapy and I have Imka twice a week. I have since apologized for my rude behaviour and she has been most gracious. But I still can't remember much of anything; my brain is still, as they say, in a fog.

Sandy, my ICU nurse, comes upstairs to visit at least twice per week. I am always grateful for her visits, as somehow she has a very comforting presence. Plus, she's been filling me in on my Jamaican heritage. So far, I know that there were seven national heroes, and the only female among them was Nanny of the Maroons. Also, there are fourteen parishes: St. Thomas; Kingston; St. Andrew; St. Catherine; Clarendon; St. Ann; Manchester; St. Elizabeth; Westmoreland; St. James; Hanover;

Trelawny; Portland; and St. Ann. Sandy is from Oracabessa in Portland but she's been in America for the past seven years, while Shane is from Spanish Town, St. Catherine. Also, there are three counties: Cornwall, Middlesex and Surrey. We have a prime minister, not a president, and a governor general.

Sandy has also been sneaking in Jamaican food and fruits for me, and so far I've had: tamarind, guinep, pineapple and Otaheite apples. Apparently, there is a thriving Jamaican community in New York so you can get almost everything here, like *back home* as she puts it. She keeps promising to bring me watermelon but that hasn't materialized yet and for some reason I am so excited at the thought of having watermelon. I am always so disappointed when she shows up without it. Last week she brought me ackee and salt fish with fried breadfruit. At first I refused to eat it because I thought it was the disgusting eggs that they sometimes serve for breakfast but she convinced me to try it and I am so glad she did. Yummy! Sandy said the next time she bakes she's going to bring me Rum cake or Black cake. I cannot wait.

I have come to look forward to our talks; she has taught me a lot about life and living. She has gone through a lot in her life and she is not ashamed to share it.

I asked her why and she said, "Our experiences are for the greater good, to help someone else. Not just randomly but when the occasion calls for it. For instance, I wouldn't just go in the subway and start broadcasting my business; the police would come to get me and place me in a facility. But like how we're here and engaging with each other, that's how I share. So we should share them. Yes, man."

That last part always makes me laugh because of her facial expression and her hand movements. That's the other thing I like about Sandy, she is always so animated. Also, she says that there are lots of Jamaicans in New York, they sometimes meet for a lime and they do a potluck. I had to question her about a lime and potlucks because I don't believe I have ever heard those words before. She laughed and said, "Don't worry, me never know those words either, until I came to America." We both laughed. "One day, when you are back to yourself."

Back to myself. I am starting to think that will never happen. There must not have been anything much to me, so there's nothing to go back to. I sometimes wonder if I were as shallow as some of these girls I see on TV shows or movies. Girls who use their looks to manipulate and create division and disturbance.

"I will bring you. I know you will love it. Usually, there are individuals from right across the island representing the fourteen parishes. There is always lots of food, fun and fellowship. At those meetings we get caught up on things happening in Jamaica."

"So what type of things?"

"Politics, special events. But right now it's bad, very bad. Every time we hear news from Jamaica, it's the shooting and the killing; especially in Kingston."

"*In Kingston.* Kingston is the capital city, right?"

"Yes, Kingston and St. Andrew. They joined the two parishes a while back. Things are not like when we were growing up."

Something about Kingston sounds, seems, quite familiar.

She continues, "When we were growing up people used to look out for their neighbours. But it doesn't seem like that is the case anymore. Sometimes my heart breaks when I hear these things—"

"What about where you're from?"

"Portland? No girl, thank God the violence hasn't touched there yet. Because God know me woulda bawl. Portland is still peaceful, quiet and calm. It's like Portland is in a cocoon insulated from the ugliness of the world around her."

"It must be the trees."

"How did you know about the trees?"

She says with a look of excitement on her face.

"You told me that Portland has lots of trees, lots of big old trees, as you put it."

"Oh, okay."

She seems so disappointed. It's in moments like these that I really wish I could remember for the sake of my friend. Sandy has been just that, a friend, and I am so blessed to have her in my corner.

There is a musical knock on my door and I know right away that it is Sandy.

"Come in if you pretty." That's something she taught me to say and I die laughing every time because her response is always the same.

"Pretty or not here I come, take me as a yam and not a potato."

I don't even know how, when or why this became so funny but it is hilarious. She enters the room and right away she is a ball of energy.

"Girl, you will not guess what happen to me today!"

"What?"

"You almost hear say me dead!"

"What? What happened?"

"I was on the subway right, girl a good ting say me was early for work."

"You're always early."

"Yes, girl. I grew up with my grandmother and she was never late for anything. So I just adopt the habit."

That's the other thing I enjoy about her. Her ability to code switch. She could be talking in the Jamaican dialect and then suddenly without any warning, mid-sentence just switch to the Queen's English; in those moments even her accent changes. I swear sometimes she sounds like Imka. I said it to her once, how much she sometimes sounds like Imka when she says certain words. For example, I notice that Robin says, "*Water*" with an emphasis on the *er* but both Imka and Sandy say *Wata* emphasizing the vowel sound *a* while forgetting to mention the *r*. Sandy said, without missing a beat, "That's because we shared the same oppressors."

At the confused look on my face, she said, "Never mind, I'll explain it to you one day. Hopefully, you will start to remember soon."

The other thing I learned from her is that (I am always learning things from her and through her) apparently at this point in my recovery, I should have been discharged by now but because of my loss of memory and having had no family come forward, the hospital is trying to keep me for as long as they can. But then she adds, "Don't worry, though, I wouldn't allow you to sleep on the street."

Every time I remember her saying this, it brings tears to my eyes. She, along with the staff here, have been so kind, giving me everything and requesting nothing except that I *get well soon.*

"Girl, usually I get a seat by myself but today I sat next to some guy who had a gun. Can you imagine that, a gun on the subway? On an almost empty train, I, Sandy McLeod of sound mind and body, chose to sit next to a man with a gun to rhatid!"

"No, oh my God! Are you okay?"

"Yes, I am fine. Apparently he was on the police radar so there were undercover cops on the train. Lord Jesus, can you imagine how me madda would a bawl if anything happen to me?"

At that last comment, I couldn't help it. I burst out laughing. Her actions and facial expression kill me every time.

"Girl, it is not funny. Although I had a good laugh after because honestly if I did not laugh I would be crying right now, to rhatid." She sometimes ends her sentences with "to rhatid." Apparently, it's a Jamaican filler word and there are many more colourful ones spoken by and large by a cross-section of the Jamaican population. Sandy thinks that I might be a staunch Christian so I might not use those words. Shane shared one with me and I still blush every time I remember it. Shane sometimes says, "to raas" at the end of his sentences but that's reserved for conversations with just me and Sandy.

"So what exactly happened?"

"The police had him surrounded in the car and he didn't know and as soon as he got up for his stop, they just tackled him to the ground. I think they had cleared that particular car because usually there are a lot more people on the train."

"Wow, just wow!"

"Girl, welcome to New York City," she says with a very serious look on her face. But then she smiles and says, "Oh, I almost forgot, I brought you the melon that I have been promising you."

I am so excited. I try to hide it. "You didn't have to do that."

"Lisa." That's the other thing, Sandy changed my name from Jane to Lisa because she said, "You don't look like no Jane that I have ever seen. You are so beautiful, with all that hair, every Jane I have ever met; black or white or orange, has been grumpy and cranky which is not a good look. So from now on tell them that you prefer to be called Lisa. No more Jane a backside!" So Lisa it is.

"But why Lisa though?"

"Girl, you must really forget. Lisa Hanna, she was crowned Miss World some years ago. She pretty plus tax. We were so proud like Ms. Lou woulda say, we glad bag bus."

"Ms. Lou, who is that now? Did she win Miss World as well?"

She laughed so hard. Then she said, wiping tears from her eyes, "No girl, she was a Spoken Word artist back home from way back in the day. But she died recently." Then she adds, "Don't worry, Lisa, you soon remember. Forgive me, a so we Jamaicans stay, we love to laugh after people. We will laugh you to scorn but we are very quick to help. We don't mean anything; it is just our way."

"You know what? I believe you. Shane is exactly like this as well."

Sadly, I have no recollection of any of these people.

She continues, "You know that you are a horrible liar and a real poppyshow." We call each other poppyshow sometimes. She taught me that word, it means clown or something like that I really like the sound and the taste of it; although I don't know why. "We both know that you have been pining after this melon from the first day I told you about it. So here you go, you can thank me later because right now my shift is about to start."

She removes a glass container from a Walmart plastic bag, hands the container to me and leaves. But on her way out the door, she says, "Enjoy!" in a sing song tone.

"I definitely will. Thank you so much Poppyshow."

After she leaves, I open the container and look at the red flesh with its brown seeds, and the green skin, the juices already settling in the bottom of the container. The fragrance is tantalizing. I touch a piece with my finger and it is cool to the touch. I have been waiting for this moment for such a long time. But now I am hesitant. Why, though? I tell myself that I'll have it before bed as a bedtime snack. Sandy can pick up the container tomorrow evening, another excuse to see her. I put the container on the side table, but I can't keep my eyes off it so I tuck it in the bottom drawer. I am determined to have it at night, for some unknown reason. Is this a quirk from my past? Imka did say I should look out for things, situations or objects that trigger a response in me; so far, nothing has, except that I thoroughly enjoy every minute I spend with Sandy. It seems like we've been friends since forever and I've only known her for a few weeks.

Last week I told Robin and she said that was a good thing. She seems to believe in some type of mystic religion, which says we have all met before the birthing process but we forget because of the trauma of the delivery. Robin firmly believes that we agree to help each other on our journey prior to being born.

I said, "Robin, why are you trying to confuse my poor traumatized brain?"

She laughed and said, "Every day you sound more like Sandy."

We both laugh at that. I really love the idea of sounding like Sandy. It gives me a sense of belonging somewhere, belonging to a community, even if I cannot remember anything about that community.

"Well, some people believe it, Lisa. I'm not sure if I believe it myself. But it sure explains a lot of weird shit we see in this place."

"What type of weird shit?"

We laugh again.

"Well, you know, a woman will come in with her abusive boyfriend or spouse with obvious signs of trauma and she defends him. She'll say stuff like, *he's not always like this* or *he's a good man, he only gets this way when he's drunk.*"

"So in that case, who is helping whom, Sandy?"

She stops and thinks for a while.

"I think both of them, actually. She agreed to help him overcome his addiction and he must have agreed to help her address her low self-esteem. I really don't know and I hate to judge but that's the only way I can make sense of situations like those."

"But why do you have to make sense of their situation? Why not just accept that it is what it is?"

"Oh Lisa, you are such a beautiful soul, such an idealist."

At the sound of that word, I feel myself getting angry. I don't know why. I have to control my breathing like Imka taught me because I don't want to lose my temper with Robin. She's been too kind. She leaves the ICU on her break and lunch just to come sit with me. I am not exactly in a position to lose friends. Imka says any time it happens, I should make a note of it on my note pad. Despite my best efforts, Robin notices but she is not offended. Instead she questions, "Are you upset because I called you an idealist?"

"Yes, but I don't know why."

"That's great, that's progress, Lisa. The whys and the wherefores will come to you later."

I am so upset with myself. But at least as she says it is progress. It means I am no longer numb with an empty shell of a head.

There are a wide range of emotions there that I will tap into one day.

A knock on the door disrupts my musing. I am happy to see that it is Robin.

"Hey kiddo. How goes it?"

"I am good. Always so good to see you."

"Same here! You always look so stately in your bed. In another life you must have been a queen."

We both laugh out loud. I swear the charge nurse is going to come barging in at any moment. I so enjoy this, the camaraderie with these ladies, the ease at which we communicate. We talk for a bit but far too soon it's time for her to go.

"As much as I would love to stay with you, my queen, my mom's coming over so I have to go make supper." At the sound of *mom*, I feel a weight creep up my legs and sit on my chest. The weight crawls into my throat and a lump is activated. I am so deeply saddened. I can't even explain how sad that word makes me feel. I try to smile, "Okay, thanks for stopping by. Enjoy."

She comes over and pulls up the grey chair, "Oh Lisa, I have upset you. I am so sorry. I didn't mean to."

Before you know it, I am crying a river of tears. Oh wow! Where did this suddenly come from?

Robin holds my hand and just sits with me while I cry. After what seems like a lifetime, I manage to compose myself and tell her she doesn't have to stay.

She says, "Of course I am staying. Why do you think they invented take out?"

We both laugh again and I feel the pressure leave my chest. However, a piece of the lump remains; it is still sitting there as if waiting for the next opportunity to increase in size, like a malignant tumor. We just sit like that for a while in the silence, with the busy streets below and the activities going on just outside my door. Eventually, Robin lets go of my hands. As if on cue, we both know the moment has passed. She gathers her things quietly as though she is afraid to disrupt this sacred moment.

"I'll check on you in the morning, kiddo."

"Please do."

"You betcha."

"Robin—"

"Yes?"

"Thank you!"

"No problem, man!"

We laugh some more at her attempt at speaking Jamaican.

"You get some rest now, okay."

With that she leaves me alone with my thoughts. I feel even more confused and alone. When I woke up a few weeks ago my head felt empty like a new book. Many said I had been given a new opportunity to fill it with new memories and I was excited about that; but tonight I want nothing more than to remember. I desperately want to remember even the sad moments and keep them alongside the new memories that I am making in this new place.

I look at the time. It is now 7:45 p.m. I'd better eat my watermelon before it goes bad. There's no refrigerator in this room and I don't want to leave it in the big fridge. Sandy calls that fridge *Big Yard* because *"every Tom, Dick and Harry leave their food in that fridge"*. So I absolutely do not want to leave my melon there, not after I have been pining over it for so long. I reach for it and my hand quivers with expectation. I carefully open the lid because I don't want to spill the precious cargo. I reach for a plastic fork in the drawer, hurriedly unwrap it and attack my melon.

Why did I wait to have it? It is so delicious and tastes so familiar. I finish it in one go, seeds and everything, well most of the green skin. I allow the juicy goodness to sit on my face and run down my shirt. I feel so at peace after I am done. I place the container on my desk and I just relax and allow my mind to drift. I was so anxious about eating the melon that I think it will trigger a memory, so I lie flat on my back, breathing in through my nose and out through my mouth—a strategy that Imka taught me and I have often used when I can't fall asleep at nights. But nothing. My brain is still empty of memories. I am so disappointed that for the second time tonight, I cry.

I must have cried myself to sleep because the next thing I know it is morning and the Charge nurse is standing over me, a very pleasant Filipino lady named Philomena. She is always so gentle and motherly. I look past her out the window. I keep the blinds open so I can look down at the river. Robin says it is the Hudson River which serves as the boundary between New York State and New Jersey. I thought that was so interesting, the idea that inanimate things can have boundaries. There is bright sunshine streaming in. I have to cover my still sleep-filled eyes.

"Hi, Lisa, sorry to wake you but we got a call from Detective Dennis, wanting to meet with you at 8 a.m. So we wanted to make sure you were up and ready," she says in a heavily accented voice. Since I have been here, I have met so many people from all over the world, with many and various accents and skin tone.

I yawn and stretch. "Did he say what it's about?"

"No, he just said it's urgent."

I get busy trying to look presentable. My hair is so big, it is everywhere. I try to get it all in a bun. They cut it after I woke up but it has grown so much since then. Sandy promised to braid it for me but she hasn't had the time yet. All the while, I am dreading speaking to Detective Dennis. Time has certainly not made him any easier to deal with. He is still just as crass as the first day we met. I try to not think about his impending visit. I wish I had memories that I could reflect on instead of stressing about his visit. I am really curious about the timing of his call, why it's so early in the morning. He has never come here before one in the afternoon. But I guess we'll find out soon.

At exactly eight, I hear his loud knock on the door followed by, "Are you decent?"

His usual attempt at humour that always falls flat. By now, the bright sunshine has given way to rain. This place is so weird; it can be sunny one minute and raining hail the next.

"Yes, come in," I say as calmly as I can muster, all the while anxious to know the reason for his early visit. He enters the room and I know something has changed. I don't know how I know, or even why I know, but I know that something significant is about to transpire. I so wish that Sandy or Robin were here. Dennis is all business-like as always. But this time he grabs the grey chair.

"How are you, Lisa?"

"I am okay…"

Before I can finish: "That's just great! Well, we just caught a break in your case. As I told you before, we sent your picture to all the little towns and cities along the river where you were found, both on the Canadian side and the US side, and we just got a hit. Someone claiming to be your husband saw your picture and called our tip line. He says his name is—."

He pauses to look at a paper in his hand. A paper that I hadn't noticed before. "Rayva Barron. Does that ring a bell?"

He pauses for a reaction. I shake my head and he continues. "He is on his way to New York. I am going to meet him at the airport at 12 p.m., so I wanted to inform you first."

He says all this with a very serious look on his face. I can imagine him at work, giving orders and putting out fires. A man so utterly certain of his place and role in this life. He continues, "He says your name is Ne…va…eh, *Nevaeh*. I got him to spell it. Does that sound familiar?"

I shake my head again. My name is Heaven spelt backwards! Sandy will approve.

"Obviously, he… your husband… is quite anxious to see you. So he didn't want to wait. He is coming here directly from the airport. He said you guys live in a little town called Paris, in Ontario. Does any of this information sound probable?"

I just keep shaking my head. I see his eyes soften and he pats my hand closest to him. Just as I was wondering why, I feel the tears streaming down my face like the rain sliding down my hospital window. He hands me a tissue and clears his throat, obviously uncomfortable with tears and all other forms of emotion.

"I am sorry," I say while taking the tissue. "I am hearing about myself for the very first time from a virtual stranger and I don't even know if any of it is true. What if he is not who he said he is?"

"We checked with the police in Canada and his story is true. Immigration Canada has pictures of your wedding on file from when he—your husband—filed for you to migrate to Canada from Jamaica."

"So I am Jamaican? Did you find out from where in Jamaica?"

This time he puts his reading glasses on, which always make him look like a different person. He quickly scans the paper again. He says, "Yes, I believe you are from Portland parish—"

"Like Sandy…?"

"Yes. A town called Balcarres."

I cry some more; waves of joyful tears flood my face. I cry for joy at the knowledge of where I come from. Something so basic, so fundamental, that up to this point everyone around me knows about themselves; everyone except me. Dennis is patient with me. A quality up to this point I never knew existed in him. But I wish Sandy were here. She would be very happy to hear that we are from the same parish. I collect myself as best as I can, because while this is all good and well, there is a man on his way to see me. A man that I have no recollection of, let alone of having been married to.

I have so many questions: will I recognize him instantly? Will he trigger my memories? Did he push me into the river? If so, why? Do we have children together?

Imka says that some memories are imprinted on both mind and body; therefore, sometimes what the mind forgets the body will remember. Hopefully my body will update me on anything of relevance that I need to know about this gentleman, this Rayva person—my husband.

I am going to need all the strength I possess for this very special encounter.

CHAPTER FOURTEEN

The mid-afternoon sun is beaming down on my window, which gives off a shiny hue. It hurts my eyes so I am forced to close the blinds. Before I do, I take one last look at the river, so calm after the rain this morning, and so calming. Well, usually it is calming, but today my nervous system is in disarray and nothing will calm me. Maybe Imka will give me some of her calming meds. Today is not usually one of my scheduled therapy days but she was called in by the on-call doctor for this afternoon in case I have an episode. Thankfully she agreed to join us. But I am not really worried, because I have not had a panic event in a while. I used to get those a lot when I'd just woke up in this place, but everyone says that I have adjusted really well, all things considered. However they are concerned that today's meeting could either release all my locked-away memories or further complicate my healing process. I hope it's the former, as I am getting sick and tired of not knowing what the hell is going on. Because I cannot connect the dots.

"Hi, Nevaeh."

It's Imka. Again, as is her custom, she's only partially in the room, exactly how I feel right about now. I didn't even hear her knock on the door. Her face is radiant with joy and her dimple is outstanding. My mind is all over the place. I feel so far away from this place, so far away from myself. I wish I had just one solid memory to anchor me, to keep me from floating away into oblivion.

"Hey Imka, you heard?" I say, in no way reflecting her enthusiasm.

"Yes, I heard, so exciting! Good news travels fast around here. Your name is so beautiful and somehow I am not surprised."

"I guess."

She moves closer to me and takes my hand. A gesture that is usually both comforting and reassuring, but now it is not. Not today.

"You guess? I understand how overwhelming this all must be for you but this is huge. Meeting your husband might trigger one memory, which might open the floodgate for all the other repressed memories. And I'll be here with you the whole time, Nevaeh."

"To be honest, I am really scared, and I don't know how or what to feel. I wish I could feel joy that my husband is coming to rescue me but I don't. Does that make sense?"

"Of course it does. Things have been so chaotic for you lately. It will take time to adjust. So don't feel pressured to rush the moment."

Imka places an arm around my shoulders, almost in a protective stance. I feel the heat from her body and I instinctively hug her. I surprise both myself and her because I have never done that before. I have never thought of myself as a hugger, but here we are.

She whispers in my hair, "Everything is going to be alright. You'll see."

I shake my head, not trusting myself to speak.

She continues, "Sometimes you have to get through the tough times to make room for the good things that are waiting to flood your life."

I try to pull strength and courage from this very beautiful, strong woman who is my therapist but also more like my friend. I brace myself for the inevitable because I don't remember a lot of things, but I do know that once something has been set in motion there is no turning back. There is no turning away from it. You just have to face it head on and hope for the best. I move away from Imka and pull the blinds, taking one more look at the slow-moving river with the sun pelting its surface. I guess every day the river has to just face the sun head on without flinching, even in the wintertime. Now it's my turn to face the inevitable without flinching. I take a deep breath and collect myself. Someone had enough faith in me to call me Nevaeh, Heaven—a phenomenon that is both consistent and eternal, sturdy and dependable, so I have to rise to the occasion and live up to the strength inherent in my name.

Imka had decided that we should meet in her office, not in my hospital room, for which I am grateful. Imka's office is simple and small but tastefully decorated in yellow: light yellow paint on the wall, a small yellow couch and yellow fabric covers on the two chairs in the room. There are two blue chairs, which have been brought in from a different room specifically for this occasion. They seem so out of place in the sea of yellow décor, just like me. I'm happy that this meeting has been relocated to this room, because my hospital room suggests vulnerability and dependence. I don't want to be reminded of that, not today.

So I guess to fill the space, while we wait, I ask, "Is yellow your favourite colour?" I don't know why I have never asked this before, as this is certainly not my first visit.

She laughs, a quiet sweet sound, before she answers: "Not really, but yellow has been found to be quite soothing, and with the work I do here in my office it is important to set the right tone. Not to mention the fact that yellow is a really popular colour back home in South Africa. It is included in our flag, in cultural wear, regular wear and meals. We are a very colourful people, just like you Jamaicans."

"Included in meals?"

"Yes, we use a lot of curry and there is also yellow rice. One of my favourites."

"So can you get those things here in America?"

"Yes, but they don't quite taste the same."

"That's exactly what Sandy says about making or purchasing Jamaican food here. It doesn't quite taste the same."

"No, for some reason it never does. I don't know if it's the seasoning or the utensils used in the preparation, but it's just not the same."

"Utensils—what do mean?"

"Back home, and I am sure this might be true of Jamaica as well, there are specific pots and pans used in the preparation of certain dishes."

"Oh, okay. That makes sense." One more reminder of how out of touch I am with the world around me. I would never have thought that a pot or a pan could make a difference in the flavour of the food prepared in it. After that we both sit in silence, me with my thoughts, while Imka scans the paperwork on her desk.

"Do you miss South Africa, Imka?"

She looks up from her papers and smiles. "Yes, I do! I absolutely do, and I try to return at least once a year."

"Is South Africa different from here?"

"Oh yes, very different."

"In what ways?"

"Well, for one, our winters are never as harsh as they are here."

"I would never have guessed that you guys experience winter there."

"Most people don't. We have seasons like here. But our

winter arrives in June, from the twenty first to September twenty second."

"I guess because of where it falls along the equator."

"Wow! You remembered that, Nevaeh, about the equator!"

"I guess I did."

"That's amazing! But South Africa is actually miles south of the Equator."

"Oh, okay! So why did you come here, if you don't mind my asking?"

"No, not at all. I came here just to study, but then I was offered a great opportunity to work with a specialist in my field. I leaped at the chance, but sadly she died and just when I was contemplating returning to South Africa, the opportunity to work here came up and I grabbed it."

"Lucky for me you did. I am so happy that we met, Imka, believe me."

"Me too, Nevaeh, me too." We look at each other meaningfully.

"I hope to visit South Africa someday."

"I hope you do. You would love it. A lot of people who visit South Africa say that every time they go, it feels like going home."

The idea of going home suddenly makes me sad. I don't even know where home is anymore.

True to Rayva's word, exactly at 1 p.m. there is a knock at the door, and although I've been expecting it I almost jump out of my chair.

Imka says, "Come in," and gives me one of her winning, dimpled smiles. We both stand in preparation for the visitor. It is momentarily comforting but short lived as I take a look at the incredibly handsome man who comes in after Detective Dennis. The newcomer meets my gaze with eyes blazing with intensity; I have to look away. Detective Dennis, true to form, rushes through the introductions. The stranger comes close and tries to hug me, but instinctively I flinch and he takes a step back as if he's been tasered. He is about six feet tall so he towers over me.

Imka notices and rushes to my aid. "Hi, my name is Imka and I am Nevaeh's therapist. It's a pleasure to meet you, Mr. Barron."

He shakes her extended hand but it is my face he is gawking at. "A pleasure to meet you, Imka. But you can call me Rayva."

We all stand around like mannequins. Thankfully, Dennis takes charge of the situation again. "Let's sit down and see how much we can accomplish here today."

We all sit robotically. Dennis and the stranger both choose the blue chairs. I guess the yellow chairs are too feminine for them. Up until now the stranger hasn't taken his eyes off me, like he is trying to figure me out. I feel feverish and naked under his intense scrutiny. I want to leave, to run away and never look back. But somehow his gaze keeps me in place. How can this extremely attractive man be *my* husband? This does not make any sense.

"I've updated Mr. Barron about the state of Lisa's, I mean Nevaeh's, health. I am going to have to get used to calling you that. I've known you for three months and you've undergone three name changes."

He chuckles at his own joke, which falls flat. The others shift in their seats uncomfortably. I wish the stranger would stop staring and I wish Sandy were here. I wish I had one memory so I could flee there and hide myself in its shadow. Dennis clears his throat and continues.

"So, Nevaeh, has seeing your husband brought back any memories?"

Everyone stares at me, anxious for a response. I think I am going to cry again, or throw up. I whisper, "No, sir."

"That's okay, Nevaeh, these things take time," Imka's soothing voice chimes in. I feel like such a disappointment.

The stranger quietly says, as if we were all alone, "I've missed you, Nevaeh. I thought that I had lost you forever."

He looks so sick with worry. I feel like such a horrible person. Why can't I remember him?

"Nevaeh, we have decided that Mr. … I mean Rayva … is going

to share with you what happened on the night you disappeared, that he can somehow jog your memory. Is that alright with you?" Detective Dennis announces, because his questions are mostly statements.

I look at Imka and she reaches for my hand and nods her approval simultaneously.

The stranger begins in his deep, masculine voice. It is not a harsh sound. I could get used to the rise and fall of its resonance. I watch his Adam's apple spasm every time he takes a breath.

"You had been acting strangely for a while."

"What do you mean, acting strangely?" I hear myself say almost accusingly. He stares at me for a few seconds, which seem more like decades. He then slowly turns to Imka and says, "May I have some water please?"

He bites his bottom lip and runs his hand through his loose curls, not waves like Shane's, but big curls despite the low cut. I can see small shrubs growing on his face as if he hasn't shaved in a few days, which is not at all unattractive.

Imka says, "Yes, of course," and leaves the room promptly. Depending on the situation, Imka has the incredible ability to be as agile as a hummingbird and as slow and steady as a garden snail—when necessary. Thankfully, she is back with four bottles of water before I get even more anxious.

He takes a sip and I watch his Adam's apple react to the excess moisture. I can't help but wonder if this man could truly be my husband. Sandy would say that he's *hot like ten pepper seed.* I catch myself and turn away from him quickly. I am sure my face is red. He sees my action and seems really hurt by it. Again, he bites his bottom lip and passes his hand over his hair. This must be a nervous habit of his. I feel horrible. He must think I am a monster. How could I forget this creature, who seems like he's just stepped off the cover of *Vogue?* But then again, how could this embodiment of male perfection be *my* husband? I look at him, across from Imka, and it seems more likely that he should be her husband, not mine.

Nonetheless, he clears his throat, sips more water, then continues: "By strangely, I mean you've been withdrawn lately." He looks at his hands and sighs as if the courage to continue could be found in his strong, manicured hands. "You moved out of our bedroom and refused to… ah… be with me, like a wife should."

"Did she give you any indication of why she would do that?" Imka questions, sounding quite clinical.

"No, she just said it was something she had to do," he says, staring at Imka, and as if finding greater support there in her eyes, he continues. "Before she moved out she started saying things."

"What type of things?" Dennis, who has been unusually quiet, almost yells.

Still holding on to Imka's gaze for support he says, "Things like, *they* were watching her and that *they* were trying to kill her."

"Do you have any idea who *they* could have been?" the detective enquires.

"No, sir. I have no clue. She stopped eating the meals that our chef made and started preparing her own food. But I honestly chalked it up to a cultural preference, being that Neva is—"

"What did you just say?" I pounce on him.

"You preferred to make your own meals because of your Jamaican culture…"

"No, after that."

"I said, Neva. That's what your friends call you and I call you that only sometimes because I honestly prefer Nevaeh."

"Why? Did you remember something, Nevaeh?" Imka pounces just like I did.

"No, it just sounds kinda familiar. But I wasn't sure if it was his tone or the word itself."

"So which is it, then?" Detective Dennis asks, sounding really patient. He seems to be the most unperturbed in the room.

"I'm not sure."

He says in a matter-of-fact tone, "Go on, Rayva."

"You stopped socializing with our friends and family; you stopped combing your hair. You refused to see our family physician. You said you were fine and everyone just wanted to see your demise."

He takes a deep breath and runs his hand over his curls again. This time he brings his hand down to touch his colourful, well-defined lips. Sandy sometimes uses a liner to outline her lips, while his lips look like they have been naturally lined. We all wait for him to collect himself. He sighs again.

"What happened on the night she fell into the river?" Imka asks quietly.

Rayva looks from her to the detective and back at me.

"You guys must think that I am a horrible husband."

"No judgment here, Rayva," Imka declares.

Dennis clarifies: "We're just trying to get to the bottom of things and help Nevaeh get her memories back. It must be really frustrating for her not to be able to remember."

The last part is said with so much compassion that like Rayva I have to bite my bottom lip to stop myself from crying.

"On the night she fell in the river, I had called 911 because she came at me with a knife. The police officers were able to restrain her and I took the knife. There was so much ruckus on our street, which is unheard of in our neck of the woods. I was embarrassed so I was yelling at her. I didn't know what else to do. She calmed down for a bit but as I was explaining to the officers what had been happening, she bolted through the front door, which had been left open. Not wanting to create any further drama, I told them that I would go after her. But I didn't realize that I still had the knife in my hand which must have spooked her because she kept saying that I was trying to kill her."

In one huge gulp his water is finished. He closes his eyes and brings his hands up to his face, but instead of running them through his hair, he covers his eyes.

"Nevaeh, I didn't mean for any of this to happen. I am so sorry." He says this with his hands still covering his eyes, partially shielding his face. I guess even strong, beautiful people need a shield sometimes.

"So how come you are just coming to find me?"

"Well, when I returned and told the police what had happened, they didn't believe me. They thought that I had pushed you. They jumped into action and created a search and rescue. The whole time they had me down at the station, holding me for questioning. My dad pulled all his strings to get me out. It was a media circus for the first few weeks. We couldn't go anywhere or do anything and at the end of that week they said that you had probably died, because the current must have dragged you into the depths of the river. I've been mourning you ever since, and I was still a suspect. It is only by virtue of the fact that they couldn't find your body that they didn't lock me up and throw away the key. They blamed me for your disappearance, but not more than I blamed myself. I prayed every night for your safe return, because somehow, despite everything, I knew you were alive. You grew up in Jamaica; after all, you had access to both rivers and beaches so I know that you're a great swimmer. Plus, I don't know anyone who is stronger than you. At times I wished for your strength."

He removes his shield to say the last sentence.

"But I couldn't convince anyone to keep looking, not even my dad. He kept saying, *she's gone, son! You need to move on with your life.* But how could I, when *you'd* promised me forever. They even held a funeral for you, but I refused to attend because I was still holding out for my forever with you, Nevaeh."

I don't know what to say. I don't know if he was really trying to kill me or not. Why would I be saying those things if I had no evidence? Dennis must have read my mind.

"Why do you think that she was saying all those things about you if she didn't have any proof?"

"I think I might be able to address that, Detective, although it might be a premature evaluation." Imka says, while flipping through her notes.

"Remember that initially we had told you that Nevaeh had gasoline in her system when we found her? Well, we linked it to a disorder known as pica. Pica is a condition that is more psychological than physical and it inspires people to ingest things that they wouldn't normally eat. It is sometimes triggered by extreme trauma or great stress. Now I'm not sure but I am willing to guess that Nevaeh had been ingesting gasoline and it triggered a temporary psychotic break which is why she was suffering from delusions in claiming that someone wanted to harm her."

"After Nevaeh's disappearance, did you search her room? The one that she had moved into, that is. Did you find anything strange in her room?" the detective asked.

"Come to think of it, we did find a can of gasoline in a corner of the room. But at the time, I thought nothing of it. My dad kinda felt that Nevaeh was planning to burn the house down—"

"I would never do anything like that," I cry out in pain, being really close to tears. I stand so quickly I drop my water bottle, which startles everyone including Dennis.

Rayva reaches for my hands and this time I let him take them. "I know, Neva, that you would never harm a fly. That's one of the many things I loved about you from the minute I met you. Your deep empathy and care for all living things. Do you remember the chrysanthemums that you had planted to honour your Mother's memory?"

"Honour my Mother's memory? No! You mean my Mother is dead?"

"Yes, for a while now. Your first week at Teacher's College."

I can't help it. The tears come flooding down like a river. Again Imka rushes to my rescue.

"Okay, I think we have covered a lot of ground today. Let's pick this up another day," she says while hugging me gently, like a mother cuddling her newborn.

Meanwhile, Rayva was saying, "I am so sorry. I didn't mean to upset her. I completely forgot that she couldn't remember anything."

"We know, Rayva." Detective Dennis says. He must have been patting Rayva's back because I hear a light patting sound like fingers on fabric.

"I only meant to remind her of how much she cared for that plant like it was a living, breathing thing. To remind her of how compassionate she is."

Rayva sounds so pained, which makes me cry some more. "Alright, you haven't eaten all day. Let's get some lunch into you, young man. Maybe we can pick this up tomorrow. Let's go eat and I'll take you to your hotel," Dennis offers, sounding so sympathetic, I am tempted to look up at him.

"No, sir, I am not hungry."

"Well, let's get you a cup of coffee then."

Imka takes control of the situation. After all we are in her office. "Please go, Rayva. Like the detective said, we can pick this up another day. Nevaeh is really emotionally exhausted from hearing all those things, things that she is still unable to grasp with her mind," Imka explains, again like a mother counselling her child. I scan the room through her hair.

He leaves reluctantly, almost petulantly, like a child being removed from the playground before he is ready to go. His eyes linger on me, while I clutch desperately onto Imka, and he says, "I'll be back, Nevaeh. I am not losing you again."

With that Dennis pulls him from the room, while I cry some more. When did I become capable of creating so much pain? I am so exhausted. Imka pulls away gently and says, "I'll take you back to your room. Do you want to walk or should I order a wheelchair?"

I don't trust my feet; I don't trust myself not to run as far away from this place as my feet will take me. So I say, "Wheelchair, please." The wheelchair which I have refused for months even when my feet didn't work properly has come to my rescue.

After what seems like years, we get to my room and there's a bouquet of light pink, yellow and white chrysanthemums on my table. The scent is intoxicating. I feel like I am going to vomit. I don't even know how I know, but instinctively I know that they are chrysanthemums. The same plant that Rayva reminded me about not even an hour before. Maybe because Rayva had just told me that horrible story about my dead mother and the chrysanthemums that I used to hold dear. Imka helps me onto the bed and moves towards the bouquet. She picks up the card nestled in the midst of the soft petals.

"They're from Rayva. The card says:

To my dear wife. My forever.

I will love you forever.

Rayva." I am just full of surprises today. I hear myself scream. "Get them out of here! I hate them!"

The nurse, a short Black lady, rushes in. She says, "Is everything alright in here, Doctor?"

She must be Nigerian because she has that beautiful, rich, singsong accent marked by clearly enunciated words.

"Yes, everything is fine."

How could she say everything is fine? I am definitely not alright. I may never ever be alright ever again. I find myself screaming and waving my hands in the air. "Get them out! I don't want them!"

The nurse must have taken the bouquet because I feel the weight of their presence leave the room. Someone else enters and Imka says, "Give her three milligrams of Ativan, Dr. Walsh." One of the new interns on this floor. I hear objects being pushed around, as more people enter the room. I feel many hands on me, holding me down. This makes me scream and fidget more. This all feels vaguely familiar and terrifying at the same time. Imka is giving instructions, although I don't know what she is saying now. Her voice is lost in the jumble of all the other voices. I try to hold on to her sweet, calm voice but there is too much going on in the room, in my body.

My body has gone rogue. She won't listen to me, and why should she, when my mind is a mess, a battleground full of brokenness and helplessness? Just as I feel like my mind was going to explode from all the activities both within and without, I feel a sting on my shoulder, the hands release me one by one and then sweet nothingness takes me away. Not a moment too soon—before I hurt someone else.

I must have slept from late afternoon the previous day into this morning. I wake up feeling groggy, and my movements are slow. It takes me a while to rouse myself. Eventually, I rise with a mild headache. I feel bruised, with a fragment of a dream that eludes my grasp. It is still and dark outside. A sliver of fog hanging over the river, much more tangible than my dream.

I decide to take a shower but to do so I must exit my room. This thought fills me with dread as memories of the previous day flood my mind. Imagine wanting desperately to have some type of memory—any memory—and yet these are the ugly ones that I have managed to accumulate. I guess beggars can't be choosers. I sit on the grey chair, building the courage to go outside the door. I panic at the thought of the chrysanthemums still being at the nurses' station. They do that sometimes, keep flowers there for ungrateful patients such as myself. That thought pins me to the chair. I wish I knew why. But by then nature is screaming so loudly I have to flee my room and without thinking, I grab my toiletry bag—another gift from Sandy—and make a run for the door. I rush into the washroom, without looking to the right or to the left. I vaguely hear someone call my name before I slam the door shut behind me.

There's a shower chair there. I sit on it briefly to catch my breath before slowly undressing. I discover that I've gotten my period which hasn't happened since I've been here. Thanks to good old Sandy, I am prepared. I guess all the trauma of the previous day must have triggered it. I am happy that I am not pregnant. That would be horrible, to bring an innocent child into this mess. I wonder if Rayva and I had talked about having children. How could I have children when I was busy dosing myself with gasoline? I didn't want to accept that I was pouring a toxic substance into my body, but after Rayva said it so convincingly I have no choice but to accept the validity of that statement. What reason would he have to lie? But why, though? Of all the things, why would I ingest gasoline? I pour body wash on my washrag, which is a little slippery from not being hung out to dry in the sun. As I do so, I am struck by a thought: what if Rayva, his dad, or that chef were feeding me gasoline, and now that I have memory loss they can blame the whole thing on me? But why? What are Rayva and his family into?

But again, why? There are quicker and easier ways of getting rid of a person, and they seem to have the means to do so expeditiously and in a more clandestine manner. None of this makes any sense, because I don't have the required memories to fill in the blanks. But at least I now know that I am a teacher; teaching like medicine is a noble profession.

Struck by an idea, I turn the tap off and get dressed in a hurry. I am pretty sure there is still more than a splash of water left on my back, which soaks through my top. I don't really care. Thankfully, I don't have to wear those horrid hospital gowns that show my hindermost parts. I am allowed to wear regular clothes, and Sandy has gone clothes-shopping for me. They aren't a lot but the quality is good and they came just as I was moved upstairs. At any given moment, dressed in my street clothes, I could just walk right through the door and leave this place. No one would know. Which I have contemplated doing on many occasions, but where would I go? Who would I go with? Sandy would never agree to that unless I were well enough to take care of myself— that plus the fact that I have joined the statistical group of an undocumented immigrant. I feel stuck: stuck in my mind and stuck in this place. I must admit that I have never wanted to leave as much as I want to leave now. Rayva's presence has disrupted my once-safe haven. I don't know if I should thank him or be angry at him.

I return to my room but not before checking if they have kept the ghastly chrysanthemums, which they haven't. Sandy is waiting there for me. I am so happy to see her that I grab her and hold her tight, afraid that she will become a part of my fractured memory. But she's here and she's real and I am grateful.

When I let her go she says, "I heard that you had a rough day yesterday mama."

I shake my head, afraid to speak.

"I came to check on you a few times yesterday during my shift but you were passed out from exhaustion and the Ativan. We all made trips, me, Robin, Shane and Dr. Imka."

I am so touched by their concern that I want to cry again. However, I will myself not to. I can't afford a repeat performance of yesterday, and of necessity I have to keep my wits about me. Things have changed drastically and I have to be brave and alert, because somehow I don't trust Rayva. I don't know for sure but I get a vibe that I find quite disconcerting. He seems genuinely concerned but I don't know him that well, so he could just be acting.

"Yes, yesterday was tough. But I am better today. I even got my period."

"That's good!"

"Really?"

"Yes, it means that your body might be getting back to some type of normalcy, which might mean that your memories might be returning soon."

"Sandy, those are too many 'mights' for my liking. Now that Rayva has made an appearance, now more than ever, I need to remember."

"Why? You don't trust him?"

I look at her and move to check if anyone is outside my door. I close it. Unfortunately, there's no lock on the door because there is no leeway for privacy in this place.

"What's going on, Nevaeh? Yes, Imka told us your beautiful name. I know you had to have a pretty name, just like your face. None of that Jane Doe foolishness."

She says that and hisses her teeth and despite myself I laugh out loud.

"Why are you checking and closing the door? Did you remember something?"

"No, but I have a weird feeling about Rayva. He said I was acting weird and they found gasoline in my room. But I don't know if he's lying. I mean he could be, right?"

"Yes, he could be. But why would he? From what Imka said, he seems genuinely happy to see you and he even brought you flowers. Sorry—I heard that they triggered you yesterday."

"But that's just it, Sandy, why? Why was I so triggered at the sight of the flowers? I have so many questions. I don't even know what to believe. I so desperately wish that I could remember."

"Well, did he say anything about a family member that you could talk with to address some of your concerns?"

"No, he might have. But I freaked out when he said that my Mother had died. That hurt so badly, Sandy."

She grabs me into a fierce hug.

"I am so sorry, Neva; I wish I could have been here for you."

I pulled away roughly at the sound of that word again. Not just any word, my own pet name.

"What did you call me?"

"Neva, it's short for—"

"I know what it is short for. But there's something about how you said it. Say it again."

"Neva."

"I don't know how, but when he said it, it sounded familiar."

"You mean when Rayva said it?"

"Yes. But when you say it, it not only sounds but it feels different."

This whole time we had been standing. She pulls the grey chair which I sit on and she sits on the edge of the bed. Somehow suggesting a reverse in our positions, a symbolic change in our relationship.

She wastes no time: "So how does it sound when I say Nevaeh?"

"It sounds like… an echo."

"What do you mean, an echo?"

"I don't know how to explain it."

"Well try," she almost yells. "This could be important."

"Well, it sounds, well not exactly a sound but it feels like you're repeating it after someone else just said it."

"Sorry, you lost me there. Repeat after who?"

"I'm not sure. But it sounds like, no feels like, someone else had just said it the same way and you pick up on the sound of it and repeat it the exact same way that that other person said it."

"Life is like an echo sometimes, Neva. In that whatever you put out there in the Universe eventually comes back to you."

I laugh out loud.

"What? What's funny?"

"Girl, you sound like Robin!"

"Really? That is not funny."

"Oh shit!"

"What? What now?"

"When I said Robin, it felt like an echo as well."

"Oh wow! This is getting weird. Maybe we should call Imka. Maybe, just maybe, she might be able to help you pull those memories to the foreground of your mind."

"Yes, I had that idea while I was in the shower. One time she had suggested hypnosis but it just felt weird to have a complete stranger poke around in my mind. I mean, what if she planted memories there? But when I was in the shower just now, I remembered and it felt like it was time for her to do something; maybe not that, but something. But that might be a last resort."

"Okay, have some breakfast and I will talk with the on-call doctor about getting Imka in here today. I am happy for you. At least you have a baseline to start from. And you never know when you're going to reach a tipping point."

"What's that, now? What's a tipping point?"

"It's a term which originates in Sociology but has expanded to include many other disciplines. Basically it is the specific moment when momentum, charged by smaller actions, creates a much more significant action and swings in your favour at the most appropriate time."

"So all these echoes that I have been feeling could be preparing me for something bigger?"

"Precisely! Neva, I know you don't remember, but life is like that sometimes. Life changes in the blink of an eye, whether or not we are prepared for it, and it can be devastating when we are unprepared. Of course we never know what's going to happen and when, but to the best of your ability I want you to brace yourself, because I sense that your memories will come flooding back. And since we don't know what you might remember I want you to be mentally prepared for it. Okay! Fortify yourself with every ounce of strength that you possess."

"Yes, I will."

She grabs me by the shoulder, shakes me and yells in my face, spittle spraying my forehead—I can smell the coffee she had for breakfast, which is strange because she very rarely has coffee, she says it makes her "jumpy." At that notion Robin had laughed and said, "Well that's precisely why we have it, because it keeps us on our toes." We all had laughed raucously and unabashedly. But I sense that there will be no such laughing today. Rayva has shifted things, brought some things into clearer focus while muddling others—"Promise me, Nevaeh! This is serious. Your life might depend on it."

"Yes! I promise! I will!" I mumble, suddenly frightened as a result of her earnestness.

"Good! I am deeply concerned that you don't trust Rayva. He is your husband, and despite your memory loss, he shouldn't be the one to evoke fear in you. That is making us all quite worried for your safety. Plus, I have been hearing from the nurses that he is *bootiful*!"

Despite ourselves we laugh, but just a chuckle.

"What do you mean?"

"I am not sure, but you just shouldn't be afraid of your spouse. He should have brought a happy vibe with him. I think he should have been the one to trigger the echo that you've been talking about, not me. Therefore I am worried about you, about what we don't know about you and what might have truly happened to you."

"Yes, Sandy, that makes two of us, mama."

*   *   *

After Sandy leaves, when I have had a chance to process our conversation, I start to feel anxious again. I really do not want another shot of Ativan so I do my breathing exercises to block a full-blown panic attack. I really need to keep my mind clear and focus, just like Sandy said. So I decide to focus on my breathing and fill my morning with the mundane, which includes my very bland breakfast of cold eggs on toast (I hate eggs in this place), a lukewarm cup of tea and much peering out the window, observing the river. I wish I could just jump in this river and be carried away to another time and possibly another place; forgetting all that happened yesterday and waking up with brand new, beautiful memories.

Following breakfast, I watch a little TV (which I don't usually do). I am happy when there is a knock on the door. I instantly know it has to be Imka. Seeing Imka literally lifts my spirit. I'm not going to lie; a huge part of my anxiety was fueled by the fact that I desperately wanted to speak with her.

"Hi, Nevaeh. How are you doing today?"

"I'm better seeing you."

We both force a smile. Imka has that weird habit of standing with half of her body in the room and the other half outside. As if she's been so programmed to check with her head first if it's safe enough for the rest of her body to enter a space.

"Yesterday was rough. I am so sorry that you had to go through that but I am really hoping that, although quite traumatic, yesterday's events will trigger memories." She just gets right down to business today. No warming up. No getting the car in gear. The introduction of this new dynamic causes me to sit up straight in my bed and pay attention to her: to her body language and facial expression.

"Yes, I was thinking that myself, and I was wondering if there's something that you could do to trigger some of those memories. Because I desperately need to know if what Rayva was saying is the truth and the whole truth, not just a part of the truth. As you know most good lies have a fraction of the truth sprinkled somewhere in the discourse."

As if waiting to be invited in, she brings her whole body, her whole being, into the room. At her urgency, I swing my legs over the side of the bed facing her, bracing for what she has to say. "I am happy you've said that, Nevaeh, because I have something to share with you."

"Yes, what is it?"

"Detective Dennis came back yesterday after dropping off Rayva at his hotel and said he felt your unease the moment Rayva walked into the room. He came back to have a talk with you, to see if he could strike a chord in your memory. Those were his words, not mine. But by then you had been sedated. So he's planning to come back today minus Rayva, who came back a few times yesterday as well, wanting to speak with you. But each time you were asleep and we obviously didn't want to disturb your sleep, which was already restless. I suspect that he's going to return by lunch time today; therefore, the detective wanted to speak to you before Rayva gets here and without his knowledge."

"But why? Did he say anything to you?"

"No, just that he had a hunch that something was off—I mean we all could feel that something was off. And I think that's what your body was reacting to. I don't think it's so much the chrysanthemums. Although they might be linked to an unpleasant memory as well; maybe the death of your mother. We can't be sure without time to assess your thought processes. So after Rayva leaves later today, we can have a talk about what he said and how that made you feel. Alright?"

"Alright."

"The detective should be on his way here by now, so try to rest, even just close your eyes."

She turns to leave and I remember what else I wanted to say to her.

"Oh, Imka."

She turns around and returns to my bedside. "I wanted to tell you that I got my period this morning."

"That's great," she says, clasping her hands together and holding them up to her mouth.

"Yes, but that's not all I wanted to say. I also—"

Before I could tell her about the echoes that I have been experiencing, almost like small tremors in my body, the detective knocks twice and pushes his way in, so abruptly that I have to catch my breath. Maybe because I thought he was Rayva, whom I am not yet ready to see.

"Hello, ladies. Sorry to disturb you but I absolutely need to speak with Nevaeh before Rayva gets here. We have an officer sitting at his hotel and I've just got word that he has left. He must be on his way here, so we don't have a lot of time to do this."

He does not even allow us to greet him. He launches into his reason for being here: "I was concerned about the story he gave about you being afraid, Nevaeh, so I did some digging. I kept asking: why would an intelligent young woman all of a sudden be afraid of her own husband? A husband with means and who sponsored her to live in Canada? As it turns out, there might have been a reason for you to be afraid."

"Maybe I should leave you two to it, then." Imka turns to leave again.

"No, Doc, I need you to stay because I am going to need your help with this plan that I have."

He pokes his head outside the door and pulls the door closed, much like I had this morning. Imka and I look at each other, the suspense hanging like a rich, ripe fruit in the room. I can almost smell the excitement emanating from Detective Dennis. To think that I'd thought to calm myself using the mundane this morning. When he is satisfied that the coast is clear, he lowers his voice. It is a very weird experience; his voice sounds like it is rebelling against being forced to whisper, having been programmed to yell all its life. I almost laugh at the thought of his voice fighting to be loud, but now is definitely not the time for that. He seems to have come here with a specific purpose in mind.

"So, we were able to learn that Rayva and his father, Rain Barron—also known as RB—are currently under surveillance as a result of some suspicious activities surrounding their ventures. They are heavily invested in the chrysanthemum plant."

Imka looks at me and takes my hand, squeezing it gently. Dennis continues without missing a beat.

"They source it primarily from Jamaica because apparently that market has not been regulated by the government, at least not yet. The chrysanthemum is used for its medicinal value, which is all dandy until people go missing, and the body count is growing."

"What does that mean, Detective?" Imka asks, and I am glad because I am caught between wanting and not wanting to know.

"There is a growing body of evidence to suggest that they have been testing their products on people without their expressed consent. Some very high-risk individuals, like drug addicts and prostitutes. The FBI has had them on their radar for the past year—"

"Wait, the FBI? Why would they be concerned about what is happening over there in Canada?" Imka asks, looking as confused as I feel.

"Because the Barrons, as a result of their strategic location close to the US—they live in Paris, Ontario, which is right there on the border—and possibly also their associates, are coming across and kidnapping US citizens to use in their research."

"Oh wow! That's quite far-fetched, don't you think, Detective?"

"But quite plausible, Doc. Now, like I was saying, the Barrons have obviously been tremendously cautious, so the FBI has not been able to find a way into their ventures."

"Until now?" Again, Imka asks it as more of a statement than a question.

"Yes, until now." They stare at each other as if having a telepathic conversation that I am not privy to. A battle of wits, even. I still don't even know what they are talking about. Not until they both turn and look at me at the same time.

Imka says, "Absolutely not. She might be on the verge of a breakthrough and you putting her in harm's way might sabotage her progress. She might never regain any of her memories if she is placed in an extremely traumatic situation or if she is pushed beyond her ability to cope."

"I understand that, and I am really sorry to be asking this—and I wouldn't if there were another way, but we are all out of options. These people are dangerous and we need to find a way to stop them before more innocents are killed."

"What exactly are you asking me to do, Detective?" I say with more courage than I feel.

"I am hereby requesting on behalf of both the US and

Canadian governments that you spy on your husband."

"What? Absolutely no way. I don't even know for sure if he is my husband."

"Yes, he is. We've checked. You got married five years ago in Jamaica, and you've lived in Canada for the past four years."

"What about my family members? He said my mother has died."

"Yes, but your dad and aunts and uncles still live in Jamaica."

I don't even have time to process all this.

"If these people are as dangerous as you say they are, won't that place me and my family members in harm's way? Why would I agree to do that, Detective? Can you absolutely guarantee our safety?"

"Yes, we can. We have a plan. But you have to agree first before I can inform you, because outside of that it really doesn't make sense that I tell you. Plus, most of it would have to be top secret. You cannot share any of this with anyone, not even Sandy. You too, Doc, this is confidential."

"I need time to think," I say, while grabbing my throbbing head.

"I do understand, Nevaeh, but we don't have the luxury of time. Any minute now Rayva could walk through the door and, being your legal spouse, request that you be discharged into his care. Once that happens we can no longer protect you. You are a legal citizen of Canada, you don't have a criminal history, you don't even have a credit report. If you leave here and go missing, there's nothing we can do. But if you agree and stay here we will grant you full citizenship and immunity right away so that we can protect you."

"This is all too much. Imka, what do you think I should do?"

"Just like you, I need time to think this through, to weigh the pros and cons of the situation."

"Ladies, we do not have the luxury of time. Time is of the essence. Primarily because, one, he doesn't know for sure if you are only pretending to have memory loss—"

"But I am not lying, though. Why would I pretend to not remember? Having amnesia is horrible. It feels like I am constantly nauseous but unable to throw up."

"Look, I believe you. I honestly do. I just think that you are a decent young lady, a teacher no less, who in some way got swept off your feet and landed in the wrong family. This happens more times than we care to count."

"My question is, Detective—" it's Imka's turn to interject, "do you know for certain that Rayva is involved? What if it's just his father who is crooked? Isn't it quite possible that he knows nothing about the disappearance of all these innocent people? I mean, we've seen the guy, he looks so genuinely concerned about his wife. It was heartbreaking to watch."

"Look, that might be true. But the way I see it, this would be an opportunity for Nevaeh to put him in the clear."

"I still don't know, Detective. I don't even know myself yet, let alone know this man. Quite frankly, he is a complete stranger to me. I don't feel anything remotely romantic towards him. So how am I going to know if he's lying or not? I won't know, and that will put me in even more danger, wouldn't it?"

"Yes, but like I said, once you I agree, we would pull out all the stops to protect you, but you absolutely must agree and be a hundred percent committed to this venture. Before we are able to expose our hands, so to speak."

"Alright, I think we should allow Nevaeh and Rayva to talk undisturbed, and then depending on how she feels she'll give you her answer. As much as I feel for all those poor souls, I really do not want to jeopardize her therapy or her life, or the lives of her innocent family members living in Jamaica. She has come a far way, and I feel certain that a breakthrough is imminent and I just cannot risk a relapse. As my patient, her needs come first, and I am sure you understand this."

"Yes, but you would have a police officer with you at all times, dressed like a civilian or someone in the healthcare field. Trust me, Nevaeh and Dr. Imka, we've done these sting operations many times, and we have a very high success rate in protecting our undercover operatives."

As if on cue, on that last comment his cellular phone rings. Imka and I jump at the sudden intrusion.

"Yes, okay. Alright. I'll let her know." Before closing his flip phone he announces, "Rayva is on his way here. He's currently on the elevator heading towards your floor. I have to leave right now because I don't want him to get suspicious. That might push him to enact an endgame that none of us are prepared for."

"I am so sorry, Detective, but I cannot agree, not until I have had a chance to process all that you've said. Like you said, I am just a teacher, not a spy. I need time to collect myself so I can make a rational decision. I don't want to just act out of fear. I want to, like Imka said, weigh my options."

"Which I think is only fair, Detective. We can't expect her to just throw herself into this without having had a chance to sift through all the information that you've so hurriedly provided."

His phone rings again; this time we are more prepared. He says, "I really have to go but I'll hang around in case there's anything and I have to intervene. Whatever you do, ladies, please don't let on that you know anything about what Mr. Rayva Barron has been up to. Indeed, Nevaeh's life might depend on it."

With that very dark admonition and a look of foreboding, the Detective slips out the door, an action that seems to have been perfected over time, leaving both me and Imka to face the music with Rayva. Thankfully, she's here with me. After all that Detective Dennis had just said, I don't think I would have had the fortitude to face him alone. Pretty soon, there's a gentle tap on the door. We both look at each other and after a deep breath, I say, "It's open. Come in."

I'm not too sure exactly what I have just given access to me and to my room.

Rayva seems taller than he did yesterday. I am not sure if that's a good sign or not. He greets Imka and then moves toward me and kisses my forehead. I hold my breath as his moist, soft lips linger on my face. I am almost panicking that he might try to kiss my lips, but he doesn't. Maybe because Imka is in the room. His smell is clean and so deeply masculine, and his cologne is both pleasant and familiar. I don't remember this smell from yesterday. He stands back and looks intensely in my eyes and again holds my gaze as a substitute for my hand.

"How are you, Rayva? Did you sleep well?" Thankfully, Imka comes to the rescue.

He looks at her and then solemnly says, "No, I haven't been able to sleep for the past three months, not since the night Nevaeh went missing." He still carries that aura of a petulant child.

I mumble, "I am so sorry," and look away from him.

He continues, "I thought for sure I would have been able to sleep last night, but after hearing about your—" he pauses and I look up, just in time to see him look away, as if searching for the most appropriate word. Afraid of being distracted he has to look elsewhere. "—episode… I couldn't sleep. I would feel horrible if anything happens to you because of me, Nevaeh. You are so sweet and so pure. You are the very best part of me."

I don't know how to react to that. I search inside myself to see if his presence or his words stirs an echo in me. I even close my eyes but all I see is darkness. A darkness which doesn't exactly match this handsome face in front of me. He continues, and I get the feeling that while he is being honest about his feelings, he is gauging my reaction as well and that he is overdoing it just for a reaction, even a suggestion of a reaction; almost as if he's testing the waters of my endurance. Does he really believe that I am pretending?

"Have you eaten today?" Just like that he switches gears on me. I don't know how to react. But I shake my head. "What did you have for breakfast?"

"Excuse me?"

"What did you have for breakfast?"

"I had cold eggs on toast, but I mostly had the toast, because I didn't like the eggs."

He laughs a little too loudly and Imka and I clasp hands. Certainly not the reaction I was expecting. Seeing the identical surprised look on our faces, he says, "Nevaeh has always hated eggs, especially scrambled eggs."

So he is testing me, testing to see if I really do have memory loss. But why would he feel the need to do that?

"Do you remember my sister's friend, Betsy?"

"No, should I?"

I am really getting angry at his sick game.

"No, just trying to jar your memory to help you remember things, you know, put things into proper perspective?"

"So that's been your plan this whole time, to jar my memory by just springing things on me, not caring about the impact they might have on me? Does that mean you don't believe my diagnosis sir?"

"Now, Nevaeh, I never said that."

"Not directly but your line of questioning does, sir."

"I am sorry," he says while trying to hold my hand, which I pull away as gently as I can. I'm not about to make nice with a complete stranger who thinks I'm a liar.

"I see some things haven't changed, have they? You're still dead set on embarrassing me. I'll never be enough for you, will I?"

"What the hell are you talking about?"

"This, your pulling away from me," he says, shouting.

Imka raises her hands and declares, "Okay guys, time out! There's no need to shout, Rayva. I am going to have to ask you to leave if you continue to upset my patient. Do I make myself clear?"

"Yes, you do."

"She's had a very rough few days and I don't want anything to set back her progress."

"Does that mean she's been remembering things?" He asks breathlessly.

He jumps on Imka's last comment, seemingly forgetting everything else that she said before that.

"No, not yet, but I feel that, judging from her reaction to the chrysanthemums, it's only a matter of time before she starts to remember things."

He looks from me to Imka then suddenly says, "I was coming here to take her home with me today. I am tired of us being apart."

We both say, "*No!*"

"I would strongly advise against that, Rayva. Moving her at this juncture in her therapy might do more harm than good."

At the thought of leaving here, leaving my friends, to go with a stranger, the tears just erupt from me like a waterfall.

"I am sorry, Nevaeh. I didn't mean to yell. I really love you and I have missed you so much. I don't know how I would live without you. But I hate when you push me away and it seems like every time we have an argument you retreat further and further away from me. I just want everything to be the way it was during our engagement and even after our wedding."

"I'm trying, Rayva, but I just can't remember. I don't know what you want from me."

By now I am fully sobbing. How can he be so selfish, wanting to take me away from here without caring about the impact that it might have on my fragile nerves and overall recovery?

"Nothing!" he erupts. "I don't want anything from you. I just want you to be okay, I want us to be okay."

This guy is either yelling at me or plying me with sweet nothings. What is up with him? I cannot deal with his volatility at all. What if I *made* him become this way? I cry some more.

Imka says, "Maybe you should come back another time, when

Nevaeh is not so upset."

He looks at her for a while then turns to me. "Is that what you want, Neva?"

"No, but you are so upset with me and I don't know why. So maybe it's best you leave and come back another day when you've had some rest and I have had a chance to process all that you've said."

I cry, holding his sharp gaze the whole time, tears flowing onto my shirt like the watermelon juice.

"Will that help, Doc?" He turns to Imka.

"Yes, but I think it's of equal importance, Rayva, that you rest. You haven't slept in a while and that can seriously impair your judgement. So why don't you return to your hotel, get some rest and maybe then you and Nevaeh can have a more meaningful conversation."

"Have you eaten yet?" I chime in, genuinely concerned for this stranger who professes his love for me while being angry at me at the same time.

"No, I haven't. I just had a cup of coffee."

"Coffee is not food, Rayva."

"I know. You always say that."

"Really?"

"Yes."

He smiles tentatively and I smile too. There's no way this guy is a killer—or is he just a smooth criminal, like MJ said?

"Okay. I guess you're in good hands, right?" He says, looking from me to Imka.

"Yes, everyone has been so kind to me. Hopefully you'll be able to meet my friends, Sandy and Robin."

"Robin?"

"Yes, why?"

"I don't know if this will help. But you had a friend once named Robin, who disappeared on her seventeenth birthday. Apparently you guys went to Blue Mountain Peak and she never returned. This has haunted you for years, as you somehow feel quite responsible for her passing, although you've never said why. Do you remember your friend Robin?"

"No, I don't. But—"

"But what?" Imka joins the conversation.

"But what, Nevaeh?" Rayva echoes.

"Nothing. I just felt really close to Robin from the first day I met her."

"So it might be her, then. Maybe somehow she migrated to the US and became a nurse."

Imka laughs. "No, this Robin is white and grew up in San Bernardino, Texas. At least as far as I know."

"Alright! It was worth a try though," Rayva says, laughing at himself and looking sheepish, revealing perfect teeth.

"Thanks for trying. I appreciate the effort."

"See, that's all I want to do, to help you. All I've ever wanted to do is help you. Nothing more and nothing less."

I say, "Thanks! Believe me, somewhere inside me there's a girl who remembers and is extremely grateful for all you've done. But please just give me a chance to locate her and bring her back."

"Always a poet, eh, Neva!" He smiles and strokes my cheek tenderly. I don't flinch this time because his touch is not completely horrible.

"Okay, Doc. I am going to go but you best believe that I am going to check on my favourite girl every day. And I am giving you one week, exactly one week to bring her memory back. After that, I am taking her back to Ontario."

The last part is uttered more like a threat; there is no smiling at that point. Imka instinctively takes a step back. I feel obligated to deflect all this animosity that I have managed to bring into her life, their lives really.

"Well, as long as I am not only your favourite girl, but your only girl, you can visit every day. All day if you like."

That charming smile that had been reined in so unceremoniously is now given free rein again, effortlessly, in the blink of an eye. What have I gotten myself into? Who is this person? So sweet and loving in one instant and then boorish the next? What the hell?

He heads towards the door, which is not that far away in the tiny room. Then as if shot by a memory gun he stops suddenly, and says, taking something from inside his jacket, "Oh, I almost forgot. I brought you your diary, which I haven't read, by the way. I scanned the first page and realized what it was and closed it right away. I felt that maybe there is something in it that will jar your memory, although my dad didn't think so. By the way, my dad says hi."

He hands me a small, brown leather-bound book. Again, the last part seems innocent enough, but bears the undercurrent of a veiled threat—or at least that's how I hear it.

"Please greet him for me and everyone else that I might know but have forgotten. Hopefully, by the end of the week I'll be able to remember everyone and *everything* about our life together."

I emphasize the *everything* because if he thinks that he can threaten me then I am just the one to play his game. His threats are beginning to get on my already shattered nerves. I don't know much about myself but I do know I do not take kindly to threats, veiled or otherwise.

He looks me over, really looks at me, like he's weighing me on a scale that only he controls. Then just like that, just as suddenly as he appeared, he leaves. After Imka checks to see that he has really left, we both make fists to control the tremors in our hands. Imagine him having the ability to have that impact on Imka, a woman who has mastered deep breathing. He ought to be ashamed of himself.

Eventually Imka says, "Nevaeh, while I cannot tell you what you should or shouldn't do, I highly recommend that you work with the detective. This young man, your husband, appears to be very unpredictable, which might make him a danger to you.

As well, I think he displays manipulative tendencies and he has mastered the art of gaslighting, all characteristics of a narcissist. So, more so for your sake, I think you should assist the detective."

"I don't exactly know what all those things mean, but I couldn't agree more, Imka. What have I gotten myself into?"

"I'll explain those terms to you the first chance I get, but for now get some rest. I'll send you some lunch. Then you can hopefully meet with Detective Dennis. We need to get this plan on the road, since he plans to take you back to Ontario after a week. It really doesn't give us a lot of time to plan."

"I hope the Detective is as good as he claims to be."

"Yes, me too, Nevaeh. Me too."

I sigh and shake my head simultaneously.

CHAPTER FIFTEEN

Diary of Nevaeh Francis Barron (Tuesday, Nov. 2004) My first winter in Paris, Ontario

I have not been writing as often as I had planned. I have been going on walks when the days are "nice," as the Canadians like to say. Paris, Ontario is a beautiful, quaint little town, straight out of a Lifetime Movie, with miles between L-shaped houses. The spaces between the homes make me ache for home and our tightknit community. And to think I hated the proximity of the houses. At first I was enraptured by the distance and loved the wide-open spaces, but I soon realize how isolating those spaces are. People have lived here for years and never met their neighbours; how deeply sad. The houses are all uniquely designed but they all wear the same brick structure. In the summer, they seem to have hired the same gardener, as they all have identical plants and gardens lining their front lawns.

Today I decided to go for a walk along the river. I still love the river; obviously, it's not the same as back home with the natural waterfalls spraying water in your face and the green rich foliage framing the falls, but it will do for now. I so wish that my friends, Claire, Bridget, and especially Robin were here. We would have so much fun. We would liven up this place and add a touch of colour that is sadly missing. Rayva's family is the only black family in this area. I rarely see people, let alone children, but when I do they stare at me like I'm an alien with three heads. I find that to be both strange and sad. I miss my family and friends so badly, and to think I avoided them for so many years and tried to bury the memories that we shared; now all I have are those same memories. I miss Mommy and Grandma but that's a different kind of ache. An ache that I carry in all my waking moments and sometimes in my dreams.

Being in Canada is a very lonely experience, especially as an immigrant. Yes, my husband and his family are wealthy, and they've managed to do well for themselves and help poorer communities both here and abroad as much as they can, but still this place can be cold and unwelcoming. Plus, I have learned the history of the Aboriginal peoples, and of course this place and all it represents still bears the smear of the blood of the original people who lived and breathed, loved and died right here in these lands. Sometimes I imagine that their spirits still push back against foreigners like myself in an effort to right the wrong that was done to them in the past. I also think that their rich history is similar to the original inhabitants of Jamaica: the Arawak, the Taino and the Carib Indians. I wish humanity would get to a place where they see souls and not bodies: bodies age and rot but souls are eternal. Souls represent all that's good and perfect in the world because souls came from a place of perfection. Plus, the soul is eternal, so when in doubt consult your soul because the soul always knows.

I love Rayva so much. I'm happy that our souls connected. I never thought that a man like him could or would ever love someone like me so completely. I think Mommy would be pleased despite the angry dream before our wedding day; I still have not been able to figure out that dream. I guess that dream is just a reflection of my unworthiness. He treats me like a queen. Sometimes it's overwhelming to be so adored especially after all I've done. I am wholly undeserving of this life that God has handpicked for me. I swear it's my mother and grandmother's prayers which have brought so much undeserved grace and favour to my life.

Blessed and hugely favoured!

Diary of Nevaeh Francis Barron (Summer 05)

Today I spoke to my dad (as the Canadians say). He's not doing too well and it breaks my heart that I am not there to help him the way that he helped me; thankfully my aunts Sabine and Sebouney are there to help him out. I still worry because my aunts are not young either. Even now, sometimes I am so angry at them for spending all their time in Kingston while my mother struggled to take care of their mother alone. Sometimes I think if they had helped in a more tangible sense my mother would still be alive, she would not have worked herself to death. But then I think that I have become them in a sense, living abroad to create a better life while they take care of my dad and they are happy to do it so that my life can be better. I guess that's how my Mommy felt about taking care of Grandma, she didn't see it as a burden or an obligation. For her it was a great pleasure, an act of love, to give back to the person who gave her life.

Since I have been here in this isolated place, I have been able to do a lot of soul-searching and reflection; especially since I don't have any access to charcoal, so I find that I am able to think clearer without it. However, I do think that I am going to need a substitute and really soon. I can already see that life in this idyllic setting is anything but ideal. Plus there's a lot of work that needs to be done in terms of working on my marriage. Rayva is so kind and loving, I feel useless because all I do is sit around and look pretty. They have servants to do everything: the cooking, the cleaning, the gardening. I have never felt more useless in all my life. So I have vowed to help him in any which way that I can, even if I have to compromise a little. And to think that in my younger days, compromise was an expletive for me. I guess the older you get the more you put things into their right perspective. Rayva has always maintained that perspective is everything.

I went for a walk by the river after I spoke to Dad. It is summer now and the river is breathtaking. I've discovered that this river is called the Nith River and it empties into the Grand River, which flows through most of the small towns in Southern Ontario and empties into the northern shore of Lake Eerie. Rayva's dad Rain said that Lake Eerie sits on the international boundary between Canada and the US. This means that, if you follow this river all the way south, you can end up in states like Ohio,

Michigan and New York. I have been to New York once since I've been here, but it wasn't a pleasure trip as Rayva and Rain were meeting their business partners and I went along for the ride in their private plane. Something else I wish that I could share with my friends, but I have put so much space between us that I think the space is as large as the spaces between these L-shaped houses in Paris.

Rain agrees with me that Paris is beautiful and he believes that it is centrally located and quite useful for their business. They work with a pharmaceutical company to extract all the healthful benefits of the chrysanthemum plant. Back home we use it to cure colds and the flu. Rain believes Paris has the best of both worlds to offer; by that he means the best of Canada and the US. Sometimes I wish I could tell my friends how beautiful Paris is in the summer, spring and fall. That is among the many things I have discovered and so wish that I could share. Also, that it looks like a town straight out of a movie or a fairy tale, or both, in the winter, when all the trees that have lost their leaves are covered by snow. The snow will take some getting used to but I am mesmerized by it every single time. Being from the Caribbean I don't exactly look forward to it but I love to see the first fluffy snowflakes falling. I sometimes try to catch them with my tongue. Rayva laughed so hard the first time I did that. We both fell in the snow.

At first, Rayva used to hang out with me and we would go for walks and dinners in Toronto and fly back in the late evenings, but their business is doing so well that sometimes he is gone for weeks. I am always so lonely when he is away. Sure, his family is great and they are always so kind to me, but it is not the same as having him here.

I wish I could get back into teaching, but both Rayva and Rain are dead set against that. They say I just need to work on making beautiful babies. But that's a sore point for me. I've already lost two babies and I really don't want to try anymore. It's too painful. I don't even want to talk about that with anyone, not even with Rayva, which is unfair because I know both him and Rain (the whole entire family) are hurting, but I just don't want to deal with it anymore. I am tired of losing. I have lost everyone I love and I know this time it is definitely my fault because while I couldn't find charcoal, I found a substitute. I know it's bad for me but I can't help it. Whenever

I am stressed I resort to it. I know my life is full of luxuries that so many people only dream about, that I never had the courage to dream about, but that luxury comes at a cost to me and I don't drink wine so I have to find a substitute. I don't smoke either, although Rayva has offered on many occasions to teach me how to smoke weed. I decline because back home only a certain class of people smoke and that is not my class. But it's strange, because here in Canada it seems like only the super-rich smoke. It's funny how when you don't have a lot of money you think that having lots will solve all your problems, heal all your brokenness, make everything good, but I have come to realize that money doesn't solve everything. It mostly either teaches you how to conceal your problems well, or it magnifies your problems to the point where they become uncontrollable. To be honest, I never dreamed that a poor, country girl like me could ever live like this, but fate has smiled in my favour and I am embracing my good fortune. I refuse to be ungrateful.

Anyways, I am trying to get my dad here for treatment but for some reason Rayva is dragging his feet. This guy has access to so much wealth, including a private plane, but he's unable to expedite the process to get my dad here. Rubbish! He just doesn't want anyone in their business. But my dad wouldn't care. Anyways, Rayva gives me lots of money to send so that he can get the care he needs, but it's not the same. I want to visit but the time is just not right.

Diary of Nevaeh Francis Barron
Homesick Chronicles
I have not been sleeping well. I so miss Balcarres. I have lived in Ontario for a while and I have come to really love the life we have here. But I miss going to Buff Bay, Hope Bay, Shrewsbury, Fellowship, Manchioneal (I have always loved this name and this town) and Mount Pleasant with my friends, for no other reason but just to explore our beautiful parish. I miss the rivers that I can actually swim in: Somerset Falls, Swift River, Reach Falls, Buff Bay River and Spanish River. Having been here for I while and I have come to understand a few things, I would never enter the Nith river, not even if my life depended on it. I miss the beaches back home. There are very few beaches in Ontario but none compares to Boston Beach, Frenchman's

Cove, Winnifred's, San-San, Titchfield and Long Bay; not even one. Not to mention going on a day trip to Monkey Island and visiting the Folly Ruins, going to Reach Falls, Blue Mountain (despite the tragedy that happened there which still haunts me to this day) and the Blue Lagoon. Rafting on the Rio Grande was never my thing, but today I wish I could go there and eat some real-real food: festival, bammy, fish, jerk pork, rice and peas, oxtail, stew peas, curried chicken, curry goat, stew chicken. I am literally salivating right now.

We do have a 'chef' and he does try, but dear Lord nothing compares to cooking outside on the wood fire and baking cornmeal pudding, sweet potato pudding, and toto. Mind you, I have never baked a single thing a day in my life, but I watched my mother and aunties bake enough so I remember the joys and the sweet smells. Oh, and the coconut and peanut drops and the gizzada. I really need to take a trip. Maybe I can smuggle some charcoal back here, because the substitute is not working. It is making me sick. Some days I feel confused. I am fighting with Rayva all the time now and I know it's not me. It is the substitute. Like Prince Hamlet said to Laertes, it is my insanity that offended you, not me, Hamlet, never me, Hamlet. In fact, like Hamlet, I am as much of a victim of this substitute as Hamlet was a victim of his insanity. Sadly, like Hamlet who chose to put on an "antic disposition" I chose my poison and, much like insanity destroyed Hamlet, my poison is destroying me and the life I have come to love, little by little. I cannot just nod and smile anymore; my poison won't let me. I can't just agree for agreeing's sake; my poison won't let me.

I wish I could share this with someone, but whom? No one will understand this weird compulsion. A compulsion which has cost me so much, but still, I can't let go. It took my babies but even yet I can't let it go. Just let it go, Nevaeh, just stop. I wish I had my Obeahman here, maybe he could talk some sense into my thick brain. I keep telling myself that I don't take a lot, just a small amount at a time and I don't do it every day, I'll go for weeks but then I feel stressed and overwhelmed and I have to, I have to!

At this rate, I am going to wreck my life and my marriage. I've spent all my life trying to rescue people, especially Rayva. Who is going to rescue Nevaeh? Who is going to rescue me from myself?

CHAPTER SIXTEEN

Today is a dull day; it's been raining since last night. I genuinely used to love the rain but today it is not helping. I have never felt more sad and alone. A part of me wishes that Rayva had not come here, had not recalled a life for me that I might never remember. I was so exhausted yesterday that I couldn't even meet with the detective. After lunch I spent a few hours reading my diary, hence my exhaustion. I'd desperately hoped that it would bring back memories; now I wish that I had never laid eyes on the cursed thing. I see a list of people and places that I bear no resemblance to or recollection of. I feel like I am prying into someone else's life, and although there's lots to cover, there are so many pages missing, so many missing years and months that I cannot make any kind of meaningful connection. How did they go missing? Did Rayva remove them to hide a truth? But why would he bring it to me if he had removed the pages? He could have kept its existence a secret. He didn't have to give it to me. I don't know what to think. There are a few pages at the back that I will get to soon because I am anxious to put the broken pieces of my life back together again. I am still hoping that I will find some answers here in this diary; after all, nothing happens by chance or happenstance, does it!

I paused and cried for two babies that I had never met and might never remember. It hurts so much that I might never remember the exact moment that I discovered their existence, their tiny heartbeat. I don't even know how far along I was when they died. I don't know what they might have become and it is the lost potential that I grieve for. I also grieve for my inability to feel any kind of maternal inclination for their lost memory, and their demise is my own doing. What kind of monster am I? How could I harm my own children? I may never become a mother, ever, and I grieve for that as well. I grieve for a Mother and Grandmother that I have no memory of. I will have to trust that if the old me ached for them then they must have been special; that I will take with me to the grave whether or not I ever remember them. Because, after reading all those deeply personal and thoughtful narratives and not being able to find a connection, I am starting to give up hope that I will ever remember anything of my old life. Maybe those echoes I felt were a trick of the mind. Maybe I have been such a horrible friend, daughter and wife that I don't deserve to remember what I had, because I didn't deserve any of it. I didn't deserve those people because it seems to me that all I ever have been was a disappointment to them and their memory.

Rayva visited me early this morning as he promised, just to check on me. He looks more relaxed. We didn't fight this time. It seems to me that he is the type of person who gets frustrated when he doesn't have a plan and doesn't have control of the situation. Therefore, now that he has a plan to take me back to Canada in a week's time, without a thought as to what I want, he is definitely in a better place. He asked if I read my diary and I lied. I don't have the energy to fight with him so I said no to avoid asking about the missing pages. Plus, I think he would only lie to me, that that's how he found it, and I have no way of knowing if he is telling the truth. I have to push those thoughts aside, though, because the detective is definitely coming today to discuss his plan and I will need to be both focused and alert.

"Hi, Nevaeh."

"Oh, hi Robin! I didn't see you there."

"I knocked a few times. May I come in? If it's not a good time, I'll understand."

"No, that's fine. Come on in. I am so happy to see a friendly face."

Robin comes into the room and pulls up the grey chair. I have been looking out the window, watching the river, which is angry, having been disturbed by all the rain. I know exactly how she feels. I feel exactly the same way. It's as if I was just starting to put some order in my shell of a life and here comes the rain, Rayva by name, to disturb my already chaotic existence.

"I can imagine. I hear you've had a rough few days."

"Rough is not the word, Robin. It seems like my nervous system has been experiencing one shockwave after the next, and I don't know how much more I can take."

"You are a strong girl, Nevaeh; you can do this."

"Can I?"

Robin takes my hand and gives me one of her Robin smiles. I haven't seen her in a few days and it's like we've been with each other for ages. That's one of the things I have learned about having real friends: distance means nothing. We can pick up a conversation from exactly where we left it the last time and it feels like we were always together. Maybe that is something that I needed to learn so God created this specific struggle in order for me to grasp it in my thick head.

"Yes, you can. Over the last little while I have seen you learn to walk, learn to talk, learn to take back your personal power. I don't think there is anything that you can*not* do. I think it's the Jamaican in you. I see Sandy like that as well. She is never afraid of a challenge, never afraid to look fear in the face and kick its butt. You come from great stock, Nevaeh. Oh, by the way, I love your name. Your parents must have really thought long and hard about what to name their precious child. There is a greatness in you that you haven't even began to tap into yet—"

"Wait! Say that again."

"What?"

"The part about greatness."

"Some people will do anything for a compliment."

"Haha! I'm serious."

"What? Why?"

"It sounds really familiar. It feels like an echo, and please don't ask me to explain it. That's the best I can do, to just say it's an echo."

"There is greatness in you, Nevaeh. What was your maiden name?"

"Francis."

"There is greatness in you, Nevaeh Francis. Just hold onto it. As humans, in most of our communities, we have been socialized to accept our weaknesses and struggle with them, but never our strengths. We are mostly taught that admitting strength is a shortcoming similar to the sin of pride. But it is not true, Nevaeh, because all of us possess complex nervous systems and we are also made up of strengths and weaknesses. So instead of focusing on weaknesses, you should accentuate your strengths. Never downplay your strengths, O beautiful one."

"Thanks for saying that, Robin, because I don't feel particularly strong—at least not today."

"But you are, my love, you are. And because you are strong in and of yourself, you don't need me, or your husband, or Imka or Sandy, or Detective Dennis—you don't need any of us to rescue you. You are fully capable of rescuing yourself, whether or not you have any memory of the self you need to rescue."

"You always know just what I need, Robin. Thanks for being

my friend. I will never take that for granted ever."

"You are welcome! Now tell me more about this echo that you've been feeling."

"I can't really explain it fully."

"Try me."

"Well, I have been hearing, no feeling, sounds in my body. Sometimes someone says something and I feel it in my body, like I have experienced that same reaction to the comment before."

"You mean like déjà vu?"

"Yes, but not exactly. The way I understand déjà vu works is that you feel like you've experienced the situation before. Correct?"

"Yes."

"But with me, it is not that I feel like I have experienced the event or situation itself, it is the reaction to the situation that I feel like I have encountered before. Do you follow me?"

"No, sorry! I don't understand."

I sigh, frustrated with my own inability to explain. "Okay. For instance, that night when you talked about your mom, I cried, remember?"

"Yes, I remember."

"So I have come to realize that I wasn't reacting to the idea of a mother, or even the absence of a mother, but my tears were a direct reaction to the emotion of sadness that I had sensed before when my Mother died."

"Okay, so you are reacting to your own reaction in the past?"

"Precisely."

"So you're a drama queen?"

We both laugh so hard that my stomach hurts.

"Yes, something like that."

"That's amazing! You must be a deeply empathetic individual to be able to react to emotions like that, and I believe that is progress. In the grand scheme of things, it might not be the memory of a big event like the death of your mom or your wedding day but it is a start, which means that your body is building momentum.”

“What does that mean, momentum? Sandy said something similar to that as well.”

“It means that, instead of remembering everything all at once and being overwhelmed, your mind is feeding you bite sized information, bit by bit, by way of emotions. Because you did say that your nervous system is in a shambles right now, so instead of bringing back all the memories at once and shattering you even more, your mind is measuring out how much you can stand at a time and when your body, mind and soul are in sync, your memories will coming flooding back: the big memories, the small ones, the sad ones, the happy ones!”

“But what if I am overwhelmed by all the sad ones? What then?”

“Well, that’s why your body is feeding them to you in small chunks, in echoes as you call it. So that when they all come back you’ve already had small doses, so they won’t overwhelm you.”

“Wow! Like a warm-up before a grueling exercise?”

“Yes, the human body is an amazing organ, capable of far more than we have been able to tap into. I don’t think we have yet experienced the maximum potential of our bodies.”

“That’s why the Bible says that we are fearfully and wonderfully made.”

“Oh, yes.” Robin says this while laughing and hugging me.

“I see you have been reading the Bible I gave you.” Robin is, weirdly, into Christianity and other religions at the same time.

“I have. Some of it I don’t understand but I find it comforting to read. Plus, I have been locating scriptures that deal specifically with healing and those that deal with the mind as well.”

“Which one is your favourite?”

“You mean which scripture?”

“Yes.”

“Well, there are a few. But I find myself reciting the one that talks about the fact that God hasn't given us the spirit of fear but of love and of power and of a sound mind. Robin, I really need to have a sound mind, especially right now."

"Yes, I understand."

"No, I don't think you do. The detective is going to ask me to accomplish a task that I don't think I have the skills or the frame of reference for. Sorry, but I can't say what it is. I can't even tell Sandy. Of necessity Imka will be a party to it because she will be playing an active role in my treatment but we can't tell anyone else. It wouldn't be safe."

"That's a whole lot to take in, Nevaeh."

"Tell me about it."

"But I know you can do it. You have that greatness in you from your people."

"Imka calls them "the ancestors."

"Absolutely, you have the strength of the ancestors."

"I like to believe that I have the strength of God and the ancestors."

"Hold on to that belief, kiddo. I don't know what it is but you're gonna do great and make us all proud."

"Thanks, Robin."

"No problem. I have to go now."

"Okay, but before you go, I wanted to ask you—earlier, you said something about being empathetic. I didn't want to break your chain of thought so I didn't ask you then, but what does it mean to be empathetic?"

"It is a deeply complex idea, but I am going to try to explain it to you as quickly as I can and maybe we can talk about it next time."

"Okay. As long as you don't leave me hanging, or else I am going to think about it all day and like I said, I cannot afford to be distracted. Not today."

"So, we call people who are not only in touch with their own emotions, but also the emotions of others, empaths. These are very uniquely-gifted people who can literally feel what other people around them are feeling. They call how and what they feel a vibe or energy."

She uses air quotes around the words "vibe" and "energy."

"So they can always tell when something is off, when a person is not who they are pretending to be."

"But Robin, sometimes I can't trust how I feel—how I am I going to trust how other people feel?"

"Over time, you will be able to trust how you feel. I think there's a lot of learning around being an empath and with time, when you have a better understanding of yourself, then you will learn to trust yourself and trust your feelings. As the empaths say, *vibe never lies* and they have come to trust vibe more than the facts as they are presented to them."

"That's a lot to think about, Robin. But I think I get the gist of what you are talking about. Thanks so much."

"You are always welcome. Gotta go! Duty calls!"

"Bye, enjoy your shift."

"I always do."

It is always like a breath of fresh air talking to Robin. It just fills up my lungs and inflates my ego. Dear, sweet Robin, there is no malice in her or place for foolishness. Just like Sandy, she is a very sharp shooter and God knows that is exactly what I need right now: honesty and truth. She is so knowledgeable and always willing to share. That's an interesting idea—me being an empath—I have never heard that before, but now that I think about it it reeks of truth. I am going to start paying closer attention to how I feel. Maybe that is what will trigger my memories, like a key, and that's a clue my body has been sending me all along through these echoes.

I am going to ask Imka for a book (no more of this notepad foolishness) and start to record my feelings so I can process them. I believe she has referred to this in our sessions as journaling. Before, I was dead set against the idea because, for one, I didn't think I had any thoughts to record, and two, I was so afraid that someone would find it and judge me, but I am in a state of utter desperation. I am so anxious to find and rescue myself that I don't even care who reads my deepest darkest thoughts; especially since it might help someone to locate themselves in this world that has a way of misplacing people.

"Knock, knock! Are you decent, Nevaeh?"

"Yes, Detective, come on in."

"Hey, how are you feeling today?"

"I am feeling a bit more solid today, less like I am standing in quicksand. Thanks for asking, Detective. And how are you feeling today?"

"To be honest, Nevaeh, I am as tired as a dog but the work must go on, right?"

"Yes, sir, and you are doing a wonderful job."

Detective Dennis blushes at my last comment. It is the first time I have stopped to notice his smile. His teeth are actually perfect. I cannot believe that after so many weeks we are having such a very human moment. I guess we have both started to see each other as individuals: before I was just one of his many caseloads and he was just the crass Detective who caught my case and I had to tolerate, but today he is a person and so am I. It has made a huge difference, and it has really helped me to finalize my decision.

Because, despite what I had said to Imka, I had still been hesitant. I hadn't wanted to put my life in the hands of a man I didn't trust, but I believe that I've just experienced a breakthrough with him. I can sense in his energy that he genuinely wants to help and he is deeply invested in this case, not only to arrest the Barrons, but to also restore my memories.

"So, Nevaeh, have you given much thought to what I said yesterday?"

And there we go, he's back to the business at hand. He is as constant as the river flowing outside my window. I smile because his consistency is reassuring, especially in these uncertain times. He smiles at me as well and it is a genuine smile, one filled with hope.

"Yes, sir, I have."

"Are you in?"

"Yes, I am in!"

"That's great! For what it's worth I know this decision didn't come easily given the short time we have to work with, so I really appreciate your courage."

"I don't know about courage. It is more a case of desperation on my part."

"Well, whatever it is, you are a really brave young woman and your family should be proud. Plus, sometimes desperation yields courage."

"Thank you, I appreciate you saying that and I am sure they would as well."

"Let's get started. I will get the Doc in here so that I can prep both of you at the same time. Therefore, we won't waste anytime going around in circles. Does that sound like a plan?"

"Yes sir, it does."

"Okay, I'll be right back."

A few minutes later Imka is back with the detective. She seems really tired. I can't believe the disturbance I have created in these people's well-ordered lives. No wonder Robin called me a drama queen, and although it was said in jest, it is a very apt description of the life I have lived over the last few months, from what I can gather from my diary.

"Oh Imka, you look tired!"

"I am, I was on the phone until late last evening with one of my colleagues in South Africa because of the time difference. They are six hours ahead of us—seven in the fall."

And here I was thinking that it was my fault that she was tired.

"I was talking to him about your case."

So it was my fault.

"I had an idea about how to help release your suppressed memories and I needed a second opinion. I'll explain it to you after we've debriefed with the Detective.

"Let's go to my office so we can talk there."

We all march out the room. We go, not to her office, but the cafeteria. The detective reveals, "On my way to call Imka a thought occurred to me, that now that Rayva has access to you, he might have bugged your room."

"What?" I am truly shocked by this.

"Now, mind you, it's just a hunch—but given what we know I thought it might not be prudent to reveal this plan in a room that he has easy access to. Also, he's been in Imka's office, so I just prefer to be cautious until we can do a sweep of your room for bugs. Your office as well, Imka."

"And what if you find it? What will happen then? Plus, wouldn't we have seen him place a bug somewhere in the room?"

"No, not necessarily. There are really small devices nowadays that are easy to place and hard to trace. The protocol would be to leave it, because if we removed it they would realize that we are on to them. You and everyone who enters that room would just have to be very careful. Either that or we would try to move you to a different room on some pretext about your changing health requirements."

"This gets more complicated by the minute, doesn't it?" Imka verbalizes exactly what I am thinking.

"I'm afraid it does, and this is exactly what happens when you are dealing with organized crime. The dynamics are fluid so they are always changing. They are seemingly always ahead of us so we have to step up our game."

By this time we have passed all the rooms with their high single beds and their shared windows, and take the elevator to the ground level where the ICU and the cafeteria are located. I am blessed to be able to have a room all to myself. I can hear all the sounds from the machines in the ICU from the hallway.

I definitely do not miss the ongoing beeping that I have come to associate with the Emergency Department. At this time of the day, the cafeteria is usually full of hungry patrons: visitors, hospital staff, and patients alike, and today is no exception. I am doubtful that we should have this specific conversation here. Dennis reads my expression.

"It is an ideal setting to have our talk. We'll just choose a table out of the way and order some food. Therefore, if anyone is watching, it will look like three people having lunch just like everyone else here. So what would you like, ladies, my treat?"

"I'm not sure. I'll have to look and see what they have."

"What about you, Imka, what would you like?"

"I am not really hungry so I'll have a chicken salad."

"Alright, let's go order our food and meet back here, then we'll find a table."

"I'll go with you, Nevaeh, to help you choose. All this might be a little overwhelming for you."

"I do feel overwhelmed. All the people, and the noise. Plus, I have not had a choice in my menu options in a while, so this might take some time and I know we don't have the luxury of time."

She links our arms and we walk together to place our order in the crowded room. I eventually settle on a steak and cheese sandwich which I thoroughly enjoy after months of eating hospital food. No offense, but there is no cheesy goodness in their meals. I devour my sandwich so fast and ferociously that Dennis must have feared for the packaging.

"Would you like another one, Nevaeh?"

I am so embarrassed, but his concern is both humorous and well-meaning so I laugh with my head thrown back. I feel like I have not laughed like that in a while. They both join me in laughing but Dennis is a whole lot more cautious than Imka and me. That good belly laugh breaks the proverbial ice so that we can get to work. Imka finishes her salad and Dennis drains the final drops of coffee from his disposable paper cup. I take a moment to look around so many seemingly unbothered faces, strangers becoming friends—much like our small group—long-time friends having lunch, people who seem to be on a date. It is such a refreshing change of scenery from my dreary and dull hospital room. I feel like I could just sit here for hours and watch people enjoy a meal, a cup of coffee, a bottle of water or just a good conversation shared among friends or colleagues.

There's something in me that has missed this so much. I feel so content here, more content than I have felt in a while. It must be all the positive energy in the room, despite the setting; so much so, that I feel like whatever it is that Dennis is going to request, I could actually do and do it well. He must have read my thoughts again as he clears his throat and begins.

"Well let's get started, ladies, because there is no telling when Rayva is going to come back to visit Nevaeh and above all else we do not want to spook him. We don't want him running back to dear old dad, who on further investigation we've come to realize is the head honcho. In the greater scheme of things Rayva is just a small fry. We believe that this is a deliberate act, not only to protect his only heir but because Rain is a smart man. He knows that he will not be able to continue what he is doing forever, so he has shielded Rayva. If anything happens, he will take the fall and Rayva will be left to take care of the family business."

"So, does that mean Rayva is not involved?" I feel a tinge of excitement to hear that the man I married is not a monster.

"Oh yes, he is just as culpable, but they have made a contingency plan designed to protect him in case things goes south."

"Oh, okay."

Imka sees the disappointment in my eyes and takes my hand. But I think they are both wondering how involved I have been in the Barrons' misdeeds. I am wondering myself. I really would like to announce my innocence but I don't know for sure. Now I am wondering if this plan of Dennis' is going to land me in jail as well. But he did say that I would get full immunity and full citizenship as well, so I guess they might have ruled me out as a suspect, or just maybe that comparatively I am a smaller fry than Rayva.

I don't know how Dennis keeps doing this; he must really understand humans a great deal because he addresses my unease: "Nevaeh, I don't think you have any cause for concern, because you are not named in any documents, you have not been mentioned in anything that would link you to any wrongdoing. So I think you're in the clear. Rayva, for what it's worth, might have been shielding you from all of this."

"I guess you're right. Thanks for saying that."

"You're welcome! Now let's get down to business."

"Nevaeh, maybe if we finish in good time, we could go for a short walk outside. Would you like that?" Imka comes to my rescue again.

I can't contain my enthusiasm. "Yes, I would definitely like that."

They both smile at me like very loving parents.

"This is the plan." Dennis says this in hushed tones while instinctively glancing around. This time his voice doesn't sound weird—not at all. He sounds more practised in this type of covert operation. "We are going to replace Nevaeh's right earring with a similar one containing a tiny microphone that will be recording all your conversations. It is completely voice activated so when you're going about your regular business it will not be recording. By that I mean taking a shower, answering the call of nature, none of those things will be recorded. They have designed it in such a unique way that it will not be intrusive in your regular life. But another benefit is that in addition to the agent that will be in close proximity at all times, at the first sign of danger if you say *that's strange* three times in quick succession that will be our signal to come get you immediately. Like I said, someone will always be listening, and not too far away either, so you will be protected. If you ever feel unsafe at any point, just say that and we will come rescue you right away. Is that clear? I want you to understand that your safety is paramount and we're not going to ever throw you to the lions, walk away and look the other way while they devour you."

"Yes, I understand."

"Do you have any questions?"

"I do actually."

"Yes?"

"What type of things are you looking to record?"

"Anything that might be incriminating or might lead to other things that are incriminating."

"I see."

"So does she have to do anything? Are there specific things that she needs to say to get Rayva talking?"

"That's a great question, Imka. Actually at this point there's nothing specific that she needs to ask. Primarily because we don't ever want Rayva to think that she is seeking information or trying to lead him in a specific direction. The fact that she has amnesia is a great win for us, because she can innocently ask questions. We are hoping that in his quest and hurry to help you retrieve your memory, he might be more liberal and open to sharing general information about your lives which we might be able to use to link the Barrons to our investigation. So, Nevaeh, you never have to feel pressured to question him about his business or work. If the conversation goes there naturally, that's fine, but you do not need to ask about that. The important thing is not to tip him off or piss him off, so he doesn't do anything rash."

"So don't tip him off and don't piss him off. Got it."

We all laugh at that.

"I will offer you this one tip, though. Rayva Barron is a man who is quite comfortable with being in charge; it is what he is accustomed to. So try not to fight with him. Also, use your feminine wiles to create a place of comfort. Try not to frustrate him either. Let him feel safe with you. The last time you flinched at his touch; please try not to do that because if you are combative he will be defensive, so he might not be in the mood to share."

"So you mean I have to sleep with him?" I lean forward and whisper.

"Well, if it gets to that—after all, he is your husband whom you've not seen in a good while. That might lead him to a level of intimacy, to the point where he shares things with his wife."

"But I don't know him. How can I sleep with him?"

"It might not come to that, but be prepared. That's all I'm saying."

"Alright! Well, if there are no more questions, I will take you up on that offer to go for a walk, Imka."

"Well, I have one last question. What is my role in all of this? You said I will have to work with Nevaeh?"

"Just that you continue to be her doctor, keep a close eye on things and update us if you notice or overhear anything suspicious. I think since Rayva has met you and has some type of rapport with you, he won't be suspicious if you are hanging around Nevaeh, so to speak. Also, we wanted to include you because our aim as well is to aid in Nevaeh recovering her memory, which might be more beneficial than any sting operation."

"Got it."

"Okay ladies, since we're done here, let's go for a walk. The walk and the fresh air might be helpful to all of us, but more so to Nevaeh."

With that we leave the cafeteria crowd behind. Seemingly just three friends who came for a bite like everyone else, had a great conversation but now must of necessity be on their way to other appointments, other meetings.

CHAPTER SEVENTEEN

As it turns out, the stroll had been inspired. The late afternoon sun, people going about their regular lives, was a welcome change from being in the hospital all the time; so wholesome. Somehow my head feels clearer and my purpose more well-defined. It turns out that Detective Dennis is quite the conversationalist after all. This is definitely why we should never judge a person by their shell, because it is the soul that counts: indeed it is the soul that's paramount.

While they spoke, I listened, at first enraptured by the sights and sounds around me but then I slipped away and started to tune into myself. At first it felt weird delving into my mind—being both present and absent at the same time—but I felt a compulsion to be alone with my thoughts, to dissect my feelings. As if this moment, where I was at this time in my life—in both a physical and metaphorical sense—was all that mattered. I was surprisingly not discomfited by things to come racing ahead in my mind, neither was I inundated by things that had happened; I was both present and available to myself, to my emotions, and it somehow just felt right.

Eventually, I will need to discuss this with Imka. I don't know if I'll have the words, but Imka is really good at sorting through feelings so I am sure she'll understand.

When it is time to return to my room I am not at all bothered, because all of a sudden I no longer feel like I am in prison and that's because I am no longer a prisoner to myself. I have momentarily given myself permission to just be, and it feels organic, like my soul has been nourished. The detective leaves us at the entrance to the hospital and gets into a yellow cab from there. I ask Imka, "Where is his car?"

She smiles and explains, "It is pointless to have a car in New York. On this side, the traffic is not too bad, there are still trees and fewer people, but in the city it's a different experience all together."

"You mean there are a lot more people in the city than we passed today?"

"Oh yes, this is not even a fraction of the people who live and work in the city. For obvious reasons the hospital has been left in this location, but you never know what's going to happen next, or when."

"What do you mean?"

"Well, New York City is growing at a rapid rate, with more and more people moving here for school and for work, so eventually of necessity they might need to build more houses near the hospital and its environs."

"I really hope they don't cut down the trees. I don't think I knew before today how much I love trees, how happy they make me."

She smiles at that last statement. By then we are back on my floor.

"You must be exhausted. I'll just walk you to your room so you can get some rest."

"Actually, I am not tired at all, and there's something I wanted to talk to you about. If you are up to it that is. I know you said you were exhausted earlier."

"No, I'm good. It turns out that the walk was all I needed to clear my head and shake off the fatigue. I was actually planning to get some paperwork done before leaving for the day."

"Okay, well, if you don't mind I will walk with you to your office."

"Are you sure? You've had a pretty hectic day."

"Yes, I'm sure."

"Let's go then."

We make a U-turn at my door, once again linking arms, and head towards her office. By the time it takes to get in the elevator and sit in her yellow chairs, the digital clock on her desk flashes 3:33. I don't think I have ever seen that before.

"Look, Imka! Look at the time!" I scream, afraid it will change before she has a chance to witness it. She laughs and seems just as excited to see it as I am.

"That's amazing, Nevaeh!"

"Have you ever seen that before?"

"Yes, I have."

"What do you think it means—it must mean something, right?"

"That is generally referred to as number sequencing and there are schools of thought that postulate that seeing specific numbers in a sequence has great significance."

"Oh, really?"

"Yes, some people believe that they are angel numbers, reminding us that we are never alone as angels are watching over us, or that we are about to either create real change or make a change in our life."

"As Robin would say, that's awesome!"

"Indeed it is, Nevaeh. Would you like some water?"

"Yes, please."

"Okay, I'll be right back."

"I'll be here."

Once again, I don't know how far away this fridge is but she is back in a flash. We both have a few sips and remain quiet for a moment, just to let the instant of peace and tranquility symbolized by the yellow chairs and the number sequence wash over us.

When the time is right, Imka asks, "So, Nevaeh, what did you want to talk to me about?"

I like the fact that she doesn't clear her throat before speaking. I have come to despise that action so immensely. For some reason it makes me anxious. The other thing that makes me anxious is people pacing, not walking, or moving around to get things done, but just pacing back and forth. I don't even know how or why but it just does.

"Yes, I wanted to talk to you about something which I have been experiencing."

"Alright."

She sits back in her chair, not in a slouching way, not too relaxed either, but a posture that indicates that she is here and she is listening.

"So, I don't really know how to explain this. I have said it to Sandy and Robin, you know, just to clarify my thoughts." I take a deep breath and another sip of my very cool and refreshing water.

She nods and smiles, encouraging me to continue.

"I have been experiencing what I call echoes."

I look at her to see if there is understanding in her eyes. But all I see is encouragement, so I tread on. She's done this many times before, where instead of asking questions to lead the talk she remains silent and offers encouragement through a smile or a nod.

"By this I mean that sometimes people might say something or perform an action and I feel like I have experienced my *reaction* to their action before."

"You mean like déjà vu?"

"No, not quite. This is kinda hard to explain. But basically, it is not the situation that I react to, but I somehow react to how I felt at the time of a similar situation."

I reach for my water bottle and ask simultaneously, "Does that make sense?"

"Yes, I think I get it. By that you mean, you don't necessarily remember the situation itself but you remember how you felt during a similar experience in the past, so it is the emotion that is attached to the situation that you currently react to."

"Exactly. So, for want of a better word, I have been calling these experiences echoes, but I sense them rather than remember them. They sometimes feel like little tremors in my body."

"That's great, Nevaeh. I think what is happening is that your body is aligning with your mind and soul so you're being fed information in a specific way that your mind knows you can relate to. Apparently, you have always been in touch with your emotions, and at any given moment you know and understand how you're feeling, even if you can do nothing about it. Your body is aware of this, so it has found a way to communicate with you and give you what you need in the moment. That's actually brilliant!"

"It is?"

"Yes! I think it means that, by tapping into your rawest and purest emotions, it's the only way you're going to recover your memories."

"See, that's exactly what I was thinking this morning as well. Remember when you spoke to me about journaling and I said no? Well, I think am ready to do it now."

"That is good to know. Remember this morning when I told you that I had a talk with my colleague? That's exactly what we spoke about. But we were more interested in you recording the experiences that make you feel anxious—"

"Or triggered?"

"Exactly! But listen to you now! I think your plan is better, and instead of recording the experience itself, I think you should record the emotions that come with the experience."

"That's what I was thinking, too."

"This is indeed a breakthrough, Nevaeh. But the other piece that I would add is, remember when we were talking about your being present, and by that I mean generally? As human beings we tend to avoid harsh emotions by not being present, by distracting ourselves with work, with play, through various substances; just in a bid to not feel sometimes. Because emotions are sometimes tough to deal with. So over the years, as humanity has evolved, we have learned to practise different avoidance strategies. But the research is now showing that sitting with ourselves, through yoga and meditation, are all great strategies to aid in stress management and just life in general. Nevaeh, in your specific case, I would therefore suggest that you not only record the emotions, but I also want you to sit with them a while, no matter how harsh and painful. Be present and available to the emotions, listen to your body, observe the work that that specific emotion is doing in your body. Do not push back against the pain, but instead push back against the desire to push back against the pain. Lean into the pain, let it guide you, let it teach you.

And I am not in any way encouraging sadistic behaviours, but I think in your specific case this will help to unlock memories. I also believe that the memories are intertwined with some very strong emotions. Because you, me—humanity in general—have been programmed to avoid them, so that is what comes naturally, and that is what you actively do, without even being aware that you're doing it: when the memory comes, linked with the emotion, you block them both, because the emotion feels too intense. It feels almost like the situation just happened yesterday, so you block it, and by blocking it you delay the process of recovery. I think quite possibly that will be the solution to getting your memories back. Do you see what I mean, Nevaeh?"

"Actually, I do. I think I understand clearly what you're saying. Because it happened to me last night."

"What do you mean? What happened last night?"

"Well, Rayva brought my diary, that's where I got the idea to take up journaling. So I read some of the entries, but not all of them; plus, some of the pages are missing…"

"What do you mean, missing? As in someone has crossed out the entries or are the pages gone?"

"The pages are gone."

"What do you think happened to them?"

"I don't know, and I didn't want to mention it to Rayva because I did not want to start a fight."

She sighs and captures an unruly strand of hair and puts it back into place with the other well-behaved ones.

"That's interesting, though. Do you think you should allow Detective Dennis to have a look at it? It might be useful, seeing that you don't really remember the events, they might find something that might help—"

"No!" I yell, scaring myself in the process.

"You don't have to, Nevaeh," Imka says, gently and calmly.

"I know, and I might show it to him. But I think I want to finish reading it first," I say, and look away. I wish she had a window with a view of the river, with a view of anything. So I just look around the small room at the many certificates on the wall.

"Is there something else, Nevaeh, that you're not saying or don't want to say?"

I fight back tears. But I have come this far, I might as well say it. What if it will help me remember? But what if she judges me?

"I don't want you to judge me," I sob into my hands.

"No one is going to judge you, Nevaeh, especially not me. And if you're worried about me telling anyone, whatever you tell me here, as long as it is not about harming yourself or anyone else, then it is sealed by doctor-patient confidentiality. Now what is it, Nevaeh? Saying it out loud might help; you never know." She sounds so concerned it almost, just almost, breaks my resolve and my pride.

"It might, but it is so painful to say and I don't even remember when or how it happened."

"Well, no pressure, then." She passes me a tissue box from her desk. "You don't have to say it until you're ready to say it, okay?"

"Okay."

"Now what were you going to say about the diary?"

"Yes, I was going to say that reading the diary gave me the idea about journaling; to see if I could trigger my memories because of how I reacted to the strong emotions in my diary."

"That's a very good idea, Nevaeh."

With that said, I feel the need to flee, to flee her office, to flee the moment. But then another thought hits me: that I cannot keep running from pain, suppressing it, and running from myself. Quite possibly running is what got me into this situation in the first place. Running is possibly why I married Rayva, why I ended up in the river: just to escape my situation.

I stand to leave and Imka stands with me: solid, stable Imka, who is always gracious. But I am riveted to the spot, like nails have suddenly appeared and pinned me to the shiny square tiles. I cannot move. Maybe my body is telling me that it is time. Not only time, but the most opportune time, to speak my truths regardless of the repercussions. Maybe my body is just tired of running. Maybe my mind is saying it is high time I stop running. It is time I face situations like a big girl.

My mind goes back to the story of Esther in the Bible that Robin had given me. I thought at the time I read it that she should have run away and hidden in the palace; certainly, there must have been many places to conceal herself, rather than take on such a mammoth task. But she didn't. She searched inside herself and decided that *the Lord had brought her to the Kingdom for such a time as this*. She trusted God's timing and that made all the difference to her and to her people. Maybe it is my time to trust the timing, to do something right, something that the generations to come can be proud of. I need to stay put, stop running, and slow down in order to accomplish something much bigger than myself.

I sit back down on Imka's yellow, soft chair that seems to cuddle me, welcoming me back with open arms. I help myself to a tissue from the box and blow my nose, and without saying a word Imka takes her seat in her yellow chair across from mine. The blue chairs are gone, returned to their place of origin, so it's just the yellow chairs that remain. I compose myself the best way I can. I sit erect in my chair, presenting an image of poise and a composure that I do not possess. And just like that I hear myself telling her what is probably one of the darkest secrets of my life.

"Remember how you said that gasoline was found in my system?"

She nods, encouraging me with a faint smile. Her dimple doesn't even join in this time.

"Well, my diary states that I didn't have any charcoal to… ah… eat… when I was stressed out. Apparently, that was my way of dealing with stress. Charcoal. Not all the time…. But just sometimes. So I found a substitute…. Ah… I think that substitute might have been the gasoline."

There, I said it, and I don't want to look at her. I don't want to see the judgement in her eyes. So, I look at my hands. I touch my hair that I'd managed to enclose in a bun this morning and then look back at my hands. I know I have to just say it, at this point; there is no returning from this moment unscathed. Whatever judgements she has of me have already been set in cement, so there's no point in withholding, running, or turning away, leaving my task incomplete. This whole time Imka has been really quiet, the whole room is really quiet, like life has paused so that I can come to this point, where I can pay attention to what's real and what's true. As if all my life I have been afraid to verbalize, because saying things make them true, make them real.

Imka's office has been strategically placed in a quiet area of the hospital, so naturally there is very little disturbance by way of noise. But the silence is claustrophobic, like it's a testament to a code of silence that I have lived by all my life. I am finding it hard to breathe because all of a sudden the air is heavy.

So I have to just say it, before all the air in the room evaporates. "My babies died and I killed them."

For the first time since my confession, Imka speaks. "I am terribly sorry to hear that, Nevaeh. That's absolutely horrible. But what do you mean?"

I trust myself to look at her, to just sneak a peek, but what I see in her eyes stops me in my tracks. All I see is compassion and I can't bear it. I don't deserve her compassion. So, I tell her the truth; then maybe she'll see the kind of monster that I am and won't waste her compassion.

"I ingested the gasoline that killed not just one baby but *two!*" I basically scream the word "two."

Imka leaves her soft, cushioned chair to come around to hold me, to hug me to take the pain away. And I weep, loud, ugly, snot-filled sobs, sobs that not only shake my body but Imka's as well. However, she doesn't let me go. She holds me like a mother holds a child, like I should have held my children in my body instead of allowing them to die. I push her away and throw myself on the floor, screaming and sobbing and screaming some more.

Imka is calling out to someone and before I know it there are others in the room, lifting me and holding my feet and arms in place, and I feel a burning in my left arm. And suddenly the darkness comes, and sleep takes me to a place where I cannot harm myself or anyone else.

CHAPTER EIGHTEEN

I awake suddenly and try to look around, but I am blinded by the blazing lights hanging over my bed like sentinels standing guard in case I attempt to flee. I cover my eyes and allow them to slowly adjust to the glare. I look around and I am back in my room. I am not alone. I look closely and I realize that it is Rayva. He is sleeping in the grey chair. He looks so uncomfortable and so out of place in this small grey room, in the even smaller grey chair. It is not that he is corpulent, not at all, he is tall and slender, but even in his sleep he fills a room, he takes up space. I think of calling his name, rousing him from his slumber, but then I think, what's the point? I don't really have anything, pressing or otherwise, to say to him. So I just close my eyes and let sleep take me away again. They must have given me a lower dosage of Ativan or maybe something of lesser strength because I am not as groggy and my mind doesn't feel as heavy as it did the last time. Sleep at this point is a mere suggestion, an invitation, insinuating peace. I graciously accept and momentarily

I am asleep. I know I am asleep but I am fully aware of the twists and turns of my dream world. Have I always known how to navigate my dream realm?

I float in this space and I like it. I cover long distances and I visit faraway locations. I pause above a river, big and beautiful, with lush green trees covering it everywhere. It has small cascading waterfalls. I want to dive in, but somehow I know that this is neither the time nor the place; maybe next time, I tell myself. I continue on my nocturnal excursion.

I get to a small house that sits on top of a hill. Instinctively I know I can pause here. Here I can rest. I go through the roof, not the door. That's the funny thing about dreams; any and everything is possible. I see people moving about: two women, mature women, and an older gentleman. But they are not the souls I am here to visit, because in a room off to the side are two other women, one lying on the bed, covered under a light white sheet that is the colour of her hair, and the other sitting in a rocking chair.

They both smile as I enter as if happy to see me. They feel very familiar, this whole place like I have been here before. They do not use their mouths but I can hear them clearly. The older one says, *how are you child?* While the not-so-old one, beaming with pride, says, *I have missed you, my child.* I didn't notice before, when I entered, drawn by their aura, but there are two babies in the room. They are peacefully asleep, one swaddled on the bed, closer to wall in the corner, while the other sits comfortably in the arms of the woman in the rocking chair. I tell them without using my mouth *I haven't been fine in a long while but I am fine now.* They both smile, one a toothless smile and the other a gap-toothed smile.

Then the woman in the chair, the one with the gap teeth says, *it is well, my child, because a people who know their God and know themselves shall do great exploits.* In that instant, peace washes over me and I know that my visit is over because I have heard, accepted and internalized what I came to this place to hear. There is no judgment here in this place, only peace. I could dwell here forever but I know it is time to go; it is time to do great exploits. I wave my farewell and they nod in agreement as they seem to move in harmony with each other.

The next time I awake I am hit by a different light, the natural light streaming through the window of my hospital room. This light is less harsh on my eyes and I welcome it. I sit up in bed, covered in peace, and look around me. The grey chair is empty and I am alone, so I take the time to memorize my dream, every minute detail: the smells, the sounds, the feels. I soak up everything, especially the feelings. I should write it down but I don't want to, I want to hold it in my mind. I want to hold on to the feeling of peace that has chaperoned me back from my sojourn, to nail it down in my memory so it never escapes. The memory of the little house on the hill will become my happy place.

"Good morning. You look radiant, my lady."

It is Rayva, and he ismiling at me with his perfect teeth.

"Good morning, thank you. I feel good."

"That's wonderful," he says, embracing me with his eyes.

"I woke up last night and saw you in the chair. Why? What happened?"

"Just as I came out the elevator, they were wheeling you in here. Apparently, you had a session with Imka and you had another episode. They wanted me to leave but I refused, I decided I wasn't leaving—not this time. I am so sorry you had a rough day…."

"That's very sweet, Rayva. Thank you! I really appreciate that."

"You are welcome, and that's what husbands are for. You might not recall this but many times I have told you that no matter what, I am here for the long haul. The forever after!"

I feel my face go red but I don't look away. We just stare at each other, me soaking up this moment, adding it to my new collection of blissful memories. Memorizing every feature of his pulchritudinous face. *Oh my, where did that word come from?* However, since life necessitates that all good things must come to an end, we are disturbed by the nurse coming to check my vitals.

"Good morning, sleepy head. How are you?"

It is Philomena, with her warm smile, which she offers to me first and then to Rayva.

"I am doing well. I feel rested."

"That's good. Okay, I will just take your blood pressure and then the doctor will be here to check on you. After that we will get some breakfast into you. Does that sound like a plan…?"

Rayva interrupts her: "Instead of *your* breakfast, can I just take her down to the cafeteria, and enjoy a good breakfast with my beautiful wife?"

Philomena pretends to take umbrage. "What are you saying, Mr. Barron? That our breakfast is no good?"

Rayva struggles to explain. Philomena and I laugh at how serious he looks, trying to clear himself.

"Don't worry. Let's hear what the doctor says first."

"Okay." He sighs with relief.

Half an hour later, I am showered, changed, and sitting in the cafeteria with my husband. However, something else is sitting with us. I fight it because what I have done and what I am doing is for the good of the cause; the exploits that I need to accomplish.

As soon as I had slipped into the bathroom to shower, I realized that someone else was there. I turned to leave and a nurse whom I had never seen before stopped me and in almost a whisper declared: "Hey, don't leave and don't scream."

"Who are you?"

"I am agent Rose Marie Chambers, and I am here to replace one of your earrings with this one." She reveals an earring identical to mine, yet which is not mine.

Overtaken as I was with peace, I had momentarily forgotten Detective Dennis' plan. I wanted to say no to agent Chambers, but I knew I couldn't. So we'd switched my earring before I got into the shower and by the time I had stepped into the cold wet shower, she was gone. Hence the guilt sitting next to us; more so, next to me. But I decide to just allow myself to sit with my emotions, instead of repressing them or resisting. In turn, and in time, I will find a way to befriend guilt and make him work for me. But for now, I will just enjoy my breakfast and learn my husband again: learn his moods, learn his mind, learn his ways and his triggers. Maybe that will help in this thing that I have to do. Because who knows what role, if any, I have played in the disappearance of these innocent people. I probably need to correct a wrong that I have quite possibly helped to inflict. Thankfully, guilt doesn't stay for very long, because where there is peace there is no guilt. But I do suspect that guilt will come and go from time to time. That's fine; we will learn to live in tandem.

*　*　*

"Hi, Imka, Philomena said you wanted to see me. Is now a good time?"

"Hi, Nevaeh, good to see you. Please give me ten minutes to finish this session and I'll see you, okay?"

"Alright."

I wait outside in the tiny waiting area. A professional like Imka sure deserves a bigger space. Pretty soon I hear voices. It's Imka and her patient, a short white guy who is balding from his crown. I have seen him around; he always seems so shy, with his head leaning to the side. Some people have real problems, I guess. Finally, it's my turn.

"Come in, Nevaeh. Thanks for waiting."

"No problem."

"So how have you been feeling?" she asks, as we both take our seats, Imka behind the desk and me across from her. The yellow chair seems to welcome me back again, bearing no animosity from the last time I was here.

"It is so amazing the difference that a day makes. I feel good, to be honest. I think I'm in a much better place than yesterday."

I share with her the reason for the peace that swaddles me; at least a part of my dream, about the two women and the babies.

"What do you think it means, Nevaeh?"

"I think those ladies could be my mother and grandmother, and those babies are my babies that I lost. I think my mind is trying to make sense of my losing all of them, or maybe God is saying that they're all at peace so I shouldn't punish myself. I must forgive myself. I am more leaning towards the latter. What do you think?"

"I agree, because compared to yesterday, you seem so tranquil."

"Thank you. I feel at peace."

We are quiet for a few moments, just soaking up the significance.

At an appropriate time Imka asks, "Still no memories?"

"No, not yet. But I am being patient and letting them come when they're good and ready."

"Excellent! That's the best way to approach things, because though they say that procrastination is the thief of time, and though they are correct, rushing a process is just as dangerous. They also say: more haste less speed."

"Thank you, and sorry about last time. I was just so overwhelmed I couldn't help myself."

"That's quite alright. That's what I wanted to talk to you about. I wanted to discuss the last session in which you spoke about your babies. Again, I am so sorry for your loss."

"Thank you—it still feels weird. It must have happened; it was written in my diary and in my handwriting but I just can't remember the event. However, I do feel the sadness that's attached to the event, so I guess it did happen to me."

"I wanted us to go over some strategies to deal with the grief because, as Mooji said, feelings are like visitors: they come and go. So currently you're experiencing peace, and that's awesome, but we need to prepare you for the next time sadness comes, guilt comes, or any such negative emotions choose to visit."

"Who is Mooji?"

"He is a spiritual teacher who was born in Jamaica, went to the UK, traveled to India and now shares his views about spirituality with anyone who will listen."

"Okay, nice. I will check him out at some point."

As always she is warm and encouraging; no judgement. I am not even sure I deserve her kindness. I don't even know why I was dreading meeting with her today.

"I wanted to show you something; come with me."

"What is it?"

"It's more like a demonstration, Nevaeh. Follow me to my kitchenette."

"So this is where you keep the bottled water that miraculously appears all the time".

"Yes." We both laugh like old friends.

She takes out a glass from the top shelf of the small cupboard, places it on the counter and pours a bottle of water into it, until it spills all over the spotless floor.

"What's going on, Imka? Why are you doing that? Stop!"

"Nevaeh, that's how emotions are if we keep them bottled up for too long; eventually, they overflow and there will be a mess everywhere. Do you see what I mean?"

"Yes, I do." She grabs a mop from a corner of the room and wipes up the mess.

We return to her cozy office and talk at length, first about my ingesting charcoal, and then the gasoline.

"That was a coping mechanism, your way of dealing with complicated emotions in a complex world; trying to take charge of situations in your life. Therefore, now we need to brainstorm strategies for you to implement in stressful situations, seeing that stress is a natural part of the human condition. There is absolutely no way of getting rid of stress altogether. We just have to find ways of dealing with it so that it doesn't overwhelm us. Consequently, it is imperative that you, me, everyone finds healthy ways of dealing with stress. Does that make sense, Nevaeh?"

"Yes, it makes perfect sense. Especially because of what happened to my babies. None of that would have happened if I were more responsible."

I feel the tears threatening to overwhelm me again. But I am determined to keep them at bay. I do not want a repeat of the last time I was here, sitting in this chair. I feel the need to fight to maintain my peace.

She explains, "Of course you should take responsibility for your actions, but without punishing yourself so harshly. Show yourself the same love and compassion that you would show to someone else in a similar situation. You have to forgive yourself, Nevaeh. The way I see it, you were doing the best you could in the situation and at the time, but now that you know better you should find ways that enable you to do better. Plus, we still don't know exactly what happened yet, since you still can't remember. Did you think of asking Rayva about what happened?"

"Yes I did, but I decided against it. I still haven't finished reading my diary and since I don't know what I might discover, I just don't want to bring it up with him yet."

"I guess that makes sense. But remember in all of this sting operation, your health, your mental wellbeing, comes first, okay?"

"Agreed!"

"Do you have any questions for me, Nevaeh?"

"No, I think everything is clear. But I have to admit that talking about my pent-up emotions has really helped; I don't feel as hollow anymore, especially with regards to my babies that died. Thank you."

"You are welcome! That's why I am here. The first day we met, I promised that I was going to do everything in my power to help you get well again, and I meant it."

I leave her office feeling like a huge weight has lifted from my shoulders, with a secret promise to myself that if Imka is committed to helping me get well, then I should be just as committed. The next few days are spent in a flurry of activity. I go for short walks, not treading too far from the hospital, sometimes with Rose Marie, other times with Sandy, Robin or Imka. The only person I haven't seen lately is the detective. Rosey, as we have been calling her, has said it is best he stays away so that Rayva doesn't become suspicious. So far he hasn't said anything incriminating, although I can't be sure because I don't know what the FBI knows and I don't know how much I know. I still can't remember, but I am at peace with that aspect of my life. I have accepted that when the time is right and when I am ready the memories will return. In the meantime, I am making new memories, taking my good days along with my bad days while applying a one-day-at-a-time methodology. I haven't opened my diary again, not since the last time. I tell myself that I will, soon, but I am not going to rush. I'll take my time and do it when I am ready.

It's a rainy night and after Rayva and I leave the cafeteria he decides to return to his hotel and call it a night. I agree because I feel kind of tired myself. He wants us to go out for dinner at a more upscale establishment than the cafeteria, and like Philomena I take umbrage, but I don't think I am ready for that type of adventure. He hasn't brought up taking me back to Canada, which I am grateful for. He says I look happy, like when we had just started dating, so I guess he is content to stay here a while because he believes the treatment is working. However, I did overhear him engaging in a very heated telephone conversation with his dad. I asked him what happened and he said I shouldn't worry about it. But I think his dad is getting frustrated with Rayva and me being in New York; he is pressuring Rayva to take me home.

Every time I think that he might just come over here and create such a ruckus that we have to leave, I feel a huge lump in my throat. I have to do my deep breathing exercises and do the hand shake (extending my arms and shaking them vigorously), releasing the tension in my body before it expands and takes on a life of its own. One of the many strategies that Imka and I have come up with to relieve stress, and so far it has been working. I just have to remain consistent.

By the time I get into my bed, it is pouring outside. The night nurse comes to check my blood pressure and to inform me that Rayva had called to say he had gotten to his hotel safely. All the nurses and a few of the doctors have a crush on him. I have to admit that I feel really special and lucky that this hunk of a man has chosen me for his wife. I still don't really trust him, but the more time I spend with him the harder it is for me to associate him with any wrongdoing. Even Sandy has come around to saying that *he is quite a catch*. She doesn't trust him either, I can see it in her body language when he's around, because we still don't exactly know what happened the night I fell into the river.

I watch the rain beat against my window for a good while, but the lightning and thunder scare me so I have to close the blinds. The wind is loud as well, as if all these elements are competing for pre-eminence. I think the rain is the superior force because it feeds the rivers and the lakes, and those bodies house many organisms that wouldn't survive without the rain. I am tired but not really sleepy, and I don't want to watch TV because they only have two channels: sports and news. Rayva had offered to pay for other channels but what's the point, since I don't watch TV enough to make it count? What I really want is to go shopping for a few novels to pass the time. I guess tonight is the night I will return to my diary.

CHAPTER NINETEEN

Nevaeh Francis Barron (a few weeks before Christmas)
I've only been here for a few years, this is like my 4th Christmas in Canada and believe me it is not the same. I miss the food back home more than any other season. The Barrons are black but most definitely not Jamaicans. They are 7th generation Canadians from Nova Scotia. Their wealth comes from successive generations working hard to ensure that they leave a legacy. That makes me feel so horrible, thinking that I might not be able to give Rayva children, but these days he is so perfectly distracted that children are the last thing on his mind. Well, at least his sister Summer is pregnant. I can't even bear to look at her, which makes me feel so bad because she has always been so nice to me. When I just came, it was her job to take me shopping and get me acclimatized as Rain called it. I don't even know how I would have managed without all her help. Now all I do is avoid her, now when she needs me the most, just like I started avoiding Ms. Linda when she got sick. It is not fair that she or this family should suffer so much, not them. They are the kindest people I know. They seem like a version of my family back home, the rich version. It seems like all I do is avoid, avoid,

avoid, avoid. I avoid talking to Rayva about the babies and Rain has been extra nice since then so I avoid him as well. I don't need pity. He says some things, the most important ones take time.

(Christmas)
I just wish they would allow me to cook sometimes. But they say it wouldn't be fair, me taking away the chef's job. I wish I could just go home for a visit, even for a week, but Rayva says he needs me here. I fully understand.
His mom, Ms. Linda, died last week, melanoma stage four.
She went so suddenly; no one could have predicted that such a vibrant, beautiful woman would have been gone so soon. I feel like I've lost my mother twice. Not many people have been as blessed as me to have had a mother-in-law who loves them unconditionally. I did not deserve her love. Each time I lost a baby, she moved into the room across from mine, in our wing of the house, so that she could take care of me. I don't know why someone as horrible as myself should be so blessed and highly favoured. To say that I miss her smile and her laugh is an understatement.
Both Rain and Rayva seem to blame themselves. I guess they are suffering from survivor's guilt. I know exactly how that feels.
I keep wondering how come the products that Rayva and Rain are making using the chrysanthemums couldn't help her. Didn't they say that it had worked on other people? Why not her? I guess when it's your time to go it's just your time. Plus, I think the doctor found it too late. Poor Ms. Linda suffered so much. I couldn't stand it, so I stayed away. It's strange how few people attended the funeral, considering how many people they know.
Anyways, it wouldn't be fair to leave Rayva at a time like this. He seems so fragile, like a little boy these days, always clinging to me. I cannot imagine what Rain must be going through right now. I just stay away from him because up until now I didn't even know that he had a short temper. Losing his wife must have triggered it.

February
I didn't write through January because there was just too much going on and so much sadness, sadness seems to be sitting on top of the house. Summer

lost her baby, their first. I avoid her even more than before now. I don't know what to say to her. At least her baby died of natural causes; meanwhile, I killed mine and Rayva's.

To say that February is a cold month would be the understatement of the year. Thankfully, it is the shortest month. Things have definitely not been the same since Ms. Linda died. That beautiful soul, gone too soon. To think that I yelled at her the week before she died and told her to mind her own business. I wish I could take it all back. Rayva says she understood that the loss of our second child was seriously impacting me.

Anyways, I am really concerned about Rain. Since Ms. Linda died he is a changed person. The sweet, mild-mannered man has become pure evil. It seems like anger and pain have made him bitter. How is that possible? I literally feel darkness overshadow me whenever he walks into a room. How could someone change so abruptly, with no warning? Also, he's gotten so moody that you can never tell what mood he's going to be in. These days, I just keep my distance. Especially because I've got my own problems.

(What THE What ???)

There was so much confusion today that I don't even know what to think anymore. Hence, my desire to write; maybe in writing I will be able to process what is truly going on here.

The police came by. Of all the houses and all the things that could have happened here that was the last thing I was expecting. They said three bodies washed up on the river, so they're checking all the houses. I definitely did not see that coming, not in this neighbourhood. I wonder whose bodies.

I didn't hear all they had to say. Rain threw me out of the room immediately and I left because I do not want to piss him off, worse than how the police showed up at his house. That doesn't ever happen!

I wonder what is really going on. Things have been going downhill since Ms. Linda died. There's no more happy smiles at the dinner table, just coldness. I even feel this coldness creeping in between Rayva and me, which he blames me for. I had to move out of our bedroom. I cannot stand the coldness and the long silences. It is driving me to use more and more of my substitute, so I have to be by myself.

My moving out of our bedroom has really angered Rain. Yesterday he gave me a stern warning about leaving his son, his exact words were: "Do not abandon my son or you will not live to regret it." His words, not mine, and it wasn't even what he said so much as how he said it. But I really have no intentions of leaving Rayva, I just need to figure out what's going on because I find all the whispering stressful. I keep thinking that they are talking about me. For instance, yesterday I was going downstairs for lunch and I heard Rayva and Rain whispering. There's no other word for what they were doing, but as soon as I knocked the talking stopped! This never used to happen. First of all, there was no whispering, there were smiles and laughter all around. The other new thing is Rain is always clearing his throat as soon as you enter a space, he does it and the talking stops and it's always just him and Rayva now. They've removed everyone from their orbit and it's basically just the two of them against the world. It is so extremely annoying I can't begin to tell you. That and pacing! Oh my God, his pacing is driving me insane! It is making me so anxious that I can't keep a solid thought in my head. Some days I just want to leave. But where would I go? I feel so stuck in this place! This huge house and nowhere to run.

I couldn't help it. Yesterday after dinner I confronted Rayva and asked if everything is fine with the family business. He got really defensive. He wanted to know why I was asking that out of the blue and what I had heard and who I had been talking to. All this from the person who is calling me paranoid! Oh, the nerve!

I don't know how but I think I should be the one to get to the bottom of this. Things have changed so drastically that it is mindboggling. How could things go from fairy tale perfection to a continuous horror movie? Every single day there is something else, and ever since the police came we now have security guards guarding the house. Why? To what end?

I am just a simple country girl and while I might not know much, I know enough to know that something ain't right as the Americans would say. And I think I know just the plan to get the ball a rolling. Just like Prince Hamlet, I am going to act like I am crazy, caused by all the emotional stress and see what I can figure out.

WHY IS THIS HAPPENING TO ME,
TO MY NEW FAMILY?
WHY ARE THINGS LITERALLY FALLING APART?
I CAN'T STAND THE WHISPERING ANYMORE!
?????????????????????????????????????
?????????????????????????????????????
What did I just hear!
What did I just overhear!
This is definitely not happening! Something is definitely not right!
What the hell is going on?
Rayva refuses to speak to me about this and I think it is important.
Why won't he speak to me?
He says it is none of my concern. But don't I have a right to know?
Did Rayva, did I hear correctly that someone has died from the meds?
But who died from the meds?
I wonder if it was Ms. Linda?????
Something is off with both Rain and Rayva.
I need to figure out what it is.
Things have not been right since Ms. Linda died.

CHAPTER TWENTY

After reading my diary, I could not sleep. I just tossed and turned all night, and the rain didn't help; as a matter of fact, it got to the point where it was more thunder and lightning than rain. Now I am so conflicted; the Barrons are wonderful people who have just hit a bump in the road. They have lost so much. Indeed they have suffered a lot. How can I continue to betray them like this?

I should inform Detective Dennis of the things in my diary, but how can I? What would I say? This diary lacks context without my memory to fill in the blanks. Maybe I should have a talk with Rayva, but what would I say? Maybe I should just give Dennis the diary and let him sort things out. Clearly, Rayva must trust me, and I don't think he read the diary, maybe he just scanned it or he wouldn't have given it to me. Maybe they thought I was going crazy so they just left me alone. So if that's the case, what exactly did I discover, then? Could I have done something wrong in my fake insanity?

"Hi, Neva."

"Oh, hi, Sandy, I didn't see you there."

"Yes, I knocked and you didn't answer. Is everything okay?"

"When has anything been okay with me, Sandy?"

She moves closer to my bed and holds my hand.

"You've come a far way, girl, since they brought you in here. Don't give up now."

"I guess."

"Oh, before I forget. Rayva left a message that his father is flying in so they are coming to visit later today."

"What? His dad is coming?"

"Yes, that's what the message said. Why, is there a problem?"

"I don't know. It just seems weird that his father is leaving all his business ventures just to come here to see me."

"Well, maybe he has business in the city so he's just going to kill two birds with one stone."

"I guess that makes sense."

"Well, duty calls. I'll check on you later."

"Thanks, Sandy. I appreciate that so much. More than you'll ever know."

She comes back and gives me a hug.

"No problem, girl. You are my parishioner. I have to take care of you. Plus you kinda cute and you've grown on me."

"Like fungus." We both erupt into laughter.

"No, like fern in Fern Gully." And then she's gone.

I remember her telling me about Fern Gully, though—in St. Ann. It sounds like such a relaxing place. Apparently there might have been a river there once upon time.

I so wish I could talk to Sandy about all this but I can't, and even if I could, I wouldn't want to put her in any danger. It's funny how you can just meet people that you instantly click with and just know you will love them forever. Just like Rayva, despite my misgivings, I will love him forever.

Sandy leaves and I return to my thoughts. Somehow the idea

of Rain coming to visit is instantly terrifying for me. I feel my anxiety rising and he's not even here yet. I definitely need to speak to Detective Dennis. As soon as I think that, Rosey steps into the room without even knocking. She beckons me to follow her. I know she wants us to meet in the bathroom. We almost never talk about this operation in my room. I grab my toiletries and follow her to our rendezvous location. Something is up. Philomena stops me in the corridor to remind me about Rayva's message and to tell me that the neurologist wants to run a few more tests to see if there have been any changes in my brain. I honestly just say okay to all she says because right now that is the least of my concerns. It is my heart that I am most concerned about.

I get to the bathroom and she is pacing!

"Rosey, please don't pace. I can't tell you how annoying it is."

"Okay, you've said that before. I'm sorry. But something big is about to happen; that's why Rain is coming to New York. I spoke to some of our people in Ontario and they just got word that Rain has been in touch with his people, and he's coming to meet with some high-profile people in the city."

"Did they say why?"

"No, just that he plans to 'diversify his business interests'."

"But what does that mean?"

"We're not sure yet, but we have a hunch."

"And are you going to share that hunch with me?"

"No, not at this time."

"Oh I see. So I have to share all my personal conversations with my husband with you, but you cannot share your info with me. Is that how it works now?" I am yelling and I don't care.

"Shhhhhhh! Keep your voice down, Nevaeh! What has gotten into you?"

"Nothing! Absolutely nothing!"

"It's not safe, okay, we don't want to put you in harm's way."

"What do you call this?"

I say while pointing to the earring that is not my earring.

"That's for your protection as much as it is for gathering intel. You knew full well what you were getting into. You were fully briefed!" Rose sounds as frustrated as I feel.

"Was I?"

"What's that supposed to mean?"

"I don't know Rose, if that is even your real name." I stare her right in the face when I say this. "I don't know what is going on here!"

"Of course it's my real name. Nevaeh, is everything alright? Did you even get any sleep last night? Would you like to talk with Imka?"

"No, I do not want to talk with Imka. I just want you to get the hell out of here so that I can take a shower. Is that too much to ask?"

"No, I'll leave you to it."

She backs away slowly, with both hands raised, careful not to further upset me. She looks at me as if suddenly she doesn't know me anymore and I have grown two heads. I probably should not have yelled at her but this whole thing is too much for me now. While vigorously brushing my teeth I take a look at myself, a good look. My eyes are red and I look tired and haggard. I can't meet Rayva looking like this. He's bound to know that something is wrong. After all, I did turn in early last night. What have I gotten myself into? It seems like I just look for trouble and jump right in headfirst. Maybe I should have a talk with Imka before I meet up with Rayva and Rain at the same time. Maybe the FBI has got this all wrong. Maybe the Barrons are just into what they say they're into. I don't even know. I definitely need to speak with Imka, and the sooner the better.

I don't even eat the cold breakfast. I rush out the room, leaving Philomena yelling, "But you have to eat, Nevaeh!" I don't have the time nor the stomach. Something is wrong. I can feel it. I have to talk to the only other person in this building who knows what is happening. I don't even knock. I just barge right into her office. She is talking to the same shy guy from the other day. He can wait. He won't die.

"Nevaeh! What is happening?" She says surprised at my sudden appearance in her office.

"I need to talk to you right now, Imka!"

"Can't it wait, Nevaeh? I have a patient right now!"

I hear him say quietly, "I could come back later, Doc. It's not a problem." He gets up to leave and Imka gets up as well.

"No, Danny. You stay. Nevaeh can wait her turn."

She says the last part through clenched teeth. Great! I have managed to anger Imka. Now is not the time to get her angry, not when I need her help the most.

"Okay, I'll wait." I say with a sigh. Feeling quite defeated.

"Alright! Have you had breakfast yet?"

"No, I don't want their cold eggs!" I snap.

"Well, go to the cafeteria, go order something."

"But I don't have any money."

"Just tell them I sent you and they should put it on my tab. I'll see you in twenty minutes."

I leave but I am not going to beg for food. I'd prefer to go back to my cold eggs. I wait for her in the cafeteria. The ladies have gotten to know me so they bring me some tea. I protest but they say it's on the house. Great—more kindness, more undeserved kindness. After what seems like twenty-four hours Imka approaches my little table in the corner. The same one we sat at while we were being debriefed by Dennis. I didn't even see her until she was standing right beside me. My mind is doing cartwheels. I almost jump out of my chair.

"Nevaeh, what is going on with you?" She pauses and when there's no response she proceeds.

"You owe Danny an apology. That was quite rude and inconsiderate, you barging in like that. I would never just abandon your session for anyone else, why would I do that to any of my other patients?"

She says all this using one breath, her eyes blazing. She is really pissed, and who can blame her?

"I am really sorry, and I will apologize to him later. But this can't wait, Imka. I really need to speak to you about this."

"What? What has happened, Nevaeh? Are you alright? Is it Rayva? Has he said something incriminating?" As she fires questions at me she pulls up a nearby chair.

"No—well kind of. Here, read this."

I just thrust my diary at her. It is easier if she reads it and then I'll explain. One of the ladies who works in the Cafeteria brings Imka a cup of tea and a warm muffin. I can smell the rich spices and the raisins. She sees me looking and offers to bring me one. I am grateful. I didn't know I was hungry until I saw Imka's breakfast. Usually they don't serve people here, you have to choose what you want, but I think we've become regulars and they seem to like us. While Imka eats, sips and reads, I look outside through the huge glass windows. It has stopped raining but it is still overcast. I think it is still raining somewhere, I hear the distant sound of thunder. After a while, less time than I anticipated, Imka looks at me and says,

"You have to show this to Detective Dennis."

"But that's just it. I can't. Don't you see that, Imka?"

"Don't I see what, Nevaeh? Clearly these people are dangerous and they cannot be trusted."

"But although I don't clearly remember, there it is in my own handwriting. I said that they were kind to me. Doesn't that count for something? How can I repay them by betraying them?"

"But right there," she points to one of the pages with the words crossed out, "In your own handwriting, you said that something was going on. And what about those sections that have been crossed out? What does that tell you? Did you cross it out or did they do it? Who knows, maybe bringing you this diary was a trap, to see how much you know or to discover if you are indeed faking!"

She suddenly looks at me like she's just seeing me for the first time.

"Nevaeh, where are your earrings?" She almost whispers the last word.

"I left them in my room." It's my turn to whisper.

"Why, Nevaeh, when *it* is for your—"

"I know, I know! My protection! But I wanted to share this with you first before deciding what to do with it. Also, Rain is flying in today. He is coming to see me later this evening."

"Oh! Alright! So how do you feel about that?"

"I am terrified at the thought that he is coming here to see me."

"Shouldn't that tell you something, Nevaeh? Plus, this," she shakes my diary in front of me.

"Yes, I know, but…"

"No buts, Nevaeh. I thought you said that you were going to trust your emotions to guide you. You are a very intelligent young woman, Nevaeh, use your head!"

"Am I though, really?"

"Yes, really. Now is not the time to be using your heart; you have to use your head."

"But I thought you said I should listen to my emotions."

"Your emotions are warning you, that's why you're terrified, and I think you should listen to what they are trying to tell you. Quite possibly they are warning you about things that are about to happen, based on things which have already happened. You should listen."

"But what if I am wrong? What if I am just nervous to see Rain after all these months away?"

"That is a distinct possibility, but somehow I think there is more to it than just nerves and you should—"

Before Imka is able to finish, the cafeteria door bursts open and Detective Dennis almost leaps across the floor to get to us.

He seems angry! Great, I've managed to anger the two people who are my biggest support system. There are a few customers in the cafeteria. They look at him, then at us and look away quickly. He is right next to me in a flash trying to whisper.

"Nevaeh, why aren't you wearing your earring? I thought we had agreed that you were going to do this!"

He sounds really angry, like he's really fed up with me. I don't know what to say, so I just look at Imka and she just looks back at me, and Dennis looks from me to her, like we're all engaged in a game of tennis. I understand that she is not going to share anything with him. She thinks it is my story to tell. I have to think quickly about how much I want to share with Dennis. He pulls up a chair from a nearby table. An indication that none of us leaves here unless I explain. I close my eyes for a few minutes, just to get a sense of the vibe and how I feel about sharing with him. Everything in me is screaming *tell him everything!* But how can I tell him everything when I don't even know anything?

I take a deep breath and sigh. When I open my eyes Dennis is looking at me like I have finally lost all my senses. Imka is as calm and steady as ever without even trying, and not wanting to tell my story, she sends me positive energy.

"Well, Rayva brought me my old diary."

"Oh, and you never thought to share this with us?"

"No!" I yell. The few people around look at us again.

"Why, Nevaeh? I thought you had agreed to share any intel you might unearth."

"Listen to you, 'intel'! This is my life we are talking about here. You are asking me to spy on people who have been my family and have treated me well."

"Is that what you read in the diary, or did you remember that?" For the first time he glances at the little brown book on the table between us, like an ocean.

"I read it."

"So how do you know it's true?"

"Because it is my handwriting!"

He sighs and proceeds more slowly and calmly. "Look, I can't tell you what to do and I can't make you do anything that you don't want to do. But these people are dangerous. They have proven that time and time again."

"So arrest them, then."

"We need proof, Nevaeh. Hard-core proof! They are so well connected that we cannot afford to screw up, neither can we afford to have circumstantial evidence. We need hard-core proof, facts! We will have every mayor and governor from here straight to Calgary after us if we don't dot all the Is and cross all the Ts in this case, and most certainly heads will roll for this, so we cannot afford a screw up."

He pauses and takes a breath, and gets his handkerchief out and mops his face; not just his forehead, his whole face. His face is turning red from all the effort being exerted, either to not kill me or to explain this to me. I don't know which I find more offensive.

"Do you understand this, Nevaeh? Now if you're not up to this, then maybe we should just part company, and you can return to Canada with your husband. We'll find some other way of nailing those bastards."

I'd almost forgotten that Imka was sitting there until she says, almost in a whisper, "The ball is entirely in your court now, Nevaeh. What do you wish to do? Whatever you decide, I will support you; you are still my patient. I made a promise to help you and I will. But at the same time, I don't want you to put yourself, me or the hospital staff at risk."

"So what are you saying? That I should leave? That's not much of a choice, then, is it?"

"No, I am not saying that. I am saying you need to think more critically about this situation."

"Don't you think I know that? That's all I've been thinking about!"

"Okay, I understand that you are stressed and you're conflicted, so take some time to process all this." The detective pauses and lowers his voice even more, then continues: "But please bear in mind that Rain is coming to New York, and our intel suggests that he is not coming for pleasure."

"I know that. Rosey told me."

"Yes, so just meet Rain and then decide from there how you want to proceed. After that if you want to continue working with us then that's fine. You can also give us the diary if you wish but if not, you are free to walk away and forget that this conversation and the previous ones ever happened. We will return your earring and be on our way and you'll be on your way with your family."

"Does this sound reasonable, Nevaeh?" Imka asks, looking quite stressed.

"Yes it does."

"Okay. I have to leave now. But you be safe, Nevaeh. Take care of yourself and whatever you do, do not mention to Rayva anything that we have told you. I'm afraid that might expose you to some serious danger."

"I'm not crazy, Detective. I wouldn't do anything so foolish no matter what I decide."

"I don't think he means that you're crazy, Nevaeh, he never said that. He just wants you to be safe. We all do."

"Alright."

The Detective leaves and Imka and I just sit there for a few minutes. The weight of my decision seems to be resting on both of us.

"I wish I could just go away from here for a while. To just think, to just sort my thoughts out."

"I know. But sometimes life doesn't afford us the luxury of just walking away to think. We sometimes have to just think on our feet. I know that's hard at the best of times, and it's made especially more difficult seeing that you can't remember a lot of the details. But I would say just trust your intuition, trust your instincts to guide you in this situation. Your brain might have forgotten but I am sure your body remembers."

"I will."

"Alright, I have to get back to work. Do you need me to walk with you upstairs?"

"No. I'm fine."

"Okay, let me know if you need anything. And please promise me that you will take care of yourself, Nevaeh."

"I will. I promise".

She pats my shoulder and then she's on her way, leaving me alone to figure things out. Suddenly, I am struck by utter exhaustion. I had forgotten that I hadn't gotten much sleep last night and Rain is on his way to the US. I'd better go upstairs and get some rest if I am to function later. I still don't know these people, not Rain, not Summer, not Miss Linda; not even Rayva. I hope and pray that I am not choosing the wrong team in this whole mess.

*   *   *

I stagger out of the cafeteria, with the ladies behind me yelling, "Get some rest, Nevaeh. You look tired, dear." My legs are lead-encrusted. I don't even know how I get to my room. This must be what Shane meant when he told me about muscle memory, that information is not only stored in our minds but in our bodies as well. As soon as my head hits the pillow, I am out like a light.

Again, I am pulled into a dream world. A reality that is similar to the waking world but not quite. This dream world seems more like a shadow—everything, every space, is covered in shadow. I am floating in the air again, but this time it is more like flying. Also, this time I cross three oceans, not just one like in my previous dream. I am panicking in my flight, but by the time my feet hit the land of three oceans, I am once more awash with peace. This peace seeps up into my feet and floats up all the way past my heart and into my mind. I am so at peace that I could cry. It feels like all my life I have been waiting to meet this sensation, which seems to be the mother of all peace. I want to stay and look around but I am not allowed to; *not yet,* at least that's what I hear echoing in my mind. As far as the eyes can see it's a panorama of colours that titillate all my senses. But by way of the dream world protocol it's hard to tell what's real, what's not and what is from me and what is for me. But for now I am content to just stand and look as far as I can at such a beautiful place. I could literally die here and all would be well. There are lush green trees, rivers, mountainous areas and unique landscapes all just inviting me to stay.

After a while, I hear the wind calling my name, and when I turn towards it I see that directly above me is a flock of strange birds, circling. They are huge and their feathers are jet black but stunning, despite their tiny red heads. They move in tandem, as if it's a ceremonial dance, with their wings touching. As I continue to observe them and search for the direction of the wind that had been calling my name I feel myself being shaken. Naturally, I think it's the wind but then I realize that someone outside of this sphere is calling me to attention. I awake and I am back in my grey room with its grey chair. I forage inside of me, grateful that the peace is still there, but it is muted, it doesn't feel as vibrant as when I was back in the dream place. I look around; the sun is way lower than before I went to sleep and Sandy is standing next to me.

"Sorry to wake you, girl, you looked so peaceful. My shift is ending soon but I wanted to let you know that Rayva called to say that he's going to JFK to pick up his dad and they'll be here in about an hour, depending on traffic. So I thought you might want to freshen up before they get here."

"Yes, sure. Thanks for waking me, Sandy." I yawn and stretch. "I was having such a peace-filled dream, if I had stayed there, I might have slept for all eternity."

She looks at me in a strange way then declares, "That sounds like the sleep of death, Nevaeh, you better be careful."

Without even thinking, without sifting through the ideas in my head so that I can sort facts from fiction and compartmentalize, I hear myself asking: "Sandy, do you believe in dreams?"

"What do you mean?"

I sit up and Sandy helps me to organize my pillows so I can prop myself up. "I mean do you believe that our dreams are sometimes trying to tell us something?"

"Yes, sometimes. I don't dream a lot and most times when I dream I don't remember, but any time I get a morning dream—"

"Morning dream? What's that?"

"It's a dream that happens anywhere between 4 and 7 a.m., I always remember those vividly and they always seem to come to pass!"

"What do you mean come to pass? Like they happen for real?"

"Yes! One time, when I was trying to find a full-time job because I had been doing temporary assignments here and there, it started to wear me out not knowing where I would be from one day to the next."

"That would wear me out too. I think I prefer consistency and stability."

"I know, right? Anyways, I was really stressed out about that, so before I went to bed I called my mom back home and told her that I wanted her to pray for me. I was quite specific about what kind of job I wanted. So I told her, I wanted a job that's just one bus ride away, in a huge hospital, working with all different types of people, where there is no toxicity. Because, let me tell you, girl, I have worked with some crazy-ass people in my life and it ain't fun to leave work exhausted and return exhausted because of all the drama that keeps you up at night. I also told her that I wanted a place where I can make a difference in even one person's life, where the staff can work as a family in helping our patients not only to heal physically but emotionally and mentally as well. Because sometimes, Nevaeh, some illnesses manifest in a physical way and we treat the symptoms, but really the root cause is an emotional wound that won't heal just by medication alone. And sometimes the wound is so deep-seated that it takes months if not years to heal."

"Is that what Imka meant by a deep-seated trauma, which can trigger not only our response in specific situations but can cause illness in our bodies?"

"Exactly! That's what I mean. Back to this dream I had. So I fell asleep in tears although I knew my mom was praying. But before I hung up she said, *No worry, it's going to happen because your request is not selfish.*"

"Wow! I'm getting goosebumps!"

"I know, right? So the next morning I had a dream that someone called me and gave me directions to a place that I didn't know about. When I woke up I questioned the dream but I wrote down the directions because I didn't know what they meant. I planned to ask Mom later in the evening. But in the meantime, I was late for a job assignment. But the dream sat on me all day; no matter what I was doing the dream was always there in the background, playing like an FM radio in the background of my mind."

"So what did you do?"

"Well, the dream was bothering me so much that instinctively I knew that I would not be able to sleep that night unless I did something about it. So that evening, after work, I followed the directions I got in my dream and it led me here, straight to this hospital. At the time I didn't even know that there was a hospital here; it was the last stop on my bus route. The same bus that I have to take to get home but since I would normally get off like five stops before the end of the bus route, I didn't know this place existed. When I got off the bus, I was shocked. So I walked in and I met Robin. Her shift had just ended and she was on her way out. But she was so friendly that I was instantly drawn to her."

"That's exactly how I feel about her."

"She said hi and I said hello, we got to talking and I was wearing my scrubs so she knew I was in healthcare, so she asked me what field and I told her that I am an ED nurse. And because she was so warm, because she exuded such care, I just told her my situation. She told me that this hospital is in need of ED nurses and I should apply. I told her that I had a copy of my resume with me. She said I should leave it with her and she would ensure that it got to HR. But to be honest, despite her warmth, I left feeling like *Oh well, at least I tried.* I didn't think she would do that for me because why would she do that for a stranger? I mean let's face it, she's a white woman with privilege and I am a black woman with a strange accent. So I just said, whatever. Plus, she had prefaced it by saying, *I can't make you any promises, I can only pass on your resume because I don't have any say in who gets hired or not.*"

"At least she was being honest and she didn't get your hopes up. So what happened?"

"Wait, nuh, I am getting to it. Two days later, on one of the days when I wasn't working. I get a call saying that I should attend an interview. But I had handed out so many resumes that I didn't even know which one was calling and even after they gave me the address to this place, it still didn't even click, not until I got here and walked through the front doors. The interview went well and they said that they would check out my references and then get back to me. I was really happy about the interview and the fact that I was even asked to attend one, but I still didn't think I would get the job."

"But why? It was specifically what you prayed for and all the signs pointed to it being your job, your dream job."

"Nevaeh, there is a thing called disappointment, and that has the potential to stop you in all your endeavours."

"What does that mean?"

"Neva, I had been disappointed so many times in the past, by things that I thought would have happened but didn't; so much so that I just shut down and stopped hoping, stopped dreaming. I was so stuck and stagnant, but I couldn't move until I started to dream again, to hope again—to feel worthy of my blessings. You see, how I understand it, God is never going to give you something that you are not ready for, because to do so would be just as destructive as not giving it to you in the first place. There's nothing more destructive than a little man with a big blessing or a little mind and a big blessing. It will destroy the mind and destroy the person. Therefore the blessing—the miracle that you prayed for—will sometimes manifest itself only when you are ready."

"Wow! That sounds inspired!"

"Indeed, inspired by hardships and tribulations. The other problem is a thing called imposter syndrome. Do you know what that means, Neva?"

"No, I don't think so. I don't think I have ever heard that term before."

"Basically, what it means is that you don't believe in yourself, in your strengths and abilities. You perceive yourself as less worthy and far more incapable than other people see you. To that end, you live in mortal fear of other people discovering that you are unworthy of your station in life. You believe that you got there by some fluke of nature and by some other act of nature you will be found out and exposed. Therefore, the fear of being found out and exposed holds you captive to mediocrity, to living below your means, your station in life; it kills your dreams, strips you of your potential. Because, let me tell you right now, fear is a bully, Neva. Fear holds you hostage in your own mind and the only one who can release you is yourself. You have the keys to freeing yourself and taking back everything that fear has stolen, everything that was rightfully yours but you gave up, because you felt like an impostor in your own life. It is like Bob Marley said, "Emanicipate yourself from mental slavery. None but ourselves can free our mind.""Oh wow! That's so powerful and deeply profound. I felt that, like literally."

"It's one of those echoes again?"

"Yes it is. But it feels different. I guess it feels like what Imka terms as 'resonating.' It is resonating with me, reverberating throughout my whole being like a tremor."

"That's awesome, because the body never forgets."

"Muscle memory."

"Yes, muscle memory. So, to cut a long story short because I know you have to meet your bootiful maan and his dad..."

We both giggle at her comment about *your bootiful maan.*

"I eventually found the courage to believe in myself, because it doesn't matter how much people believe in you—unless or until you start doing the work of healing and start believing in yourself, their belief cannot and will not help you overcome yourself. Because most times, if we choose to be brutally honest, it is mostly us. We get in the way of ourselves. It is not our parents or our siblings or our coworkers, it is us. We make our lives more difficult because we are sometimes filled with self-hate, triggered by unforgiveness. I have found that it is less difficult to forgive someone who wrongs me than to forgive myself. Can you imagine? Myself, the self that I go to sleep with, I wake up with and I spend all my waking moments with, I refuse to love and forgive. So I have learned to do it—and trust me when I say that Imka is amazing, sometimes she teaches me lessons even without intending to. She has taught me how to love and pardon myself for doing things that I've done that I am not proud of, reminding me that I was doing the best I could at the time and it was all about survival, while stressing that once you take responsibility for yourself, you forgive instead of reprimand. Did you know, Neva, that sometimes we punish ourselves by sabotaging and thereby withholding good things from ourselves?"

"Yes, we humans can be our own worst enemies. To the point where we need to be rescued from ourselves."

"So true, girl. That is resonating with me so much, Neva. Big time. I am happy I came to this hospital, because of the people

I have met: Imka, Robin, Shane, Philomena, even that Nigerian girl that we hardly get to see anymore, what's her name again?"

"You mean Ngozi?"

"Yes, her. Neva, you are really good with names, and trust me, your memory is sharp!"

She says, "sharp" with a huge emphasis on the P. It sounds like an explosion coming out of her mouth when she said it.

"Of course it is, most of my memory files got deleted so I have room for more memories!"

"Oh Neva, you are so poetic! No wonder you're a teacher. I bet you're an English teacher."

"Come to think of it, I don't know. I'll ask Rayva."

"Oh dear, look at the time," she announces while looking at her wristwatch. The one she got from her ex, that she continues to wear despite the trauma he put her through, just because she likes it. "I have to run, but what about your dream?"

"Oh yes, I was so captivated by your tale of struggle and survival that I almost forgot. Well, in my dream, I dreamt that I went to this place and it has three oceans…"

"You should talk to Imka, but if my memory serves me correctly, don't quote me on this, but that sounds like South Africa. I believe it's surrounded by the Atlantic, the Pacific and the Indian Oceans. My Geography might be a little off though."

"Oh! Really? Anyways, it was so peaceful there, I felt peace crawl up my legs and into the rest of my body, but then I heard my name in the wind and when I turned around I saw a circle of birds with their wings touching."

Sounding quite concerned, she questions, "What type of birds, Neva?"

"I'm not sure. They were jet black with tiny pink heads, or maybe red, yes, it was red. The birds had red heads."

She looks at me so seriously. Instantly, I know that the tone in the room has shifted; her look is so intense I am compelled to look away from her and look out the window at the gathering darkness. The bright lights overhead magnify the darkness—so much so, that I have to look away and, having nowhere else to look, I look at my hands on my lap, on top of the thin white sheet.

When I can stand it no more, I demand: "What is it, Sandy? Why are you looking at me like that? Did I say something wrong?"

She picks herself up off the grey chair that she has been occupying and comes to sit on the edge of my bed with one leg dangling haphazardly above the floor. She leans into me so that I smell her fading perfume and pronounces, "Neva, those are not good birds."

"What do you mean, Sandy? You're scaring me."

"I'm sorry to frighten you but back home we call those birds 'jancro' and they are scavengers. They eat dead animals, any dead thing really, it could be human or beast; they don't discriminate. That is not a good thing to see in your dreams. The rest of—"

"What do you mean not a good thing to see in my dreams?"

"Well, back home there is a theory that if and when you see these creatures in your dreams, since they represent death in the waking world. Then to see them in the privacy of your own dream world they foreshadow death."

"What?"

"Yes, I'm sorry, Neva. I don't make the rules. It is never a good omen. Just please promise me that you will be careful, okay girl?"

"Yes, I will. I promise."

"Sorry, but I have to go now. I don't want to miss my bus. I promised my neighbour that I would babysit for her tonight so that she could catch an extra shift at work."

"Alright! Do what you have to do, just please do me a favour."

"Sure, anything."

She is so close I can almost see myself reflected in her dark brown eyes.

"When you get home, please call your mom and ask her to say

a special prayer for me. Can you do that?"

"Of course, Neva. From the first day I met you, I told her about you and she and her church people dem have been praying for you ever since. They even had a fasting service for you."

"Really?"

I am so deeply moved by the thought of complete strangers praying for me that one tear escapes and just runs down my left cheek.

She says, "Of course, Neva. That's why us humans are here, to look out for each other and render assistance when and as much as we can."

I am so overwhelmed by the kindness of strangers that I can't even speak, can't even thank her and her mom properly. But maybe it's for the best, because maybe I don't remember or haven't collected enough words to thank her properly. Knowingly, she squeezes my hand closest to her on the side where the tear still smears my cheek and then she's gone. There's no need to say anything else when all that needs to be said has already been said—some voiced, while others are said in a different realm— yet heard, nonetheless.

I don't want to think about death and dying, yet instinctively, even without thought, I put my earrings back in and head to the bathroom for a shower. I am just going to do whatever I need to do to get through this evening. No more feeling worthless and acting useless in my own life; there's just too much at stake. I don't need to have dinner here because tonight I am going to "paint the town red." Rayva's words, not mine. I asked him why red and he said that's the only way to do it, the only colour worth applying.

I had intended for my shower to be quick but I lingered and allowed the water to wash over me, rushing down my face, my hands, down to my feet, imaging that the cold water—I like cold showers and I don't know why—is washing away all my imperfections. I wish I could also wash my hair but that is a task for another day. I need a whole day to sort through my big hair, which gets tangled so easily and needs a whole lot of love and attention to coax it back to manageability. Sandy said when I first came here my hair was really knotted so they had to cut some of it but since then it has grown back and reclaimed its place in the world.

Soon enough I am dressed and waiting in my room. I free my hair from the customary bun and allow it to roam free for the evening. Rayva has mentioned a few times that he likes to see me with my big hair out. I am wearing a red top that Rayva brought for me, and a pair of black jeans that he also bought for me. I don't have any make-up; I only have a red lip gloss that Sandy has given me, which I apply liberally. The Jamaican nurse who comes to check on me is duly impressed; apparently, I "cut a dash," whatever that means, and I am too preoccupied to start a conversation.

I've discovered since I've been here that most people, but especially Jamaicans and Africans, can't just explain things—they have to tell you the whole backstory, name all the players, list all the conflicts, before they get to the climax. Tonight I do not have the energy for another story. Plus, seeing how I constantly live in my empty head, I cannot afford to be taken off guard when Rayva and Rain get here. So I'll have to find out about this dash that I have managed to cut at a later date.

I must have dozed off, because I am startled by a knock on my door. By the time I figure out what is happening the door is thrown open like a flag being tossed in the wind. Then I come face to face with the purest evil that I have ever encountered. The face looks like an older, more weather-beaten version of Rayva, but he looks too vile to be even a remote relation. It is not that he is hideous; it is the fact that he is angry. That is the first impression that comes to me of this man, my father-in-law, the one who was kind to me but now doesn't seem that kind.

Rayva comes in right behind him. He stands about a foot

taller than Rain, because this must be his dad. Seeing the look of confusion or terror—or both—on my face, he pushes past his dad and takes my hand.

"Dad, why did you have to do that? You could have knocked and waited. You've frightened her. What is the matter with you?" He smooths my hair as he speaks.

"Have I?" he says, without releasing me from his incensed gaze. As if this act of terrifying me were deliberate.

"Are you alright, Nevaeh? I'm sorry he frightened you!" Rayva says, while holding me close to him in a protective posture. Eventually Rain comes in, bringing his whole evil presence into my tiny, grey room. I don't want to look at him, but not to would be telling. After he spends a few brutal moments appraising me, I feel battered all over. He asks, "How are you doing, Nevaeh? We've missed you at home."

Since I have been here, I have learned a lesson or two about tone. One of the first lessons I've learned is that some people ask how you are out of genuine concern, while others ask for other reasons. Rain asking how I am doing would definitely fall under the "other" category. I am about to respond, but I am crippled by fear. Rayva must sense it, and declares, "Terrified, that's how she's doing, Dad. I told you to be gentle with her, as she is in a really fragile state, but as usual you don't listen to me. You never listen to me, Dad."

The last part sounds like the cry of a wounded child. Rain comes closer and barks, "Of course I don't listen to you, because you are weak, just like your mother!"

Every word in that sentence is punctuated with such rage and bitterness that I have to look up at Rayva to see if he has been seared by the words of his only living parent.

In turn, anger rises in Rayva; I can feel it emanating from him. I cling to him, not wanting him to respond or react to the hate being thrown at him, at us. But it seems that my hold is not strong, or I am just not enough to contain him. Rayva suddenly pulls away from me, I think he is going to punch his dad and I scream, "No! Don't!"

He stops short and punches the wall instead. Instinctively, I throw my legs over the edge of my bed and rush to Rayva's aid. I'm thankful for my tiny room. His knuckles are bruised—an ugly red mark spreads rapidly. His dad looks at us and says, "Just like old times eh, both of you ganging up against me."

Somehow I find the strength and the voice to say, "We are not against you, sir."

"Sir? Is that what you are calling me now? Sir?"

And the strangest thing happens—Rain laughs so loudly that he bends over. This is really beyond me. In all my imaginings of what would happen when we met, this doesn't even come close. I am at a loss for words.

I look to Rayva (his eyes sparkling with rage) and then look back at Rain. I then realize that his eyes are not amused, they are still as cold and dark as when he entered my room. A part of me begins to pray that Detective Dennis and his people are still listening through my earring. Eventually, after Rain is able to contain himself, he takes a step towards me, moving past Rayva to get to me and whispers in my face, "Where is that Goddamn diary of yours?"

I must have momentarily forgotten about the diary, my diary, because my first instinct is to question. "What diary? What are you talking about?"

"Your stupid diary that you kept locked up in your room. Rayva told me that he found it and brought it to you. The fool that he is!"

"So if it is *my* stupid diary why wouldn't he bring it to me and why would you want it?"

"I don't have time for games, Nevaeh. I didn't come all the way here to play with you, eh. Those days are over, long gone." He waves his hand in a dismissive gesture to emphasize "gone."

"Oh, really?"

"Yes!" He screams in my face, spittle temporarily blinding me. I want to wipe it but I don't want to touch his spit. So I wipe face on my shoulder so it goes directly on my new red blouse. Before I know it, Rayva is pulling me out of the room and his dad is trying to pull me back in. We all struggle until Rayva and I are outside the door. Rayva pushes me and says, "Get out, Nevaeh. Go find Imka and stay with her!"

"So you're choosing her over your flesh and blood?" More of an observation than a question.

"Dad, she is my flesh and blood, remember, husband and wife become one. Has Mom been gone so long that you've somehow forgotten that?"

Rayva stands exactly between me and his dad, all the time pushing me to leave. But I am so confused at the sudden attack that I cannot move. Imka would really love the irony. Nevaeh who is always running is frozen in place by fear and shock.

"Dad, this is neither the place nor the time."

Rayva has lowered his voice and has taken a less combative stance. Meanwhile, through my peripheral vision I see that people have stopped doing what they were doing and are frozen just like me, looking at the very novel scene unfolding in the most unexpected place.

I start to say, "Rayva let's go. I'm not leaving you!—"

The whole time I was looking at Rayva but he was looking at Rain, watching his actions, gauging his moves. Then I see something creep into Rayva's eyes, something that I don't ever remember seeing there; it looks really foreign and out of place there. It looks like something that would have been more comfortable in my eyes. I wonder if fear has transferred from me to him. I hear people gasping behind me and I vaguely hear *gun*! That's when I hazard a look at Rain and notice that he has something glossy in his hands. Again, it is such a novel thing in a place such as this that it takes me a while to register that Rain, right here in this hospital, a place of healing, is hold a weapon of mass destruction. It is a small object but the closeness and the bitterness of the person holding it magnifies the small instrument. I find myself saying,

"This is strange! This is strange! This is so strange!"

Rain takes a step back and so do Rayva and I. Rayva has one hand holding me and he holds out his free hand in a posture of surrender; instinctively I do the same. He says more like a plea, "Come on, Dad, please just put away the gun. Do not make this more than it has to be. I am sure Nevaeh has her diary and she will be happy to hand it over to you if you just put away the gun and allow her to go get the diary. Alright? Does that sound reasonable, Dad?"

"You fool! You think I am just going to let her walk away like that, leave us the way your mom did?"

"Dad, stop saying that, just stop. Mom got sick, really sick, and she died. She didn't just leave us by choice. I have told you to stop telling yourself that. Now you've internalized it and you actually believe that Mom left us. Who is the fool now?"

I pinch Rayva, for him not to provoke this very unstable man, who looks like him, and looks like his dad, but is very much not like his dad.

"*Fool!*" I hear Rain roar; we'll see who the fool is. "Don't you see that she's going to be the one to bring down this whole family? Because she can't just leave things be and keep her mouth shut?"

"Dad, this is neither the place nor the time. Can you just please wait until Neva is doing better, then we can talk about it? I really don't want her to relapse, okay?"

"It's too late for talking, son. Now Neva,"—he says 'Neva' in a mocking tone—"just pass over the diary so that we can end this. You are causing a scene and you are preventing these good people from getting their work done!" Again, he waves his free hand at the people around us but I don't dare look at them, I am too focused on the object in his hand.

At his comment and mocking tone, I feel myself getting

angry. "Me, I am the one that's doing this? You're the crazy man with a gun!"

Again, a monstrous, ugly sound that is supposed to be laughter erupts out of him. How can he take something so pure and beautiful and make it so ugly? Just as quickly as he started laughing he stops and raises the gun. Without warning Rayva pushes me to the ground and stands in front of me. But before I can get to my feet, I hear an explosion. This time it is not Rain's thunderous laugh, it is a shot from his tiny gun. I attempt to stand but I can't even move and my ears are ringing. I look up, Rayva is still standing, still looking at his dad, holding his chest, the blood starting to seep through his white shirt. He has a look of terror on his face.

He manages to croak, "You shot me, Dad! ... Why?"

The 'why' is but a whisper, but I hear it, and then Rayva falls to the ground still holding on to his father's gaze. I find myself now cradling his head, sobbing, loud ugly sobs, almost as ugly as Rain's laugh. Rayva closes his eyes and at my scream he opens them and looks at me and says, "I told you that you were my favourite girl."

I manage to utter, "I know, your only girl."

At that he smiles, and red, ugly raw blood comes out both sides of his mouth, like a fool I think *he's ruining my clothes. How are we going to go for dinner now*? He struggles to breathe, then continues, "I told you that I will always protect you, Neva. I'm sorry I didn't sooner." He coughs up more blood and then says, "I love you." He closes his eyes and his head twitches and falls to the side, away from my red blouse and then I feel his soul leaving his body. I picture his soul being at peace, looking down at the mess and then leaving, leaving to go where all the other souls go when they leave this place.

I am still weeping and wailing. Suddenly, I feel myself being dragged unceremoniously, dragged on the floor, away from Rayva. Rayva's head falls off my lap and hits the floor with a thump. I don't even know what's going on. I look away and I see people holding Rain. I think *where were they before things came to a head?* I am pulled to my feet roughly and I look up and see that it is Detective Dennis. I try to beg him to help Rayva but he whispers, "He's gone, Nevaeh! He died protecting you, now we have to get you to safety." I nod in response, all the while pretending that I know what is happening. Like this was all a part of the plan that we had hatched a few weeks ago. I try to pull away and run back to Rayva but the detective holds on to me roughly and says, "Let him go, Nevaeh! Now we have to move! We have to get you to safety!" I want to tell him that Rayva's soul left and he's empty without it but everything is moving too fast.

I don't know where he's taking me, which place could offer safety or solace, because in that moment I feel like I will never be safe again. I will never know peace, no matter how hard I try to hold onto peace in my dreams, in my mind. In that moment, I feel the weight of guilt sitting on me like it has moved in for good this time. I know for sure that I will never be healed, not now, not ever. It doesn't matter where he takes me, how far he drags me from here, I will always see, feel and smell Rayva's blood on my hands. I will always know that he died because of me, he died protecting me, and that's a huge gift and a tremendous burden to give to someone.

Nevertheless, Detective Dennis holds on to me. By now I am bawling, kicking and screaming but he still continues to hold on to me, as if his life depended on him holding me. I want to look back at Rayva, run to him. All I keep thinking is that Rayva is bleeding on the ground, his body has been left on the cold ground without his soul and I have to go to him. After all, am I not his wife? He did this for me, so I have to offer him some comfort. But as adamant as I am to see Rayva again, the detective is just as adamant to prevent me. Just when I think I am about to lose my mind, just when I think my mind is going to fly away like Rayva's soul, I feel a sting in my arm and darkness embraces me and holds me just as tightly as the detective.

PART 3

CHAPTER TWENTY-ONE

I wake up, and try to sit up while fighting the grogginess that threatens to engulf me. I think someone is trying to talk to me. I think it's Imka, at least it sounds like Imka, but she sounds really far away. I think that I am going to wake up in my hospital bed and then we're going to have a talk about my memory loss, but she sounds so far away and I am so tired that I have to go back to sleep. I'll talk to her when I wake up tomorrow. I'll go see her in her office, sit on her yellow chair and she'll give me a bottle of water from her kitchenette.

The next time I wake up, I feel like we're moving slowly and my head feels weird. I am sitting with my chair reclined and I am wearing a seatbelt. Where is my bed with its thin white sheets? Where is the grey chair? Where is the river? It's been replaced by other seats that recline, blue ones with flecks of white or grey. My nose feels stuffy, and my ears are blocked as well. I look around. I think I'm in a plane but I am not quite sure. And why would I be in a plane? This doesn't make sense. I try to think back to when I might have gotten on a plane but all I can see is Rayva's blood on the floor, pooling around his head and chest.

I have to get someone to help me but who should I get? I remember hearing Imka when I woke up before, so I call out her name. At first my voice comes out hollow and I feel like I have to yell to be heard but then desperation infuses it with strength and I shout, "*Imka!*"

Abruptly, I see her coming towards me. She looks like she just woke up as well. She looks exhausted. I feel so bad but I need to talk to someone, I need to know what is happening. I need to know why I'm in a plane. "Imka, where am I? What is happening?"

"It's okay, Nevaeh, you're safe now. Go back to sleep, I'll let you know what happened when we land."

"When we land? Where are we going?"

"Don't worry, Nevaeh. Just close your eyes and go back to bed. I will explain everything to you later."

She declares all this while walking back to her seat, just a few feet away from mine. She is holding on to the chairs as if she's at risk of falling. She sounds so tired. Sleep is not far from me either, so I close my eyes and allow sleep to reclaim me. I tell myself that Imka is here with me so everything will be fine.

The next time I open my eyes, I wake up to Imka's sweet, gentle voice. I make a mental note that she doesn't sound as tired anymore. She's shaking me gently and saying, "Wake up, Nevaeh. We're here!"

I yawn and stretch and try to sit up straight, but my seat is in the reclining position. I look up at her. My ears have deceived me; she looks as haggard as I feel.

"We're here."

"Where are we?"

"In Cape Town."

"Where is that? Cape Town?"

"Cape Town is in South Africa."

"What?" I spring up out of my chair, bumping my head on the compartment above me.

"Why are we in South Africa? What is happening?"

She walks away with a sigh and starts removing bags from the compartment next to where I just hit my head. Just from her body language I gather that at this point I could be bleeding to death and she would still be content to remove the luggage, as if that were the singularly most important task she has to accomplish and right now. I guess exhaustion is keeping her focused on just one task at a time.

I suddenly scream, "*Answer me! Why are we here?*"

Unexpectedly she seems to snap. If I look carefully I think I'd see steam coming up out of her head like a kettle when it reaches its boiling point. She drops the bag she is holding and comes to stand in front of me. I think she is going to punch me in the face. Then she takes a deep breath and as calmly as she is able to muster, hisses: "Nevaeh, please stop this, okay? I will explain everything that you need to know as soon as I have showered, eaten and had a chance to rest. All you need to know right now is that you are safe. I know that you must be frightened, but have I ever done anything to harm you, Nevaeh?"

She seems to be struggling to contain herself. I think this is definitely a first; I have never seen this side of her before. I shake my head, afraid to speak lest I upset her even further. I seem to be having this effect on people these days: first Rayva, then Imka, the detective, Rain and now it's her turn again.

"Alright."

She nods in approval of my answer. Again she takes a deep breath and commands:

"Just grab a few bags and let's go. I haven't showered or slept properly in forty-eight hours, and I am really not myself when I haven't slept well. So let's do this as expeditiously as possible. As soon as we exit the plane there will be someone there to assist us."

I stumble out of my seat but I have to shake my legs one at time to activate them. I guess I've been sitting for quite some time. Plus, Ativan sometimes has that effect on me. I guess they gave me a whole lot of it for this flight. Imka said forty-eight hours. No wonder my feet are still relaxing. Thankfully it doesn't take them too long to warm up and start working properly. I can't believe that I'm in South Africa. How has that happened?

In a flash, my mind takes me back to the scene where Rayva was bleeding on the ground and his dad, his own father, was standing over him with a gun, looking so lost as though his mind left along with Rayva's soul. I bite my bottom lip, close my eyes for a moment and take a deep breath to settle myself. After a few minutes I am able to grab a few bags and follow Imka, as I see her disappear around a corner. I think she is disembarking without me so I run after her. Well, stagger is more like it.

She goes down the makeshift steps before me, and I see two women and a man standing with her and they are shaking hands. By the time I catch up to them I am out of breath. Plus, the sun seems so bright that I have to drop one bag so I can cover my eyes. The gentleman steps up and says, "Here let me help you," and takes my bag. First one lady, then the next, and finally the gentleman with my bags at his feet, all introduce themselves. I think they are Angel, Tembe and Aaron, but I can't be certain. At any rate, I register how much they sound just like Imka. Imka must have told them my name because they address me by my name. I'll ask Imka about their names later.

While I am sorting them out in my head Aaron declares, "Sanibonani, Nevaeh. Imka says this is your first trip here."

While he is saying that, Tembe and Angel vocalize with one voice: "Sanibonani! Welcome to Cape Town, South Africa. We hope you enjoy your stay here in our beautiful country." They say this as if this is their one job and they've been doing it all their lives. Their accent sounds just as beautiful as Imka's, but deeper. I guess that's because she's been living in the US she has lost some of her accent.

I manage to mutter, "Thank you."

They all smile at me, and say again with one voice, all three of them this time, "Lovely accent!"

I think one of the girls asks if I am American. Imka jumps in and tells them, "No, Nevaeh is Jamaican-Canadian." I've never thought of myself as Canadian before. Actually, I don't even know, seeing that I only just recently discovered that I am a Jamaican from Portland. I soon realize that I feel a deep longing for Sandy. I wish she were here and hopefully I'll get to see her again soon.

Imka hurries things along and gradually we make the trek into the main building, into the airport. They check our paperwork; apparently, Imka has my passport. She's thought of everything. I try to remember when we had planned to visit South Africa but nothing comes to mind. I decide that I'll just wait and see what she's about to say. I try to do a quick inventory of what has happened but all I keep seeing is Rayva's lifeless body on the floor. Since I am among strangers in a strange land, I will myself not to fall apart. While Imka talks to the people across the desk, sometimes in English, punctuated by laughter, and also in a language that I have never heard before, I do my deep breathing and resolve to remain calm and just act normal. I tell myself that everything will be fine, I am with Imka after all, and she's thought of everything. So meanwhile, I'll just focus on my breathing and let her take care of business for now.

We get into a taxi that seems to have been waiting to take us to the hotel, not too far from the airport. I so desperately want to ask Imka for an explanation but as soon as we enter the taxi and she gives the driver the name of the place, she falls asleep and I really do not want to disturb her. She is sleeping so soundly that she snores. I close my eyes as well but all I see is Rayva's blood. So I open them quickly and look out the window instead. At first we pass some industrial buildings and then we pass a cluster of houses. They are painted in as many colours as the rainbow: vibrant blues, many shades of pink, yellows and reds. I close my eyes on the reds, as they remind me of that scene in the hospital not too long ago. The taxi driver must have seen me looking through the window.

He says, "It's summertime now, so you'll enjoy your stay in Cape Town." His voice is rich, made more charming by his accent. I smile at him in the rear view mirror. "It's beautiful all year round but especially in the summer." I smile again and return to looking out the window. Soon enough, we pull up to the hotel. It is called the Providence Hotel and Suites.

After spending the last three months in a hospital, this hotel is a luxurious change. It is nestled among the most glorious trees I have ever seen. Off to the side and spreading all the way to the back, they are in full bloom, spreading purple, white and light pink blossoms everywhere, and I swear that you can smell them all the way to the airport. Trees and lush, green, well-manicured hedges create the illusion of a gate along the front of the hotel, keeping it incognito; you definitely would have to know where you're going to find this place. We share a two-bedroom unit and each bedroom is huge and has its own en suite. There is a kitchenette, with a small refrigerator and a stove, much like Imka's at the hospital but about two times bigger, a work area equipped with a computer and a printer, a huge balcony that overlooks a pool, and a private beach. The balcony is twice the size of Imka's office at the hospital. I am in heaven. Just from standing on the balcony and taking in the invigorating scene I feel the tension in my shoulders subside; there are trees for miles. I take a deep breath, filling my lungs with the clean fresh air. I close my eyes and imagine myself running along the beach, carefree and certain of my purpose and destiny. Imka joins me on the balcony.

I don't even notice until she remarks, "Beautiful, isn't it?"

"Breathtaking is more like it."

We stand and stare for a moment, both lost in our own worlds, until there's a loud bang on the front door which startles us. But somehow I am not scared; the setting is too serene for fear. Fear seems to be letting go of my shoulders, even as I look at the trees and the beach in the distance. Instinctively, I know that there's no need to fear, here in this place surrounded by nature.

"Oh, that must be room service. Are you hungry?"

I've been so distracted by my thoughts that all this time, I'd forgotten how hungry I was until she mentions the word.

"Famished."

"Me too."

I remain on the balcony while she opens the door, and right away my senses are assailed by the most delicious scents I have ever encountered. I think, *if it smells so good from all the way out here the taste must be divine.* Imka addresses the attendant in a quite musical language, with a series of clicks. We will definitely need to talk about this language. We bring chairs to the balcony along with the cart, which looks like a lavish buffet compared to how I've been accustomed to eating over the last little while. Imka observes, "That's glazed chicken, that's fish, that's beef," pointing at each alternately.

Without looking away or missing a beat she continues, "Remember when I told you about yellow rice? Well, here it is." She sounds so over-joyed just by saying those words. There is a separate shelf on the cart with a rich variety of fruits and vegetables, pastries of different textures and colours, and red and white wine in a bucket of ice off to the side. I am not even sure I should be drinking wine based on the fact that I had been heavily sedated—I hate to think about it—after the incident.

We fill our plates and eat in silence for a while, then after we've both taken a sip of our red wine, Imka notes, "I think my eyes are bigger than my stomach. I ordered more than we can manage!"

I say, "You think?"

We both erupt into laughter, the sound of which orders any residue of fear and tension to leave and we are once again ourselves: patient and doctor, but also friends.

"I know you must be wondering why we're here."

"That's an understatement, Imka. I am dying to know why we're here!"

"Well, bringing you to South Africa was always a back-up plan."

"A back-up plan? What do you mean?"

"I know it must be confusing for you, and you obviously have a lot of questions, but can you please wait until I'm done? The power nap in the taxi helped some, but I am still really tired. Be that as it may, I don't think it is fair to you to keep you in the dark for much longer or ask you to go to bed and wake up not knowing what has happened. Okay?"

"No it wouldn't, and I would definitely not be able to sleep— unless you have more Ativan."

She giggles with her wine glass poised close to her lips. "No I don't, actually."

"Alright! I will!"

I place my wine glass on the floor next to my chair, bracing myself; once again, wanting to hear and yet not wanting to hear what has brought us so abruptly to paradise. But she is right, I don't think I would be able to sleep without the benefit of hearing what brought us here, so far away from Sandy and Robin, from Rayva and Detective Dennis, from Portland—from everything and everyone that I have come to know in a short while.

"Like I said, coming to South Africa was always going to be a back-up plan but—"

"Wait, I know I promised not to interrupt, and I won't. But just tell me one thing first."

"What's that, Nevaeh?"

"Are you really a doctor?"

She laughs, throwing her head back. It is such a refreshing sight that I laugh along with her.

"Yes, I am a doctor."

"Okay, because I honestly don't know what to believe anymore after all I have seen in the last little while, and here you are talking about a back-up plan."

She takes my hand. "I am so very sorry about Rayva, Nevaeh. That never should have happened."

"I feel so guilty, Imka. I can't help but think that it was all my fault, that if Rayva hadn't come between me and his dad he would still be alive…"

"But then you would be dead, Nevaeh. Think about it: Rayva chose. He chose you! In that moment, he knew he had to make a decision and he did. And also, his dad chose. He chose to bring a loaded gun to a hospital, to visit a patient, with the obvious intention of using it if he didn't get his way—or, quite possibly, he was still planning to use it even if he got his way. I know you're sad and you will be for a long time; after all, he was your husband, whether or not you remember him. And don't forget, Rain was your father-in-law for a while, and as you've stated in your journal he was kind to you." She takes a breath and looks out at the trees.

"But like I said, he made a choice. Try not to beat yourself up about things that you cannot change, and things that you have no control over. Will you promise me that, Nevaeh?"

"Yes, I'll try! Okay, so what about this back-up plan that I wasn't included in?"

"Sorry about that as well, but it was for your own protection."

"Oh yes, everyone is always trying to protect me."

She seems genuinely hurt by my ingratitude.

"I'm sorry, Imka. I don't mean it like it sounds but I just don't know anymore."

"Well, that's understandable. Now back to what brought us here, and do not interrupt or else I am going to fall asleep before I tell you anything. This wine is having its way with me."

We both laugh out loud. In fact, I feel the same way. I feel really mellow from just a few sips.

"So, when you'd just come to us at the hospital, we didn't

know anything about you other than that you had washed up and you were wearing some pretty expensive earrings."

I touch my ears.

She explains, "Yes those are yours. The Detective took his back. Anyways, after Dennis had sent your picture all over the north and south borders close to the river, he got a hit (his words not mine) that you had reported an incident to your local precinct in Paris, Ontario."

"What incident?"

"Ne…*va*…eh!"

"I'm sorry, I won't interrupt anymore."

"Apparently, you had made some allegations against your father-in-law, that he had raped you."

"*What*? Did Rayva know?"

"We don't know what Rayva knew. But this allegation had sparked an investigation into your father-in-law, and that led to the police on your side of the border making some startling discoveries. Apparently that is when they started to notice some discrepancies in his business dealings and business associates, which all started just around the time of the death of his wife. Therefore we realized that you were in a lot of danger, and we had to find a way to keep you safe until you got your memory back." She pours a little more wine, then continues.

"Also, when Rayva came and told us about the day you fell in the river, we knew that the police weren't at the house only because you had been acting strangely, but quite possibly because of the rape allegations as well. That's why they were there, and that must have pissed off the whole family, bringing the police into the situation. Apparently, you had reported the rape six months prior, but based on Rain's connections they did their homework first, so they were planning to bring him in on the rape charges and then turn their attention to his business affairs whilst they had him in custody. But after you fell into the river, they turned their attention to finding you, because their case was pretty much dead without their star witness."

"So why was Rain so angry about my diary? I didn't see anything about the rape in it."

"I'm not sure. But I think when you disappeared, he went to search your room, found the diary, removed all the pages that mentioned him and left it there. Then Rayva must have told him that he had given you the diary, not knowing what he had done, and he panicked—not knowing whether or not he had overlooked anything, and not trusting your diagnosis of trauma-induced amnesia, he came to retrieve it. I think after you have rested you need to review that diary; there might be something else in it."

"But I don't have it with me. It's back at the hospital!"

"Yes, we ensured that it was packed with your other things before you got on the plane. We left in a hurry but we made sure to cover our bases."

"So what happened to Rain after, you know….after he shot Rayva? Did they arrest him?"

She nods and reaches for the wine bottle and offers me some.

"No thanks. I've had more than I should already."

"Me too, but I've not had this brand in a long time. It's a local brew."

"I can imagine. You must be so happy to be home."

"Yes, I am. I only wish it were under different circumstances."

"I feel the same."

She looks at me really somberly and says, "Nevaeh, despite everything, please try to enjoy this trip. Try to relax and remain in the moment instead of worrying about things that are outside your control. Please promise me. So many dream of travelling to a distant land and here you are. So please enjoy it. It is time you make beautiful memories because, with all the trauma you've experienced and continue to experience, who knows if or when you're going to get your memories back."

Even as I agree, more to pacify her, I know that it will not be easy.

"So if Rain has been arrested, why are we here? With him in jail there is no danger, then, is there?"

"Well, that's what I said as well, Nevaeh. But the detective said that Rain has made enough friends in high places, for all the wrong reasons, who would kill their mothers if they had to. Once again, his words, not mine. So while Rain might be locked away, he does have enough pull to ensure your death before his trial. Plus, even if he is too traumatized to be so inclined, his friends definitely won't be. Like Rain, they do not know how much you remember or if you are just lying, putting on a facade to cover yourself, so they will come after you in the interest of self-preservation. I'm sure, at least to them, it is nothing personal."

"But so many people saw him shoot Rayva—they don't need me for that. Do they?"

"It's not just the murder charge, it's the other charges as well. The fact that people have gone missing who were presumably linked to the research and distribution of his products. Products that are backed by huge pharmaceuticals, so therein lies the danger. These people have made insane amounts of money off a product that is potentially tainted, so they have to protect their own best interests. I think the product is good but the detective speculates that there might have been a few bad batches, which might have led to unintentional deaths. They do not want this coming to light, ever! Especially now with Rayva gone. You might be in far more danger than ever before. Do you understand now why we had planned to bring you here and why it was necessary to accelerate the process?"

"I think so, but it is a whole lot to take in."

"I know. It took me a while to grasp the details as well and I had a little more time to process."

"So won't they be looking for me?"

"Yes, in the US, Canada, and Jamaica maybe, but not here."

"But won't that put my family in danger?"

"It might, though it is you they want, not them. But the detective has thought of that and contacted the Jamaican police. He also dispatched a few of his own people on surveillance of the area where your family members live, so they should be safe. But I really think these people are more invested in finding you than the people closest to you. They believe that it is you they have beef with, not your friends or family members."

"They might use them to smoke me out, so to speak."

"They might, or they might not. Let's not think about that until we have reason to, okay?"

"Alright."

"I know you have been placed in a difficult position, and you must be scared out of your mind, but you still need to recover your memories. Being stressed and worried will not help." She places a hand firmly but gently under my chin. "Promise me, Nevaeh. South Africa is beautiful and some have found its aesthetics therapeutic, so please promise me that you will not miss the opportunities for growth that present themselves to you while you are here. Okay?"

"Okay! I promise."

"Well, if you don't have any more questions right now, I think I need to shower and go jump into that luxurious bed that keeps calling my name."

"Just one more question. Do you know if they had a funeral for Rayva?"

"I'm not sure. I'll ask the detective when he calls."

"Alright."

"Oh, that reminds me," she says, getting up. She quickly goes into the unit and returns with two phones and hands me one, a blue phone. I am thankful that it is not red. I will never be able to look at red the same again, ever. I didn't even know they made phones in colours other than black; hers is purple. Even though she is exhausted—I can see the tell-tale signs in her face—she is still agile and swift, not only in her actions but also in her thinking.

"Do you know what happened to my phone that they found on me when I came out the river?"

"No, come to think of it. I must ask the detective, or you can ask him when next you speak. These are special phones that they gave to us so that we can be reached at any time, night or day, in any location."

It feels weird holding a cellular phone. I can't ever remember having my own phone, although obviously I must have.

"Okay, I'm going to turn in. Are you coming?" she says, while wheeling the cart back into the unit.

"In a little while. I want to soak up this view some more."

"It is pretty, isn't it?"

"Indeed! Quite possibly just what the doctor ordered."

We both smile at each other knowingly.

Afterwards, she leaves and I take in the view but my mind is bursting at the seams with the information she just shared. Rain had raped me! That's so disgusting! I wonder what Rayva thought of the whole thing. I also think back on my diary entry about the death of Miss Linda and I think—no wonder Rain became so resentful, angry and bitter. Miss Linda quite possibly was treated with one of the tainted batches, so maybe that's why it didn't help. It hadn't worked as it should, not at all, and he blames himself. Rain had probably discovered this afterwards. The guilt he must have felt left him reckless, bitter and brought out the odiousness in him. It had crushed his soul and changed him into a monster.

If nothing else, I know about guilt; I know the fragility of the human mind and the impact of the weight of guilt. Still, he needs to be held accountable for violating me, and possibly others. I will personally see to that, if for nothing else, he is held accountable for what he's done to Rayva; that I remember clearly and will never ever forget as long as I live. That is forever etched in my memory like the grains of sand on the beach below. Rayva did not deserve to die like that, no one does. At least, Ms. Linda's death was a horrible accident but Rayva's was both deliberate and intentional and I can never forgive him for taking the man I loved and the one who loved me.

CHAPTER TWENTY-TWO

Despite myself, I sleep like a baby. I guess, like Imka said, the wine had its way with me. I wake up and open my windows, which are on the same side as the balcony, and look out at the picture-perfect scene unfolding in front of me. I feel a strange kind of feeling, one that I cannot readily identify because it is so new and foreign to me. I think I will talk about it with Imka as soon as she is awake.

I decide to do my deep breathing exercise, but I am already so at peace in this idyllic setting that I do it more out of habit than anything else. I get a feeling that something is going to happen today, but I don't know what. I pray that nothing disastrous happens to ruin my mood and memory of this place. As Imka has specified, I am here to heal and collect felicitous memories. In a very short time I have accumulated too many sad ones.

While I am deep in thought, trying to assess my feelings, I hear a gentle knock on the door, followed by:

"Are you awake? May I come in?"

"Yes, sure! Come in."

Imka, with her regular habit of being halfway into my room and halfway not, says, "Good morning, did you rest well?"

"Good morning, yes I did! The wine had its way with me."

We laugh conspiratorially and with that she brings her whole body into the room.

"I thought you would like to go for a walk before we have breakfast."

She must have seen the hesitancy in my face, so she adds: "We don't have to go very far, just to look around. I think the walk will be beneficial to both of us. Also, it's to help ground you in this new environment and experience."

"Okay! I can do that."

The fact is, so far almost all my actions have been planned out for me, so it is really weird to be called on to make decisions for myself, even one as simple as going for a walk. A new awareness creeps into my mind and body: *I am now free to make my own choices, my own decisions. Also, no one is coming to save me, so I have to save myself.* With that new knowledge comes a new discovery: I am now free and I don't have to be afraid anymore, at least not here.

Imka is saying, "Alright! I'll leave you to get dressed. We can go shopping as well, to get you some more clothes."

But I am already thinking that I am going to be wisely selfish and enjoy this trip that God must have picked out for me. Because, although I can't remember, I don't ever recall feeling so much at peace and free from fear and guilt. As I arrive at this new understanding, more weight leaves my shoulders. I feel them fall from the pressure of the weight leaving.

I am dressed and ready to go. I don't have that many options anyway. We stop by the breakfast bar (as they have named it) and we each grab a muffin. There will be plenty of time to indulge after our walk.

"So who is paying for this impromptu vacation?"

Imka looks at me and swallows her muffin. "The FBI is."

"That's great, then."

We head through the gates. I hadn't even realized until now that this hotel actually sits on a little hill. We head downhill, amazed at the rich, green foliage. I hear the birds chirping and I smell the rich blossom of the fruit trees around us. This place reminds me of somewhere, but where? I am not sure, but I am grateful for the affinity that I feel. We make a left when we get to the gate; the sun is just coming up and it is a cool morning. We walk towards the back of the hotel. The scene is complete with light purple petals on the ground lining our way, like a bridal train. A sign of welcome, much like the word "Sanibonani." The luxurious scent is intoxicating.

"Nevaeh, this tree is called a Jacaranda and they blossom in the summer."

"They are beautiful."

"They sure are."

"Let's go over here. There are a few other flowering trees."

We get off the original path, past a canopy of greenery, and go through a clearing. There in the clearing is a rainbow of colours: purple, yellow, pink, white and red. She points to the yellows and says, "That's called a wild laburnum, and these are tree wisteria." In reference to the purple ones.

She walks a few more paces with me right behind her. "These white ones are called Cape chestnut." Turning away she says, "I am not too sure, or possibly I just don't remember, what those other white ones are called."

"Those pink ones," she says, pointing straight ahead, "are known as the pompon tree. We used to pick them as children and call them our bridal bouquets."

Imka laughs like a little girl and I can see her running around with her friends.

Not wanting to look at the blood red trees I ask: "So did you grow up in Cape Town, Imka?"

"No. I actually grew up in Port Elizabeth, which we

affectionately call PE. It is a seaport city and it is in the Province of Eastern Cape."

"Okay, so you have provinces, just like Canada?"

I say that without even thinking.

"Yes, just like Canada, but we have nine but I think you guys have—"

"Ten… I think. To be honest, Imka, I don't even know how I know these things about the provinces and stuff."

She clasps her hands and brings them up to her face and says, "Do you know what that means, Nevaeh?"

I shake my head.

She says, "This could be the first sign that your memory is coming back. Isn't that exciting?"

"Yes—it is! Wow!"

"Let's keep walking and talking, and maybe you'll remember more."

Just like that I have a new revelation. I realize that this is the ideal place for my memories to return; plus, the feeling I couldn't locate in myself earlier this morning I realize it is called bliss. I am so at peace, especially out here among these breathtakingly beautiful flowering plants. I am in a state of bliss.

I feel panic creeping in at the moment as well, but I take a deep breath and plant my feet firmly on this land, South Africa by name, grounding myself. I refuse to undo so much of the work that Imka and I have done so far, because this memory didn't just pop out of nowhere—it came from days, weeks and months of doing the work to get to this place, where I can remember that Canada, like South Africa, has provinces, but whereas South Africa has nine, Canada has ten. I notice that Imka has stopped and she is saying something.

"Are you okay, Nevaeh? Do you want to turn back now?"

"No, Imka, I am fine."

"Alright, but please let me know if you are experiencing sensory overload, because after being cooped up in the hospital it is quite possible."

"Yes, I will. But no, I don't want to leave. Back there, I was just grounding myself, savoring the moment, celebrating a victory which might be minute to some but ginormous for me!"

Imka smiles knowingly and takes my arm, just like that afternoon when we first went on a walk in New York. We pass the morning just walking in this meadow, only speaking when it's necessary, with the understanding that silence is welcome and has a place in our discourse.

As we venture deeper and deeper into the forest of trees, we pass little bunnies, hopping to their destination, little animals scurrying to get out of our way, a few birds stopping to look inquisitively at the strangers invading their sanctuary, and still a few other animals (ones I don't ever recall seeing) sniffing in our direction. I guess they discern that we are friends, not foes, who come in peace, and they move on with their lives. Soon it is time to return, because the sun is telling us that it is mid-morning, and although there is no set schedule our bellies announce that it is time to eat. So we leave with the understanding that there is healing in nature and we will return someday. While we walk back, I think, *this place feels so familiar.*

It is when I hear Imka responding that I realize that I had broken the silence and spoken my thoughts aloud.

"Yes, this land indeed feels familiar, because the Earth is old and it was made by the same Creator who used the same material to colour our world. So there is memory in the land and sometimes it feels familiar to us, it feels like we have been here before because we have walked along a path that the Creator used the same material to make before."

"That's so profound, Imka, and it makes so much sense. Because just like how humans have memory so does the land around us. The land remembers."

"Yes, it does."

"That's so amazing and encouraging."

"Yes, why is that, Nevaeh?"

"It's encouraging because if the land, an inanimate object, has the ability to remember, then that's an indication to me that I too will remember. I will remember the good and the bad."

"Yes, I think you will. Especially because you are in a space that is so peaceful and you feel safe. I also believe that your brain has been waiting on this calmness in you to release your memories."

We get to the gate and walk up the hill in silence once more. We head straight to the dining room. There is no more breakfast but they are setting up for lunch so we have organic sweet tea while we wait.

"This tea is called honey bush, Nevaeh. It is grown exclusively in the Western Cape and we export it all over the world."

"It is delicious and calming."

She smiles proudly.

"So you were telling me back there about growing up in Port Elizabeth?"

"Yes, I grew up there with my parents and two brothers."

"You're an only girl?"

"Yes, which is pretty much like being an only child. The boys were always off doing their own thing, which gave me plenty of time to figure things out on my own."

"You grew up alone then?"

"Not quite! I had a lot of cousins, and my parents adopted a girl from Soweto, who had lost both her parents in an accident. Her name is Shale and we became real sisters. Despite our age difference—she is five years younger than me!"

"That's great! Where is Shale now?"

"She works in Johannesburg, and I plan to meet up with her as soon as the opportunity presents itself."

"Where are your parents now?"

"My dad died a few years ago and my mom still lives in Port Elizabeth with one of her sisters."

"Are we going to Port Elizabeth?"

"Of course."

"Excellent! I can't wait to meet your family, Imka."

"I am sure they will love you, Nevaeh."

Soon the buffet is spread and we help ourselves to small portions, unlike yesterday. Before you know it the room is filled with people and chatter in various languages. We talk about the languages, and she says that South Africans speak eleven different official languages and she had actually been speaking Xhosa when I had observed her the day before. Which she is not quite fluent in, but she understands much more than she speaks.

Imagine that—eleven different languages. I imagine a scene where they are all angrily or happily describing an incident in their own mother tongue. That makes me smile inside.

We finish and head upstairs for a shower. I decide to treat myself and wash my hair. Come to think of it, the humidity that had given me frizz in New York is thankfully absent in Cape Town, at least in this tranquil location.

While I'm towel drying my hair, Imka knocks and says, "Nevaeh, Detective Dennis is on the phone. Are you decent?" She is still outside the door, and I can't help but smile at the jab at the Detective. I'm dressed in a plush robe provided by the hotel.

"Yes, come on in. I'm just towel drying my hair."

"Oh wow Nevaeh! So much luxurious hay." She puts the phone on speaker and places it on the bed between us.

"Hi, Nevaeh. How are you doing?"

"I'm doing well, Detective, all things considered."

"I know, but you're a strong lady and Imka is wonderful, so I know you'll be fine."

"Yes, she absolutely is."

There's a respectful pause and then he says, "You might be there for a while. The DA's office doesn't want to rush the case. They want to make sure that they have all their ducks in a row first. Also, we will be collaborating across jurisdictions so that might lengthen the process. But just sit tight. You're in good hands and in a safe place."

"Yes, that's great to know, but what about my family: my dad and my aunts?"

"On the night that you guys left, we sent a few of our people to Balcarres as well. So far, there hasn't been any strange movements, but we will continue to keep an eye on things on that end. Try not to worry." And as if an afterthought, "Remember your health. We need you to be well and healthy, but you need that for yourself more than anyone else. Just be kind and gentle to yourself, okay, Nevaeh?"

"Why, Detective, you're starting to sound like Imka!"

He laughs heartily and says, "Guilty as charged, human by association."

We all laugh, but then I remember: "What about Rayva? Did they have a funeral for him?"

"No, not yet. The DA is waiting on the autopsy results to release the body to—" I know he is searching for the info on his desk, I hear papers being pushed around.

I supply the answer, "To Summer, his sister."

"Yes, that's it. Summer."

"Alright Detective, we'll talk to you soon. Please keep us posted," Imka interjects.

"Yes, will do! Take care, ladies."

"Wait!" I yell. "What about Rain?"

"I was hoping you wouldn't ask. He's in bad shape—"

"What do you mean?"

"The doctors said that he experienced a mental breakdown after he shot his son. So they say he is catatonic and might be for a really long time, although it's hard to tell. This means that we will need your memories and testimony now more than ever, Nevaeh." For emphasis he repeats, "Now more than ever."

With that, there's an ominous click and he's gone.

"What does that mean...?"

"Catatonic?"

"Yes."

"It means that although he's awake, he is unresponsive. He's just staring into space, seemingly oblivious to his environment and the people around him."

Imka must have seen sadness crawl back into my eyes after our lovely morning. "Are you alright, Nevaeh?"

"You know, I don't quite remember her, but from what I read in my diary Summer was good to me. I can't help but feel great sympathy for her. In one go, she has lost both her father and brother, after recently losing her mother and child. It must be horrible for her right now!"

"That is horrible, Nevaeh, but please don't take this on. This is way too much, and neither you nor I want you to undo all the progress that you've made so far. It wouldn't serve you to do so."

"I know! I am trying, but still, I feel for her."

"Yes, that's fine. It indicates that you are human, but just don't take it on. Don't carry it around on your shoulders like it is your burden to bear, because it isn't. Rayva wouldn't want you to, either. He sacrificed so that you wouldn't have to, so use this second chance wisely and handle yourself with great care. It is what Rayva would have wanted for you."

"I guess."

This whole time she has been standing close to the door, always close to the door; now she comes to sit with me on the edge of my bed and looks at me for a while. Then she says, "Nevaeh, I get the distinct impression that before this amnesia, you used to take on everything, take on everyone's load, even loads that were not yours to carry. You felt obligated to bring dead weight with you everywhere, including into your new life with Rayva. That must have been a very crowded marriage: him with his family woes and you with your past."

I sigh. "I guess."

"That is no way to live, Nevaeh. It is great that you take responsibility for your part in a situation, but you need to learn how to sift a situation and discern which parts you're accountable for and which part is not yours to take with you. Plus, even with the parts that are yours, you need to know when to let go of them, let go of the shame associated with the memory. Sometimes things happen outside of our control and we have to just accept that and move on with our lives. Life doesn't ever sit around and wait for us. It leaves us behind. If you don't learn to do that you will forever be carrying burdens that are not yours to carry. Besides, there comes a time when, even if you're culpable, you have to forgive yourself and let it go!"

All this time I have been trying to avoid her sharp, brilliant eyes; suddenly, she gently touches my chin and I have to face her.

"Nevaeh,"—she lowers her voice significantly, almost to a whisper—"when we go on a plane, the rules are very clear about maximum weight, correct?"

"I guess."

"Well, the plane is made out of sturdy metal, yet it is man-made, so if the plane has a maximum weight, why do you not think that humans have a maximum weight as well? I mean, think about it: why do you think that sometimes good, decent people just suddenly snap, just lose it and commit unimaginable atrocities? Look at Rain, for example. You said he was kind and gentle. My theory: they've reached their maximum weight! Simple! They have carried their weight for far too long and keep adding to it, and then their mind and body just give way under the pressure. I think with everything that you've been through, you've finally reached your maximum weight and that's why your body deleted some of your memory files. But I think that you are strong and noble, and eventually you will regain your memories, but you have to learn the lesson about your body's ability to accommodate your maximum weight. Okay?"

"Alright."

With that she gets up and retrieves her phone, which had been placed on the bed between us.

"I'll leave you to tame your beautiful mane. Then we can go look around Cape Town later, if you feel up to it."

"Okay, but I feel really exhausted. I think I'm going to take a nap. I'll let you know how I feel later."

"Okay, just take your time. No rush."

She walks to the door then pauses, as if in deep thought.

"That's a good sign, Nevaeh."

"What is?"

"Learning to listen to your body. Your body will always tell you what it needs and when it needs it. You just have to get into the habit of listening."

She closes the door and leaves after that. Between her and the detective, they have certainly given me a lot to think about. So I finish my hair, quicker than I thought I would and snuggle in the richness of the fabric of my duvet.

I actually sleep longer than I thought I would; I wake up at dusk. I go to check on Imka and she is sitting on the balcony as if ready to greet the approaching darkness. She is so focused she doesn't hear me approach until I sit down on the comfy floral chair next to hers.

"Hi, Nevaeh. Are you okay? You were in such a deep sleep that I didn't want to disturb you."

"Yes, I'm fine, just tired," I say, yawning and stretching. "Excuse me."

"It's called jet lag. I fell into a coma shortly after you did."

We both smile at her euphemism. We gaze out at the trees, so peaceful and soothing. The tide is coming in on the beach. I imagine it washing away today's problems and misgivings to make way for tomorrow's.

"Oh, I almost forgot. Remember I told you about my adopted sister, Shale? Really my sister. Well, she works at the Apartheid Museum in Johannesburg, and she was able to get some time off sooner than we thought. So tomorrow we are flying to Joburg to meet up with her. I think we'll just spend a week there and then come back here. Are you up for it?"

"So we're leaving here?" I say, sounding like a whining child. Because I don't want to leave the tranquility of the trees, the scent of their blossoms and the solitude that cloaks the beach; all of which seem strangely familiar and soothing. I am already attached to this place. It seems like my heart, body, soul and mind have come into agreement that this is what I have been in need of for a really long time.

"Oh, not for long. We'll use this hotel as our base, so to speak. We will always come back here, but I want you to experience as much of South Africa as you are able to."

"Okay! Sounds good, because I really like it here. So peaceful and soothing, which feels really familiar."

"Yes, it is. And you know what, Nevaeh, not to take away from the blissfulness of this place, but there are a lot of places in South Africa that will offer you that same sense of peace."

"Alright."

"Let's go downstairs for dinner and then come back to pack quickly."

"You know Imka, I really could get used to this."

"What do you mean?"

"This jet setting lifestyle: yesterday or the day before, New York, today Cape Town and tomorrow Johannesburg. That's the life, eh?"

She laughs so hard she holds her stomach, wiping her happy tears, and she says, "Yes, that's the life, Nevaeh."

We eat quickly, pack and still have enough time to watch a movie: *Air Force One* with Harrison Ford. This movie shows the strength and courage of the Americans, and how committed they are to their country and ideals. All the dramatic pauses, the sounds which foreshadow danger, the brainstorming and problem solving: I feel so alive. I literally cannot remember when I have done all these very normal things. This trip is indeed exactly what the doctor ordered. Just thinking that tomorrow at this time we will be falling asleep in a different city gets my blood pumping and my pulse racing. I have to catch my breath.

We wake up early the next day. A taxi picks us up at the hotel, drives us down the hill and, just a short distance to the gate, I see a little bunny dart across the road. By the time I yell, "Stop!" the driver has hit his brakes and thankfully I am wearing my seatbelt. Even so I bang my head on the passenger's seat in front of me. I feel weird, like something has shifted or come undone in my head.

The driver stops and asks, "Are you ladies okay?" He seems really concerned.

He gets out to check, but the lucky bunny is long gone.

"Are you okay, Nevaeh?"

"I think so. I feel weird."

"What do you mean?"

"Are you ladies alright? I am so sorry about that."

"My head feels heavy."

"Do you want to go to the hospital?"

"No, absolutely no hospital!" I yell more loudly than I had intended.

She smiles knowingly. "Well, I don't see any bruising or a bump. So I guess you're just shaken, but if you start feeling nauseous please let me know."

"Why? What does that mean?"

The driver interjects. "Are we going to the airport or the hospital ladies?"

"The airport," Imka and I say together.

"If you feel nauseous it might be a sign that you have a concussion."

So we're on our way again. At first I look out the window but then I discover the start of a headache so I close my eyes, take deep breaths and just relax as much as I can. I try not to think but just remain in the moment, just leaning into the headache. I accept the pain without judgement or fear, without thinking about ways of fixing the problem, just letting it be. This must be what acceptance feels like—no assumptions or preconceived notions—no jumping five days ahead of myself. And just like that, all my memories come flooding back. In the short time that it takes us to get to the airport, I remember everything: my little house on the hill, the one from my dream in the hospital, Claire, Bridget, Shalk, Mommy, Daddy, Grandma and Robin. Even things I wish I didn't have to remember, but I embrace them. I feel like I have had a fever this whole time and when I bumped my head, my fever broke. But I suspect that this was more of a psychological shift, a relocation of my energies rather than a physical conveyance. I am simultaneously crying and laughing, after all these months.

Imka is panicking: "What is it, Nevaeh? Are you alright? Are you hurt? Should we go to the hospital?"

The driver keeps looking back in his rear view mirror. "Is everything okay, ladies? Should I stop and pull over?"

I say, "Absolutely not, sir, everything is fine, not perfect but fine."

At this he shifts in his seat and both him and Imka look at each other and then at me like I have finally lost it. But I don't want to tell her yet. I want to just savor this moment. Maybe I should just wait until we return from Johannesburg to tell her. That wouldn't be fair or kind to her, though. I decide to tell her when we get to Joburg, as she calls it.

All the old memories, the old longings, the old aches come back to assail me; however, I don't see them through the same eyes. I am more equipped now, fortified, so they are all welcomed. They are no longer villains or demons come to assail me. They are part and parcel of my journey, they are the things and the people who made me who I am; so no, I am no longer afraid of them, and neither am I weary of them. I have so longed for this moment, the moment I remember who I am, that I don't even care how much some of these memories hurt—as a matter of fact, even the painful memories have lost their sting. They no longer hold me hostage. They no longer have the power to oppress me, because I am seeing them with fresh eyes. It is not even like I am seeing them for the first time, but it is simply that my perspective has changed.

I revisit each person I have lost, including Rayva, and I say a proper goodbye to each of them. In my mind's eye, I see myself hugging each of them: Shalk, Mommy with her gap-toothed smile, Grandma with her grey hair, beautiful Robin, Miss Linda, my two babies and Rayva, who is no longer covered in blood. He's just Rayva, the way I'll always remember him. My husband and hero, who tried desperately to rescue me from myself.

We get to the airport and I have to shake myself out of my reverie. We have places to go and people to meet, and finally I can participate fully in the moments that will come. The whole entire me, not just selected parts but the whole me. I feel like doing a dance like we used to do in that little church back home.

"Nevaeh, what has come over you? You look different and you keep smiling. Is everything alright? You really frightened the driver. I think he thinks you're crazy," Imka concludes, after we collect our bags from the trunk of the car.

I laugh so loudly, several people close by turn and look at me and I swear they are shaking their heads, like I have lost every ounce of my mind. Little do they know that for the first time in a really long time, I have finally recovered my mind, all of it: the broken part, the whole part, the part yet to be discovered, it's all there fully intact. Imka seems notably embarrassed, her cheeks turning red, which makes me laugh some more.

"No, Imka," I say after a while, wiping my eyes. "I have not lost it. I am fine."

I hug her so tight she fights to free herself.

"What has gotten into you?" she demands through clenched teeth.

She turns red and I see a muscle pulsate in her left temple.

"Maybe I should call Shale and cancel and get you to a hospital. We might have to wait for a long while for you to see a doctor but with your history I don't want to take any chances. Quite possibly you might be concussed. Do you know what that means?"

"Yes, Imka. I'm an English teacher so I know fully well what that means. Anyways, I was going to wait until later but I don't want you hauling me off in a straitjacket so I might as well tell you now. I've gotten my memories back!"

"What? When? How? Are you sure?"

"Back there when I bumped my head in the taxi."

"Are you serious? Oh my Lord! That is wonderful, Nevaeh!"

"Yes it is." We are laughing, jumping around and hugging. I am pretty sure we're both crying. This brave, beautiful stranger who became my friend, who is a lot like Robin. In her, I see who Robin might have been if she had lived to fulfill her dreams and become all she should have been.

"You look fine."

"Not crazy anymore?"

We laugh until we have to put our bags down again. A few people have almost bumped into us.

"Watch it, lady," says one guy, looking from me to Imka like we're in the wrong place.

By the time we get to our gate they're boarding, and we have just enough time to show our passports and head to our seats. We find some space to put our travel bags in the overhead compartment, that being our only luggage since we won't be in Joburg for that long. We find our seats, watch the flight attendant do the safety demonstration and then we're on our way.

"So tell me, how do you really feel?" Imka asks, with her head pressed back firmly against the seat, with a huge, dimpled smile.

"To be honest, I feel like I am just coming up from under water, like my whole body has been submerged for a really long time, and somehow I am just able to break through to the surface so I can breathe again. It's eerie because I also feel like I am just coming out of a fever; like I've had a really high temperature and it just broke. When I was a child, I had the measles and I had a fever for three days. The whole time my mom had been making me tea with hibiscus leaves, which usually works, but for some reason this time it didn't help. My parents were so concerned that the fever wouldn't break until, eventually, someone told my mother to pull up the vervain plant, the root and everything, wash it thoroughly and boil it; that did it, the fever broke. So that's how I feel now, like I have been having a high fever for a long time and it just broke!"

"That is just wonderful, Nevaeh. I am really happy for you."

"Finally, I feel like a normal human being again!"

She just smiles at me.

"But does this mean that we have to return to New York right away?"

"No, at least I don't think so. But for sure that will change the dynamics of this case and quite definitely place you in even more danger."

"So what are we going to do, then?"

"For the meantime, let's just enjoy this huge victory and our impromptu vacation. We won't tell the detective because that might place him in danger as well."

"What do you mean, put him in danger? That's the last thing I want to do, you know that, right?"

"Yes, more than anyone else, I know that."

She shifts in her seat, trying to find a comfortable position but gives up and continues: "Well, by now Rain's associates must know that the detective has been working closely with you. They must also know that if anyone should know where you are, he definitely would. Therefore they might try to torture him to get your location, because as far as I know not even Rose Marie knows where we are. She's just been told that you're in a safe place and in order to continue your treatment I had to go with you. But if they know for sure that you have all your memories back there might be a greater urgency to eliminate you, so to speak."

I picture the detective squirming in pain with blood dripping from his light brown hair. I shake my head, trying to dislodge the image.

"No, we cannot share this info with him then, not yet."

"So let's agree to keep it under wraps, at least for now."

"But what if I accidentally say something and he discovers that I have my memory back?"

"When and if that happens we will deal with it. It also depends on whether the time is right, then we'll tell him. But for now, just continue to enjoy your vacation."

"Can you imagine?"

I can't contain myself. I punch the seat in front of me and the guy turns his whole body around to see me, I offer him one of my most disarming smiles. He just shakes his head and pulls up his seat, away from me and my exuberance.

"I am in South Africa, home of Nelson Mandela. Do you think we'll see him in Joburg?"

She laughs so loudly I can see her back teeth. "No, I don't think so. He's gotten old and he doesn't make that many public appearances anymore."

The two-hour flight goes by in a flash. Soon we are grabbing our bags. We get a taxi and he takes us to a hotel. This hotel is not as fancy as the Providence, neither is there a beach or trees, but it is enough that I am here. We take a nap and refresh ourselves and prepare to meet Shale. I am so excited, and a bit anxious, to meet someone from Imka's family, someone who has known her their whole life. I suddenly miss my dad and my aunts a whole lot. I miss Jamaica terribly, and my friends. I vow that as soon as this whole mess is over, I am going to get on a flight and head to Jamaica. I don't care where the money will come from.

"Imka, do you think I could possibly call my dad?" I ask while we wait on another taxi to take us to the restaurant where we'll meet Shale.

"Yes, I think so, but there's about a six-hour time difference, so your dad might be asleep now."

"He must be so worried. I have never gone this long without calling him before, and I don't really know how I'm going to explain the prolonged absence of a phone call to him without giving too much away. Because above all else, I do not want him to worry about me."

"And at his age he shouldn't have to. But as a parent, Nevaeh, it's his prerogative to worry and it doesn't matter what you say or how you feel, he will worry."

"And how will I explain Rayva's death?" I ask, tears about to erupt.

"Don't cry, Neva. Everything will be fine," she soothes. "Just tell him he died suddenly in an accident, and you're too upset to talk about it right now."

"My dad, in fact my whole family, really love—I mean loved—Rayva. They fell in love with him before I did."

She just squeezes my hand gently.

We get to the restaurant and Shale is waiting. Beautiful Shale. No, she is stunning; she has beautiful dark skin, like Bridget and Claire, full naturally pink lips which she highlights with gloss and a lip liner pencil, and large expressive eyes. When we are introduced, she hugs me like she has known me for years. I feel guilty for feeling nervous about meeting her.

I feel daring, so we order a seafood platter. The most delicious seafood I have ever had. I practically inhale everything I put on my plate. It is such a refreshing change from hospital food, and also a throwback to the seafood in Jamaica.

I try not to think about sweet, sweet Jamaica, about how far I am from my homeland. So in an effort to not cry in this very posh restaurant, I ask: "So how long have you worked at the museum, Shale?"

"I have worked at the Apartheid Museum since it opened

about five years ago," she says, with her wine glass in midair. So stately, with her long slender fingers, polished to perfection.

"Oh wow! That must be both exciting and stressful at the same time."

She laughs and throws her head back. Imka and I join in.

"It is, but it is very rewarding."

"How so?" Imka questions.

"Well, I get to help curate pieces of our people's history and put them on display for the world to see. Because, as you know, some would like to erase it. But as horrible as apartheid was, it is still a part of our history and to erase it would be to erase parts of who we are as a people."

"That's very true, Shale." Imka beams like a proud parent.

We eat in silence for a bit. Then Shale says, "Imka, I know you have not been there since we opened, but would guys like to visit while you're here? I can get you complimentary tickets."

"Are you sure? Because we don't mind paying."

"How much are the tickets, though?" I ask, more out of curiosity that anything else.

"It's sixty-five rand."

"Imka, about how much is that in US?"

"About five dollars."

"What? And I thought the Jamaican dollar was weak."

"How much is the value of the Jamaican dollar?"

"Right now I don't even know. All I know is that if I send my dad one hundred Canadian, he gets lots of Jamaican for it. But our dollar is so weak that it doesn't accomplish a lot, unless you have millions."

"I almost forgot that you had lived in Canada for a while."

"How is living in Canada?" Shale questions. "I hear it is very clean."

"I think that's one of the first things people hear about Canada, that it is extremely clean, and it is very clean. A beautiful place to live, but like everywhere else they have their own issues—and a dark past."

"What do you mean?" Shale asks, putting away her fork, ready for a story.

"Well, for starters, they ran the Indigenous peoples off their land and pushed them on to Reserves. And they have applied strict rules to keep them there."

"What do you mean? What kind of rules?" Imka asks, looking very concerned.

"Based on past treaties, they are entitled to monetary support from the Federal Government; however, if they choose to leave the Reserves, they are no longer entitled to some of those benefits, so to speak."

"That's horrible, and I bet they took all the fertile lands and gave them the worst pieces," Shale says, sipping her white wine.

"It is horrible. But stealing their land is not even the worst part. The powers that be took their children—"

"What do you mean, took their children?"

"Well, what's the best way to rob people of their history?" I don't wait for a response. I just continue, "Take their children, teach them your way, don't give them a chance to learn their language, customs or history—and that will lead to what I call the great forgetting. Because, let's face it, most of our cultures have rich oral histories, that's how we pass on our traditions to the next generation in the absence of a system of writing. But when they take the kids, indoctrinate them, teach them their way, their language, and tell them that the way of their foreparents is primitive, then that's what leads to the great forgetting."

"Yes, Nevaeh, you are absolutely right, and that is—" I get the sense that Shale is going to share more but Imka interjects.

"Alright, ladies, enough depressive talk for one evening. Let's leave that conversation for another day. And yes, Shale, we'll accept your offer. Just tell us when."

"I already made the arrangements, so you guys can visit tomorrow."

"Okay, sounds great."

"Well, ladies, the night is still young. So what next?"

"Shale, the night might be young, but currently I am not feeling that young. Maybe, as the Americans would say, I'll take a rain cheque."

"What about you, Nevaeh?" Shale asks, looking optimistic.

"Sadly, I must agree with Imka. I am not feeling that young tonight."

"It must be the jet lag, ladies," Shale says sympathetically.

"It might be! I promise that we will go paint the town red with you some other time. Okay Ms. Shale?" I use the same line that Rayva had used. I feel a stab of pain my chest where my heart sits.

I can't believe that it has only been a few days and so much has happened; just like the rainy season back home, when it rains it certainly pours. At any rate, I say this more to appease myself than anything else, but deep down I know it is a combination of events, not just the jet lag. I don't know how much Imka has shared about me with Shale, but if I know her well, I will say not too much. Also, I suspect that Imka has rejected the invitation on my behalf. A whole lot has indeed happened in an insanely short time and I still need time to process. I haven't had a chance to, yet. Plus I have had a headache all day, ever since I bumped my head, but I am so ecstatic to have had all my lost memories come flooding back that I refuse to let a headache slow me down. Imagine living with the knowledge that a huge part of you is missing but you don't know how to recover it; that's how I have been all these months. I have been feeling like I lost a limb.

That being said, I have to admit that it is indeed karmic, because I spent a huge part of my life hoping to forget, deliberately forgetting and galvanizing aid to forget. Then it got to the point where I would have gladly, graciously, and gravely given up my soul to be able to take a stroll down memory lane; especially during those days cooped up in the hospital. Thankfully it did not come to that—giving up my soul. The fact is, until someone has lost something really valuable and has it returned to them without pomp or pageantry, fear or favour, it's virtually an impossibility to explain the great delight of getting their treasured possession back.

Ironically, until this great misadventure happened to me, I did not realize what a treasure-trove my memory is. I didn't stop to consider that that is where I keep all my loved ones, those who have transitioned and those who are still here, but we've either lost touch or circumstances prevent our commingling. Really, even just to call up a memory at will to escape a sticky situation is both a God-given gift and an unsung blessing.

We part company, promising to meet up in the morning at the museum. I don't know what to expect at an Apartheid Museum, but I am excited to be here on this journey with these two wonderful souls. Come to think of it, why would anyone voluntarily celebrate such a horrific aspect of their history? This would be the equivalent of Jamaicans creating a Slavery Museum, but from what I remember about Jamaicans, I can safely say that that is not going to happen, at least not any time soon. We are a proud, rebellious, creative, intelligent and resilient people, who stop at nothing to make our dreams a reality. But highlighting that part of us is not on the cards, or at least I don't see it.

On our way back to the hotel, I think of all the beautiful souls who have either been permitted to enter my life or have infiltrated my walls. I think of Miss Shalk, who in retrospect was not a horrible person; I just saw her through those eyes. I heard her comments through the channel of disrespect. The mind is really powerful and capable of creating monsters or angels out of people. It just depends on the occasion. Shalk was just doing the best she could; shaming was what she knew, and that's what she was trying to use to get me out of my slump. A slump, I now understand, that had originated from the charcoal that I had been ingesting. I did not know it was so harmful. How could I have known? Growing up, a lot of the neighbourhood kids used to eat charcoal, some even used to eat dirt. Even pregnant women used to eat those things. However, I think I went a little overboard in that regard; hence, my dependence on a substance to get me through harsh times. Like all substances that create an illusion of safety, it easily led to an addiction.

Clearly, even the most benign substance has the potential to be destructive if not taken or done in moderation, because after all charcoal is just trees; baked trees. I suspect this applies to not only substances, objects, flora or fauna, but it applies to humans as well. Plus, Shalk was not only mean to me, but she was also strict with all of us; unlike some teachers she did not subscribe to the notion of having a favourite, and for that she should have been applauded and not ridiculed. In my own practice, as a teacher, I have always endeavoured to be fair and kind to all my students and I know for sure that I do not practise partiality, so for that I credit Shalk. Also, I realize that people can only give out of what they have, what they know; therefore, by the time I became a teacher, I knew better so I did better.

The next day is a bright and sunny day in Joburg, with a gentle breeze and not even one cloud in the sky. We meet Shale for breakfast at a quaint little restaurant near her place of work. I just have toast and more sweet tea, since I don't know what to expect from the museum. It seems ironic to me that we are eagerly revisiting a history that has no place in the present and is therefore best left in the past, but at this point in my journey I am quite open to new knowledge and new ways of thinking and being.

We get to the museum and right from the get-go the entrance is symbolic of the apartheid era. There's a gate for *Europeans only, Blacks and Non-Blacks*. This idea seems so out of place and out of touch with the reality of the present that I wonder if I really want to go through all the exhibits.

But I think, that was the old me, the new me is a lot more

open-minded. So we go through all of them, examining each, like a scientist looking at a ground-breaking specimen. We do not speak, as if we've all agreed that this is a sacred moment. As it turns out, this museum is not only about apartheid, but it also traces the history of the South African people and ends with my favourite exhibit: "A Place of Healing."

This is a place allocated for reflection and is indicative of the South African landscape, with flora and fauna indigenous to the area. Again, as if predetermined, all three of us find a space and create an invisible ring around ourselves in this rich oasis, and just take a moment of introspection. Both Shale and Imka shed tears, and although I may never know why, it does seem fitting and appropriate because I do not see shame in those tears—I see strength, beauty and resilience derived from great pain. Come to think of it, South Africans could easily be my people.

In that moment of my own introspection, I see my life parallel to the events as depicted here in the museum, and like never before I am filled with so much gratitude that it feels like a weight on me. It seems as though, where fear has resided all these years, gratitude now sits and has filled every cell in my body. Leaving this place, I vow to never be afraid, to never ever be ashamed of my past and to always be grateful for the present that the past has afforded. I now realize, I guess I have always known, that there is no point running from the past; however, holding it up in the light of grace, looking it squarely in the face, embracing and extracting the lessons, is the only way to grow and develop without carrying baggage with you.

After an emotional release, in our own unique ways, we promise to meet with Shale for dinner. Although it's her day off, she'd wanted to get a few things done. But in the meantime, Imka and I need to have lunch; having not had a solid breakfast, I am famished. The nearest restaurant is about three blocks away so we decide to walk. It is still a beautiful day; a gentle breeze moves us along without being too pushy. We are both in our own unique realm, with a mutual understanding and appreciation for silent reflection—on the exhibits and I guess on our life as well. We both order steak and mashed potatoes; no wine today, at least not yet. I still have the residue of a headache from yesterday.

"So what did you think of the museum, Nevaeh?" Imka asks, while cutting through her steak with a ferocity that is both alien to her and quite becoming. I guess she is just as famished as I am.

"To be honest, at first I was skeptical about going."

"Skeptical? Why?"

"I was just not sure of what to expect, and when we heard about apartheid on the news back home and learned about it in school, it just never seemed like something to be celebrated."

"And now, having seen the exhibits first hand?"

"Well, I get it now."

"How? What do you mean?" She places her utensils on her plate, rests both hands on the table in a protective gesture and pays attention to me as if I am the most important person in the room.

"Well, I have sort of drawn parallels with my own life. In the sense that there are many things that have happened, that brought me great shame and chronic pain, but just like the idea of the museum—"

"What do you think is the idea behind the museum?"

"The whole notion that you should not be ashamed of your past, but rather you should learn from it and allow others to learn from it as well. If, for nothing else, to prevent others from making the same or similar mistakes. Because really, no one should be made to feel embarrassed for doing things that they quite possibly had no control over...."

"That's great progress, Neva! I am so happy you see things that way because—" She pauses and looks around, which causes me to look around as well. But no one is paying attention to us; everyone is engrossed in their own discussions and meals.

"Because what, Imka?"

"Because I wanted to talk to you about something that happened to you. Now this might not be the most orthodox place, but let's face it, there is nothing conventional about our situation."

We laugh knowingly.

"By the same token, if you do not wish to discuss this now, it is no problem, okay? I am always here whenever you're ready."

"Alright."

"Remember when the detective said you had reported a rape?"

"Yes, I remember; not only the report but the incident."

"Do you think that you might want to talk about that now? We can if you're ready, but only if and when you are."

"Well, now is as good a time as any. Plus, I might even have to say it in open court, in front of a bunch of strangers, so this might actually be a practise run."

"Happy you see it that way as well."

"Not just since my memory came back, but even before that, I have been seeing a lot of things in a whole different light. From a completely different perspective—"

The waiter interrupts to offer more water, which I accept, happy for the distraction while I put my thoughts together. I've known I would have to talk about this eventually, but I had not expect it to be here and now. I think now is as good a time as any. I look out the double windows and see the mountain in the distance and people walking around, happy people with a history of sadness. However, either they or their foreparents were brave enough to face their ugly past so that it wouldn't haunt their present.

"I've not really been focused on the rape, because I sort of removed myself from the event, so that it felt like it was happening to someone else, by someone else."

"What do you mean? Remember when we spoke about disassociation?"

"Yes!"

"Is that what happened?"

"Maybe, I don't know for sure. It might have been the shock."

"So you never saw it coming?"

"What do you mean? Are you blaming me?"

"Oh, absolutely not, Neva. I would never do that. But what I am asking is: did Rain seem like the type of person to do something as horrible as that?"

"No, absolutely not! When I first moved to Canada, they were the perfect family. I thought I had died and gone straight to heaven. Every single one of Rayva's family was wonderful to me, but somehow I felt underserving. A girl like me did not deserve any of it; not after everything I had done. Like you said, I brought baggage with me."

She reaches for my hand and just gently squeezes, her way of encouraging me to speak, to unload without interruption. I know that later she's going to ask about what I have done, but I am still not ready to deal with that yet, so in the interim I'll talk about Rain. It's more recent and somehow comparatively easier to report.

"I felt like I had somehow managed to bamboozle my way into someone else's life; I was living someone else's dream. We used to do everything together, you know, me and Rayva, Summer and her husband Robbie, and Rain and Miss. Linda.

"They were so in love, like two teenagers. They went for walks, held hands. My parents were in love, but I have never actually seen much show of public affection, so Rain and Miss Linda's romance used to embarrass me at times. But then everything changed when she got sick. He became moody, especially, when the medication he had helped to make was helping others and not his wife, the great love of his life." I pause to have a sip of my water.

"I had my own issues, and I had been around death and dying enough to know that, regardless of her optimism and Rain holding on to hope, she wasn't going to make it. When she died

Rain was beside himself, he was inconsolable, and I felt so bad for him. Over the years I have not dealt with death very well, so even in this I was stoic, because again, my own issues.

"Rain started to nitpick every single thing that everyone said and did. He yelled at Rayva and when I tried to defend him, he turned on me. By then Rayva and I were having our own problems; mainly me, I was at the heart of it. Anyways, I had moved out of our matrimonial bed after a huge fight, and one night I heard a loud bang on the door which woke me up. It continued and I was angry because I thought it was Rayva so I opened the door and confronted him, but it wasn't Rayva, it was Rain. At first I was confused. He smelled of brandy—I will never be able to get that scent out of my head."

I reach for my water and I see that my hands are shaking. Imka takes both of my hands in hers. I take a deep breath, shake my head to clear my thoughts and continue. I've gotten to this point, so why stop now?

"He pushed his way in, held my hands in one of his while he locked the door behind him. The booze and his own personal hell empowered him. He had nothing left to lose. He threw me on the bed, ripped off my night gown, pushed my legs apart and forced himself into me. Instinctively, I kicked and screamed and then he put a pillow over my head. I literally thought I was going to die. So I kept really still and imagined myself swimming in the river back home. I tried to temper that horrible memory with one of beauty and peace. I always choose the river."

Imka comes around to my side and hugs me. But I push her away. I cannot accept her pity here and now, or else I am going to cry uncontrollably, and I am among strangers in a restaurant so I will not allow myself to accept pity or fall apart. She understands the gesture and returns to her place across from me, and I drink more water and force myself to continue.

"After that, he just left me on the bed. At first I tried to deny that it had happened, but that didn't work. Then I tried to forget that it had happened, and all my life I have mastered the fine art of forgetting, of disregarding my memories. However in this case I couldn't, I just couldn't make myself forget, because it was too physical. I think because it wasn't a purely emotional wound, it was physical and emotional; all the signs were there so I couldn't just delete it from my memory."

"What happened next? How did the police get involved?"

Imka's voice seems so far away, just like when I woke up on the plane.

"I decided to have a shower, but before I did I wiped myself thoroughly and placed the towels along with the bed linen and my night gown in a plastic bag in case I wanted to take action later, after my head cleared. I was even willing to let it go because I couldn't stand the shame of other people knowing. But what made me decide to tell the police was Rayva—"

"Rayva encouraged you to tell?"

"No, the opposite! He didn't believe me. He thought I was lying. I even showed him the clothes in the bag but he still didn't believe me. He just kept saying that I was trying to cause problems for him and his family. Eventually, I got really angry and I decided to actually create the problem that he was accusing me of making. I went to the police and told them my story multiple times. At first I thought that they did not believe me. They kept sending me from department to department, person to person, and I was so angry that I decided that I would see this through to the bitter end. By then, I didn't think I had anything to live for; like Rain I had nothing left to lose. My second baby had just died, shortly before Miss Linda, and I was just not in a good place emotionally. Now that I think about it, what with ingesting gasoline, coupled with everything else that was going on at the time, I now understand why I was in such a foul place. Looking back at it, jumping into that river is the best choice I made in a really long time."

"Why was that the best choice, seeing as you could have died?"

"It led me to Sandy, to Robin, to you and to South Africa: all you guys have rescued me from myself. I was doing serious harm to myself, not just then but for a long time. I was destroying myself slowly in an effort to forget my pain and grief and shame."

"Why do you think that was happening?"

"I felt unworthy, despite all my blessings, and like Sandy said, I was suffering from a thing called imposter syndrome. Therefore I couldn't see my worth, I couldn't see my value, which led me to sabotage myself, sabotage my marriage. Rayva was so good to me, and his family were as well. At one point, I wondered if I deserved what happened to me, what Rain did—"

"No, you absolutely did not. No one deserves that."

"I know that now, but at the time it tied into the narrative of self-loathing that I had bought into and that I kept feeding myself."

"Is that why Rain was so angry, because he thought you had evidence of the rape in your journal?"

"I don't know. I think he was probably shaken by the fact that the police were investigating his business and he wanted to blame someone. He has been angry for a long time, ever since Miss. Linda died, and I think his anger turned to bitterness which led to everything that has transpired so far. He was angry with himself for not being able to rescue the love of his life, so he gave up on himself, much like I did, and started making horrible choices. I guess he was self-sabotaging as well. I think also that he came to realize that she had possibly ingested some of the tainted medication and blamed himself for that immensely. He just couldn't ever forgive himself."

"Do you think that you can ever forgive him for what he's done?"

"If you had asked me this up to yesterday, I would have said an emphatic no, but now I think that I am willing to consider the possibility of forgiving him."

"Why? What has changed?"

"You guys—meaning you South Africans."

"What do you mean?"

"Well, in order for you guys to have gone on with your lives and not only survive but thrive despite your horrible past, someone had to decide to forgive to let healing in. Correct?"

"Yes, that's true. Plus, it helped that there was a Truth and Reconciliation Commission. Do you remember that exhibit?"

I nod in acknowledgement.

"Therefore, I think that definitely helped with the healing process. But in your specific case, what if Rain never finds the courage to apologize for the wrong inflicted against you and Rayva—will you still find the strength to forgive him? Because as you've rightfully said, forgiveness is the only door which allows healing in."

"I think I will. Knowing me, I will."

"Please don't get me wrong, Neva. I am not insisting that you forgive the person who has wronged you. No one should do that. I am just saying you should forgive, but only when you're good and ready—while bearing in mind that forgiveness is for you, not the person who has wronged you."

"Yes, believe me, I get it! I grew up with a mother who fully believed in and touted the benefits of forgiveness. So, like you said, when I am ready I think I will. Because you know what, at this point in my journey, I am so grateful for my life. To actually get my life back on track, I feel like I've got a second chance that I am not about to waste, and neither am I going to give anyone permission to live in my head and control my movements. I have allowed the ghosts of the past to do this for years, and I am just sick and tired of being sick and tired, so I am no longer open to allowing that to happen anymore."

"Good for you, girl."

"Thank you so much, Imka. I don't think I would have been able to get to this point without your support. You are one of the few people that I have ever called a friend."

"You are most welcome. I am happy to call you my friend as well. Your strength is admirable. I must say that I have not really had a patient who has made so many strides in such a relatively short time. I am so impressed and honoured to be your friend and therapist. But do you want to know what is great about our friendship?"

"You buy me as much food as I want, and pay for my hotel and taxi fare?"

We both laugh so loudly that the people around us look at us and seem to laugh along with us as well.

"That too! But unlike your other friendships, whatever you say to me is covered by a strict, formal confidentiality agreement. Technically, as you are my patient, we shouldn't really be friends because of ethics and such, but under the circumstances I don't see how we couldn't be."

"That's a bonus right there, knowing that I am never alone. In the past, I have had some sturdy friends but I didn't recognize that in them until now."

"Yes, it is. Now let's go to the hotel so you can get some rest. You must be exhausted after the emotional day you've had!"

"Indeed I am, but I know that it is all a part of my healing journey and I am going to be okay. Decidedly, feeling exhausted is way better than feeling numb."

It turns out that Imka was right; I sleep like a baby that whole afternoon and I would have happily slept all night if Imka hadn't woken me to get ready to meet up with Shale. Again we had an awesome time. Sadly, there is not an actual beach in Joburg, only a man-made one, so we invited Shale to come with us to Cape Town to enjoy the ocean with us. At first she was hesitant, because she didn't want to impose, but in a few days it would be the weekend so she couldn't come up with an acceptable excuse.

Imka and I—but mostly just me—spend the next few days sight-seeing. We go clothes shopping as well, and find a hair braider to tame my hair. For the first time she tells me about her brothers. I can see how much she adores them. But in a lot of ways we are a lot alike in that she grew up alone, being the only girl, and I grew up alone being the only child. We visit the botanical garden, the zoo, an indigenous nursery, a theme park, and for the first time ever in my whole life, I visit a night club. Mommy must be turning in her grave right now, but I decide that I have to live my own life and not wait on others to live it for me.

When I was with Rayva, I had a long list of *don'ts*, which mostly frustrated him, but he loved me enough to accept. I wonder how much more rewarding and pleasant life might have been if I had had more *dos* and less *don'ts*. Currently, I am so intoxicated with the desire to live that I don't even care who approves. My only wish is that Rayva were here to enjoy this new found perspective with me.

Ultimately, the time comes for us to return to Cape Town, to our beautiful hotel. Imka shares her room with Shale; after all, they are sisters. As much as they try to include me, I know that there are special memories that they share which will always be private to them. The first night we are so exhausted that we have a light supper and crawl into bed. No one stirs until about eleven the next morning, but since we have no plans we just chill until lunch time. We revisit the buffet table and have a feast.

Between mouthfuls Shale announces, "We should go visit Table Mountain."

Imka retorts, "That's an awesome idea. I have not been since high school."

"Same."

"What's Table Mountain?" I ask, sipping my freshly-made drink of passion fruit and pineapple; no wine today.

"It is a mountain that overlooks Cape Town and is a part of a national park," Shale explains.

"Okay, sounds interesting. I have not been on a hike in a long time." As I say this, I reflect on my last trip to the Blue Mountains and the painful memory attached to it. I have to shake my head to remain present.

"Yes, it should be fun. Hopefully I can get to the top." Imka ponders.

"What do you mean?" Shale and I ask at the same time.

"I don't know about you guys, but I am certainly not as young and active as I used to be. Plus, being in New York, I have not been as active as I should be. I take a taxi almost everywhere, not to mention the elevators at work."

"Are you scared, Sis?" Shale teases.

I join in, making chicken sounds, which triggers laughter in all of us. This comradery so reminds me of my friends back home that I can't even hide it.

Good old Imka is so in tune with my many moods that she notices. "Are you okay, Nevaeh?"

"Yes. Of course I am fine… it's just that… this, us… reminds me of my friends back home."

Shale says, while simultaneously gently rubbing my hand, "Aww! That's alright. I hope you'll see them soon."

"Yes, I hope so too." I sip my drink to avoid the compassion in their eyes.

"Okay, so let's do this hike tomorrow morning, before I change my mind," Imka announces.

We decide to get some things for the hike, so we go shopping and just use the opportunity to stroll around the city. I have to pinch myself. I still cannot believe I am here. I used to hear so much about Cape Town on the radio back home and here I am, front and centre, in Cape Town. We head home, shower and get a light meal at the buffet. Some of the people have become accustomed to seeing us. They even stop to say hi and question where I'm from because of my accent, and only for that reason, because in a lot of ways I look a lot like so many of them.

This whole place so reminds me of the sense of community in my hometown, Balcarres, that I can't even explain it. The warmth, the food, the trees—bliss. We decide to watch a movie.

I am not too sure which, because the whole time I am thinking about this trip to Table Mountain and reflecting on a similar trip many years ago. When the movie ends I barely make it my room and I fall into a coma.

In the middle of the night I am awoken by a scream which I think has come from me, but I sit up in my spacious bed and listen for a while and I realize that it is coming from Imka's room. I think that maybe Rain's associates have discovered our hiding place so I listen for a gun shot, and after not hearing any, or any loud talking, I rush to the room next to mine. I find Imka just cuddling Shale. I feel like I am intruding on a private moment and my instinct is to extricate myself and give them privacy.

However, Imka requests, "Please get her some water, Nevaeh."

I move as quickly as Imka had a few weeks ago in a different city, in a different room, in a different context. I return and Shale is shaking like a banana leaf in the wind, a full-blown panic attack. Imka offers her the bottle of water and she grasps it with trembling hands. Imka soothes her like a child and tells her to take deep breaths, while simultaneously stroking her back. A few minutes later Shale is doing a little better and I turn to leave; again the weight of the moment is thick with intimacy.

But she says, "No, Nevaeh, please stay. Thanks for the water."

I pull up a chair and look at my hands while they sit in the middle of the bed.

When Shale is able to speak again she says, "Thanks guys. I thought I had this under control."

Imka and I say, almost at the same time: "That's fine."

The good Lord and Imka know that I have had similar moments.

I feel like a story is coming so I wait, but there's only silence and quiet breathing. Then suddenly Shale shatters the silence and says, "Nevaeh, I don't know if Imka has told you this, but I watched my parents die when I was really young, and sometimes I get flashbacks in my deepest sleep that shake me to my core."

"No she didn't! I am so very sorry to hear that."

"Yes, it was an automobile accident. I was really young but I was in the back seat with them when it happened. I don't even know how I survived." She clears her throat and somehow I don't hate it as much when she does it.

There is more silence, since I don't know what to say, and Imka says nothing because apparently she is not in her role as therapist here, but sister and friend. Eventually, the silence is pounding in my ears and I feel like I must say something.

"That must have been horrible for you."

Shale looks at me as if she had forgotten I was in the room.

"Thank you! It was for a while, even now emotionally it's exhausting, but then Imka's parents adopted me and that has been one of the greatest blessings of my life. Indeed that has made all the difference for me."

She hugs Imka tight as if she's afraid of letting go and whispers in her hair: "I don't know what would have happened if they hadn't rescued me. I suspect that they not only rescued me from a bad situation but they rescued me from myself; from a life of poor choices."

I didn't even need to ask her for clarification, I can only just imagine because I know only too well what it means to be rescued from myself. I am so impressed with Shale, how readily she shares this traumatic event with a virtual stranger. This sharing circle, if you can call it that, really seems to help, because soon she seems better. It's as if she has been relieved of a substantial burden, as if in sharing her story she has allocated the weight of the burden evenly in the room, none having more than the next.

After a moment of less weighty silence, Imka declares, "Well, if we are going to go on that excursion tomorrow, we all need to get some rest because we have to leave early."

"How early is early, though?" I ask.

"Like around 6 a.m. Any time after that is too late."

With that we bid each other goodnight and soon I am back in

my bed, afraid to sleep lest I conjure images that I would soon forget. However, fortified by Shale's bravery, I eventually turn off my bedside lamp and I am out almost before the light.

Imka wakes us up at 5 a.m. and by 5:30 we are already in a taxi. The morning air is cool and refreshing and reminds me of my house back home on top of the hill. There's a bit of fog but I see the sun peeping over the horizon and according to the weather channel it is going to be an amazing day for our trek.

We are wearing white T-shirts and grey shorts. We'd decided to dress alike just in case one of us goes missing—actually Imka's idea—she's thought of everything. By 6 a.m. we are throwing our backpacks on our backs and checking out where to buy the tickets for entry.

"So what type of animals are we likely to see on our journey?" I ask, wanting to hear and yet not wanting to hear.

Shale excitedly lists: "Tortoise, mongoose, porcupine, a species called the Table Mountain ghost frog and oh, snakes!"

That last one stops me in my tracks. "What? Snakes? You do know that I am Eve's great, great, great-grandchild, so I don't do snakes?"

Imka starts to make chicken sounds and we laugh until we have to hold our sides.

"Alright, alright," I say, recovering.

We start our trek, the crisp morning air nipping at our faces.

"Don't you have snakes in Jamaica?" Shale asks.

"Absolutely not. We have mongoose, because they brought them there to get rid of the snakes and the mongoose did a really great job. So apart from snakes, what else is Table Mountain famous for?"

Imka shares, "Well, it is considered spectacular enough to be named one of the wonders of the world—unofficially though."

"That's cool. So can we drive up the mountain?"

"Yes, but where's the fun in that?" Shale questions.

Looking at her happy-go-lucky demeanour one would never

have guessed that this girl had had a meltdown last night. The human spirit is quite indomitable. Again, I draw strength from Shale and decide that I am going to put my last memory of Blue Mountain Peak out of my mind and enjoy the mountain. I am actually striving to replace the old one with the new. I still can't help but reflect on my friends: on Robin, then Claire, and then Bridget. I wonder how Claire and Bridget are doing. A sudden wave of homesickness hits me, which feels like nausea. I quickly look around to see if the ladies are watching but they are too preoccupied in taking pictures of the flora and fauna.

I ask quickly before anyone can figure me out: "So is there a river in the mountain?"

Shale says, "Not quite a river but there are streams; five in total."

"That's awesome! We should check them out. I love rivers."

"This route that we are taking will only allow us to see one."

"That's fine, as long as I get to see one; any one will do."

As the morning wears on we rest, eat our snacks, take pictures, talk, laugh and tread on. This trip is more and more reminding me of the one I took when I was younger. The higher we climb, the more my anxiety rises. I feel bare, like the saying goes back home: *the higher monkey climbs, the more he is exposed.* I really did not think that I would be having this reaction. For the most part, I calm myself by looking at the plant life and asking questions. Every so often we hear scurrying in the bushes and I look intensely, but thankfully the only things we encounter are lizards—mind you, I hate them too—but I hate snakes more.

"What do you call those ones?"

I say, pointing to a flock of birds, reminded of the ones from my dream, which had foreshowed Rayva's demise.

"I think those ones are called the orange-breasted sunbird," Shale declares, sounding uncertain and looking to Imka for confirmation.

"Yes, that's their name. Mind you, I don't really know a lot about birds, but I know those ones because of their exquisite beauty."

"They are stunning." I try to capture them on film.

Their rich colours, orange, green, blue and brown, glisten in the mid-morning sunlight. I try to remember seeing one of these birds back home but the only one that comes to mind is the doctor bird or hummingbird as they are commonly called.

"These birds remind me of the hummingbird back home, but the hummingbird is quite small, more elegant, and it moves faster."

Shale stops suddenly where two roads meet. We almost bump into her.

"What do you call these ones?"

We stand close to her to see what she has found. It is a small yellow chest bird with brown feathers covering its back, just sitting there on a tree stump as if sunbathing.

Imka offers, "I think those are called the Cape Siskin, if my memory serves me correctly."

We also encounter breathtaking plant life. Invariably, becoming more exquisite the higher we climb. I feel like the plants reach out to embrace me. I gadually feel the stress seep out of my shoulders. We stop once more before we summit the mountain to eat and refresh ourselves. When we reach the flat top of Table Mountain, the name made more explicable; we take more pictures and look down at the picturesque landscape and I think, "There is a God." The smooth and even surface is nothing short of amazing; an architectural wonder, so vastly unlike our Blue Mountain Peak – which protrudes upwards. The vast expanse at the top makes me dizzy, with an intense sense of being exposed, left without covering and nothing to hold on to. This lack of shield, strips me to my core, leaving me naked, open and unmasked. The view is so imposing, I stagger a little.

I am stunned to hear Shale say, "Absolutely." Apparently it was more than just a thought.

We look around, take in more of the lush scenery and then decide to call it day. On our way down I start to feel like I can't breathe and then in my mind's eye I see Robin's backpack. I try holding it together for as long as I can and then the tears come gushing down. It is Shale who catches me before I faint. I wake up later in the shade of some trees, which form a cocoon around us. My face is wet; I guess they must have doused me with water, hopefully from my water bottle.

"Are you alright, Nevaeh?" Imka sounds really worried.

"Yes, I am." I try to stand but my legs are weak and wobbly.

"Well, you don't look alright," Shale says, helping me to sit up instead of trying to stand.

"What happened back there?"—Imka again.

"It was nothing. I must have been dehydrated. I'll be fine in a few."

But the more I declare that I am fine is the more uncertain they both look.

"I don't think you're fine, Nevaeh. You even feel feverish!" Shale says, touching the back of her hand to my forehead.

Imka digs into her backpack. "I think I have some Tylenol. You should have one with some of your water."

"No, I'm fine. I don't need it," I protest weakly.

They both start to question me and poke holes in my theory. I feel the beginning of a headache and I am still dizzy. I feel so weak and overwhelmed. I can't hold onto myself; I feel myself slipping away. I tell myself that if I don't tell them, despite the fact that it is a clear beautiful day, I am going to be struck by lightning. This high in the mountain, I am pretty sure that we are close to God, who knows all I've done, even if I have never allowed myself to verbalize it – even if I have spent so many years suppressing it – that it feels like it never happened. They try to lead me and as we are walking or scrambling along like three crabs, I think, "But God knows. He knows that I killed my friend."

Both Imka and Shale stop abruptly in their tracks and say,

"What?"

That's when I realize what I have said it aloud. I have said it aloud for the very first time ever. Not even Rayva knew what I had done. No one knows. Not even Claire and Bridget.

Shale says, "It must be the fever. She's hallucinating. We have to get her to a doctor."

Imka shoves the Tylenol in my palm.

"No, I am fine. I don't need this."

They help me to lie on my back in a patch of green grass. "But you're roasting with fever, Nevaeh. How can you tell us that you're fine?" Shale sounds like she's on the verge of tears.

"Plus you're delirious, you're talking nonsense. A sure sign that you have an extremely high temperature. You need to take this until we can figure out a way to get you off of the mountain."

Imka sounds like she's about to join Shale in shedding tears. So I decide that they deserve to hear the truth, whatever the consequences. But I don't want to tell them while I am lying down; I don't want any pity. So on this beautiful day with birds chirping and flying overhead and the flora and fauna watching from their secret places, I share something which I have never allowed myself to ever say.

"It is not the fever. I am actually telling you guys about something that happened many years ago, which changed me and my life forever. I made myself forget the details, but when my memories came back all the details came flooding back to me."

They both take one of my hands without saying a word.

"My best friend Robin always wanted to have her birthday party at a fancy restaurant and then all of a sudden she wanted to have it in the Blue Mountains with just the four of us: her, me, Claire and Bridget. The Blue Mountains are the highest point on the island. It is much like this mountain but it peaks instead of being flat at the top. The terrain is a lot more treacherous, especially on the descent. So while we were having lunch, she announced that she was pregnant and she was planning to run away to the

Maroon settlement to live with her Maroon boyfriend."

They look at me questioningly so I know I have to pause and give context. "The Maroons are the descendants of formerly-enslaved Africans and some of the Indigenous people on the island; I think the Taino Indians. They are Jamaicans but they live in their own communities and have their own system of government."

Imka interrupts: "That sounds like the Orania people in the Northern Cape. They believe in maintaining their authenticity in language and culture and since they have a non-confrontational approach the central government leaves them alone to make and institute their own laws."

"I swear Jamaicans could be South Africans."

They smile wanly. I take that as a cue to continue.

"Anyways, our other friends must have known or at least suspected because somehow she had started looking weird to me in the weeks preceding that day. But I was so naïve, so idealistic, that I would never allow myself to even consider that possibility. I mean, Robin was the smart one, the one who had her head screwed on right, the one we called upon to help us make tough decisions. She had her whole life ahead of her."

I look at each of them, pleading with them to understand my actions, when up to this day I still did not.

Imka, silent up to this point, says in a tone that I don't recognize, "Go on, Nevaeh."

"Our friends seemed like they had accepted it. They weren't willing to confront her and talk to her about it, talk some sense into her."

"But you wanted to speak some sense into the situation," Shale concedes.

"Yes, that's all I wanted to do. But she was so stubborn that she wouldn't listen. So the plan was that when we got to a really treacherous point she would say she wanted to pee on account of the fact that it's cold in the mountains, then we would all go our separate ways to pee and then she would just disappear and we literally would not know where she went. Ergo, we couldn't tell her mom or anyone. Despite the fact that I had a horrible headache—I felt nauseous and dizzy—I decided that I would just make one last-ditched effort to make her see reason. The others left us, according to the plan, but I remember that we were yelling and screaming at each other. She was saying that it was her life and I couldn't tell her what to do with it. I asked her about her mom who had had her own struggles with depression. She said that her mom would be fine. Then I said, what about me, and she said, *you have your Obeahman to ensure that the greatness in you manifests.*

Seeing their mutual confusion, again, I feel the need to explain the Obeahman reference.

"So an Obeahman is a person, male or female, who uses dark magic to grant your wishes. However, this one was different; he read scriptures and washed me in a concoction made of herbs. Also, those people are rumoured to hear directly from the ancestors, and they can foretell the future and help you to fix problems in the present."

Again more questions in their eyes. Maybe I am not doing such a good job explaining myself.

"It's a long story, and one for another time, but I was having some problems with my Literature teacher so I went to see the Obeahman to help me with that issue."

Shale nods, an indication for me to continue.

"Now we all, all four of us, had vowed never to speak of that event ever again because I was still raw from it and I had felt responsible for everything that happened after that visit. So her saying it was a huge betrayal, and I felt in that moment that I couldn't trust her and I said as much. I called her a hypocrite and a whore and she got mad and shoved me, and I got mad and shoved her back. At the time, neither of us realized how close we were to the ledge of a precipice, and after I shoved her, she slipped and I tried to catch her but I couldn't grasp her hand—

and if I had, I would have gone over the edge with her."

I pause and allow the tears to come like a torrential downpour. In that moment I cry more than I have ever cried before. Huge sobs that shake all three of us. It feels like I've been crying for ages but I know it has only been for about ten minutes. After that I feel spent and cleansed all at once.

"I didn't tell the others," I continue, looking at my sneakers, covered in dust. I reach for a sip of water, then persevere.

"I just allowed them to continue to think that she had left, just like she planned. But the problem was I didn't see when her red backpack fell. It must have, because when the others came they found it and decided that something had gone wrong so we needed to get help. At first they searched and I helped them. I can't believe that I actually helped, knowing what I had done."

Shale breaks the mutual silence: "But it sounds to me, Nevaeh, that as horrible as it was, it was an accident—"

Imka chimes in, "I think in order for you to be culpable there must have been intent, a pre-determined intention to kill. But from all you've said, it was unintentional. Like Shale said, it was a terrible accident, not a murder…."

"Yes, but she died at my hands. It was all my fault. I feel like I pushed her. If I hadn't been so, so needy, and selfish, and let her be like the others, none of it would have happened. She would be with her boyfriend and baby right now in Maroon Town."

"But that's conjecture, though, Nevaeh. You are merely speculating. You don't know for sure that any of those things would have happened. Do you?" Imka as always the voice of impeccable reason.

"No, I guess not. But because of me, my selfishness, my clinginess, both her and her baby died."

"Oh, Nevaeh, that's a whole lot to carry, and we're going to have to talk about this some more. But in the meantime I think you should find a way to talk about this with your other friends. I think they have a right to know and be allowed to grieve properly."

"But don't you see? I can't. I can't even look at them, look them in the eyes. From that time, our relationship has never been the same. When the incident just happened, I willed myself to forget, but I would remember from time to time exactly what had happened and I couldn't get it out of my head. Especially after my babies kept dying. I felt like it was karma, like I did not deserve to have any kids of my own. Poor Rayva!"

"Is that why you moved out of your matrimonial bedroom?" Imka sounds so sympathetic. I don't even deserve her sympathy.

"Yes, that's primarily the reason."

"Do you remember us talking about maximum weight?"

"Yes."

"I think that is a whole lot for you to have been carrying Neva, for all these years. I don't know your friend, nor the circumstances surrounding her passing, but based on all you've said, I think this was an awful accident."

Imka, level headed as always but I don't really want to hear that right now. I want to stew in guilt, it is what I deserve, not tendereness.

"Yes, Neva, this was an accident, just like my parents' accident. There's nothing that anyone could have done to prevent it. No one could have foreseen it either. Therefore, it's rather pointless to question the whys and the wherefores and keep punishing yourself. I can say this because for a really long time I suffered from survivor's guilt. If it had not been for Imka and our family, I don't even know what would have become of me. I kept asking, why did I survive and they didn't? But there's no real answer for that. We never know exactly why things happen the way they do. Sadly, sometimes they just do. You are going to kill yourself carrying this load that is far too weighty for any one person to lift, let alone carry."

Shale's impassioned plea is quite moving but I still want to make amends.

"So what happens now? Do I tell the police?"

"Well based on what you've said, you all searched and there was no body recovered. Correct?"

"Yes."

"So how are you going to prove that a crime has been committed?" Imka asserts.

"I saw her fall over the ledge. I made her, I pushed her."

"Yes, you did, and I think you have punished yourself enough. So I think you should converse with your other friends, and as difficult as this is you should strive to forgive yourself so that you can live a healthy life without regrets. Continuing to punish yourself is counter-productive; it doesn't serve anyone. Okay?"

I nod, not trusting my voice. I still feel so undeserving of their kindness. I would have much preferred that they were mad at me. It's going to take me a really long time to see things from their perspective. But I think that they are right; it is time to discuss this with Claire and Bridget. I am sure they too have suffered as a result of my actions.

I try to get up and they both take one of my arms. I can't help but wonder how many secrets have been revealed and kept hidden in this mountain over the years. My legs feel less wobbly so I think I can trust them to get me down off of the mountain. To think that this day had started out with so much promise and I ruined everyone's day.

"I am so sorry, guys."

They both ask the same question: "Sorry for what?"

"I ruined our beautiful trip."

Shale says, "Nevaeh, don't be silly. I know we only just met, but I feel like I have known you since forever. Besides, even if I did not know you, you're a person in pain so it is my good pleasure to help you as much as I can. Regardless of what we've done, or haven't done, or have allowed to happen, we are still human beings worthy of love and compassion."

"No, not me! Rayva should have just allowed me to die. I am not worthy of his sacrifice."

"What?" Shale looks to Imka for clarity.

"Rayva is her husband and he died in a terrible accident recently."

Shale just holds me and I feel her rather than hear her crying in my braids. I can't help it, with her crying and Imka stroking my back, I cry some more. After we are both spent she lets go and I feel, just like last night, that a weight has been evenly distributed. But now it's my weight that has been shared among us. I feel less heavy and more balanced for the first time in a really long time.

CHAPTER TWENTY-THREE

Imanage to descend the mountain without incident. I am forced to stay in bed for a few days. At first we think that the fever and my other symptoms are as a result of an insect bite but I check and there's not even a scratch on me. But according to a few bystanders (we saw them while we were leaving) I must have developed mountain fever because of the altitude. I have never heard of such a thing but apparently, although Table Mountain is not that high, it is a possibility. It clearly depends on the individual and the things going on in their body at the time—hormones and such – or in my case a guilty conscience.

Inevitably, I am forced to use these few days in bed for intense introspection and soul searching. I make some hard choices as well, because as Mommy used to say, *all things work together for good, Nevaeh, it might not be at all good, not at all. But believe me, somewhere in there it is working for your good.* So far she's been right. When I do an appraisal of my life I come up with: she died, I planted chrysanthemums, I met Rayva through those chrysanthemums, we got married, I went to Canada, almost destroyed myself and my marriage, I was raped, jumped in the river, met my new friends, and here I am in a beautiful, luxurious place with two very dear souls. So much goodness that I don't deserve. It must be because of my Mother's prayers; grace and favour have cloaked me.

Indeed, all things work together for the good of them that love God, and despite myself one thing has remained constant—and that is my love for God, and clearly His unfailingly reckless love for me. For that reason I have come a far way in a short time, and to God be the glory, as Mommy used to say. Getting my memories back, forgiving myself, sharing and taking responsibility for the things that have happened, I have healed a whole lot from many traumatic experiences, and I just want to keep getting better. I want to feel whole—I don't know if there was ever a time when I felt whole—but I have tried brokenness so now I want to experience what being whole feels like.

I make the tough decision to speak with my friends back home. This is a situation where I should have talked with them face to face, but my current circumstances do not allow for that and the coward in me is grateful for that fact. I have reached out to Bridget, to whom I had given my cell phone before I left, and she still has the number although the phone broke; symbolic of our bond. I cannot believe it and I even surprise myself by remembering my old number. We have a telephone meeting today and she is going to have Claire with her. She said that they will go by the river, which will be just like old times. It is late afternoon in Cape Town and it is just morning there, but I guess they sensed the seriousness of the situation and wanted to make it meaningful, so the river it is.

They pick up on the first ring, and I am startled by Bridget's voice; she sounds the exact same as she always has, and so near. She says, "Hello."

I reply, "Hello."

And she exclaims, "What happen, girl?"

It is just like old times. Except that it isn't, because we are all older and wiser and I would not have made the same mistakes again.

Claire comes on the phone: "Hi, Neva! How you do girl? Long time!"

She sounds the same, too. It feels like the years in between never happened.

Very quickly we fall into a rhythm. I think they are sharing the same ear piece; they each have one in one ear. I hear their steady breathing. I can almost picture them. I am pretty sure they are sitting on the banks of the river side by side; shoulder touching shoulder. It is the only river in Balcarres and it is surrounded by rich, lush greenery and features small waterfalls.

"How are things, Claire?"

"Not too bad, girl."

"How you do?"

"I'm good. I am trying not to complain."

"That's good because no one will listen."

We all laugh out loud. I hear people in the background.

"Are you guys still at the river?"

Bridget explains, "Yes we are, but Balcarres is not a small community anymore. It has grown so much. You would be surprised."

"Oh, really?"

Claire proclaims proudly, "Yes, but it's still pretty, that has not changed—".

"And it never will." Bridget completes her sentence.

Such a nostalgic moment; I am almost brought to tears, but I promised myself that I am going to be strong and get this done. It is like an event whose time has come and there is no getting around it or evading it any longer.

"So can we talk privately then?"

"Yes, of course," they both say.

Claire says, "So how is Mr. Rayva?"

"Bridget, you didn't tell her?"

"No, I couldn't. I felt like she should hear from you first."

"Why? What happened?"

"Claire, Rayva died recently—"

"Jesus! What? How? What happened?"

"It was a terrible accident and I don't want to talk about it right now, okay…?"

"I am so very sorry to hear that, girl. Wow!"

"Maybe another time when I call, if you guys will speak to me after this."

"After what? Neva, what is going on? Are you in some sort of trouble?" Claire is starting to get impatient. That much has not changed.

"No, no! Well not really! But I wanted to talk to you guys about something that happened on the night that Robin disappeared. Please promise me that you will bear with me and hear me out until the end, and then you can ask questions, or whatever comes naturally."

I imagine them making eye contact and looking worried.

"Promise." They both say.

"A swear."Claire reiterates.

"So, I'm just going to come right out and say it."

Before I proceed I clear my throat and take a deep breath, inhaling through my nose and exhaling through my mouth; fortifying myself and my resolve. I reach for my water bottle for support. I look around my palatial room to ground myself in the moment.

"On the night when we were descending the peak, when you guys went to pee, I was arguing with Robin and I pushed her over the precipice." There, I have said it now let the chips fall where they may. There is a thunderous silence on the other end. I think I have lost connection or they have hung up on me. I yell, panicking that they have abandoned the call, abandoned me! The irony is rich.

"Hello!"

"We're still here!" Bridget exclaims. Sounding way more serene than I expected, to the point where I wonder if they heard me. I panic and gulp loudly at the thought that I might have to repeat the whole ghastly tale. I sip more water, letting the coolness settle me.

"But you didn't push her. It was an accident. She shoved you, you shoved her back and she slapped you across the face and the momentum from the blow sent her over the edge. You tried to… rescue her—"

"Wait, Claire! How do you know this?"

"We heard the shouting and we ran back together, it was pretty dark but you had that little flashlight in one hand and it was pointed directly at Robin. We couldn't see the ledge either because darkness was all around the two of you. It was only after it happened we realized how close you guys had gotten to the edge and the fact that we almost lost both of you. We came back in time to see it happen but we were shocked into silence. Even Robin, she didn't even scream because it was so sudden. But by then it was too late. There is nothing any of us could have done. It was all a terrible mishap, an accident." Claire discloses, all in one montoned breath, sounding defeated.

"But you guys never said anything. You helped me look for her, or I helped you to look for her. "How? Why?"

Bridget interrupts, "Neva, it was a terrible accident like Claire said, and in that moment we had a choice to make and we chose—"

"What choice was that, Bridget?" I can't believe they've known all this time and have never uttered it or tried to use it against me.

Claire explains, "We had already lost one friend and we couldn't afford to lose two. Therefore, even without saying a word to each other; instinctively, we both knew that we would never tell. We would never mention any of this to a living soul. It was an awful, awful, horrible accident and we couldn't lose you, too…." There's a crack in her voice and she swallows hard for balance and takes a breath. Bridget interjects, "What would have been the point?" Claire concedes, "Although in many ways, we knew we had—"

Bridget asserts, "But we also knew that you would always come back to us. We knew that you would always blame yourself but we've hoped and prayed that eventually, you would come to realize that this was an accident and accidents happen, and find a way to forgive yourself so that you can heal—"

Claire jumps in, "That's exactly why it is called an accident, Neva, because no one could have predicted it. No one could have prevented it." She is corroborating what Shale has already said.

"I am sure you didn't go to the mountain with the intention of killing anyone."

Also what Imka had expressed.

"Of course not! I would never! Now I feel horrible to have put you guys in such a terrible position. You shouldn't have had to choose—"

"We would again." Claire sounds resolute.

"In a heartbeat," Bridget echoes. She is so utterly resolved and sure of her choice, a tear escapes me despite my grip.She gathers momentum,"It was our choice, and we would do it again under similar circumstances. Think of it, if the situation were reversed and it was Robin who was standing frozen to the spot and we had to choose, it would have been the same choice. And you guys know that I loved, still love, Robin with my whole heart, I still think about her, about her smile. But I also love you, Neva, and I know you loved Robin as well. That's why you were fighting with her, to keep her with us, when we just gave up and accepted her decision. You fought to keep her on our behalf when we were too cowardly to do so."

"Sometimes I wonder if things would have turned out differently, if both me and Bridget had joined with you in speaking some sense into Robin. And then I think it might and it might not have, so why dwell on a possibility that is no longer real, no longer attainable?"

Claire has clearly spent some time thinking about this; they both have. Meanwhile, I tried my best to suppress and forget, to flee. I do not deserve my friends. "Oh wow, you guys! You did that for me?"

As if on cue, they both say, "Yes."

Bridget continues, "For all of us, really."

"And I was so mean to you guys?"

Bridget says softly, "We knew it was the pain and guilt, we know that that wasn't you."

"That's why we were quick to forgive you, as we knew the weight of the burden that you must have been carrying." Claire offers, sounding close to tears.

"So what now, guys? What do we do now that the truth is out, out in the universe?"

There is more silence and then Bridget says quite soberly, "We go on!"

"After all, that is what Robin would have wanted. She was all about having a bright future, moving on regardless of the situation. Remember what she said the day when we discovered that Shalk had died?" Claire concludes.

"Indeed. I actually met someone who reminds me so much of her."

"That's God's way of telling you that it is time to move on, and let dead things go! I know, you know, we all know that we will never forget Robin: the lively Robin, the sensible Robin, the go-getter Robin, but what we need to let go of is the dead Robin!" Claire again echoes words of wisdom.

"That's deep, Claire! When did you get so smart?"

We all laugh, a little uncertainly at first but then raucous and loud. Then there is more silence, not uncomfortable, but germane to the occasion.

Then Claire explains, "I've been through a lot, I'm still going through it, but if nothing else my situation has taught me wisdom and has brought me closer to God, to the point where I don't even allow it to stress me anymore. I have come to recognize and accept that God has a plan for all of us. He didn't just send His Son to die and then abandon humanity. As the song goes, *the hotter the battle the sweeter the victory.*"

Bridget jumps in, "A real talk dat, Claire, but some of us want success without having any struggles. If you or I have, or anyone has, successes without struggles, there is nothing to ground us so we are just wanton, like Mama used to say."

We all laugh at the memory of her mom.

"How is your mom, Bridget?"

"She is doing well. It took some doing but she finally accepts that she cannot save my father, so she left and we are now living together. The best years of our lives!"

She sounds so hopeful; I can't help but smile into the phone.

"That's great, girl. So happy for you and your mom. How about you, Claire? How are you and your family members doing?"

"We're doing okay. I don't know if you heard, but Mama died…"

"No, I didn't! So sorry to hear that, girl."

"Yes, it's life. And I don't know if you remember but she has been kinda dead to us for a long time now. But I am still with my aunts and everybody is hearty, so we have a lot to be grateful for. Me especially, that I have always had their support."

I feel a stab of pain, although I know that that wasn't her intent. I hurt, because I should have been there more for them, even if in a financial way. God knows I had enough money to do so. I still have some in a private account that Rayva had disclosed to me, he said just in case anything happened to him, I would be taken care of.

Good old Rayva, always looking out for his favourite girl, his only girl.

"Yes, we all have a whole lot to be grateful for," I admit meaningfully.

There are a few more minutes of catching up. Both Claire and Bridget are now registered nurses and are working at the hospital in Port Antonio. They still live at home, though, and travel to work every day. Bridget had changed her mind about being a teacher because she felt like being a nurse would be more aligned with her nature. She is happy she took some time out to work and then figure things out. I agree, because teaching is not for everyone; it is indeed a calling. I am so happy for them.

When all is said and done it is time to go, and we make plans to chat again soon. This time for sure I know I will keep my promise. We also plan to have a private memorial for Robin, just the three of us, when I am able to sort things out and get to Jamaica. We say goodbye and I feel like I am floating. I feel so small in a big world; I am so humbled. This whole time I thought Robin's death had been my load, my burden that I was inextricably linked to for eternity, but the whole time my friends had been sharing the weight. I am beyond grateful to God for my friends that He picked for me. I can never thank Him enough, or repay them, but I intend to be a better person, to honour them and the memory of my loved ones; mainly Rayva, who died trying to rescue me.

Next on my to-do list is to call my dad. We speak for a long time, with my aunties in the background asking questions and adding bits and pieces here and there. They all weep for Rayva, as I knew they would. But I know that eventually they will accept his passing because they are strong people who have come to accept that in the midst of life there is death. Death will not destroy them. Apparently my chrysanthemums are blooming again; they are once more the talk of the town. I guess Mommy is proud of the strides that I have made. I share with them the dream I had about flying to Jamaica and seeing Grandma and Mommy; they all declare that, *that is a good dream.*

Before I hang up, the realization strikes me that my aunts have never divulged any information about the curse that Sabine mentioned in passing many years ago. I figure while I'm at it, I might as well clear up this mystery, which has been bugging me all these years from time to time. Aunt Sabine takes the phone after a moment of deliberating with the others; apparently, Daddy knows about it as well.

"Well, we were hoping that you would not ask but since you have, we might as well tell you. But please keep it between us and don't keep thinking about it either, okay? You promise?"

"Yes, Auntie." Now I am not too sure that I want to hear. I don't want to be keeping secrets anymore, but it is what it is and there's no turning back.

"So, I don't know if you've heard about the Obeahman who live in our area?"

My heart skips a beat. "Yes, Auntie. What about him?"

"Wait nuh!"

"Sorry Auntie, I won't interrupt anymore."

"You better not, or else I am not going to tell you. So anyways, that man is your uncle, my Mother's first-born child. She had him really young—"

"*What?*" I can't help it. But I guess she understands, as she proceeds with the narrative.

"Yes! It's true! So because she had him really young, she gave him a way to another family in another parish to take care of him, because you know they were well off and never had children of their own. Anyways, to cut a long story short, they sent him away to 'Merika for schooling cause you know they could afford it. He was supposed to study medicine, but instead the bwoy decided to become a Obeahman. We heard that he even traveled to Africa but I don't know where, 'cause you know Africa is a big place. Naturally, the family disowned him when he returned and set up him balm yard. Can you imagine, after they had invested so much in him? So from that time, people in the community said, because of his actions, none of us would ever amount to much. We would never go to college or anything like that. And you know what, from the day he moved back here to Balcarres Mama was sick until the day she died. Some people said it was the shock and shame, others that that bwoy did something to his mother out of spite because he felt like she abandoned him. So we pledged never to mention it ever again—"

"Oh wow!" Talk about a turn of events.

"Yes, my dear, so that is the story. But please don't put it on your head because people also say belief kill and belief cure, so that's why we never tell you. And guess what, Nevaeh, even without knowing you have broken the curse. You have made us so proud, girl."

"Thanks Auntie! I appreciate all the support over the years. I just have one last question, and I will never ask again or repeat this story. I promise."

"Yes, what is it, my dear?"

"The Obeahman, what is his name?"

"You know, I don't know. Hold on, Sebouney might remember."

I hear her transferring the phone and my dad asking her if her mouth is tired from talking so much. Good old Dad, he's never lost his sense of humour.

Aunt Sebouney takes the phone and she says, "I am not sure, but I think that they used to call him James before all this. Now I am not too sure what they call him."

I hear my dad saying in the background, "The man is a herbalist, not an Obeahman, there is a difference—"

Aunt Sebouney, still holding the phone, yells at him, "What is the difference poppyshow, tell us?"

He takes the phone and elaborates, "Listen, Star Gurl, don't listen to them. Your uncle—because that's what he is, your uncle—he uses herbs to heal people. But Jamaican people too superstitious so they have to add that negative kind of spin to it. Look, man, I have never heard that this man has brought any harm to anyone. People question, how him look so young and fresh the few times he ventures out? You know why…?"

"It's the herbs!" I supply.

"Exactly. The man lives cleaner than a lot of these so-called Christians and he eats clean as well. I have heard that he is a vegetarian and only eats what he plants. The only thing he sends the guy over there to buy is fish. That is the only thing that he eats that they don't raise or plant themselves. So of course he looks young and fresh every time. There is nothing wrong with dat. Don't mek people fool you, Nevaeh, this guy is a decent fellow. In fact, I'll tell you this much, when your mother was over here sick, he offered to help and she rejected his help. He even offered to help his own mother as well. But because everyone in this family seems to be afraid of what people will say, they flatly refused. Who knows, your mother could possibly still be alive today to see you pass the worst, but she chose. Nevaeh, she chose. Now you must choose what you will do with this information, you have to decide if you are going to make old wives' fables destroy your future, your bright future, or you are going to continue to grow and prosper. It is on you now. No one else can make those choices for you."

With that said, he says it's time to go and I bid them farewell. Dear old Dad, the voice of reason and clarity. Now everything makes perfect sense. My mother's warning, no absolute fear of, the "Obeahman," the Healer not taking payment but accepting herbs, the free bath, instructing me to read my Bible, him giving me the chrysanthemum plant because he knows the inherent healing properties. Also, telling me about *ukuu*. He must have learned that in his travels. This all makes perfect sense. Also what Dad said, about having a sound mindset and not allowing what people say to live in your head and destroy you, makes a whole lot of sense too. My uncle is a herbalist of the highest order. I am honestly so proud. He definitely was and is ahead of his time. When I return to Jamaica, I must make an effort to meet with him and talk; if he will see me that is. Also, I guess what I felt for him when we met was a familial connection, a blood bond, deep calling unto deep; nothing more, nothing less. The soul does know and remember even when we are oblivious or when we forget. This life is so funny and filled with twists and turns.

I intend to keep my promise to check in with my friends and family members more consistently. I owe them that much consistency. I don't share with any of them that I am in South Africa—not my family members or Bridget or Claire—as that would have required too much explaining and might just place them in harm's way. Luckily, the detective gave us phones with North American numbers so no one would be the wiser to my specific location. But for now, I know that they are all safe and are keeping their heads about water and it is enough; it is enough for me that they are there for me when I need them, even when I don't think I do.

The following week, Imka and I do some travelling. We visit many picturesque and surreal places, and for the first time in my adult life I am actually present for all of it. We encounter small and large streams, numerous waterfalls of varying sizes, and we visit the ocean. It turns out that South Africa is surrounded by two oceans, not three. But as Mommy used to say, *dream nuh walk straight*. We see many animals endemic to the areas we visit: squirrels, lizards, flamingoes, among many others—we even spot a baboon. Plus, a rich plant life that is mind-blowingly beautiful, plants that I have never seen before.

Despite all the wonder of this place, it is the river that I yearn for, which keeps calling my name. Eventually we plan a trip to one of the rivers in Cape Town, even though I am a little worried about the memories that the river will conjure up for me: I always choose the river. I think in a lot of ways, I really want to go because I want to weigh the measure of my healing. The way I see it, if I fall apart after entering the river, I know I still have a lot of healing to do. But if not, then I will know for sure what being whole feels like. That will become my measuring-rod for growth and healing.

We plan to go in the early morning. Shale comes too. At first I take in the vastness of the river and smell its freshness, I touch some of the plants that frame its banks. Then I dive in, head first. I resurface and I feel invigorated. I feel like this river, in this faraway land, is a part of my being and has always been a part of me. As I move around, catching my balance, flexing my muscles, my body remembers how to react in the water, and in the gush of the river I hear the sound of welcome, *Sanibonani*. Then I know for sure that I am whole and it is well.

I know that there are still obstacles to overcome; after all, there will be a trial and I will have to testify – I guess dad was right about me being a star girl – among other hardships unforeseen, but I know that whatever comes my way: I will overcome. Before, I used to be so afraid of struggles, afraid of the future, I used to tense up just thinking of what possibly might be, but now I get it: struggles are part and parcel of the human experience and they are mostly handpicked, with growth being the ultimate endgame.

My uncle James once told that there is *ukuu* or greatness in me, which I have never actually allowed myself to accept or activate. But now I am willing and ready to embrace all of me: the good, the bad, the ugly, the beauty and the greatness that is in me. Embracing fully the notion that I will mess up again someday, but it is in forgiving myself that I will heal, and it is in healing that I will grow and evolve and fulfill my purpose or purposes here in the earth. In fact, future generations are depending on me to rise to the occasion and be the best possible version of myself that I can be.

And now I can, now that I have been rescued from my personal hell, rescued from myself.

ACKNOWLEDGEMENTS

Rescued took me a while to write. I found it to be the most challenging, therapeutic and cathartic of all my books to date. The emotional content was draining for me, and I often felt exhausted after a writing session. As usual, I hope this book will be just as therapeutic and beneficial for everyone who chooses to read and digest its contents.

By way of special thanks, I want to mention my 1N–3N WhatsApp CREW for always reminding me of the richness of our Jamaican heritage and the vastness of our culture, through anecdotes shared and the discussions we've had over the years. In particular, thanks Sunil Williams for your technical expertise when I thought that I had lost three quarters of this book; big up you damn self. Also, thanks Fredrick Nelson for always being the voice of reason and a strong source of encouragement whenever I need it most.

I'm thankful and grateful for my family far and wide, my friends whether or not we've been in touch over the years, and above all to the Almighty God for His grace which sustains me and holds me together, even on days when I feel like I am going to lose it and come unhinged. I am eternally grateful.

Shalom my friends! I wish you peace, love and light!

AN ODE TO CHANGE

Kareen Lopez Samuels

They came looking for me,
All the while not knowing that that was the old me.
They came looking for the old me,
And wondered why I didn't jig to their song like a puppet on
a string.
They mused on my lack of triggers, probed to find where my
smile was shrouded.
That was previously permanently plastered all over my face—
before—like a clown.
All the time not knowing that that was the old me.
Now I, loving, let all my feelings in and feel all my aches and
pains.
No longer do I flee from pain, as in them is gain.
As I have experienced enough pain to know that it hurts as
much as it heals.
Sometimes, my musing leads to tears, a smile, a laugh, or even
trepidation,
But I still allow all of it in.
Sometimes I go slow with myself, yet at other times I move at
warp speed.
In the face of numbness, I was unrecognizable to myself.
Now, I take all of it in; except the indignity of indifference.
That was the old me.
I have questioned my very existence,
My own sense of value and worth.
Now, I choose to acquiesce only to my own need to just be.
Today I embrace all of me.
Like a dead tree, suddenly spouting new leaves,
Yes, this is the new me.
They came looking for me,
But found out that that was the old me.

ABOUT THE AUTHOR

Kareen Lopez-Samuels hails from the small island of Jamaica. A teacher of English by profession, an educator for over twenty years. She is the author of *Zimera* and *They Were Here Before* both published in 2020, an editor, a reviewer and songwriter. The first child and only girl for her parents – Winston and Beatrice Lopez (mom deceased). She completed a BA in Linguistics from UWI (Mona), an MA in Language, Culture and Education from York University, and an Honours Specialist in English from the same institution. She is currently employed to the Peel District School Board. She currently resides in Brampton, Ontario along with her husband and two girls.

For feedback, comments, etc., please contact Kareen via one of the following:
Website: toishma.com
Email: kareensamuels@yahoo.com
Instagram: @toishma
Twitter: @toishma